A stunning tale about the deeply entrenched conflicts between a white mother and her biracial daughter.

Mama's Child is a story of an idealistic young white woman who traveled to the American South as a civil rights worker, fell in love with an African American man, and started a family in San Francisco, where the more liberal city embraced them—except when it didn't. Together they raise a son and a daughter, but the tensions surrounding them have a negative impact on their marriage, and they divorce when their children are still young. For their biracial daughter, this split further destabilizes her already challenged sense of self—"Am I black or white?" she must ask herself. "Where do I belong?" Is she her father's daughter alone?

As the years pass, the chasm between them widens even as the mother attempts to hold on to the emotional chord that binds them. It isn't until their daughter, Ruby, herself becomes a wife and mother that she begins to develop compassion and understanding for the many ways that her own mother's love transcended race and questions of identity.

Also by Joan Steinau Lester

Nonfiction

The Future of White Men and Other Diversity Dilemmas

Taking Charge: Every Woman's Action Guide to Personal, Political & Professional Success

Eleanor Holmes Norton: Fire in My Soul

Fiction

Black, White, Other: In Search of Nina Armstrong

Mama's Child

A Novel

JOAN STEINAU LESTER

ATRIA PAPERBACK

New York London Toronto Sydney New Delhi

ATRIA PAPERBACK

A Division of Simon & Schuster, Inc.
1230 Avenue of the Americas
New York, NY 10020

First Atria Paperback edition May 2013

ATRIA PAPERBACK and colophon are trademarks of Simon & Schuster, Inc.

For information about special discounts for bulk purchases, please contact Simon & Schuster Special Sales at 1-866-506-1949 or business@simonandschuster.com.

The Simon & Schuster Speakers Bureau can bring authors to your live event. For more information or to book an event, contact the Simon & Schuster Speakers Bureau at 1-866-248-3049 or visit our website at www.simonspeakers.com.

Designed by Jill Putorti

Manufactured in the United States of America

10 9 8 7 6 5 4 3 2 1

Library of Congress Cataloging-in-Publication Data
Lester, Joan Steinau.
    Mama's child / Joan Steinau Lester. — 1st Atria pbk ed.
        p. cm.
    1. Mothers and daughters—Fiction. 2. Racially mixed people—Fiction. 3. Domestic fiction. I. Title.
    PS3612.E8195M36 2013
    813'.6—dc23

                                                                    2012029271

ISBN 978-1-4516-9318-8
ISBN 978-1-4516-9319-5 (ebook)

For Carole

Foreword

Alice Walker

For those of us who went South in the mid-sixties to challenge American apartheid in Georgia, Alabama, and especially Mississippi, being able to look back at that decade from the perspective of fifty or more years is an astonishing accomplishment. I know I was not alone in thinking, at the time, that there was probably no way I would survive those years of car and house and people shooting and bombing; no way any of us would emerge, whether in body, soul, spirit, or mind, unscathed. And we didn't.

But we went, I believe, because we felt the most exquisite love imaginable: love of black people who were risking everything to make a better life for themselves and their children, love of the few whites who dared stand with them, love of the children, whether white or black, who we saw becoming distorted human beings, capable of continuing and refining the cruelty or submission to cruelty their parents and the general racist society taught them from birth.

At this point in my life, fifty-odd years later, I have to laugh, if sometimes bitterly, at how naive we were, how hopeful, how fragile.

But then again, as the people liked to say in the Southern states, you just never know what God has in mind! We thought, I think, that we were destined to break new ground between the races, by loving, uniting with, sometimes marrying, persons of "the opposite race." That this might be, for the heart, for the spirit, and for the American psyche at large, a major contribution to collective growth. We had no idea. No idea that, decades into the future, it would be the relationship with our children that would most sorely test us.

These children, born at a time and sometimes in places none of them would ever choose to live, would later critique everything their parents had done, and find us wanting. For we were focused on "changing the world" at a time—their childhoods—when they rightly felt we should have been focused solely on attending to them. That, precisely, is what many of us were struggling to achieve: a society, a world, in which our children had everything they ever dreamed of needing, including our full and undivided attention, adoration, protection, and love.

In this the most vulnerable, the most passionate, the most honest and brave of books, I see the humor of some of our early Movement fears: that "the white woman" would run off with "our" men. That she would then have "everything," as she seemed to have already. That she could not, would not, suffer, as we did, having been left with our empty arms. That her children, though brown, would adore her whiteness. How mad this all seems now, reading this book. And yet, it was a very true phase of our passage.

Our passage into what?

Our passage into what it takes to make true sisterhood. And truly human, beings. Our realization that our pain is not only a shared pain, those of us whose children have divorced us, in the millions now ("Estrangement between children and their parents has reached epidemic proportions in the United States" a recent sentence leapt out at me from newspaper or Internet); it is the same pain.

One of the reasons I value writers is that the best of us will worry the scab we sometimes grow over our wound until the wound bleeds, if necessary, before the entire world, as we trust we will somehow, having wished harm to no one, including especially our children, bring healing to ourselves, to anyone suffering as we are still, or have done, and to them. It is a testament to the Universe's wisdom that it sometimes will unite just the right craftsperson with just the right wound, so that, through riveting art, everyone can examine it.

In this novel "the white woman," at last standing in the truth of who she is, undefined by parents, lovers, spouse, or children, finds she is free. From that freedom she connects solidly with people of color, black women, other white women, children of every hue, and with her own spirit of resistance and pride.

It is a beautiful vision. And well worth having done the necessary work of going to the Deep South, at its most troubled and dangerous, to gain.

Temple Jook House
Mendocino
September 16, 2012

1990

Ruby Jordan's fingers tingled, she was that eager to write her farewell.

Half an hour later, wrapped against a wind studded with sleet, she shoved the letter to her mother into a mailbox on Williams Street. The lip of the blue box swallowed the envelope addressed, formally, in her best script, to Elizabeth O'Leary, 1507 Ashby Avenue, Berkeley, CA 94703, as if it were any ordinary paper. She listened to the lid clank, stared at the metal box, and bit her lip as pain pricked her chest. But as quickly as the sting jolted her it vanished, leaving only a familiar wash of longing that rose like acid. She swallowed it down. *Not now*, she swore to herself, *not on my own personal Juneteenth.* Her mama had told her that white people used to have a terrible saying: "I'm free, white, and twenty-one." *Well*, thought Ruby, snapping her fingers as she strode down the block, *I'm free, Black, and twenty-three. Catch me if you can.*

PART ONE
1978

CHAPTER 1

Elizabeth

"I need to see you today," Gladys, the New Harmony School director, growled into our answering machine. "We've had an incident." Her deep voice intimated this was no ordinary farewell meeting for Ruby's final days of sixth grade. "Looking forward—" her gravelly voice murmured, as if she hadn't just raised my anxiety.

Solomon had his own full schedule that day—*like every other*—so, given the urgency of "see you today" and "incident," I called Inez to teach my Merritt College class and, sweating, navigated Ashby up to Telegraph and turned right toward Oakland. At Sixty-fifth I angled left toward the brown shingled house our group of community parents had converted to a school, building an addition nearly every year.

Pushing through the noisy halls filled with children's voices, I slid alone into Gladys's office. Her secretary, Laverne, waved her hand toward the small battered chair facing Gladys's desk.

"She's running a little late, but she'll be back momentarily. Take a load off."

Laverne's soft shoulder-width Afro brushed my cheek when she patted my arm. Why, I wondered after she left the room, had she done that?

After squeezing myself into the chair—had I gained that much weight?—I scrutinized the posters filling the wall: a white woman in an orange-print skirt held hands with a black sister in slacks over the words WOMEN HOLD UP HALF THE SKY. An oversized UNICEF calendar featured a blue globe ringed by multihued children. GIVE! the calendar urged. And everywhere paintings, blue, red, green tempura paint slathered across butcher paper, bright yellow suns lighting the upper corners of landscapes. Several papers bore titles. I saw a curling, faded paper labeled RUBY'S FAMILY: four stick figures hovering under the ubiquitous bright yellow sun. Three of the figures were brown, one was colored pink.

Gladys bustled in, trailing smoke, chattering before she cleared the doorway. A squat woman churning energy, she started out, "Ruby's such a talented girl." She swept aside a space on her desk, rummaging for an ashtray. "So vivacious. I remember our talent show when Ruby was, what, in fourth grade, when she brought down the house with 'Over the Rainbow.' Remember? Such a bright child. So lively." She tapped out another Camel from her pack while scanning a pink message slip, not waiting for an answer before she rushed on. "Yes, such talent."

I listened warily, shifting in my undersized chair. The principal hadn't called me in to discuss Ruby's lovely voice and bright disposition.

"And smart. But Ruby is having problems." Gladys plunged abruptly to the reason for her call. To my thirty-five-year-old eyes, the woman was ancient. *A relic from the old breed of progressive educators, fifty at least.* Though I'd been part of the parents' committee that hired Gladys Holland six years before, she hadn't been my choice. Her confrontational style grated, and, along with Solomon and several others, I'd advocated for a slender, soft-spoken African American woman from Portland, arguing that the students needed a different role model, one they rarely saw in a position of authority. I wondered if Gladys knew. Still, I had to admit that during her tenure the school had prospered. She'd hired terrific teachers, kept parents involved, and was an ace fund-raiser.

"That girl is going to have problems when she gets older, too." Gladys, who was under five feet, peered across her desk, bobbing her head to emphasize her words.

"I-I don't think so," was all I could stammer.

"I'm worried about her. Something unfortunate happened this morning in the bathroom."

"What?" My heart pounded. "Is Ruby okay? Where is she?"

Gladys tapped her fingers on one of the papers stacked on her desk. "She's back in class, but she had an altercation."

"An altercation?"

"From what we gather, another girl accidentally opened a stall door too hard and knocked Ruby down. Ruby dug her nails into the girl's scalp and made a racial slur." Gladys stopped and stared at me. "She called her a white bitch."

I was speechless.

"What concerns me is that Ruby chose to couch her reaction to this accident in racial terms, as well as with violence." Gladys gave me a long level gaze and spoke slowly. "She's almost twelve, a critical age when she's trying to figure out who she is. She won't fit in the white world. She may not be accepted in the black world. She's going to have a difficult time finding her place."

I shivered. "Ruby is black. That's where she fits," I said, fighting tears. *She's normal, leave her alone!* I glanced at the One World calendar on the wall, with its children of many nations holding hands around the globe, and crossed my legs and arms, trying to shut out the warning voice.

"But you aren't. And you're her mother. She's a sensitive girl, and she's going to have some major challenges," Gladys repeated, her head bobbing. I wanted to tear it off her neck.

"No, she isn't. And how do you know what happened in the bathroom, what really precipitated this 'altercation'?"

"They agree, Jenny pushed open the door and Ruby leaped up and attacked her."

"Jenny?"

"Jenny Lee."

The name wasn't familiar.

"She came in the middle of the year; she's just in fifth grade." Gladys looked at me accusingly, as if *I* were now wrenching small children's scalps in bathrooms. "That's another issue. But school will be out in three days." I could almost see her wiping her hands of the incident—and of us. "Since Jenny wasn't injured, even though she was shaken up, I'm inclined to let it go at this point in the year. Both of them are back in class and it's certainly not the first physical altercation we've had, although the first for either of these girls. But mostly, Elizabeth, I wanted you to know how concerned I am about Ruby. Why would she call Jenny a white bitch? Why would she have such a racial chip on her shoulder? These are things you and Solomon need to think long and hard about." Gladys picked up a yellow file folder while she kept her hooded eyes on me. "Before she goes to junior high school."

Shut up! I'm sick of this school, anyway.

"Do you talk about race at home a lot?" Gladys asked, peering at me as if I were a lab exhibit.

"We're very involved with black liberation," I said. "For a long time," I added, remembering the Vietnam marches where Ruby, gripping my hand, had chanted along with the crowd, *"No Vietcong ever called me nigger!"* I didn't want to tell Gladys about the Black Panthers who'd filled our home for years, toting their guns. I flashed on an image of our old friend Stokely Carmichael, now Kwame Ture, tall and elegant, who practically oozed "death to the white man" from his pores whenever he visited California and crashed on our couch. Or fierce Bobby Seale, who used to bounce Ruby on his knee and now teased her as "my girl." Or how could Gladys understand who Ralph Featherstone was to us: shortly after Ralph's last sing-along in our kitchen when Ruby was four, a car bomb in Maryland, probably planted by the Klan, blew him to pieces. We displayed his photo on the living room shelf as a memorial, along with a framed tribute written by his new wife. Yes, Ruby knew his story. We considered Ralph one of our martyrs, one of the several we'd known personally, as a family. I didn't tell Gladys any of this, or that we were angry all the time. At whites.

"But you're white." Gladys squinted, clearly puzzled. "Isn't Ruby part white?"

"Being African American is a political definition," I said, trying to still my racing heart while words flowed out automatically. "As all racial categorizations are. She's seen as black by our culture. Anyone with 'one drop' of 'Negro blood' is black, according to Southern courts. We want Ruby to have an identity that fits the one the culture puts on her."

"I don't know, you have a confused young girl here." Gladys, usually so poised, so aggressive, looked baffled. As if Ruby were the first biracial child she'd ever encountered.

"Well, the culture is messed up about race!" I grew heated. Perspiration beaded under my arms. "Biracial identity is an attempt to fade out of blackness. Solomon and I are clear. Ruby is black."

"But she has lots of strengths," Gladys said, as if to counter a flaw: Ruby's unnamable, confusing racial designation. She shook her head and stood, extending her hand. "We wish her luck, and of course we'll be sending her records on to Martin Luther King Junior High."

I grasped her hand, gave a numb smile, and fled her office, weaving my way through students until I sank gratefully onto the school's front steps, dropped my head in my hands, and burst quietly into tears. "Ruby's fine," I kept whispering. As if the more I said it, the truer it would become.

*   *   *

"Hey," I called out later that afternoon, still exhausted from the meeting when the kids straggled home after Ruby's pickup soccer game, which Che had gone over to referee. They trooped in making a racket. Rosa and Cesar leaped and yelped, as they did whenever anyone appeared at the front door. If it were Ruby or Che, the barking intensified until the kids stroked their shaggy backs. Rosa yipped full volume at Che until she got her rubs; then, once she'd thoroughly licked his face, cleaning up microscopic lunchtime leftovers, she was his noisy black shadow, her toenails clicking on the floor.

"How was the game?" I peered around the wall separating the living room from the kitchen, wiping both hands on the blue BRIGADISTA SANDINISTA apron tied around my waist, and scrutinized Ruby, trying to beam that maternal X-ray I'd read about. She looked the same as always.

"My team lost, four to one." Ruby plopped onto the oak hall bench and reached down to take off her cleats. I saw her glowing face, golden apricot under the grime and sweat and the matted curly hair that flew all around her head. *How could anyone believe my fairy child has problems?*

"But I made the goal." She lifted her head, the sun through the glass door glinting off her braces, and she rolled her lovely brown eyes up at me so I could see her pleasure. At moments like that, when our eyes locked, our connection was visceral. She smiled, and my heart unclenched. Fight or not, Ruby was fundamentally okay.

"Where's Daddy?"

"Teaching. Wow, you made a goal." I stepped closer. "Too bad you lost. Was it fun?"

"Kind of," she mumbled, head down as she untied her shoelaces. Her legs had grown so long, so fast—at five foot seven she was nearly my height—that every pair of pants she owned were highwater. "Afterward we fooled around . . ."

The rest of her words were lost among long tangles, a curtain hanging over her face. These days she'd turned mercurial: one moment she was beaming at me, the next I had to grill her to get one scrap of information. I was used to that with Che, who'd recently turned a reticent thirteen. But Ruby had ever been the confiding one, eager to press against me on the couch, lean her head on my shoulder, and pour out her heart. We were so close we'd been the envy of all my friends. Until this spring. Day by day, watching Ruby now was like seeing a time-lapsed photo of a flower unfurling: she was that different every time I looked.

"Who were you with?"

"Oh, you know, Jamylle and them . . ." Again she looked up; the brilliant smile captivated me, as it always did.

"How was school?" I held my breath.

"Fine."

"Anything special?

"Not really," she said flatly, the sullen stranger closing over her face as if a shade had been drawn.

I knew any more questions were hopeless. *Well,* I consoled myself, *we'll talk about it later.* Once Solomon and I had a chance to catch up, after dinner, we'd talk to her together.

While I turned away, Che slid back out the front door. I heard the steady plunk of his soccer ball, *thump, thump,* hitting the stoop. "Che!" I called, stepping outside with Cesar rubbing my leg until I bent to scratch him. Rosa, limping from a deep cut in the pad of her right front foot, hobbled out, whining for her turn.

"Mama?" Che smiled at me then, the same golden red tone as his sister's lighting his face, as if a special incandescence shone, like Ruby's, from under his skin. He sidled up the three steps, brushing lightly against my shoulder, hand automatically out to pat Rosa. "We had a snake in biology," he said, his deep voice cracking while his brow wrinkled. "We dissected it." His face curled closed so his lashes fluttered against his cheek. "It was dead already. Jabari brought it in. But when we cut it the guts came out." He squealed with horrified delight, until my serious teenager suddenly sounded like a ten-year-old. "They oozed out all over." He tried to gauge my reaction. "It was gross!"

Lulled by his lapse into childhood, I reached out to try for a squeeze, but he wriggled free and expertly hurled the ball against the step, bouncing it on the black and red target Solomon had painted. I heard the plunk, steady and slow, just like he was. "After you hit the target . . ." I calculated ". . . two hundred times, come set the table."

Inside, Ruby's footsteps thumped and I followed the sound to her room at the back of the house. "Help me with dinner, okay?"

"All right, as soon as I call Imani. I have to tell her one thing. It's important. What are we having?"

"Pizza—or do you want upside-down night, with scrambled eggs and toast? I have that seeded bread you like. The one that's real thin-sliced."

"Pizza!"

How many thousands of times had this been our dinner? Rotating between four or five meals, somehow pizza seemed to come up more often than any of the others. Over the stove I'd hung a colorful BLACK POWER! UNGAWA! poster, with a raised fist, next to a picture of a massive Chinese woman in red, her huge forearm wielding a giant hammer. Underneath these two Solomon had tacked an Angolan SWAPO poster; its stenciled guns loomed over the steaming vats of food I cooked, usually fresh green beans to go with pizza, or cheap spaghetti or chicken backs and wings, for the Black Panthers and hordes of neighbors who constantly filled our kitchen. Now, when the steam billowed, I strode to Ruby's room. Through her closed door I could hear her muffled voice on the phone and wondered if she was talking with Imani about the fight at school. "Ruby! Come on. Now! I need you."

She padded up the hall, skillfully chopped beans and tossed

them into my bubbling pot. "Quick, put the lid on," I told her. I sprinkled hamburger onto a frozen pizza crust, said, "Here, sweetie, spread out the meat with this spoon, I've almost got the tomato sauce done"—and was tossing a salad with olive oil, oregano, and chives from Berkeley Bowl when I felt a sweet hand massage my left shoulder. After a moment, she seized my arm and began to pull me into a dance. Ruby's eyes sparkled; in their flash I saw my familiar child. How tall she was getting, I marveled, as we swayed to the jazz beat blaring from the stereo.

"Daddy," Ruby called out hopefully when the front door clicked open. But it was Che clomping through the dining area. "Can I cook, too?" His voice cracked.

"Shoes off," I reminded. Kicking his sneakers into the corner, he ambled into the kitchen.

"Watch out, sweetie. Careful of the stove and the hot food." Soon the three of us, with Cesar wagging his tail, were creating an improvisational dance to Coltrane's *Live at Birdland*, an album I never tired of. When Elvin Jones crashed the cymbals, we clapped in unison, Cesar and Rosa brushing our legs. At the rat-a-tat of the steady drumbeat we jerked our hips, a whirling threesome of giggles crowding into the kitchen, until the boiling pot of beans overflowed, squelching the flame. Catching my breath I relit the stove and handed Ruby a stained quilted blue mitt, a wedding present from Solomon's sister, Cookie. "Here. Use this while you stir."

The aroma of bubbling tomato sauce filled the kitchen. *Yes,* I thought, stealing glances at her, *Ruby looks fine.* I knew why she'd grabbed that girl's hair—Jenny had knocked her down—and as for calling her a white bitch, my heart thumped, but before I had a chance to go further with the question I heard the front door click open, and out of the corner of my eye I saw my husband lope through the living room into the kitchen, sniffing the food. *Yes, he's still gorgeous,* I let myself notice. *Stands so erect, those fine shoulders.*

Home for once before nightfall, Solomon's still-lean body hung over me like a question mark, but I didn't say a word. Uncorking a bottle of Chianti, I felt my shoulders stiffen and my legs tighten while I silently handed him a glass. And refilled my own. Deliberately, I turned my back into a fortress and busied myself with the sauce scalding on the burner.

"Sorry I missed the meeting," he mumbled. "I tried—"

Instantly, I heard Che scoot next to his father, a habit I hadn't seen him show in years. When I glanced over my shoulder, Solomon was absentmindedly rubbing Che's curls from his forehead in the familiar way he'd used to, and, shockingly, my thirteen-year-old was allowing it.

Ruby lunged for Solomon, wooden spoon in hand. "Daddy, I scored a goal today in the game. It was awesome. Right into the corner. The goalie couldn't get near it! It was the only goal our side—"

"Sugar, that's great." He reached under Ruby's armpits and in one strong motion lifted her three inches off the ground, pulling her up to his face until they touched noses. She giggled. "That's my girl," he said enthusiastically, "you go get 'em." Lowering Ruby, he stooped a bit to rub noses with Che, too, who tried to pretend he was too tough for this "baby stuff." Then, Solomon's tone contrite, he asked me, "How was the meeting with Gladys? I thought I might catch the end of it."

"But you didn't, you missed it," I hissed. "Entirely." I turned to face him. "Like the last one. Only this was an emergency."

His face collapsed into a series of weary planes; his eyes behind his glasses hardened. "Shit," he said, his voice turned hard. "An emergency? You knew I was working. It was a critical gig. I had to drive all the way down to San Leandro to teach a master class, and the traffic on 880 was bumper to bumper. What happened?" He stepped toward me again, draping one arm tentatively over my shoulder.

I nodded toward Ruby and Che, willing the shoulder to soften, and motioned them back to their rooms. "Gladys," I whispered, catching his hand while I mouthed the words, "is a bitch."

"Nothing new there. Coulda told you that six years ago," he whispered in my ear, leaning over to nibble the lobe. "What was the emergency that couldn't wait?"

"I'll tell you later. Everything's okay now, I think. I'll fill you in on the way to the Hendrix meeting. It's tonight, isn't it? God, I can't believe those cops got acquitted. Beating up a Panther never counts." I tossed the salad, keeping my voice neutral, although in the way of long-married couples I understood exactly what I was lobbing. I glanced over my shoulder to measure his reaction.

His face tensed and tightened, pinching his features, and the telltale nerve throbbed in his neck like a steady drumbeat. "You know how the brothers—*and the sisters*—feel about us lately." His arm loosened from my shoulder until it felt as if he'd peeled away a blanket, and a chill blew over me.

Be careful, I thought. *Wait until I'm not so upset about Ruby.* But the caution never made it from my brain to my lips. "Screw them," I blurted. "If you're comfortable with me, they've got to accept us." And I jiggled my shoulders, knocking his large hand completely off. "Even Bobby?" I asked, remembering how he used to moan at our table over my stuffed pork chops, laughing about The Pig and wolfing down plenty. He'd bounced Ruby and Che on his knees for years when they were small, even joined Ruby and me singing my father's sacred old union songs, the ones I'd grown up on, inventing new verses to my favorite, "Which Side Are You On?" Together we'd belted out "Don't scab for Mister Charley, don't listen to his lies/Us black folks haven't got a chance unless we organize," and roared our solidarity together. How could Bobby not want me at the meeting?

"Christ, Red!" Solomon shook his head. "Do I have to explain it again?" He stretched to his full six foot one, straightening his spine even farther, and began to inch backward, one scuffed loafer at a time. His face was as impassive as his eyes.

I couldn't stop myself, even as I heard the whine of my voice, like the sharp swish of a falling bomb. "What's the matter, don't want to take the white-bitch wife?" *What's happened to us: The good-looking mystery man playing his soulful guitar in a Mississippi dirt yard? The slender girl in lace-up sandals frisking like a puppy, willing to do anything—"I'd get shot," I once declared to a roomful of Panthers—for civil rights? The playful couple blowing bubbles onto naked bodies, swirling the suds into patterns before lunging onto each other? Swearing, "Soul mates forever."* Warm images from the past raced through my mind even as I heard myself direct Ruby, who'd reentered the kitchen with her brother, "Don't let Cesar lick that spoon full of hamburger juice in your hand" and saw my long arm curl around Che's muscular shoulder to sprinkle garlic powder in the sauce. Che danced away, as if he were allergic to my touch.

"Elizabeth—look, I'm sorry I missed the meeting," Solomon said quietly, taking a deep breath, jerking me fully into the present. After a pause he said, "Here's to . . ." He raised his glass. "The revolution."

I couldn't tell if he was serious or not. Looking like a hollowed-out shell, the man leaned against the yellow wall next to the stove, already splattered with grease despite my recent paint job. I twisted the oven dial to 400, holding my face tight and my breath shallow. He couldn't paste us together with revolution. Not anymore. I shook my head.

"Christ!" he said, banging his beautiful head softly against the wall. "I give up."

Ruby, her face enveloped in steam, grabbed the simmering pot of beans and slammed it into the sink, trying to silence us, I knew, while Che slipped quietly out of the house. I heard the rhythmic *plunk, plunk* of his ball against the stoop. Even the dogs quieted and slunk to the living room. "Not now!" I told Solomon, tightening my jaw and nodding in Ruby's direction.

"Look, I've *had* it with you blaming me every time I can't make every single one of those damn meetings called at the most inconvenient times." He took off his glasses and wiped them on his shirt, then burst out, "And *you're* the one who said—"

"Not now!" I turned my back and threw hunks of cheese on the pizza before I slid it into the oven. *Jeez,* I thought for the thousandth time, *why am I so pale, the classic red-headed milky white?* In a political crowd my skin always screamed white, white, white, like a neon light shining out from the earth tones around us.

"Daddy, something happened today," Ruby interrupted.

"Not now," I snapped, momentarily forgetting the incident at school. "Your father and I are talking. Please. Leave us alone for a few minutes." I nodded toward the living room.

Instead of trotting off, Ruby turned to me and stretched out her hand. "The last sip? Please."

"No, you're too young."

"She only wants a taste," Solomon protested, handing her his nearly empty glass. "Here's a sip, sugar."

"Solomon!" I warned, reaching for the glass. But it was already at her lips, and before I could snatch it back she'd downed the wine in one gulp.

Within two minutes her eyes glazed over, and she nearly stumbled on her way to the table.

CHAPTER 2

Ruby

"Imani," I almost cried, clutching the receiver to my ear like a life preserver. "Jenny Lee called me a *nigger* before she slammed the bathroom door into me, and I went off on her the way Daddy would've if anybody treated him like that. I beat that girl."

"You did? Are you okay?"

"I never heard that before, not for real. It was so weird. Remember when we used to yell in those marches, 'No Vietcong ever called me nigger'? Those little banners we wore on our coats about that stupid war and those stupid signs we had to hold until our arms fell off? Well, now somebody did call me that. I can't believe it."

I lay back on the red star quilt that I've had my whole life. Grandma Jean made it when I was born, with these giant red stars on a blue sky. Lots of little stars, too, yellow ones. A corner of one of the red stars, near the middle, was torn, and whenever I lay on the quilt my finger always wanted to slide in the hole. I don't know why. Grandma Jean told me not to "worry the hole, 'cause you'll grow it bigger." She said she'd fix it on her summer visit from Atlanta, when she came every year for a month. And she promised she's gonna teach me to sew, too. My mom bragged, "I don't sew," like it was some kind of accomplishment, and Daddy didn't know how either. Grandma Jean told me all along that when I was eleven she'd give me sewing lessons, and this summer *Here I am,* I thought.

"But you pounded her?" Imani said.

"What was I supposed to do, let her get away with it?"

Mama banged on the door then so I had to slam down the phone in like five seconds and act all normal. She hadn't even noticed anything was wrong. I thought, *Wow, she's too caught up in her own Black Power politics and her stuff with Daddy to even notice me.* Even though Mrs. Holland said she was going to call my parents and tell them, but maybe she didn't? I really wanted my mom to know how scared I was when Jenny spit that word at me, when all my life that was the worst thing anybody could say. That word, it's like it has edges to it, just the sound, and it digs into your skin like somebody's stabbing you with a blade. Jenny's eyes looked mean and hard when she said it, real fast. I couldn't believe my ears at first. Before dinner, in the kitchen when we were playing, I'd wanted to melt into Mama like I used to, back when her arms circling around me made the whole world safe and cozy.

I started to relax into that feeling, until I flashed on the night when she and I took BART over to a demo in the city, a long time ago, when I was little. It was dark, with candles and peoples' faces all in the shadows, like rising out of night. The police in their blue uniforms were lined up with riot shields and helmets at every corner, like these giant faceless robots. They were so huge. You couldn't even talk to them. They were all in lines, like these massive scary walls.

We used to go to End the War marches or rallies all the time in the city. That night she and I were marching along Market Street in a crowd all jammed together. I held on to her brown coat, trying to stay by her while she lifted her sign high over her head, screaming,

"Ho ho ho, Ho Chi Minh, the Vietcong is gonna win." She yelled so loud she got hoarse, practically, by the time we'd gone six blocks. My hand on her coat froze in the fog and the icy wind that whipped down Market Street. I didn't have any mittens or gloves. Suddenly the creepy cops in their giant helmets swooped right in front of me, and they grabbed a boy with a giant Afro who didn't look any older than Che. In fact, he kinda looked like Che. They punched him. I couldn't see why. He kicked and hollered. Other protesters were kind of trying to pull the cops off him, but they twisted his arms back and handcuffed him while they kept punching him and he was screaming. They pushed everybody back and they made a ring of cops around him, so nobody could get up close and help him. Suddenly Mama let go of my hand and dashed forward. "You let that boy go!" she screamed at the cops and broke through their line. "Take your hands off him right now."

"Lady, you're interfering with an arrest—"

"I know what I'm doing. Let that child go right now, he didn't do a thing." She reached over. I could only see a little bit. It looked like she was trying to put her hands in front of where they were hitting him, on his tummy and his face.

"Lady, I'm warning you, move back." The cop who was shouting at her lifted up his nightstick and began to shove her back.

"Mama, no!" I screamed.

"When you let that child go, I will," it sounded like she said.

That was all I saw because the crowd pushed me away, everybody moving forward, and I was almost crushed. When I squeezed between people and scrambled back, I couldn't find Mama or the cops or the boy or anybody.

"Mama," I screamed as loud as I could.

A hand reached down for me. But I pulled back; the hand had a scratchy leather glove, not nice warm skin like Mama's.

"Where's Mama?" I screamed, looking up.

An old woman stared down, her eyes kind of glassy, gray hair frizzing out from a gray cap. "Child, I don't know," she said kindly. "Where did you last see her?"

"Here!" I bawled, frantically looking around the crowd. "With the cops . . ." My mother's big smile over her brown coat had dissolved into the mist along with the police and the boy. Had they gotten her, too? I'd heard so many stories of jail, of beatings. Even people getting killed, people my parents knew. That I knew, too.

"What's your name?" The stranger stooped down over me.

No words came. Only a strange cry that sounded kind of like a cat.

"How old are you?" She patted my head awkwardly.

"Eight," I managed to whimper, which was not strictly true but the next day was my birthday.

The old lady squinted and pointed a shaky finger toward a small woman bumping a stroller along the sidewalk, scowling. "Is that the person you're with?"

I shook my head as fast as I could, wanting to say, "That woman doesn't look anything like my mother. Mine has a shiny white face with bright red curls sticking three feet out from her head in all directions." And she's a giant. Plus her face is always smiling, pretty much, like sunshine, not like that woman at all, who looked like a grouch. My body shook with sobs until I closed my eyes and pictured Mama. Would I ever see her again? How would I find my way home?

"What's your name?"

I froze, suddenly remembering I wasn't supposed to talk to strangers.

"Do you know your phone number, little girl?" the old lady asked. A knot of adults gathered around us.

I nodded but I didn't say anything.

"Tell me what it is so we can call your house," she said gently.

"It's 845-5020," I choked out.

"Come with me," she said, and grabbed my arm. Her hunched-over body was strong even though she was old so I didn't have any choice. I let her haul me into a tiny pizza place across the street where she asked the owner to let her use the phone. I heard her repeat the number to herself. I hoped I was right about the number.

"I have a lost child here," she barked into the phone before she handed it to me. "She won't say her name."

"Daddy," I blurted through my cries as soon as his voice filled my ear. "Mama's lost. I'm lost." I dissolved completely into sobs. "I think the cops have her."

"I'll be right there to get you, sugar," he said quietly. "Everything's okay. You're not lost, you're found. Stay with the woman who called me, stay right there in the pizza shop. But what the hell did your mother do?" I could hear the anger rising in his voice. "Let me speak to that woman again."

The pizza guy must have called the police. Two cops in those big blue uniforms came rushing in the door and held on to me, one on each side like I was a prisoner, until Daddy came. He had to show them all kinds of ID, even though I tried to squirm away to run into his arms. Then Mama showed up, crying so hard she couldn't talk. All she could do was pick me up and squeeze me and not let go.

"What the hell happened?" Daddy asked her.

She wouldn't answer until we were in the car. "I was trying to rescue a child, a boy, that the pigs had, they had him in cuffs and they were beating him up. Like crazy people. Kicking him—"

"What did you think was going to happen to Ruby while you were the great white savior?"

"Solomon, stop it! This is no time for that crap. This is serious. A teenage child is in jail right now, who knows what they're doing to him? Well, I do know, and it isn't pretty." She began to cry again. "I knew someone would find Ruby and call you. And that they'd release me. They did, after about five minutes, right there on the street. Such idiots—"

"I can't believe you'd put your own child in jeopardy—"

"You've got a lot of nerve lecturing me about child care, Mister Never At Home—"

"I know enough not to abandon a seven-year-old on the street in a mob full of strangers."

"A mob? Oh, now the people's army is a mob? And they weren't strangers, they were comrades. Look, Ruby's fine, aren't you?" She turned to the backseat, where I sat numbly, then she said to Daddy, "I'm sorry, but it was instinct. I just ran, without thinking. Wouldn't you do the same if you saw a young brother being beaten by cops? We've got to call Albert as soon as we get home, put out the word. And tell everyone to get down to the station in San Francisco. I got the boy's name, Elias Anderson, so we can try to get him out tonight. Before they beat him to a pulp." She put her face in her hands.

"Great that you got the kid's name, Red," Daddy said. I knew whenever he called her that he was softening. "You've got good instincts."

Still they argued, all the way home, about who cared more about me. But nobody really paid me any attention. I sat alone, wondering, *Did my mother care more about that boy she didn't know than about me? How could she have lost me? Wasn't I special to her? Didn't she know how scared I was about getting lost?*

I'd always known, like since I was born, that Che, who's only a year and a half older than me, is Daddy's special kid. "My man," Daddy calls Che, and gazes until the pride practically drips down his face, his eyes get so soft. He used to touch Che's head in that certain tender way, brushing back my brother's reddish curls when he was younger, and kind of croon, "My son, firstborn child." It's been that way my whole life, and I guess I'd kind of imagined that left me with Mama, that I was *her* special one. But the night I got lost in San Francisco, even after we all found each other at the pizza place once the cops connected us up and we drove home and Mama boiled hot milk with nutmeg the way I liked it, and even after both my parents tucked me into bed and sat next to me for a long time, my body still trembled.

Now somebody had called me nigger, for real, and it seemed like Mama didn't even care.

Maybe what I thought that night when I got lost in San Francisco was true. Maybe I wasn't anybody's special child.

CHAPTER 3

Elizabeth

"Why did you tear off after dinner before I even knew you were gone? We had stuff to talk about!" I sat cross-legged on a couch under the window nursing a Heineken, lifting my left wrist to scrutinize a nonexistent watch the moment Solomon cracked open the front door later that night. Cesar, who lay on the couch next to me, raised his head. "Out again till one." I tossed the bottle into the wastebasket, where it pinged against glass. Traffic still sped by outside on Ashby, headed toward San Pablo. "Yup. Do you wonder what we did all evening after you raced out, leaving every single dirty dish behind?" I gestured toward the kitchen, the red-crusted plates on the side of the sink, the hardening spaghetti pot, the skillet still on the stove. "Did you wonder if maybe there was more to tell you about my meeting with Gladys?"

"Damn it, Red, that's when the gigs are. I can't revolutionalize the whole goddamn music industry single-handedly, can I, just because you want me home every night?" He paused. "Yes, I was at the Hendrix meeting, where it took hours to decide, but we're calling a massive rally at the opening day of the trial, if you care. In

front of the courthouse. Which I thought was so important to you."
He folded himself into the blue chair facing the street, avoiding my
eyes. His were ringed with fatigue. "Yes, I stopped in at Yoshi's for
one hour to jam. I have to keep up my connections, remember?"

"That's not the fucking goddamn point." I wobbled into the
kitchen, shielding my eyes from its bright lights, and returned with
two Heinekens, handing one over. "We never see you, and I have
total responsibility for the kids from the second they get home."

Solomon was infuriatingly silent. He could be that way. Making
me do all the conservational work.

"It's not as if I don't have a job, too."

He maintained his silence. I flopped onto the couch and flipped
open a dog-eared pamphlet. "It's sexism," I said darkly, "and it's
systematic." I closed the mimeographed booklet and pointed at the
cover price: 50 cents to women, a dollar to men. "At least we get a
good deal somewhere. We should pay half price for everything, in
proportion to our pay."

"*The Politics of Housework!* 'The Politics . . . ? Let's talk about
something serious, goddamnit, at this time of the night. Please."
His nostrils flared. "What happened at school?"

For an answer I began to read aloud, as I'd once read *The New
York Times* to him over breakfast, when every protest was a harbinger
of the coming revolution. " 'Housework remains the woman's job
and even the revolutionary man who washes dishes simply *helps*.' "
My voice rose. He sat heavily, slouching in the large chair, his black
trumpet case leaning against his leg. His left cheek spasmed, the
nerve in his neck twitching in time to the cheek. " 'The roles we
take as natural are conditioned by oppression.' If you understand
that about race, why can't you get it about sex?" I raised my eyes
only to be met with half-closed lids, a jaw clenching and unclench-
ing. "Women's liberation explains it all. You just do whatever you
want, no matter the cost to me, to the kids, to anybody, while I'm
chained here. Housewife. I didn't marry a house."

"Then do what you want to do." Wearily.

"I don't know what I want. Aside from happy children."

"And that's my fault?" His eyes were hoods.

"It's classic."

"What is this, a goddamn women's lib seminar?" He closed his eyes.

"Liberation." I rose and began to pace. "Would you use that abbreviation about any other peoples' liberation?" When he didn't answer I screamed, "What was the last demo we've been to together? The Vietnam rally on Sproul Plaza? That was a year ago! What do we do as a family? Are we going together to the rally before the trial, are you gonna sneak up to the stage with the kids like you did that time you left me alone in the crowd?" I ached, still, and it had been years. That sunny Saturday, with the fog lifted and a welcome heat, we'd rattled along Grove Street, shushing Che and Ruby, until we arrived, late, at Bobby Hutton Memorial Park, as the Panthers had renamed DeFremery. When we joined the throng pressed in front of a platform, I saw I was one of only a couple whites. We'd slipped into a spot at the back of the crowd, where I stood next to Solomon behind rows of pillowy Afros and raised fists. Suddenly, he wove forward, dragging Che and pushing Ruby's stroller as a wedge, saying, "Excuse me, excuse me." I began to follow while he pushed toward the stage until I saw him wave me back. Startled, I stopped and lost sight of them until Solomon's head popped up in front. What's that about? I wondered, shocked. When I looked at the men and women jostling for space next to me, with people packed in behind us, I was acutely aware that I was on my own, a solo white woman bereft of my usual cover.

"The white man's rule has gone on too long!" a man screamed from the stage, his arm jutting upward. I applauded, trying to ignore glares from two large women wedged next to me. "The white woman expects us to clean her filthy house and wipe her kids' nasty asses. We're done with that shit!" While the crowd roared,

fists raised, I kept clapping, desperately, wanting to hoist a sign: I'M
WITH YOU, BROTHERS AND SISTERS! Instead I smiled broadly, trying
to demonstrate solidarity. Yet I felt horribly adrift, so unlike the
cozy solidarity of the days when we'd crossed arms, clasped hands,
and sung, *"We shall overcome, black and white together, we shall overcome . . ."* How could Solomon have abandoned me in this sea of
angry blackness? What would the kids think? I tried to shrug it off,
the way I'd learned to do with pretty much everything, but the be-
trayal stung. Later, when I waited alone by the car, "I'm sorry," he'd
said softly, looking like Rosa with her tail between her legs when
she knew she'd misbehaved. "But you know how it is, honey. . . ."

"I thought we didn't settle for 'how it is.' We're trying to make
'how it is' be different," I'd told him grimly, opening the car and
climbing in. As usual, I busied myself with the kids, who were clam-
oring for snacks, and we let it drop. But a hard wedge lodged itself
between us.

Now my Bill of Housework Rights exposed it.

"I can't go to demos anymore with you, can I, in this climate?"
he muttered. "We've been over all this. And over it. Why now, when
I'm more exhausted than a dead dog? And you're half drunk."

"What about *sharing* housework, instead of *helping*?" I rammed
him. "Which is token anyway."

"Elizabeth, what is this, everything and the kitchen sink? You're
the one who's here. And when I come home, tired as I am, yes, at
one fucking a.m.—after I've been out making good money. Speaking
of the kitchen sink, all right, let's. Look at it. It's stuffed with filthy,
disgusting dishes." He pointed. "Literally stacked on both goddamn
sides. The linoleum is coated"—he poked one foot out gingerly—
"with shit. What is this, dog pee or sour milk? I could lose my
footing and never be able to get up. Black man down! Drowning in
shit." He attempted a chuckle, which further infuriated me.

"Mopping is a bourgeois trap," I snapped. "And how the hell
would I have time to mop the floor with two kids running around,

two dogs, the fucking pregnant cat that *you* dragged home, the phone ringing every fucking minute with messages for *you*—'Oh, this is important, make sure the brother gets it'—and every kid from the neighborhood tearing through. Not to mention that I do have a job. And I run over to school whenever there's a crisis. But you wouldn't know, would you? Since you're never here. Am I supposed to be raising these kids by myself?"

"Could we maybe talk about this in the morning?"

"Oh yeah, when you get up after I'm at work. Good idea; maybe a phone call would do it!"

"What's going on? Did something happen with the kids?"

"Oh, now you're worried about the kids. Great. Yes, something is going on with the kids. They're biracial, remember. Gladys says Ruby's not white, not black. And she's going to have B-I-I-G problems. Not exactly what we pictured, is it, our perfect little new world? Oh yeah, and Ruby got in a fight today." I observed him evenly. "With a white girl, a fifth grader, who knocked her down."

He shot up, his eyes fully open.

"All right, somebody pushed her with a bathroom door, from the stall, by mistake. The door opened onto Ruby and knocked her down, but Ruby grabbed the girl's hair and dug in. And she called her a white bitch."

"When did you find out about this?" He eyed me through slits.

"At the meeting with Gladys. I talked to Ruby about it tonight after you left, at bedtime. She said this girl Jenny, who's new, slammed the stall door on her on purpose."

"She's got to learn to fight."

"Fight? You mean with her fists?"

He balled one up. "Yeah, take that bitch out before she decks Ruby." He rose, crouched, and pantomimed the action, *whoosh!* right arm swinging hard, hitting, again and again. His cheek twitched while he crouched lower, punching air. "Bam. No more trouble."

"Solomon, you're out of your mind. That wasn't what it was about. Ruby's not going to fight. She's not a street kid."

"A 'street kid'?" he said slowly. "A 'street kid'?"

I gulped.

"You equate 'black' with 'street'? White girls don't fight, black girls do, 'street girls' do, and she's not black, she's not 'street'?"

"Oh, that's not it, you know it's not." I tried to soften my tone.

"Trust me, that girl needs to learn how to defend herself. She's deeper than we think. There's a lot going on inside her. But she can take care of herself. 'White bitch!'" He chuckled grimly and picked up the *Chronicle*. "Did you see what that bastard Reagan said about Nicaragua?"

"Don't change the subject. I'm worried about Ruby." I started toward the kitchen to tackle the dishes, but when I heard him behind me cursing, "Damn women's lib," the day's events rushed up on me like a tidal wave. I grabbed a wineglass and hurled it toward his head, aiming a few feet to the left. In a second he was on me, knocking me down with the palm of his hand, glancing my right temple while he hissed through gritted teeth, "Don't you ever throw anything at me!"

"I wasn't throwing *at* you," I whimpered, curled in a ball, afraid to move. "It was the wall. How could you hit me?"

"Don't throw glass," was all he said at first, into my shock, my disbelief. No one had ever struck me. In Mississippi I'd been afraid we'd be murdered, in Sacramento I'd been afraid of some racist idiot randomly attacking us on the street, even in San Francisco I'd had moments of terror, but I never imagined it would be Solomon who'd force me to the floor with a blow to the head. Weeping, I crawled to the refrigerator for ice cubes and managed to pry the freezer door open. The dogs padded in and sniffed, trying to investigate, but I pushed them down the hall, away from the shards of glass. Solomon silently helped me make an ice pack, folding the cubes into a dish towel while we sat on the floor. "I'm sorry, Red," he moaned quietly, "I thought you were attacking me. What have we come to?" We clung to each other, shaking.

"I wanted to go with you tonight," I said. "It's so hard—"

"But you couldn't," he said, cutting me off angrily, "you know that. Oh yeah, I can see strolling into the All-African People's Revolutionary Party meeting with a paleface on my arm. Great."

"Well, why do you have me in your arms right now then?"

Sigh. "We've been over this. You think the world is a fairyland, everybody's nice. It's not that way. There are dangerous folks out there. And I for one don't want to rile them up."

"Why do you hang out with 'dangerous folks' if you're married to me?"

Silence.

"Could we talk about maybe why Ruby called the other girl a white bitch?" I said, accusation driving my voice like a gun.

"Ever think about that when you call yourself my white-bitch wife?"

"What about your *goddamn whitey* songs? 'Lord, white folks and flies I do despise,/and the more I see white folks, the more I like flies.' Don't you think Ruby hears that?" I stopped. "She needs a proud black parent. Who shows her another way to be black. Without hating the honky. Somebody who's here."

He started to speak, paused, then held me tighter. Slowly, he said, almost whispering, as if to himself, "You never think about how maybe a family is holding me back."

"*You?* Holding *you* back? Hey, weren't we talking about Ruby? But if you're talking about 'holding back,' where am *I* going? Running to the grocery store on my way home from class. Is that supposed to be my destiny? Biology is destiny?"

"Cut the women's lib crap, Red. You sound like a robot. As a composer," he spoke carefully, as if addressing a slow child, "I need a certain kind of time around me . . ." He hunched his shoulders, still cradling me; all I could see in his eyes was a deep brown shimmer, reflecting the kitchen light. "Floating-mind time to experiment, to create, not this constant press of daily details. I'm an artist, and I'm always running, running to get to class in the morning, afraid I'll lose my job. . . !" His head hung over his chest.

"Well, color me black. Maybe I'm an artist, too, but I don't even have the time to figure that out. You wanted children. It's a little late now for regrets. I never agreed to raise them by myself."

He lifted his head and eyed me with silent fury, with that flash of anger I'd first glimpsed in Greenwood the day we met: June 13, 1963, the morning after they gunned Medgar Evers down in Jackson. "Shot dead right in front of his children," old Mrs. Washington, who'd housed three of us Student Nonviolent Coordinating Commitee volunteers, said grimly when she told me.

"Damn it," Solomon shouted now.

"Shh," I hushed, finger to my lips. "You'll wake the kids." The ice in the towel was leaking down my shirt; I stood to stick the pack in the freezer and run hot water to soak the dirty pans.

"I can't find a goddamn thing in this mess," he said. "Look at this—stacks of mail from the Dark Ages!" He pointed to the slab of wood in the corner, where a clutter of KPFA public radio newsletters, Panther pamphlets, copies of *Ebony* and *Jet*, and piles of mail swamped the counter. "Who can find anything here?"

Traffic on Ashby rumbled by, so we didn't hear her coming until Ruby appeared in the doorway, rubbing her eyes, her face pinched with worry. "What's going on?"

I breathed as quietly as I could, motioning her back to her room, but with lidded eyes she asked, "Daddy, what's—"

"Have you seen my glasses?" His jagged face smoothed out, as if the angry man I'd just seen were a phantom, and here was my familiar husband: genial, smooth, and handsome as ever. "Just trying to find my glasses, sugar."

Ruby stood, her face creasing, looking from him to me while I kept one hand on my forehead, trying to cover the swelling. "You usually leave them on top of the bookcase by the window." She nodded toward the living room. Yes, she would know. Whenever Solomon was home, she tracked him, I saw, although he rarely noticed. I observed again how alike they were: two lanky, intense people determined to take charge of every moment, trusting nothing to chance. Even their angular bodies reflected their fierce spirits, whereas Che and I tended toward a rounder "Hey, let's relax" body type, with Che the so-far shorter version of my big-boned body.

We spotted the elusive horn-rims where Solomon had set them high on the bookshelf, poking out from a stack of dusty books. "Go back to sleep, sweetie, everything's okay," I said, giving Ruby a hug and a gentle push. Over her shoulder she shot me a look of disbelief, but she stumbled back to her room.

Solomon carefully hooked the glasses behind his ears, pulled out his usual chair at the dining table, and reached in his pocket. During the early civil rights years we'd never smoked weed, scoffing, "We don't want to get busted for some silly-ass stuff like that!" Now I sunk into the red chair under the bay window at the front of the house with ice pressed to my face and watched him wet the fingers of his right hand with his tongue and roll a fat joint. Stray pieces of grass and sticks poked out the ends. He struck a light on a matchbox, drew a deep inhale, held the breath, and passed the joint. The dogs slouched in to investigate the smell, and then clumped away down the hall, toenails clicking.

Solomon passed me the joint and I inhaled deeply, resting my head on the back of the armchair while he stumbled back to the kitchen, heated oil, and poured corn kernels into the sizzling pot, shaking it back and forth. I heard the explosions: *pop, pop, pop*. Once we polished off the popcorn we scavenged every sweet: M&M's, Pepperidge Farm chocolate cookies, even chocolate pudding mix stirred with warm milk, until, done in, we fell onto our bed.

Dozing, half asleep, I peered from half-closed lids and saw dawn blush. When the high chirps of towhees drifted in through the open window, I pushed Cesar off the bed and, determined to ignore the previous evening's insanity, stroked Solomon's body, still enchanted by his skin changing from dark red-brown on his face to a light milky tan on the soles of his feet. His palms were laced with dark lines, as if God had inked in life lines. While he slept I traced the web on his left hand where the short lines curved, intersected. *Where is this life going?*

He woke and sleepily stretched his hand over my hips where the bones lay under a roll of flesh newly gathered around my middle, the ten pounds I'd gained in the last few years all clumped together. His familiar hands explored me until I could pretend there was no other world outside, nobody who cared about the white skin I wore, the treasonous casing covering my staunch black heart. He rubbed the soft skin inside my thighs, stroking lightly until he reached the red curls between my legs. I sighed with pleasure. "Let's turn on the light," he said, and kept his eyes on my rigid nipples while he reached inside me, massaging, circling with his fingers, back and forth, until I writhed on the bed. "Shall I stop?" he teased softly.

"No," I begged, my eyes searching his, watching the perspiration on his upper lip. *How many years have we carried on this ritual?* "Don't stop." When I tingled with the oncoming rush, knowing I couldn't hold it back another second, he rolled on top of me, thrusting hard, with a spasm—"Yes," he moaned—and we rocked, jerking our hips together, his sharp bones jutting into my soft flesh. Still panting, I felt a sizzle pulse to my feet. Solomon lay on me, inert, silent.

Afterward we lay spooned, Solomon pressing his warm body behind mine, avoiding the chilly damp spot we'd left under our lovemaking. He whispered, "Yes," again and again until we slept, curled together, reminding me, as I drifted off, of those early months in Mississippi. And I thought, in the moments before sleep claimed me, that I hadn't even had a chance to tell him about the five kittens, how Che and Ruby and I had watched them being born, one by one, in our shed. How tiny they were, how Zoe had licked each baby before they lined up on her teats, sucking. How they were piled right now in a small furry heap. Or how Ruby and Che had grown wide-eyed at the sight.

At breakfast Ruby asked, her face wrinkled in concern, "What happened?" She leaned over to gently touch my forehead, slightly swollen. In the mirror I'd been able to convince myself it might go unnoticed.

"I fell," I told her, avoiding her eyes. "I tripped on an ice cube on the floor when I was getting a snack." The bruise was already turning faint yellow and purple. But small as it was, it marked the night that tipped Solomon and me from a struggling couple to a warring one. Within days he started crawling into bed just before dawn, sleeping for another hour or two after I rose. He was home so rarely that during the entire next six weeks he never once saw the kittens mewling in the shed before we gave them away. I think he hardly knew they were there.

During that strange period when Solomon and I passed silently in the mornings, I made an effort to dance occasionally in the kitchen or the living room with the kids, desperate to hear us all giggle. I let them spin Jackson 5 records whenever they liked and put on living room shows. Che, spoon microphone in hand, was Michael jumping around. Ruby, each time a different backup brother, played pretend instruments, and my two looked like members of the family the album cover missed: bell-bottoms, puffy Afros, even tasseled vests. While the record scratched out tunes they gyrated, they twirled, they clapped and rocked and slid. "'I want you back,'" they wailed. And "'I'll be there.'" While they flung themselves from side to side singing, "'I'm goin' back to Indiana,'" thumping to the beat, I held myself erect in the doorway, amazed at these talented two. How could Solomon not want more of this? "'ABC, easy as one, two, three,'" they sang, stepping forward, back, in unison. "'Listen to me baby, that's all you gotta do.' Yeah. 'Shake it, shake it, baby. . . .' " I clapped along and roared my appreciation, especially when Che dared to shake his butt. But try as we did to keep the energy up, except for dancing moments—" 'Blame it on the boogie' "—when the music ended we were a sad trio. Even the dogs and Zoe seemed to feel the change. The three of them trooped in and out, appearing to have lost their verve. Yes, the dogs were getting on—both nearly ten—but not old enough for this sudden decline. And I didn't think Zoe's lost kittens were enough to entirely explain her stealth. We all needed something to shake us up. But what?

Some instinct guided me to the healing power of dirt. A long-handled shovel leaned against our back shed. Coated with rust, it had been left behind by the previous owner, waiting since the day we arrived in Berkeley. For eleven years it had leaned in place. One evening when the kids looked especially desolate, picking silently at their supper, I tramped out to the front yard, snatched the spade, and jammed it into a patch of dry weedy grass.

Push. It hardly went down an inch. I stepped on it, I jumped, I jabbed, I jumped again, slamming the full force of my 160-pound five-foot-ten frame on top of the shovel blade. It went down only half an inch in the hard, dry dirt. But I scraped and pushed and jabbed until I could wiggle the shovel back and forth, getting down a little deeper with each jiggle. Finally, a foot down, the earth yielded. I scooped a handful of soil deep from under the web of roots and inhaled a fine fresh odor, a scent I hadn't smelled since childhood. I jabbed again. And again, knowing that wherever I went, eventually Ruby was sure to follow.

"What are you doing? You've been out there almost an hour," I heard her call from the front porch.

"Making a garden! Come and help."

She hesitated.

"Come on, it's fun!"

Slowly she stepped onto the grass, gaping at the piles of dirt and at me, her wild-haired, half-dressed mother, as if I'd lost my mind. A hot, dry Santa Ana wind blew, even though it was only June, so maybe I had. My nerves were jumpy and my skin itched. If I didn't dig, who knows what I'd be capable of?

"Here." I wiped my grimy face with my shirt and passed the shovel. "Have a turn."

"Eeww." Ruby held it at arm's length.

"If we dig up a plot we can plant flowers, like those lilies we saw over on Sacramento the other day, the orange ones you liked, remember?"

"Oh yeah." She perked up and jumped onto the shovel, pressing it another inch into the dry dirt. Then we took turns digging, spading up mound after mound of earth until, sweaty, exhausted, and inspired, I scooped up a handful of dry dirt and flung it directly at my well-coiffed daughter. Watching the dust float through the air, spreading like a cloud, I stared, horrified, at what I'd done.

"Mama!" Her eyes flashed wide in alarm. But something jiggled loose. After a few seconds of shock, she bent down for a handful herself. Closing her eyes, she let it fly, whooping, "Got you!" And the fight was on. We hurled dirt back and forth. We tossed clumps in the air, giddy, silly, until our shouts brought Che to the door.

"What's happening?"

The dogs yelped behind him, wagging their tails, nosing the screen door open. Chasing Rosa and Cesar, he stepped out on the stoop and took a direct hit from Ruby in the rump. Soon all three of them tumbled into our dirt fight. Cesar turned out to be a champion digger, spraying earth with his paws. We snorted and howled, astonished at our dirt play. Dripping sweat and dirt, while Che and Ruby were hidden in a fog of whirling dust, I pulled out and turned on the cracked hose and aimed, spraying until we were soaked, dripping, smeared with mud. We laughed so hard I peed in my pants, but it didn't matter. I just hosed myself off. When the dogs were coated with mud, I sprayed them, too. By the time night fell, the three of us, streaked and grimy, our arms draped over each other's shoulders, stood on the stoop and looked back at the yard. We'd dug ourselves a good-sized mud plot. But more than that, we'd dug ourselves out of our funk.

We each had our own strategy for coping with the stress of our brittle home. While mine was to break all the parenting rules and lead us in spontaneous mischief, Ruby's was perpetual motion. She charged out of the house every day with Imani, running off to school or soccer or music lessons. Or she slammed into her room, restless, and slammed right out again, determined to be in constant movement, as noisily as possible. She still stopped long enough to perch on the edge of my red easy chair, and maybe lean into me, but only for a minute; by the time we'd settled in and begun a chat, she jumped up, whirling into the kitchen to check for a snack or pleading homework. After years of our sharing every thought at length, I missed our easy, lazy companionship, now that this dervish had taken over my daughter's body.

Che grew ever more quiet.

CHAPTER 4

Ruby

A boy on the plane from Atlanta, where my parents made me go all of a sudden instead of Grandma Jean and Grandpa Jonah coming to us like they usually do, gawked at me across the aisle. In an obvious way.

But that wasn't anything new. White people always stared. They couldn't stand it when they couldn't figure out my race, which they never could. My golden skin (that's what Mama calls it) and nappy hair confused them, and at eleven, almost twelve, I dressed in real cool clothes. I'd seen how much better people treated me if I wore a sharp bright red blouse, ironed, real crisp. What a difference my outfit made. Mama, who basically played sharecropper, that's what Daddy said about her overalls, or she wore raggedy batik skirts that dragged on the floor—she didn't get it. At all. She disapproved of my lipstick from the second I started wearing it, scanning me, looking annoyed. "You're a dupe of consumer culture." Last week she bought me a peasant blouse, bringing it home for no reason, saying, "I saw this on Telegraph Avenue and I thought you'd like it."

"No. *You* would like it," I told her. How could she be so dense?

The white cotton blouse was smocked with blue and red embroidery, hearts and flowers, big puffy sleeves. "That's not my style at all." It was hers.

Do you ever see me? I wanted to ask. Sometimes I felt like an exhibit who was supposed to prove she was a perfect mother. Or how close we were. *Who do you see when you look at me?* I wondered. *Am I the black version of you that you wish you could be?* I wanted to say all this. A lot of it was stuff I'd heard Daddy say, but I knew it would only make her cry. I'd watched that happen when a black person told her something she didn't want to hear. I hung up the blouse in my closet and hoped she'd notice I never wore it. Which didn't happen. Instead she forgot all about it. Maybe someday she'd start noticing what *I* wanted.

The white boy across the aisle was like all the others. "What are you?" He leaned over.

"A zebra," I wanted to answer but I said, "A person."

"No." He was embarrassed. "No, I mean, where are you from?"

I knew what was coming but it made me mad so I said, "Berkeley." West Berkeley. Or North Oakland. Our house was right on the border.

"No," he tried again. "Where are you *from*?"

I was in a bad mood so I said, "Berkeley," again and frowned, trying to scare him. I'd found out that most white people scared pretty easily. "What do you mean?" I wanted to make him stumble around.

"You look so exotic. Are you Mexican? But you don't sound Mexican."

I finally told him, "My dad's Black and my mom's white," and watched the relief on his face. He assumed then that he knew where to place me, but he had no idea who I was. Just like Mama.

God, I was sick and tired of having to explain my racial background all the time. Anyway, that boy kept eyeing me. I didn't know what that meant: Could he suddenly turn threatening or was he only curious? Mama said people stared because I was beautiful, and she acted as though I should enjoy it, or at least ignore it. She had no idea what it was like when I could see men's eyes get so weird. I wanted her to understand, so she could say, "I know *exactly* what you mean, and this is how *I* dealt with it." Sometimes I wanted her to be black so bad tears came to my eyes, 'cause Daddy really didn't get this either. It was a lonesome feeling.

Black people always knew who I was. They didn't have to figure out the details. I guess they understood how mixed we were.

I think my parents sent me off so fast—they told me one day and I was packed the next—because they were falling apart. Che refused to go with me. He'd said he'd stay over with Jabari, his best friend. They sleep over at each other's houses practically every weekend. So he got to do something normal while I got shipped off. But I didn't put up too much of a fuss 'cause I love going to Grandma and Grandpa's. Once before I flew there alone, when I was ten, and the stewardess gave me as much soda as I wanted, 7-Up was my favorite, which I was hardly ever allowed to have at home—"It will rot your teeth"—and she gave me some wings to pin on the blue blouse my grandma made me while I was there. She sewed it exactly the way I wanted it, too, with a high collar that stood up around the neck. It was so cool.

I felt real comfy at my grandparents', and they told me a lot of history, too, about civil rights and stuff like that. "It didn't all start in the sixties," Grandma told me in her gravelly voice one day. "Naw, it didn't all start in the sixties like people think." She jerked my head, braiding my hair. "Or the fifties. Your great-grandmother and I sat at a white lunch counter in . . ." Her fingers tightened, pulling my scalp while she calculated. We sat in her living room, a cozy "front parlor," she called it, me on a footstool, and she was squatting behind me on the couch with her knees holding me. That room felt like it was alive. A bright yellow and orange and red kente cloth hung over her piano. The couch and the chair, a big stuffed one, were covered with a different kente cloth, with small dark blue squares. I loved the ebony sculptures, too. A whole group sat directly on the floor, a flock of crouching women that I thought of as ancestors, like great-grandmothers, actually. The walls were filled with African masks, painted the brightest red, black, orange, all kind of designs. In one corner she had a dark cabinet, like a shrine, with framed photos of her people and Grandpa's. "I was ten, so, 1928. Can you picture us?" She yanked my head back. "Little colored girl dressed in her Sunday best, pigtails flying, and Mama with her white gloves. We didn't get arrested either. Just ignored, until I had to use the toilet." She chuckled. "Oh, it didn't all begin in Greensboro on February 1, 1960. Those brave boys stood on a lot of shoulders. Rosa Parks wasn't the first to refuse the back of the bus, oh no," she said, tying rubber bands into my hair.

When Grandpa Jonah heard her tell the story, he came stomping in from the front porch, kind of gruff like he always talked, with a low deep voice. "Damn night riders! But we got 'em, my brothers Joseph and William did, with the Arkansas Southern Tenant Farmers. Yup. They were organizers. And I worked with 'em from the inside." He winked. "From the school, I funneled grant money to 'em."

He looked a lot like Daddy: same broad nose, tall, skinny, dark. Not like Grandma Jean, who was as light as me, with a lower lip that jutted out and "a belly and a butt," she liked to say, lifting her elbows and kind of dancing in a circle to show them off.

"They organized those farmers for seven years," Grandpa Jonah told me, holding himself erect, arching his back just like Daddy, and wearing the same sharp clothes. "Colored and white together just like now. Nope, that's nothing new." Even before that, "when I was your age"— he raised his hand, palm down, to show his eleven year-old height—"I wrapped my head with cloth to make it look like I was an African, ha, and we sat downstairs at the movies with the white folks instead of up in the balcony. Even though in the balcony we got to throw candy over the edge on the crackers, if we wanted to waste our sweets!" He slapped his thin thigh. "Back then your grandma here wore dreadlocks before any other woman in Atlanta," he bragged. "Last year, the folks down at the Chamber like to have a fit when they saw that nappy hair. She's right, it didn't all start in 1960 or with the good Dr. King in the bus boycott. We been at this a long, long time, sugar. Lots of different kinds of folks."

That day, Grandma Jean tried to lock my hair, too, but even though she rubbed in buckets of oil and I cried buckets of tears, I kept begging, "I want to look like you," but the curl wasn't tight enough.

"You're fixin' to give us enough salt for a salt lick," Grandpa Jonah said, wiping away my tears with the handkerchief he always carried. "Salty, salty dog."

Flying home, I wondered who would pick me up at the airport. I kind of hoped for Mama. I wondered what was going on between her and Daddy, with them fighting all the time. If I had her to myself in the car, maybe she'd tell me the truth.

But it was Daddy hollering, "Ruby!" waving over everybody's heads while I scrambled up the ramp. I wished he wouldn't do that with his deep voice that filled the whole place. He sounded practically like Grandpa Jonah, only louder. Everybody stared at us. "Give me some sugar!" he called out, opening his arms. When he kissed my cheek and his sweater brushed against my face with that pipe tobacco smoke, that kind of woodsy smell, I was glad to see him anyway.

"How's Grandpa and Grandma?" he asked, pulling my green suitcase out of my hand. It was new, plastic with a real leather handle, and I didn't want to scratch it. He led the way through the crowd. I could feel his hand twitching as he tugged me, and his right eye blinked in a funny way when he bent toward me. Was he nervous? Was he mad at me? Had something terrible happened? I couldn't answer him with the crush of people. A double stroller with a screaming kid blocked our way until we scooted around them. It was good that Daddy was holding my hand, pulling me, 'cause my own sight began to smear. It was like raindrops were falling one by one on my eyelashes. Once we climbed into the car I couldn't stop them.

"Ruby? What's this?" In our family, being tough was expected. Suddenly, to my surprise, my father threw both arms around me. I sniffled and leaned into his shoulder.

"I don't know," I tried to say, but I couldn't stop crying.

"Everything's gonna be all right. We'll talk about it when we get home. We're still going to be a family. You're going to be fine." He gave me a lopsided smile, one I'd never seen before. The way he said the words, like he was forcing them out, like it wasn't true at all, made me not believe them one bit.

And deep inside I knew at that minute that I wouldn't be fine.

CHAPTER 5

Elizabeth

"Divorce." Once the word sliced the air, we sat stunned in the dining room. "Divorce?" Solomon echoed, looking whipped. We hovered in our old midnight spots, facing each other across the table in a rare rendezvous. "I can't believe that after fifteen years, coming through . . . the crucible of the Movement," he faltered, "we're finished." His long thin fingers clasped his fork, ready to dig into a late-night lasagna, but the silver hung motionless above his plate until he put it down. "Women's Liberation has fucked with your brain," he declared softly, tears streaking one cheek, while he bowed out of the kitchen.

"It's not because of Women's Liberation we can't get along," I called after him, too weary of our circular arguments to continue. Instead I followed silently into the living room; I stood leaning against a wall, watching while he opened his alto sax case, plucked out the metal mouthpiece, licked the reed, and blew without attaching the saxophone. I heard a sputter . . . then a pattern, coalescing into "Amazing Grace." Only the tempo gave it away without the sax. He blew slowly, low and sad, leaning back while I stood, tears clogging my throat, in the archway. *"How sweet the sound . . . I once was lost . . ." I wish I could burn my way back to you. There's nothing to say; we've worn a groove of trouble so deep, a wave we can't climb over. "Save a wretch like me."*

Was it only fifteen years ago we met? I'd never seen a dark-skinned person cry before the night Medgar Evers was killed, never saw how the shiny tears layered a transparent sheen over brown skin. That first morning in '63, when I opened the screen door to peer outside at my new home in Greenwood, Mississippi, where three of us SNCC volunteers were staying, I heard the sound, a mellow voice and the plink of a guitar, before I saw the source. Then I made him out, a gorgeous dark man with high cheek-bones, a finely chiseled head, and horn-rimmed glasses resting on his broad nose. He hunched on a bench in the yard with one leg splayed out, crooning, *"Wade in the water, God's gonna trouble the water."*

I watched him lean over his guitar while I stepped off the porch, making my way down a short flight of rickety stairs onto the yard, feeling self-conscious: a big-boned twenty-year old in wrap-to-the-knee leather sandals and green sundress, copper curls frizzing over my shoulders nearly to my waist. Ever since I'd been a kid I was tall for my age, and solidly built; usually I felt about as graceful as a bull in a china shop. The yard was a dirt patch with one white camellia bush, nothing like the lawns I'd grown up with in Cleveland, even in my part of town. There the noon whistle blared from the nearby Fisher Body plant where my dad worked, the shriek so loud everything stopped at our house and we had to cover our ears, but even we had a small grass lawn. Waves of Delta heat rose, creating an aura around the man. An orange cat curled under a bush and a mangy dog scuttled by, its tongue hanging.

"Solomon Jordan," he said in a deep voice, leaning forward and extending his arm. "From Atlanta. Been here a week. Gonna save the race." The bitter tone was leavened with a low chuckle.

"Lizzie O'Leary." I grasped his warm brown hand. "From Cleveland. I got here last night on the bus. To teach at the Freedom School."

His face relaxed, his full lips suggesting a smile before his eyes flitted down to his strumming fingers. Sparrows warbled from a nearby branch, throwing back their heads and pumping their tails while I stood wiping my forehead.

"Welcome," he said, still strumming and humming. "Welcome to Faulkner country. As written by Kafka," he murmured almost under his breath. "It's a tough day. And this is a tough place. 'Mississippi Goddam.'" He began to hum, kind of moaning until words formed: "'Hound dogs on my trail,/School children sitting in jail,/Black cat cross my path,/I think every day's gonna be my last.'" Again the tight crooked smile while he slipped a broken piece of glass, a bottleneck, onto his finger and slid it up the neck of the guitar, back and forth until a sound I'd never heard before, a throbbing high-pitched vibration, made me want to sway my hips and dance, and cry, too, in this strange, frightening country of Mississippi.

"I've been waiting all year to come," I said, looking around. "Wow, you've read Kafka? I love him. But isn't Faulkner strange enough without Kafka?"

"You don't know Mississippi." That sardonic grin. "We all read *Metamorphosis* at Morehouse, even musicians. I graduated three weeks ago. Free as a bird."

I must have looked blank because he explained, while he continued to strum, "It's a Negro college in Atlanta where my dad teaches and I spent four years as a prisoner." He riffed on the guitar; it sounded like a drumroll heralding an announcer. Then: "One of the premier Negro colleges in the United States." He resumed his normal voice. "I was a Tigershark. Swim team," he added, after my look of incomprehension. "We have one of the best. Divisional champions."

"Oh. I majored in English Lit before I dropped out."

He looked quizzical.

"Money. I wanted to come down here so bad and I needed four hundred dollars. So I got a job at Woolworth's. I picketed them every Saturday and worked the lunch counter Monday to Friday, nine to five, behind enemy lines"—I gave a half-grin—"until they found out. After that I was a lingerie clerk at Penney's. Not too many jobs for English Lit majors, especially ungraduated ones. But I got the money."

"Why did you want to come so bad?" He stopped strumming and looked up.

"I had to be here. When I was growing up all I heard about was my uncle volunteering in the Abraham Lincoln Brigade, in the heroic Spanish Civil War," I half mocked. "But this is our fight."

His broad forehead wrinkled, his eyes squinted, and I could see the gears working, puzzling it out.

"Fighting the Fascists," I prompted. "Everyone came from all over to support the elected government, the one Franco took over. This is my chance to be part of the Movement, to do my part."

"I'm impressed," he said, the hinges of his mouth releasing into the broadest smile yet. "You're a brave soul."

I blushed until my flaming face matched my hair. But it was true. I was brave; I had to be. I'd grown up on persecution stories: my father's mythical Irish ancestors, who dug peat and starved and knew the fairies; his sacred UAW union, Fisher Body Local 45. And my mother's *bubbes* and *zaides,* forced by pogroms from one country to another until her uncles and aunts and cousins were butchered. These tales, told so often they formed my cellular structure, had led me to believe that a wronged people was always right, forever cheered on, and that my place was by their side.

Beads of perspiration wet my forehead and dribbled under my breasts. Unsure what to say next, I tried a safe, neutral topic. "Boy, it's hot."

"Don't call me boy!" He leaped up, dropping his polished guitar so fast dust rose. His eyes smoked through the glasses. I wasn't expecting him to be so tall, or so lean.

"I wasn't calling you boy. It's only an expression. Just a word," I faltered, stepping back.

"Not to me. I'm a grown man. A man!" His voice was a razor. "It wasn't just a word to Medgar who they killed like a dog. And called *boy* every time they kicked him. Don't you ever call me boy."

"I won't. I didn't know. I'm sorry." My brain blotted the word *boy* forever from my speech. *That isn't what I meant! I'd never call Medgar Evers a boy. Or you either.*

His lips tightened to a slice in his wide face.

"I'm sorry," I repeated, wilting with apology as every ounce of my coveted Beat persona leached from my body. I was just a white girl after all.

"Listen, Red, sorry if I bit your head off. Like I said, tough day." He turned to his guitar and began to sing. " 'If I feel tomorrow like I feel today . . . I'm gonna pack my grip, make my getaway.' 'St. Louis Blues,' " he muttered before he started a tune with words that sounded like " 'dead,/Evil spirits all 'round my bed.' " Soon he dove into a driving, pulsing rhythm that surprised me by making my underpants wet. " 'If your man gets personal,' " he sang with his broad Southern accent. I found it hard to breathe before I escaped back into the house.

The next day I asked, "Sol, please teach me guitar." Lifting my face I expected his lopsided smile, but instead I saw fear tighten his face before a mask settled. He looked away before he said sharply, "Solomon, not Sol."

"Sorry," I gulped.

"All right," he agreed, his voice softening. "I'll teach you. But you'll have to practice."

"I will," I pledged. "I promise I will."

"You're on, Red."

Then I was his pupil. Each sweltering evening, after we tramped dusty roads trying to coax the locals into registering for the Freedom School, we sat on the worn bench. He gave me lessons while Mrs. Washington, who owned the weathered house, tended us from her porch, rocking, keeping watch, a guardian for the courtship she must have known was budding. Her shrunken frame pushed back and forth, a rhythm for our songs, like the gentle swoosh of a drum. Soon my sore fingers could pick out "Freight Train" and "Black Is the Color of My True Love's Hair." Sitting side by side on the bench or a patch of grass, we sang, my thin soprano riding above his bass. When he pressed his hands against mine, guiding them onto the strings, I trembled.

Solomon was a fine teacher, patient with my mistakes, ordering my fingers into proper positions with his: rich brown against parchment pink twined on the strings. Each day Mrs. Washington rocked, soothing our romance. Out of the corner of my eye I saw another volunteer, Bessie, a girl from Boston, watching, too, saying nothing but following us with her stare. Just the way the white people did in town. Their eyes raked over my body until I stood naked every time I strolled into Holly's store for a Coke. Everyone, dark and light, gave me that blank, surly look if Solomon was hovering by my shoulder.

Still, every day we knocked on doors, alternating our opening lines, knowing the answers before they came: "Do you have children eight to twelve for our Freedom School? It's free." I skipped along next to Solomon's loping walk, struggling, even with my long legs, to keep up while we talked of Faulkner and Kafka and Thomas Mann, all the great writers we were reading, until we heard the sputter of an engine approaching. Whenever a car full of white men slowed, crawling next to us, spitting dust in our mouths and words we didn't want to hear in our ears, we choked down a stomach-clenching fear. While we couldn't dare hold hands, we gained strength from each other's company. Once when the fear got too bad and I threw up after we crept back to the house, Mrs. Washington wiped my clammy brow with a cloth.

Within a month Solomon and I spent all our time together; around others I simply looked away, keeping my gaze on my beautiful man. Or my handmade sandals. At the close of summer we clambered up the steps of a Greyhound bus and headed out west to Oakland, California, where everything was possible. Like two paper boats tossed in a raging pool, we held hands and jumped, singing, "God's gonna trouble the water"; the storm we were calling forth would surely cleanse our bloody land.

Now, though, fifteen years later, we could hardly cleanse ourselves, much less the nation. I watched in grief, unable to move, while Solomon deliberately, stiffly, reached into the hall closet and unfolded our green wool blanket with the black stripe, spreading it carefully on the couch. *My parents sent us this blanket from their trip to Canada,* I thought numbly. He lay down fully dressed except for his shoes, sank into the soft cushions, and silently cut the light.

In the morning, on Solomon's way out of the house, he pecked me good-bye before he ambled over to the breakfast table to slap Che's shoulder and kiss Ruby on the top of her head. Ruby groaned, "Daaad," before she rushed out the door, book bag flapping. Che simply sat quietly and watched his father close the front door before he crept out.

How did they know?

I shuffled heavily back to the kitchen, turned on the gas burner, and poured a can of Campbell's chicken noodle soup into a crusty pan, not bothering to scour traces of rice left in a ring. When I lifted a spoonful of broth to my lips, the smell gagged me. Gusts of fog blew by the windows, shrouding the house. Rosa lay at my feet, a tired bundle mirroring my mood. I tried again, but when I felt my stomach lurch I stumbled to the toilet and vomited, wave after wave. *What have we done?* Throwing on a pair of jeans I wobbled out the door and rushed to BART in a daze, hurrying to teach my English as a Second Language class. For hours I numbly responded to student questions, my mind on automatic.

After school, when Ruby and Che burst in the door, I stared at them bustling around the hallstand while they untied sneakers, shoved, squealed, and dropped their books before they ran off again: Ruby to Imani's, Che to Jabari's. At dinner I studied them while they reached for slices of the pepperoni pizza I'd bought on the way home. *How will the three of us do this?*

"Mama, when's Daddy coming home?"

"Don't speak with your mouth full," Che scolded his sister before he carefully split the last slice of pizza with a knife, one strip for himself, the bigger wedge for Ruby.

"Where's Daddy?" Ruby asked me. "Is he going to sleep on the couch again?"

That night Solomon loped slowly through the front door at midnight, shivering with the damp night chill. I flung myself at him and hung on, pressing against his black leather jacket.

"Jesus, Red, I'm scared out of my mind to live without you." His voice was flat, stayed flat and drained through the steaming licorice tea I poured, laced with rum. Exhausted, we staggered down the hall hand in hand and tumbled naked into our double bed. *We've had this bed since we moved to California.* As if the flame in our bodies could burn away daily life, we fell on each other, hoping our heat could glue the broken pieces together. We clung, weeping on and off, until morning. It was a Saturday; at noon Ruby banged on our door.

"We're talking," Solomon answered quickly. "It's private."

"Are you sick?"

"No, sweetie," I said, in as soothing a voice as I could muster.

"What's the matter?"

"Nothing, we'll be up soon," I cooed.

"Hold me," Solomon whispered.

"I can't believe we can't make this work."

"I'm so tired of fighting, Elizabeth, I can't keep this up."

In the midst of our tears and recriminations, we furiously made love, over and over, willing our passion to fuse this union: our promise to the future. When we sat on the side of the bed talking, his hand on my thigh, I finally confessed the vomiting and how queasy I felt every day, especially in the mornings. "Damn it, we can't let race rip us apart," I said. "We might be having another kid."

His face turned ashen; he looked as though I'd slapped him. But he said quietly, "It's not simply race, it's our personalities. Our dreams."

"I thought we made our dreams together: the New World, the kids, the revolution. I guess that doesn't include babies." I brushed his hand from my leg.

"We did . . . but I need space to be my own man." He looked sick himself. "And if you're pregnant . . ."

I waited.

"We'll deal with it."

"Deal? What's that supposed to mean? An abortion? I thought you were against those. Genocide, remember? What about Cookie, and how they tied her tubes without her permission? Or *I'll* deal with a baby. Is that what you mean? *We'll* replenish the race and *I'll* deal."

"I don't know what I mean anymore." He hung his head. A tear streaked a shiny trail down his cheek.

"I need you here, I need you home, dinners, weekends, nights, mornings, damn it. I can't raise these kids by myself. And they need a black parent, some days I just don't know what to do. I listen to

'You've Got a Friend' and I feel like Carole King is a better friend to me than you are."

"I can't do it, Elizabeth, you know it," he muttered.

Day after day, no matter how we talked or cried, we came to the same conclusion: we couldn't swim together through the turbulent waters. When my period trickled into my underpants, the brown spots of blood sealed it. "Fuck the All-African People's Revolutionary Party," I heard myself scream that night. "Fuck the revolution. Fuck you!" I crashed out of the bedroom, slamming the door. In the kitchen I threw a frying pan across the room, denting the wall. "I fucking, fucking give up!"

Before we even told the children—though they must have heard my screams—our good-natured daughter transformed into a terror. She scrawled FUCK YOU in red Magic Marker on the living room mirror over the fireplace. Over and over her scrawled words looped across the mirror, a mural of obscenity: FUCK YOU, FUCK YOU. That evening, squirming on the side of her bed, she taunted me as she'd never done before when I told her to clean up her room. "You can't make me do anything." Ruby's eleven-year old eyes scrutinized my face.

"Ruby, what's the matter?" I squinted at her, trying to understand, before she fell against me, sobbing.

"Mama, everything's horrible."

"No it isn't, sweetie, we're going to be okay," I tried to reassure her, but knowing me as well as she did, she probably didn't believe that any more than I did.

Late at night I sank gratefully into Solomon's arms, nestled in bed. "I'm afraid Ruby will be a juvenile delinquent. And what about Che? Who will guide him? Everywhere he turns—at school, here—he's going to be surrounded by women." I sat up, panicked, forgetting how little time Che already spent with his father. "Mostly white women. How's he gonna learn to be a strong black man without you around?"

We lay on our sides facing each other. "I don't know," he said. He set his mouth tightly. Then into the silence he said, "That's not the only choice." Solomon grabbed me hard and pulled me against his chest, crushing my nipples.

"Ow, what do you mean?" I pushed him off and heaved myself onto my back, shoving a spare pillow under my knees.

"I'd love to have Che live with me." Solomon's deep, composed voice in my ear surprised me with his decisiveness, his calm.

"No," I gasped, rolling fully away, facing the wall. "That's ridiculous. How would you manage raising a child? You hardly see him now."

"I'd change my schedule." His voice was soft, clear. "We could share—"

"Oh, *now* you'd change it? After all the times you've said you couldn't possibly—" I leaped from bed. "So you can have Che all to yourself? He will *not* leave this house!"

"That's not it and you know it." Solomon jumped in front of me, his face close to mine. "Doreen told us herself he's out of control." Facing me, he reached for my shoulder as if to caress it.

I pushed his hand away. "He'll settle down. I can't imagine dividing Ruby and Che." Sure as I tried to sound, I was afraid. Doreen, the director from the Tilden Park People's Camp where Che was a junior counselor in training, had indeed called the day before: mellow Che was a changed boy from last summer, she said, furiously picking fights with the other CITs, taunting them with his two favorite slurs—"Faggot" and "Nigger"—backed up with blows. Doreen suspected he'd stolen a dollar from another boy's jacket, but when she confronted him he vehemently denied it. "It's only because I've known you all for so long that I'm letting him stay and giving him another chance," she warned me on the phone. "One more report and I'm going to have to let him go."

I hadn't wanted to acknowledge Che's radically changed behavior even to myself, but the previous night, shortly after the call from Doreen, when he loped silently in the front door, his walk an exact replica of Solomon's, I was sure I detected a whiff of alcohol on his breath. I quizzed him, "Were you drinking?"

"That's licorice you're smelling," he swore, stumbling over his words, and clamped his mouth shut before he turned his head away. Che had never lied to me before.

How could this sweet boy mirror our unspoken panic so quickly, and become a demon child overnight?

"No," I told Solomon. "Absolutely not. That is not an option."

"You said yourself—"

"No."

"Che should live with a man, his father."

"I'll never split the children," I vowed. "Ruby adores him. He adores her. Just watch them for a minute. When you have a minute," I said bitterly. "Can't you see how close they are?"

"I'm only saying—"

"And what about Rosa? You can't take care of a dog, too. No, absolutely not. That is never going to happen, so forget about it."

But over the coming weeks, while Solomon stubbornly drove his case and I resisted, I silently equivocated. Like a hummingbird darting in and out of a blossom, my heart leaped back and forth about what was best for Che.

Then, on the final Friday night of People's Camp, Che stumbled home from a last-fling party with several older boys, reeking of some foul-smelling liquor. The stench rose from his mouth, his clothes, and he was barely able to stand upright. This time he couldn't deny it.

"But this is the first time," he mumbled groggily, his eyes unfocused and glassy. "It won't happen again. I didn't know the whiskey was so . . ." His words trailed away while his head nodded forward.

"It better not," I said sternly before he wobbled off to bed.

Later I sobbed in Solomon's arms. "What's going to become of him? What if the police catch him next time he's drunk? Having a white mother and a schoolteacher father isn't going to protect him. You know they beat kids to a pulp who look exactly like him." The picture of my dear son's bruised face, eyes swollen shut, ribs cracked, rose in my mind. I'd seen too many photos in the papers, heard too many stories from neighbors, from Panther friends. I knew exactly what the Berkeley and the Oakland cops did with drunken black boys. They might even kill him. The more I thought about it, the more hysterical I grew, until I was moaning like Emmett Till's mother, imagining the worst.

"He'd do better with me," Solomon said soothingly, rocking me in his arms. "I know you don't want to let him go, but, Red, it would be the best thing for him. The safest thing. He needs a man to guide him, he needs that kind of"—he paused—"male stability."

"No, I'm not going to let him go," I said loudly, shaking my head. "Male stability be damned. You haven't been too damn stable around here. And Ruby and I couldn't stand it. Che needs us, too."

"He needs his father."

"No." My body heaved. "He needs his mother."

"You want him to be safe."

"Yes," I sobbed, curling into Solomon's chest.

"This is the safest course. I know Che, Red, in a way you never can. A father knows some things." He paused and almost whispered. "These are dangerous years coming up. We have to be very careful if we want him to survive."

I shuddered. "I don't know."

Later that night I dreamt of Che knocked to his feet by police clubs, stomped, kicked, beaten over and over. Toward morning I dreamt of him tumbling into the gutter, drunk, striking his head on the curb, and awoke trembling, with an unease I couldn't shake.

Back and forth over our days and nights Solomon and I argued. "How could you want to separate a boy who's barely thirteen from his mother?" I asked, incredulous. I couldn't imagine Ruby and me in the house without Che. His sweetness, still emanating most of the time, lifted up the whole atmosphere of home. "No."

But then I'd have another terrifying dream. For two weeks I hardly slept, missing Che already, until I thought my heart would stop. I couldn't breathe.

Finally came the night Che staggered home, clearly and irrefutably high, unable to unzip or remove his own jacket. I had to put my child to bed, pull off his pants and shoes, kiss his unconscious cheek after he'd peed all over the bed, and cover my dear boy with a blanket.

"All right," I agreed, fighting back tears. It seemed best for my son to be with his father, it seemed safest, as Solomon kept promising, although inconceivably difficult for me and for Ruby.

From then on, every evening when I crawled into bed, tears squeezed out of my eyes for hours, no matter how I tried to tell myself this decision was best for Che. The agony was so piercing, colonizing every organ in my body, that I didn't think I could survive the pain.

And how would we tell the children?

CHAPTER 6

Ruby

I waited and waited after field hockey practice up on the Cal field. Usually we didn't hold it up there, but this was special, we were practicing for an exhibition game. The grass was spongy and green, like a golf course, not patchy and bald like our field. The grass was so cool I ran down the field like my feet were flying. Like I could play all day. Left wing was the coolest position anyway and I was fast. But eventually the practice ended and one by one all the other girls got picked up. I hate when that happens, when I'm one of the last to go. Imani, our goalie, kept me company until her mother, Inez, drove up. Inez leaned over to hold the passenger door open for Imani and called out, "Do you want a ride? I can drop you at home, it wouldn't be any problem."

"No thanks, but my mama's gonna pick me up after work. If I weren't here she'd worry. Thanks anyway."

So I let Inez go, and a minute after that I watched the last girl leave on the bus. That meant I was all alone. I couldn't stand it when my parents were late, it was the lonesomest feeling.

So, tired as I was by then, I walked way up the steep hill, with my bag of stuff, to stand on the corner of College Avenue and Dwight Way. "On the uphill side," Mama had reminded me in the morning. "If I'm not at the field. Keep an eye out for me. It might be impossible to park down by the field at that time of day, so if I don't make it there I'll drive by on College. Be ready to hop in. There'll be traffic."

By the time I reached the corner high up on campus I was drenched with sweat—my bag was heavy—but pretty soon the sun slanting through the clouds dried me off. Until it began to drizzle. The fog that rolled in actually brought a freaky rain. All I had on was my field hockey skirt and a red tee over my uniform. No jacket. The wet and the wind froze me to the bone. Pretty soon I was shaking I was so cold, but I didn't know what to do. I was sure she'd come any minute, so I didn't dare leave the spot, or she'd really be mad.

I stood on the curb—"the far corner, I'll be driving through the light," she'd said—and I watched every car speed by, on the lookout for our old Volvo. That car had been in a million fender benders, 'cause my mama drove like a maniac, zipping around double-parked cars trying to swipe them, I think, she couldn't stand them, and she made U-turns across any old street. She didn't care.

Every time the light changed I was sure I'd see the battered blue Volvo. I stood on tiptoe a couple of times to make sure I'd spot her, and she'd see me. But still she didn't come.

College Avenue was close to campus, near the frat houses and dorms. Students were still arriving for the fall in long lines of traffic, their cars piled high with mattresses and boxes tied on top. Every year we saw them troop in like this. Some of the guys whistled at me, shivering in my little field hockey skirt.

I began to wonder: Did she mean for me to wait down on the field? But no, I was sure this was where she'd said to meet if she didn't come in a few minutes after the game. She'd said it wheezing. Her smoking was messing with her lungs big-time, I knew. We'd done a unit on smoking at school last year, but no matter how often

I hid her cigarettes or threw them out, she puffed away and just got mad if I said anything about it. "Walk up to that cross street, that's probably going to be a lot easier," she'd told me. I tried to remember exactly what she'd said but that was it, I was sure.

Standing on the edge of the street, choking from fumes with the steady stream of cars and vans zooming by, and trying to cover myself, it wasn't easier for me. I ducked my head and blinked my eyes to clear the raindrops off my eyelashes, wanting to make sure I could see every car.

I waited and waited until I couldn't wait anymore. The sky was getting dark and I was afraid to stay there by myself. I was mad at Mama for being late, but at the same time I was scared something had happened to her, or to Dad or Che. A boiling mix of anger and worry churned my stomach.

Plus I had to figure out how to get myself home.

Since I didn't have my bus pass or money, I trudged down the hill, hauling my soggy bag while it got darker and darker and I got wetter and wetter. It took an hour to walk home. When I got there I burst in the front door, my hair plastered to my head. Glad to be home, but afraid to hear what had happened.

My mother's wild red hair frizzed around her head and her eyes had swelled nearly shut from crying. I held my breath, so scared I thought I'd throw up.

"Don't drip all over the floor," she yelled. "Take your clothes off at the door, please, Ruby."

"What happened?" I screamed, all my worry clenched into red-hot rage when she talked like everyday, like nothing special was going on. "Where were you?"

"What do you mean, what happened? I'm fine."

"You were supposed to pick me up at field hockey!" I yelled, the knot in my stomach heavy and hard.

"Oh no, oh, sweetheart, I forgot." She put her hand to her head. "I spaced on it. I am so, so sorry."

"You're sorry? How could you forget? I can't believe this." I threw down my bag and clumped into the living room, but she followed and grabbed me. She smelled like stale sweat. "No," I screamed. "You can't just hug me like everything's normal. I was terrified Daddy or Che was dead!"

She pulled back and stared at me. "Oh, sweetie, I'm so sorry, I really am." And then she turned away to walk into the kitchen. She sounded like she was sniffling.

"Is that all you can say, you're sorry?" I shouted after her. No way I'd ever forgive her. Not ever!

She stopped and twisted her head back. "Yes, Ruby, that's it, now calm down."

"No!" I bellowed, my throat hoarse from screaming, tears blocking my eyes. "I was standing for one hour on the corner of the street breathing in cars, in the rain, worrying about *you*."

"I'm sorry, sweetie. There's been a lot going on."

"'A lot going on!' How could you leave me there? In the rain! Freezing, not knowing what had happened to you? Or Daddy or Che." I wanted to throw something, but all I could do was yell, "I hate you!"

"Listen, Ruby Jordan, I do a goddamn lot for you, every single day of your life, and one little time I mess up. Cut me some slack, Ruby. Get over the drama. After all, here you are, safe at home. You made it back." And she stomped out of the room.

My jaw dropped open. She didn't ask about the practice or how I did or how I even got home, or offer to get me a towel to dry off with, or apologize again about how totally terrible I must have felt or what a jerk she was. She didn't try to comfort me at all. All she thought about, all she ever thought about, was herself.

As I stood there in shock, still trembling with anger, I flashed again on the night she'd lost me in San Francisco. Was this the story of my life, being forgotten by my mother? What was going on, anyway? I could see she'd been crying, but I wasn't going to ask. She should be asking *me* how *I* am, I thought, not the other way around! I was so mad I felt sick to my stomach.

Racing back to Che's room next to mine to get the scoop on what was going on, I called out, "Hey." Usually I was glad to see my big brother's round smiling face, but today when he poked his head around his door it looked like the face of an angel. Lately he was the one person in the family who kept me sane. Daddy, too, sometimes, but I couldn't count on his attention. Sometimes he was all there, other times I didn't know where his mind was. Like Mama today.

"What's going on with Mama?" I asked, trying to talk normally, even though I was so mad that snot was coming out of my nose and I was still drenched, shaking with cold and fury.

He didn't answer but he kind of flung himself at me, which was not like him at all, believe me, but at this moment, after Mama's weirdness, I hugged him back. Rosa lay in his room like usual on his bed, not doing anything except smelling up the room with her farts. So that was one normal thing about this day.

After that bear hug that I didn't expect, my brother still didn't speak. He reached for his NERF ball and tossed it into a hoop on the door. When it rebounded he lobbed it to me. After I ran into the bathroom to grab a towel around my shoulders and tie another one around my waist, we took turns throwing the ball up, up, and in, over and over and over. We ran in that tiny space, bumping into each other, shooting until we were breathless. It was good to just shoot hoops for a while, not think of anything except the green ball and the brown rim. We didn't have to talk, once we got into our rhythm, to stay close. While we played I forgot how my mother had abandoned me, and then acted like it was no big deal. I forgot that I told myself I could never forgive her. I forgot how I worried sometimes about what was wrong with me that made Mama not care. I forgot everything except an awareness of where Che stood, where the ball was curving high up in space, where I was, and the metal rim. Those were my four points of concentration. Nothing else mattered.

After we'd played until I fell on the bed panting, I told him, "Mama left me up at the field today. She forgot me."

"Wow," he said, plopping down next to me. "That's terrible. That's like a nightmare I once had. How did you get home?"

"I walked." I felt better just telling him. He got how scary it all was without me needing to explain. Somehow that was what finally loosened the tightness in my gut. I lay on my back staring at the ceiling while he sat there, not saying anything. He didn't need to.

"I don't know if she really cares about me," I finally said.

"You know Mama loves you, Ruby. She's got a lot on her mind. But forgetting your own kid—I thought those things only happened in movies."

His voice was so kind that I kind of softened. But even though I suddenly remembered how Mama still thumped into my room every night to kiss me good night, and stroked my forehead the way I liked it, and even though she cooked my favorite meals a lot, like anything with cheddar cheese, I couldn't forgive her.

"Yeah," I said. "Only in the movies."

He was quiet. Mama's mother, Grammie Margie, came into my mind. Grammie Margie loved to stuff me with hot dogs and mustard. And Grandpa Colin, who looked exactly like an older version of Mama, he was all wrinkled, and wore every union button ever made on his hat. That's what he gave me, a UAW Local 45 button, every birthday, along with ten dollars. As if I didn't already have all the buttons from the other years. He was the one who taught me to bake apple pies. Every time I saw him we'd bake a pie. He'd let me carve a design from the rolled-out dough, like a heart or an "N."

I'd press it onto the top crust, brush it all with butter, and it would come out of the oven looking golden, smelling like heaven.

Then I thought about my mother's brother, Uncle Joey. He lived in Chicago, "organizing metal workers," Grandpa Colin always said, his chest all puffed out. Whenever Uncle Joey visited us he rode me to school on his cool motorcycle. I'd wake up in the morning and there he'd be, asleep on the couch, his black beard sticking out of the covers.

I was laying stretched out on the bed next to my brother, thinking about our weird family, when Che interrupted my thoughts, saying quietly, "I hope Mama doesn't keep acting crazy." He sounded worried, as if he'd picked up all my fear.

"No, she probably won't," I tried to reassure my big brother. Even though I hardly believed it. But I knew one thing for sure. I could always count on Che. That was a cozy feeling. I tried to hold on to that, and not think about Mama. Che would always be here.

The next night Daddy boomed from the living room, as if we were a million miles away. "Che and Ruby! Come here." Oh no, I thought, trouble. What did we do?

When I dragged into the living room, walking as slowly as I could, he and Mama were pasted stiff as boards on our couch under the bay window. Cesar lay on the floor nearby and Zoe's tail stuck out from under the couch. Everybody accounted for. I hopped into our red recliner, which was a lot like Grandma Jean's, and Che plopped on the arm, kind of leaning down on me, teasing. I pushed him up and slapped his hand when it touched me. I had to keep some dignity.

"We haven't been a very . . . cheerful family lately," my mother started in a strange voice like an announcer's on a show. "So your father and I . . ." She stopped at the weird sound of "your father" instead of "Solomon" or "Daddy" like usual. *Who is this person she's talking about?* From then on, though, her mouth said those strange words, "your father," as if she were used to it, as if this weren't the first time. "We're divorcing," she said in her new weird way. "Your father is going to get an apartment nearby." She stopped, kind of gulping. "We're going to try an experiment, with Che spending most of his time with his father, and Ruby spending most days here with me."

"I want to be with Che," I said right away. Che got very still, the way only Che could. Like a statue.

"You will be," they said together. "There will be lots of overlapping days and nights," my alien mother said, stiff and steely. Even her wild red hair was brushed down flat instead of sticking out all over her head like it usually did. "The new apartment will be nearby, so you can spend afternoon time together, or dinners."

"We're going to try to keep it fluid," Daddy chimed in, chin up, as if he were informing us about an adventure trip we were gonna take, a hard one but basically okay.

"Oh," Che said, his voice flat. His face didn't show anything.

"Oh," I repeated. I guessed this is what people mean when they say somebody's in shock. Even though I knew the divorce might be coming, I felt like I was dangling in air, with nothing underneath. Not even a net.

"I want to be with Che," was all I could say.

"I want to be with Ruby," he echoed, surprising me, because he never said stuff like that.

And "You will be" was all we heard back.

"What about Rosa?" Che asked in a tiny, kind of scared voice that sounded like he was eight years old, not thirteen.

Silence. "She's going to stay here with us," the strange woman on the couch said. "With Cesar and Zoe and Ruby and me. You'll be seeing a lot of her, Che, when you come over."

"Don't I have any say in this?" Che asked, sounding more like himself. Mad. "This isn't fair! For you guys to decide everything without consulting us. Especially me, if you think I'm moving. Which I'm not."

"A boy needs to be with his father," Daddy started off, kind of preachylike.

Then Mama jumped in, "You know you've been having a tough time lately, Che. We think this will settle you down. And your father really wants you—"

"Don't you?" Che butted in.

"Of course I do," she said. "But we know this is the best thing. At least for now. So we've made the decision to give it a try."

"No!" I jumped up, crying. "You can't take Che away from me. You should let us have a say."

"We've made the decision," Mama said again, slowly. "Sometimes kids don't know what might be in their own best long-term interest. Even though you want—"

"*You've* made the decision. What about us? What we want? This is so unfair," I said, collapsing back into the chair. "To just announce it. He can't move."

There was silence while I sat there crying, except Che leaned over to hold on to my shoulder.

"I'm sorry," Mama said then. "I really am. We're going to try to make this work out for you two as well as ourselves."

I was too mad, too upset to say anything else. And I guess Che was, too. Nobody was listening to us anyway.

Silence again. "Well." Daddy rubbed his hands together. "For now, we're all here. It will take a few days for me to find a place." He stopped. "Do you have any questions?"

What could we ask? *We don't all have to separate just because you two are,* I thought furiously. "How come you're divorcing?" I asked, sniffling. "Why can't we all stay together?"

"It's an adult decision," they chorused again in their new group-speak.

"Why?" Che asked, and I wanted to hug him but instead I

punched his back with my fist. He wriggled away, pushing me almost off the chair.

"It's complicated," Daddy began.

"Yes, complicated," Mama repeated, paler than ever.

I noticed their bodies silhouetted against the window, two figures joined at the shoulder, his wide Afro brushing the side of her head. Che had an Afro just like Daddy's, only even bigger. Sometimes my hair puffed out in a soft halo, too, but usually I wore it in two ponytails held tight with two bands. Today those hair bands felt like the only things holding me together.

"It's a grown-up thing," Daddy tried again. "Complicated. Hard to explain." *You said that,* I thought, rolling my eyes inside my head. I'd never dare do that in front of him. My father was old school, he said, like "I may be a revolutionary, but when it comes to discipline, I'm *old school.*" Mama must have been new school, because I could definitely roll my eyes in front of her. She might not like it but she would grin, kind of, where Daddy would say, "Don't you cut your eyes at me, young lady!" and bark, "That's fifty cents off your allowance." Or "Go directly to your room, young lady, no dinner for you." But now Daddy, who was usually so sure of himself, was stumbling. His face was as tight as a rubber band stretched right before it breaks. He looked like a person I'd never seen before, a man crying without tears. "People who love each other sometimes can't live together—"

They talked and talked and didn't tell us a thing. It felt like we were in a movie where everybody pretends everything's normal while the monster crunches its way through the roof.

"I'm going to my room," Che said softly.

"Me too." I wanted to copy every single thing he said, as if this could keep him here. Like if there were two of everything he said, that would make him more real, so they couldn't get rid of him.

In a house that all of a sudden felt empty without anybody who understood me except Che, I followed his familiar shape, that strong neck on broad shoulders, to the back of the house where our bedrooms were. I wasn't ready to be alone in my room, so I tagged behind him into his. Well, it was his bedroom for now.

He didn't say anything but he began to take down one of the football posters on his wall, an Oakland Raiders one, and then he bent to scrape up all the football cards on his floor. They were everywhere, mixed in dust piles under the bed and under his covers. He knelt next to his bed sorting them, which I hadn't seen him do in years, actually. He crouched over each card, carefully smoothing it with the fingers of both hands, placing it silently onto one of his piles. He organized the cards this way, over and over, piling them without lifting his eyes from the stacks. I watched his lips move while I tried to imagine that he wouldn't be here every day.

"Che—" I started, not knowing what to say. When he looked up, I saw tears in his eyes, identical to the ones that were smearing my face. "Che," I tried again, but I had no words to say how I felt. We'd always been together, our whole lives.

"I don't want to talk," he kind of snuffled. "I want to be by myself. Ruby, go on." A major thing in our family was that everyone had a right to privacy, so even though I didn't want to I walked out of the room. He shut the door practically on my bottom. But as soon I was in the hall I knocked on his door. He didn't say anything so I knocked again, harder.

"Go away." His voice was hoarse. I could tell he was crying, something he never ever did, so I tore into the living room where Mama and Daddy were still stuck on the couch, with their traitor arms wrapped around each other.

"Che's crying," I told them, glaring as ferociously as I could. *See what you're causing, look what you're doing to us. My big brother is crying!*

"Okay." Mama's eyes were as red as her hair. "I'll come in a minute." She gave me a lame smile, like she was trying to do it but it wasn't happening, really, not inside. Not at all. "Thanks for telling me. We're gonna get through this—"

I slammed my door shut as loud as I could to let her and everybody know how mad I was. Then I heard her knock at Che's room. He said, "Go away," but she pushed his door open anyway, like we're never supposed to do, and she stayed in there a long time.

I couldn't believe this was happening. My big brother was going to be ripped away from me, my daddy wasn't going to live with us, and I was gonna be left alone with someone who forgot I even existed. I wished I had a mother who actually cared about me. But maybe that only happened on TV. I didn't know, since my parents said it wasn't "revolutionary" to own a TV or watch that crap, so I hardly ever got to watch. Only at my friends' houses. My parents didn't want me to get "corrupted."

While I lay on my red star quilt, poking my finger in and out of the hole under the corner of that one red torn-up star, I wondered what happened to kids who get their families all broken up. Would I look different in school now, so everybody would know? Was Daddy gonna love me less since he was choosing Che? How could they take my brother away?

Most of all, while I worried that hole in the quilt until the star was practically coming loose in my fingers, I wondered how my life was going to be in our weird new home, with just the two of us. Half a family. I'd always had a whole one, and now it was chopped right down the middle. Like somebody took an axe to it.

And now that Daddy wasn't living here Grandma Jean probably wouldn't even come to sew up the hole.

CHAPTER 7

Ruby

On the first day of junior high school I felt older, even though it had only been three months since sixth grade. Maybe knowing I'd turn twelve in October helped. After a little kids' school like New Harmony, where I'd been my whole life, with the same ten kids practically, junior high school was completely different. There were like a million kids at Martin Luther King Jr. Junior High. So that was good.

But at home I began to wonder, Now that it was only Mama and me, was I gonna turn white, just by the two of us living together? Honestly, sometimes I stared at my arm next to hers when we were doing something close, like lifting groceries out of the car, and every time I saw my brown skin, whew. I was still me! But it was like they'd separated us into the Black family and the Other one. Mama and I were all mixed up without even the same last names, because fast as you could say *whitey* she changed her name from Elizabeth Jordan back to Lizzie O'Leary. Which I hated. She acted like she knew exactly who this strange woman, Lizzie O'Leary, was, while I was still the same old Ruby Jordan. Only more confused. It's funny, Che never seemed to worry about color like I did even though he was the same rosy tan shade. It was his laid-back personality, while for some reason I got fixated on my parents' politics. Like you were black or you were white. Good or bad. Which was confusing, too, because Mama was white. I don't know, it all just drove me crazy, honestly. While Che never seemed bothered about any of that.

I thought about it a lot when I was in bed at night, about why, and who was I. One night, just before I fell asleep I remembered the day when I was six that Daddy and I had marched in our Panther threads, just the two of us. Maybe Che didn't want to go. He never did like mobs of people all crammed together.

"Sugar, here's a slick coat and a pint-sized beret," Daddy had said happily while he squatted down in front of me, buttoning my tiny magic leather jacket. When he carried me on his shoulders I was swept into the crowd, carried right into the center of the singing, marching people. We all raised our fists, chanting, "Black Power, Black Power." I loved it. Nobody stared at me or asked where I was *from*. "Hey, little sister," adults said, smiling, recognizing me. "Tough beret." Other kids milled around, and then these cool teenage boys, serious guys in black outfits, they kind of swaggered along the sides of the march to keep us in order.

We marched for blocks, me waving from Daddy's shoulders and shouting until we arrived at a jammed plaza by the Oakland Courthouse. We worked our way up front in a crowd full of soft 'fros. I fit right in. Then Angela Davis strutted onto the stage in her black micro-miniskirt, looking like a giant over us. She had these eyes that looked right at you, or through you. And thick eyebrows. When I saw her wide cheeks I saw a grown-up version of my face. It was weird. But in a good way, a powerful way.

"We still live with the vestiges of slavery," Angela Davis screamed out, with her high Afro making her look like a queen with a crown.

She opened her mouth wide when she spoke, saying every word like the weight of each one mattered.

I gripped my legs around Daddy's shoulders and wrapped my arms tight on his head so I wouldn't fall off until he told me, "I can't see a thing. I've got to put you down, you're too heavy, Ruby. My back can't take it." Angela Davis's voice kept coming, every word like a bullet, hard, precise. Even after Daddy set me on cement and I had to tiptoe, peeking between people to get a view, I didn't want my eyes anywhere else. The way she stood matched her words. All around her men stood on the steps with their black leather jackets, black berets, and matching white T-shirts with the leaping panther. She was a queen above us all, and we were her loyal subjects, applauding everything she said.

"We live with the unfinished work of the struggle"—clapping—"to be agents of change, righting the wrongs of the past!" The crowd roared and cheered. I got chills. When she paused, the crowd called back, "Black Power." She raised both arms while people pumped their fists and bellowed, *Black Power, Black Power.* It was a high for me being part of that crowd, just Daddy and me with nobody giving us a second look and everybody so intent, so focused. Riding home, I fell happily asleep, feeling like I'd known then who I was. Just me, little Black Power me.

Once Daddy left home and moved to Dwight Way up near the high school, I lost that whole world, with his Panther friends coming over. Even though I saw him a lot, it wasn't the same as living with him. Our lives were separate, no matter how much he pretended they weren't. I missed Daddy, the way he laughed or looked, how when he spoke he'd press his long fingers together like a tent under his chin.

I gained another world, though, because he started sending me letters with things he'd never told me before. He was not a talkative guy but he poured out a lot in writing.

October 13, 1978
Dear Ruby,

I miss living with you, my daughter. Especially with your birthday coming up! We'll be sure to celebrate at my place. Twelve. Wow! Marking this turning has me thinking about our ancestors, whom I want to make sure you know something about. They're the ones from whom I doubtless get my beat (smile) and you get your fire (double smile). They go back a long time to an era we can hardly imagine, even a few generations ago. My daddy's mother, Granny Ella, was old when he was born, at least forty. She never knew her exact age. And Daddy was forty-two when I arrived, which means he was born in 1898. (Can you believe it?) My grandmother Ella was born into slavery sometime in the late 1850s, in northern Virginia. Her mother, Rose, was a teenager and Ella was her firstborn child. Once the Civil War started and everything was chaotic, Rose made her way with baby Ella to New York as "contraband," the name for runaway slaves who made it to free territory. My daddy's got me thinking about this I suppose because he's writing it down for me, but I wanted to give you a heads-up.

Anyway, you remind me of Granny Ella, whom I knew as an old woman when I was a boy and she lived around the corner from us in Atlanta. She died when I was six. As soon as I saw you, though, I wanted to name you Ella. I knew you had that same gritty spirit. Your eyes were shooting fire (smile). But your mother was hot on Ruby, and I thought that was a mighty fine name, too. After all it was the same red color, only a darker shade, as your great-great-grandmother Rose's, and she must have been quite a woman herself to have made the trek as a teen with a baby for something like two weeks. So I was cool with your name, just like I'm cool with you.

Your ever loving and oh so proud father

P.S. What about Halloween this year? I know you're too grown to trick-or-treat, but maybe we should have a ghost party at my place. What do you say?

We did have the party. It was incredible. I got to invite Imani and Jamylle. Plus, with two of Che's friends and tons of Daddy's, there must have been thirty people crammed into his four rooms. Noisy, happy people, singing, dancing, jamming. You know when we party we don't play. Daddy and Che lived in a huge, ramshackle Berkeley brown shingle. The front was decorated like a gingerbread house, with white scalloped shingles, and the landlord had a small plot of grass on the side, with some kind of blue flower all around the edges. It was pretty. A purple passion tree spread out by the front doorway. In the spring, lilac wisteria bloomed in front of the building. It hung from a peaked roof over the front door and smelled divine. I loved that house from the minute I saw it, the day Daddy first took me over and showed me into the front foyer. A walnut staircase climbed up the back of the foyer like in those old movies of mansions, where these stairs wind around and the star comes dancing down them.

Daddy and Che lived on the top floor, four rooms with sloping ceilings, like in an attic but the ceilings were high. They had shiny wood floors and huge glass windows for a full view of the bay. When I curled up that first day in one of his beanbag chairs, I sank in and watched the sky streak gray to pink, and every shade of purple. I was grateful Daddy had stayed in our South-Central Berkeley neighborhood. I could slide over any time I wanted. Pretty soon, I was at the apartment every day for at least an hour or two, doing homework, talking on the phone, or just watching the sky change. Sometimes pink clouds skidded across like kids chasing each other, or other days the blue faded slowly to gray, with a faint green line. Sitting up in that high nest with West Berkeley spread out below me, I felt like maybe my life wasn't completely wrecked after all.

The Halloween party was a blast. We spent days decorating, making everything from scratch.

"Ruby, come and help me," Che called out when he tried to cover two coat-hanger wires he'd bent into a pumpkin shape with orange crepe paper. "Damn." It kept ripping every time we wound the paper onto the wires, until we figured out we needed to double up the crepe paper before we wrapped it. Then I had trouble with a pack of black tissue paper. I cut it and glued strips into paper chains, but the Scotch tape wouldn't hold the streamers on the wall, so they got tangled in the lamps. Eventually I brought over some masking tape from home and that stuck.

Che and I spent every afternoon up there for like two weeks after school. I'd work with him right through dinner instead of making my way down to Ashby Avenue. Then I'd have to call home. "Hello," I'd say, trying to sound sorry, because I knew it was after six when I was definitely supposed to be home. "I'll be there in an hour or two, okay? I'm going to eat here, okay?" There never was much to eat in Daddy's refrigerator—pretty much like at our house—but that wasn't the point. Our planning for the party was. I don't know what we imagined might happen, if only we worked hard enough to make the world's best-ever party. Would the Halloween magic heal all that hurt bubbling around inside us?

The crazy thing was—it did. We needed some sort of a blessing, I guess, or a healing, or whatever you want to call it, and just working so hard on the party together, we got it. In the evenings all three of us made ghosts, trying to see who could make the scariest ones. We bunched the corners of old sheets and tied them with brown packing string to make heads. Daddy let us draw with black Magic Markers on most of them. We inked in the most horrible faces we could imagine: fanged smiles and toothless grins and just mean-looking faces, as mean as we could make them, with patches over one eye and scowls. We hung our ghosts all over the apartment, everywhere, on the furniture and from the tops of doors covered with the fake cobwebs that Auntie Cookie scrounged up somewhere. She got all the sheets, too. She was always able to talk people into giving her things, just like her twin sister, Auntie Belle. Those women could talk their way out of a paper bag. We draped the cobwebs in every corner until they stuck to our hands. For a week I had gooey white webs under my fingernails, and I smelled like chemicals.

After we had the whole apartment decorated to create a haunted house, we made party games, one in each corner of the huge living room and one in the kitchen. And finally, the day before the party, we hauled in food from the grocery store: apples for bobbing, and jugs of cider we poured into a giant pot to boil for mulled cider with cinnamon sticks and floating orange slices. Daddy had red wine for the adults, with a box of new wineglasses in the kitchen. Chips in bowls, hot red salsa.

The last evening before Halloween, Che and I even tried cooking pumpkin pies, with canned filling and frozen crusts. We burned the first two in the oven that must have been too hot, up on the top rack. Once we turned the temperature down and put the pies on the bottom rack, the crust never hardened right on the second batch, but we served them all anyway. With heaping scoops of vanilla ice cream, nobody except Auntie Cookie noticed the burned pumpkin skin or the soggy crust on the wedges we cut.

"What did you do to these?" she asked, holding her fork in the air and making a wicked face. Auntie Cookie, who'd just moved from Atlanta to take a big social work job in Oakland, was a full-size woman, as tall as Daddy was and with a lower lip that hung out like Grandma Jean's, which, in her case, gave her a sour expression. She walked as if she were stomping grapes and she could turn mean when she had to, but she always had a smile and kind words for us—and for Daddy, her little brother—except when it came to food. Do not mess with her food. That was serious.

The day of the party, rain fell steadily, our first real downpour of the season. Up on the top floor we heard it pounding on the roof. We needed it. By the end of October the dry, dusty streets could choke you, and dry brown grass covered the hills. The cool rain, even such a heavy one, was a relief from the scorching days of September and October that always followed foggy August. I was tired of sweating at home in my bedroom all night, 'cause we didn't dare sleep with our windows open down there on the first floor. Even though Mama had put nails on the side of the window so you could only open it a few inches, it still felt safer to keep it closed.

The night of the party, in the midst of a raging storm that never let up, everybody arrived soaked through, shaking themselves like dogs as soon as they reached the hallway. Daddy had spread another bundle of those endless sheets in the foyer, folded into thick pads to absorb all the drips from umbrellas and jackets. People left their raincoats downstairs and padded up to our floor in their stocking feet. Daddy had a no-shoes policy in the apartment, and that muddy night nobody fought him on it.

After they warmed their hands on cups of hot mulled cider, everyone—grown-ups and kids—wanted to squeeze around two yellow buckets we'd filled with water and floating shiny red apples. Bob for the Apple was definitely the hot game that night, which surprised me, given all the water they'd just escaped. But two at a time people dipped their faces in, stretching mouths open as wide

as they could, trying to bite into the slippery apples. No hands allowed. Daddy had made sure to get extra-hard Braeburns; of course,
they bobbed away until someone pushed one against the edge of the
pail and then got a grip with their teeth. That was tricky, though—
you couldn't push too hard or the plastic bucket would tip over, and
if somebody else's head was in your way you kind of butted heads
and water sloshed all over. It was funny. If you snorted with your
face in water you swallowed some of it and choked a little, but the
fun of it was that you sprayed anybody nearby.

That night, for the first time in months, everything felt right.
The crowd was all African American, except for one white boy,
a friend of Che's who sometimes came to our house—the Ashby
one—on Saturdays. Most of the grown-ups were musicians—horn
players and composers and professors—men and a couple of women
who knew how to get down, make music, and have a good time.
They jammed all night, blowing up a storm. I don't know what the
neighbors thought but no one complained as far as I knew. Daddy
made sure there was lots of fun for us before the grown-ups got into
their music: we played Parcheesi and Crazy Eights and Slapjack and
ate our fill of chocolates, candy corn, lollipops, and popcorn balls
covered with sticky brown caramel.

For a few minutes I sat by Che. I couldn't believe that for the
first time in a bunch of years he'd made a costume, and it was a kid
one, like since he'd moved in with Daddy he was little again: he was
a crayon box, colored orange, with the Crayola design. I'd helped
him cover the spot where his head poked up on top with cutouts of
crayons, front and back. He looked so funny, and he was just drinking in the *oohs* and *aahs* over how original it was.

"Baby, however did you come up with something so clever?" a
woman with a real close-cropped Afro asked him. She introduced
herself as Elaine, like she was somebody special that we should
know. Maybe she was a Panther I'd met before, I thought.

My costume was simpler, although Auntie Cookie and I had

had to rummage through two fabric stores to find the right material for my hat. I was Queen Nefertiti "the beautiful." In my Egyptian crown, covered with gleaming gold and green fabric and strips of dark green, red, and gold braid that I'd glued in a complicated design, people said I looked just like her. Standing as tall as possible, showing off the four gold necklaces I wore, I felt regal and beautiful. That was unusual for me, since my height usually made me self-conscious.

"I've seen photographs of that famous sculpture," the woman named Elaine gushed, "and you're the spitting image." I felt her staring at me all evening.

Finally, after Che ripped off his cardboard, I unpinned my hat and stashed it on a shelf in his bedroom, where he said I could sleep that night. Special occasion. I kept the necklaces on, though. Wandering back into the kitchen area at one end of the living room, I grabbed a cup of steaming mulled cider and sipped, feeling the heat in my chest before I made my way over to the Bob for the Apple pail. Zoe followed me, rubbing up against my legs, nudging me to pet her. I'd brought her over for the party. She wasn't a black cat but she had black stripes, and I thought she lent something to the Halloween atmosphere, especially when she arched her back, her hair stood on end, and she hissed at everyone. When I asked Mama— "Liz," she reminded me to call her—if Zoe could come to the party I'd been surprised when she said "Sure" just like that. I bent down to rub her back and right away she started to purr with that deep contented buzzing sound that resonated in my chest like happy chocolate. I kept it up, carrying her in one arm until I reached the pail and set her down. She didn't want to get close to it.

One second after I dunked down into the cool bucket, holding my breath and trying not to laugh underwater, I felt another head plunge in, sending a wave over the edge. Immediately we bumped heads.

"Ow!" a woman's voice yelped, sounding like Elaine. She jerked up out of the water to massage her head with long fingers that surprised me, since she was so small.

"Ow," I echoed.

Then, sitting across a yellow plastic bucket, water trickling from our faces, we each rubbed our heads until I reached into the water with my hand, breaking all the rules, and picked up an apple. She mirrored me. We both bit in at the same time, chewing the crisp apples, not saying anything. She reached over with her free hand and offered a shake, staring in a way that made me uncomfortable.

"Hello. We met earlier. I'm Elaine Bowen." She chuckled. "I've heard about you. Wonderful things, from Solomon." I shrugged. It wasn't a big deal to me if Daddy talked to his friends about us. He hadn't said anything about any Elaine to me. But the way she looked at me definitely meant her introduction came with a check mark. *Listen up, girl.*

The party was only getting started then, around ten or eleven, with the musicians wailing full blast. After I hung around by Daddy for a while, I crept into Che's room. He was still at the party, and I fell asleep to the familiar sounds of guitars and a violin tuning, a keyboard pounding, two saxophones, one high, one low, and it felt so right.

CHAPTER 8

Lizzie

"Pack your T-shirts," I told Che quietly. "But leave a few of everything here."

We threw his clothes, comic books, records, and collection of action figures into two black garbage bags; I helped him pack up his football cards, still finding strays in every corner, and late that afternoon, when I could postpone it no more, dashing through the freezing November rain, I packed my teenage son into the car. As I splashed along Grove Street and turned right on Dwight, I watched Che gaze out the window and tried to imagine how it would be not to sniff that adolescent boy smell every day—the potent mix of sweat and hormones that filled our house—and how it would be not to kiss his soft cheek good night, when he'd let me. I wanted to turn back. But I couldn't bear to unsettle Che's world again, so I drove on.

"Knock-knock," I ventured, but when he shook his head I didn't try again to play that reliable childhood game we'd carried right into his teens. We rode in silence.

At Solomon's apartment in one of those big old Berkeley houses that were mostly subdivided, I helped Che up the winding stairs with his garbage bags. He was his usual stoic self, devoting himself to the task, bumping these giant bags stuffed with clothes up every stair. Then Cookie materialized at the apartment door right behind Solomon, throwing open her arms to Che, ignoring me as if I were an unwelcome ghost. I felt a twinge of annoyance, wishing she weren't intruding. Solomon looked so excited, more like the eager young man I'd met in Mississippi than the grim figure of recent years. It would have eased my ragged heart to keep the moment, the hand-over, all in the family—although I suppose she would have said she *was* family. Trying to ignore her, and my disappointment at her presence, I focused on Che, who'd already sprinted off to his new room, looking suddenly, from the back, exactly like his dad. The shorter, broader version.

"Che," I called, fighting back tears as I followed him down the hall. "Let me help you get settled." Solomon and I hadn't foreseen this secondary transitional moment; I wasn't sure of my welcome and how long I should stay for the unpacking, but I dove in, chattering to my silent teen, while Solomon and Cookie hovered uneasily in the doorway. His room was spartan, with a plain three-drawer dresser, a single bed, and a new wooden chest covered with football pennants. Where had those come from?

I leaned over, trying for a warm hug, but finding Che rigid and timid in his new surroundings, I scurried out, catching a glimpse of an impeccable living room decorated with brilliant fabric. In the morning I awoke surrounded by piles of soggy Kleenex on the floor, as if large, wet clumps of snow had fallen during the night.

Ruby, incredulous, sniffled all through breakfast. "How could you?" she railed, slurping milk from her cereal spoon. "How could you let him go?" She looked so mournful, such a reflection of my own heartache that I trembled, doubting my decision. Zoe, still missing her kittens, howled day and night, giving voice to our grief. Rosa limped back and forth, pacing stiffly by the front door while she waited for Che, refusing to leave her post. Only Cesar, indestructible Cesar, acted normal, wagging his tail in circles every time he saw Ruby or me. Generous treats after every meal, licked from my fingers, or a dinner plate set by my chair were a guarantee to his happiness. Rosa, when I tried the same treatment, wasn't bought off so easily.

All that day and for weeks afterward I wavered, chewing the question in the corners of my mind while I spoke mechanically to students, pondering it through my rubbery cafeteria lunch. Should I have let Che move in with his father? And why had Solomon and I split anyway?

By the time Ruby dragged home from school one week after Che had moved out, I was biting my nails for the first time in twenty years. The two middle fingers on my left hand were chewed raw, sore to the touch. I was peeling away a ragged line of nail when Ruby held up two pictures she'd drawn with colored pencils: in each, a devil with a halo of red hair rammed its pitchfork at her, piercing her stomach. She shoved the papers, one by one, in front of my face while I lay on the couch.

"What is that?" I asked, horrified, propping myself up on one elbow.

She rubbed her stomach, only saying, "It's sore," but would hardly discuss the drawings beyond saying, "My art teacher told me to draw what I felt," before she padded back to her room. Was I really that much of a monster? What kind of mother lets her child go? Even off to his father? Had I caused a terrible tummy ache in my sweet daughter?

Wanting to clutch my own stomach, I suddenly sensed the vacuum in the house as a raging whirlpool of silence that might suck me down. Desperate for movement, for sound, I wandered into the kitchen. It, too, was unnaturally quiet. At a loss, which was so unlike me—every second of my life had been jammed against the next for years—I turned on George Lewis's *Homage to Charles Parker*, poured a glass of Chianti, and slumped at the table, unable to move. Even the alto sax and then the piano on the second track, usually my favorite sections, couldn't rouse me. How were Ruby and I going to survive this blow?

Finally, after several glasses of wine, inspiration hit. What we needed was a fancy meal. Food could conquer all misery; we'd fully inaugurate our twosome household with a feast, the kind I generally cooked only on major holidays every few years. Celebrate instead of mourn, I vowed, adapting the chant of my childhood—Joe Hill's *Don't mourn, organize*—on many a picket line. Choking back tears, I set to work.

An hour later, when Ruby emerged, she carried a raggedy letter "from Daddy," she muttered, looking away. Even at the table she clutched it in her lap like a baby blanket she couldn't bear to part with.

"How was school?" I tried. The large table, without Che, without Solomon, loomed sharp and empty under my solo chatter.

Ruby shrugged and ate silently, eyes on her plate, forking food into her mouth without seeming to notice it. All through the roasted chicken I cranked out conversation: "Do you like the potatoes au gratin I baked with cheddar, your favorite cheese? . . . Hmm, aren't the fresh string beans good, with almonds and grated cheddar, just the way you like them?"

She hardly said a word, even at my minute of triumph: the banana flambé topped with vanilla ice cream and whipped cream in dessert glasses. "Hmm," she mumbled and dug in, spooning the rich chocolate sauce and sugar-coated bananas into her mouth. But as she ate the dessert, she said nothing. Gripping the long stem of a wine goblet, I tipped up glass after glass of deep red Chianti until I, too, withdrew into silence. So much for the joys of cooking.

As we cleared the table Ruby erupted, her face contorted in raw pain. "How could you do it, Mama? How could you let Che and Daddy go? How could you split our family in half?" She broke into tears.

What could I say? Her accusations echoed the ones rattling around my brain. Was life with Solomon really that tough? But didn't I deserve better? a small part of me argued back; didn't I deserve a true partner, not just a nighttime squeeze? Yet the cost was already perhaps too high. Couldn't I have hung on a few more years, at least until the kids finished high school? Seeing Ruby's suffering face was unbearable.

That night, while my daughter showered I vacuumed her room, trying to assuage my grief with the dull practicality of household cleaning, a new remedy. I charged into corners with the noisy machine only to discover two stray sheets covered with Solomon's cramped writing slipped in a crack between her bed and the wall, one crumpled page lodged under the bed. I hadn't known he was writing her; how had she received the letters without my knowledge? It was like a cereal box club they shared, exchanging the secret ring back and forth. Was she writing him, too? Tempted to read Solomon's small script, I reached for the papers, but just in time, slapped my hand away. "No, no," I said aloud, retaining some shred of integrity. Instead I cornered Ruby in the hall when she emerged from her shower wrapped in a towel. "What is your father saying to you? Did his letters come in the mail? I didn't see them."

Ruby merely waved her head and hunched her shoulders in her new signature shrug before racing for her room. In that instant the sunny child she'd been fully gave way in an angry rush to a stranger, seething with an undercurrent of sorrow and rage.

My mind raced. How could I regain my daughter's love, her trust? I couldn't bear to lose two children at once. Maybe this had all been a disastrous mistake. Could I repair it?

My anguish vied, though, with the small voice that urged: *You deserve your freedom!* And that prodding prompted our next fight.

I sank into the couch, bit my fingernails, and ran the numbers: Three meals a day times fifteen years came to over fifteen thousand meals. No liberated woman would clog her brain with such trivia. I pumped myself up. And what thanks had I gotten for it?

"Sweetie," I called down the hall. "We need to talk." My bleeding cuticles stung. When there was no answer I yelled, "Ruby!" biting another strip of skin from my little finger, forcing the pain that lay heavily in the pit of my stomach out onto my hand.

Finally Ruby appeared and inched toward me, swinging a book. "What?"

"I'm not going to cook dinner anymore," I announced in the abrupt style I'd learned from my own mother. Though she wisecracked her way through life and was renowned for a generous heart, when difficult news had to be delivered she plowed ahead, announcing it flatly and finally, virtually wiping her hands, as if to say, "Check that off the To Do list. What's next? No wallowing here. Time for a joke." After I'd survived my own adolescence, at last she'd become my bosom friend, I comforted myself—just as Ruby and I would someday be, despite our current troubles. "I'm tired of my brain being taken up with menus," I said, steeling myself from the horror creeping over Ruby's face. "Fifteen thousand, almost sixteen thousand meals! At two hours a meal—that includes shopping time, so it's a conservative estimate—that's almost *thirty-two thousand* hours." I self-righteously presented my statistics. "That's eight hundred workweeks! I've done enough for two lifetimes. . . ."

"What do you mean, 'not cooking anymore?'" Ruby, feet planted on the floor, stared. She'd begun wearing makeup and even at home dressed in sleek blouses and skirts she'd ironed, even though I bought her plenty of sensible clothes that didn't need ironing. I hardly recognized the tall, fashionable girl in bright red lipstick who stood over me aghast. She looked as if she belonged on the cover of *Vogue*, not in my living room strewn with beer bottles, hand-knit Peruvian sweaters, books, magazines, old bills.

"I am no longer the cook for this family." I sprawled full-length on the sofa. "This minifamily. Look what happened last night when I spent all that time, and you didn't even appreciate—"

"But you're the mother, you have to cook," she interrupted.

"No, I don't. Ruby, you're twelve years old. You're not a child. Kids your age work full-time in most of the world," I threw out, not sure whether that was true. Or whether I approved. But my foggy, suffering mind knew only that I had to make a statement of liberation. Maybe that would soothe the ache. "I'll make sure there's food in the house. We can always eat yogurt or scrambled eggs. Or simply see what happens. I'm through with cooking. Especially dinner. I'm tired of waking up thinking I have to defrost hamburger or wondering what we'll eat. I've had it!" How could I cope with the pain of divorce *and* the damn cat howling all night *and* miss Che so much my bones hurt *and* teach a new course on public policy at Merritt College *and* fret that Rosa's leg might never heal *and* worry about Ruby *and* cook? "My brain is stuffed. I don't want to gum up the delicate works with hamburger," I said, trying to inject some levity into the gloom that surrounded us like a toxic fog.

"You're the mother." Ruby stuck to her point. "Mothers cook."

She should have known better. "Nope. Except for special occasions. Otherwise, this mother is off duty." If she'd tried a more plaintive tack rather than that antifeminist argument, perhaps I would have relented.

But Ruby dug in and upped the ante. "If you don't cook anymore, I'm going to move in with Daddy." Her tough stance lacked only a cigarette dangling from her shiny red lips.

"Move in with Daddy?" I echoed, stupefied. "That's not up to you, Ruby."

"Why not? I thought I wasn't a child! So why can't I make that decision? You just said I wasn't a child."

"There are some things the adults still need to decide. You're not grown-up either."

"Che's there. Is it girls with the girls? And boys with boys? I didn't think you'd be for that kind of sex division." Her look held me pinned like a butterfly.

"Ruby." I sighed. "Look at it my way—"

"No. You see it *my* way for once! You lie around moping, you can't cook, except when your precious friends come over and then we have a three-course dinner and twelve bottles of wine. Like all the time. Why should I live here if you don't even care enough about me to take care of me?"

"That is so untrue. What about the flambé? What about the stuffed pork chops that you never said thank you for? What about the melted goddamn cheddar cheese stuck all over everything? Is that all I am, the invisible cook? That's the definition of *mother* to you?"

"Mothers cook," she said, sounding like a fifties caricature.

"Historically mothers have done the shit work! You got that right. But we don't want to perpetuate that bullshit any longer, do we? Isn't it about time for a change, time to transform the role into something more expansive, with a little more depth?"

She glared. "Why now?"

"All right," I relented. "How's this? I'll still grocery-shop—*as I always have*"—I gave her what I hoped was a significant look—"and I'll cook 'real meals' on Saturday nights. On weekdays and Sundays we'll look out for ourselves. It'll be easy, we can eat whatever we want: canned soup or yogurt or something. It'll be fun. Kind of like camping."

"One night a week you're going to cook?" She looked skeptical.

"Ruby, stop it. You can't talk to me in that tone. Listen, if I'm making a meal for myself, you know, something easy, I'll rustle some up for you, too."

Silence.

"But the whole point is: no commitment. I'm withering away here! Look, you're seeing a woman strike a blow for freedom." I struck a pose, fist in the air, half mocking, half serious. "You'll see: the last thing I want for you is to get tied down in a kitchen someday when you grow up, wasting your talents. You'll thank me someday."

"No I won't, I'll hate you." Ruby stalked out of the room.

We did survive my no-cooking regimen. Neither of us lost or gained pounds. Ruby began to dive into recipes for the first time, which she seemed to enjoy, producing a passable spinach quiche and several batches of granite muffins that I didn't have the heart to tell her were inedible. We nibbled on those tasteless rocks for days, until late one night I threw the crumbling remains into the garbage can. She persisted, though, and quickly became quite the baker, turning out light, fluffy pastries that filled our home with the alluring smell of caramelizing sugar and melting butter. She became so adept that everyone on the block soon counted on her freshly baked berry pies and cupcakes, bran muffins and cobblers. On Saturdays the sweet aroma of her cooking wafted out the open windows, suffusing our entire end of the block all the way to the corner at Sacramento with the scent of fresh baking. Whenever we had a neighborhood celebration, or any excuse for a potluck, roly-poly Ayanna next door would ask, sniffing the air hopefully, "Where is Ruby's peach cobbler?" That cobbler was famous. Then my daughter's unique cheese dumpling/Danish, full of egg and specialty cheeses she begged me to buy her, was another of many delicious pastries she created; her incessant baking began to smother our fragile home with an alluring bakery scent, providing the illusion, anyway, of comfort. And she developed quite a few fans who appreciated her generosity with this new talent. Ruby never turned down a request from a neighbor for a pie or cake. When I suggested, more than once, that she could make money selling her baked goods, she rejected the idea. "No, I want to give them away." She was adamant, as if the act of sharing the very home-cooked foods she felt deprived of nurtured her, too. When I pointed out that *I* actually paid for all the ingredients, she simply shrugged, said "Thanks," and went back to whipping her batter.

Eventually I did resume a bit of light cooking, but never again with the same housewifely zeal I'd carried from the fifties right into the seventies. Pleased that I'd liberated myself from the compulsion, I never suspected that Ruby was feeding Cookie stories of my culinary abandonment, embellished, I'm sure: I was probably starving the child, chaining her in her room with a thin bowl of gruel. And when I let her out, yup, colored girl no doubt cooking for Miss Ann.

What Ruby did need, I decided, rather than gourmet mother-cooked (slave-cooked) meals, was an adult woman of color she could relate to, a role model who might be able to guide her. Without Solomon around, she needed that presence. The African American women she already knew, like Imani's mother, Inez, and my next-door neighbor Ayanna, were busy with their own children. Ayanna, a painter of local renown, had four sons plus a dog, an elderly cat that peed all over the furniture and the floor, and a high-maintenance husband. Though she moved like lightning—which invariably surprised me, given her full figure—and had a finger in every Oakland arts group or political event, her days were beyond crammed. And she'd never evidenced more than the usual neighborly interest in my daughter, except when she was trying to wheedle cobbler out of her. No, it would have to be somebody new, someone with attention for Ruby, who was interested in playing a significant role in this young African American girl's life. I resolved to keep my eyes open.

One week after our no-cooking showdown, followed by a simmering standoff, divine providence handed me an exact match. Although I don't believe in such a thing as fate, it was uncanny the way she showed up: the intense, diminutive woman leading the Human Relations seminar at Merritt College gave an impression of rock-hard solidity, like earth, even though a worry line slashed her forehead. I felt instantly that I could trust her as a mentor for my daughter; even her name, Abi, bore a striking resemblance to Ruby's. Her dark hair waving around her face and with her olive skin and wide cheekbones, Abi Santiago appeared Latina, or maybe mixed race like Ruby. Filipina? I couldn't figure out her ethnicity, but her warm, sturdy presence attracted me. That evening I learned only that she attended Golden Gate Law School at night, intending to practice civil rights law.

Four days later, Abi and I sat at a small table outside The Juice Bar Collective on Vine Street, digging into our polenta with salsa, heavy dark bread, and organic salad laced with carrot strips. I watched her carefully across the green metal table and listened to her story: born Abi Min in Maui, her father was a well-known Hawaiian journalist. Her mother, from an English-Welsh background, worked as the arts editor for a newspaper there. "My last name, Santiago, came from my ex—Fernando Santiago. He's a Latin jazz pianist, the son of Eddie Santiago—you might have heard of him."

I shook my head.

"Most people assumed I was Latina even before I got the name," she chuckled. "I live on Bustelo coffee and salsa's my favorite music, so maybe I am, in some essential way."

"Amazing." I bit into a thick slice of bread, wondering guiltily what Ruby was eating. "My ex is a musician, too," I said, "and my kids are biracial." Instantly I wished I could reach out and grab the stream of words, pulling them back into my mouth: mentioning Solomon, even indirectly, opened the door to feelings I was trying to keep at bay.

"Really. Who? I know the music scene pretty well. Is he local?"

"Solomon Jordan." Such a rush of emotions when I said his name flatly like that! As if I were giving a stranger my Social Security number, but behind the code lay an entire enchanted, secret world. Sixteen years of history.

"Solomon Jordan! Oh my God, I can't believe you were Solomon Jordan's wife." Abi was clearly awed. "What a horn. Every time he plays at Yoshi's or the Keystone Korner, I try to catch him." She stared at me. "And you were his wife. Wow!"

"Hmm." Why had I ever initiated this meeting? I felt myself shrink back and drop a veil between us. Yet as we lingered over our meal, covering our compatible political histories, we discovered more parallels; by the time we arrived at dessert and after-dinner drinks—peppermint tea for me; a mug of steaming black coffee for Abi—I said, "I'd like you to meet my daughter, Ruby. She and I are at odds these days, hmm, ever since the family broke up. We're drifting apart." I felt pathetic, wanting to beg. "She's an unusual girl, quite sharp. I think you'd find her interesting—"

"I'd love to," she said, cutting me off. "I'd like to get to know you both better."

On our stoop I saw Ruby's shadow through the glass, waiting, as if she suspected already, before I did, that a significant event was unfolding. Her eyes darkened and her thick eyebrows contracted when we walked together through the door.

"Abi is a fascinating woman," I whispered to Ruby in the kitchen while I ran water into the blue enamel kettle. "You'll enjoy her company," I said in a cheery voice of long habit, the one meant to buoy her. "And she's biracial, too, a different mix."

"Is that all I am? Biracial?" she said angrily, and tramped to her room. The echo, when she banged her door, hard, reverberated through the house.

Two nights later I invited Abi over for mushroom-barley soup, my star *Moosewood Cookbook* recipe, even though I knew Ruby would object. "You're cooking for her, but you won't cook for me?" Yes, I thought, but this *is* for you. As an image of Abi floated into mind, she sparkled with energy and I felt a surprising rush of joy, as if I'd just received good news. With her long dark lashes and liquid brown eyes, she even reminded me a little of Ruby, although her wiry body, so compact, was utterly different from my daughter's lanky, gawky frame. But she was kind and funny and might be a friend for both of us.

"Why does *she* have to be coming over?" Ruby complained again in the living room just before Abi arrived. Her curly hair, tied back with the red ribbon she favored that year, blazed over a sharp black shirt and she stood in her new posture, more erect than ever, look-ing as though she were defying the world—me—to accost her. "We always have people trooping through the house. People we don't even know. It makes me uncomfortable, the way they look at me. As if I'm some kind of freak."

"Because I want her to," I snapped. *This is for you.* "You have your friends over. She's a new family friend."

Ruby grumbled, yet by the time we finished dinner she appeared relaxed, sprawling on the floor near the table with her homework and scattering our conversation with questions. She spread her pa-pers out, caressing them into the shape of a fan, until Rosa, lying next to her, rose and padded gingerly to the door, sniffing for Che. When our old dog limped back and dropped onto the floor, Ruby's papers flew up. Annoyed, she blurted, "I hate English!"

"Why?" I asked, puzzled.

"It's stupid."

"What happened? You were liking English."

"Nothing."

"Ruby, this is so sudden. Something must have happened." I watched her closely, trying to figure out why this expressive girl was acting like an inarticulate teen. Was this monosyllabic, simplistic vocabulary simply part of her sullen new self?

"The teacher stares at me," she said at last, reshuffling her papers. "When he talks to me, his eyes are . . ." She blushed.

"What?" I heard the hum of the refrigerator rumbling from the kitchen and took a breath.

Ruby's eyes pooled as she bent her head down and pointed at her breasts.

"That's sexual harassment!" Abi the law student jumped in, leaning forward. Her own dark hair, short and curly, waved around her ears, so much like Ruby's that my fingers twitched with the urge to smooth it back. "You should write down every detail of what happened, and when, and how you felt. Put down all the specifics: dates, every particular of each event. Did any of your friends see?"

"I'm not sure," Ruby said quietly.

"Ask them. If you want to make a case, it helps to have witnesses. But you need to keep a log. Dated, with every detail."

"Is it sexual harassment if he didn't say anything or touch me?"

"It could be, if he's creating a chilling environment that interferes with your learning. This is so classic!" She shook her head in disgust. "These predators . . ."

I reached out and touched Abi's arm, grateful for her attention and knowledge, confirmed in my hunch that she'd be exactly the mentor Ruby needed. Although Ruby complained later, when she strolled into the kitchen brushing her teeth, that Abi was "jumping to conclusions," I was sure Abi was onto something. We wouldn't let that slime get away with harassing my girl. No wonder she thought everybody was staring at her: he was giving her a complex about her appearance.

That weekend Abi invited us to San Francisco to hear Gwen Avery's "stomping piano blues," she said, at the Artemis Café. Somehow

I convinced Ruby to come into the city with us; maybe it was the promise of the city, with the possibility that we'd hop in for some quick clothes shopping on the way home. Once settled into the grungy ground-floor café, she and I sipped our herbal tea while we all chatted, seated among five or six tables of women. "This is an interesting place," I gushed like a tour guide, frantic for Ruby to enjoy our outing. "All women. How unusual."

"Hmm." Abi looked amused, but said little, and Ruby, as so often recently, remained silent. What was she thinking? Gwen Avery lumbered over to the piano and rattled the keys, running her fingers up and down the keyboard. "Hey, good-lookin'," she joked to a young African American woman with gold hoop earrings who sat alone at the next table. "I could be your sugar mama." The woman called back, giggling, something I couldn't make out, but her tone, and a coy little smile with eyes batting, suggested it was risqué. Gwen closed her eyes, still playing. I watched, fascinated, when she threw back her head and began to sing, "'Precious Lord . . .'" She raised her huge voice: "'. . . take my hand. Lead me on. . . . Through the storm, through the night.'" Her volume built; she rocked, she stomped, drenching the gospel music with a flavor of juke joint blues that I recognized from Solomon. "'Hear my cry, hear my call, hmm, hmmm . . .'" she growled, her eyes swiveling over to Ruby. "Brighten up, girl, get off your ass, move your feet." Ruby, startled, glanced away, her eyes flickering over to me, as if to say "Help," but Gwen didn't let up. "'When your feet can't sit still no more . . .'" she rumbled, half singing, clearly enjoying Ruby's discomfort, until she returned to her song.

I leaned over and patted Ruby's arm, whispering, "Oh, she probably just likes you and she's teasing," but Ruby, with her new abruptness, pulled away. Gwen moved on, shifting gears, lifting a whiskey-contralto in a soft, "'All my love . . . Please take all my love/Inside of you. It would be/So good for me . . . please.'" Love. My only history with this music had been during my early years with Solomon; my chest contracted when I remembered how full of expectations we'd been. An image of Solomon romping with our toddlers in People's Park opened like a movie reel in my mind, when Gwen burst out with more blues, growling again to a rocking beat, "'I wanna be your sugar mama./I wanna be your sugar mama,/every day. Be your sugar mama I want to love you in the morning . . .'" Solomon's picture dissolved into the piano melody.

Watching Gwen Avery, so obviously her own woman, I couldn't imagine this husky forty-year-old deferring to any man. I found myself staring like the day I'd met Solomon, seduced again into an unfamiliar world through music. My eyes began to take in my surroundings: the concert posters for "womyn's music" tacked to the wall, the other women in the café—young, mostly white— lounging at their small tables, a few leaning forward, listening intently. I felt nourished in this space, feeling a rush of energy that recalled who I'd been: the wild young woman I'd buried during the years I'd bitten my tongue, hoping to be seen as almost black or not seen at all. Now here I was awash in music with Ruby, who, after Gwen withdrew her attention, fidgeted quietly, although once she asked Abi, pointedly ignoring me, I thought, "Where did you get those cool earrings?"

As we left the café I leaned over to Abi, our lovely new friend who'd opened the door to this novel outing. "Thank you," I said, squeezing her hand. "What a wonderful afternoon."

"We'll do it again," she tossed off, squeezing me back with an unexpectedly strong grip.

Two steps later Ruby ducked behind me, grabbing the side of my jacket like a child, burying her face in my sleeve.

"What's going on, Ruby?"

"Don't look at me," she hissed. "Look away!"

I did as instructed, peering across the street. All I saw was a young, long-haired woman in a blue beret with an older man, gray-haired, limping beside her. "Do you know them?" I whispered.

"Shh . . . this is horrible! They saw me."

"What is this paranoia, Ruby?" I muttered, careful to keep my face pointed frontward. "So they saw you, so what?" Had the teacher's stares gotten to her so completely?

"They saw me coming out . . . of . . . that place!" she said quietly but vehemently, poking her head up and scanning the street. The couple, walking in the opposite direction, were not looking back at us.

"So what?"

"That place! You know . . ."

"The café?"

"This is horrible! That's Connie Baker. She's in my class and she's the most popular girl that ever lived. Wait until the news gets around school that I was at this . . . why did you ever bring me here?" She spat out the words, practically crying.

"Oh, nobody's going to think anything, Ruby," I said, putting my arm around her. "It's not that big a deal."

She jerked furiously away. "You can't be black so now you're going to be with—" She pointed back at the club. "With them. Pathetic. You can't stand to just be a normal mother like everybody else's."

"Ruby, think before you talk," I whispered, pulling my arm away from her. "You have no idea what you're talking about."

Somehow the three of us crammed into Abi's ancient blue MG, Ruby and I folding up our long legs like accordions. Ruby's silence was noticeable and the ride was tense, though I tried to chat with Abi as though nothing had happened. I hoped she wouldn't notice Ruby's reticence and be put off her "mentor mission," as I'd dubbed it to myself.

"Have you been to the women's bookstore in Oakland?" Abi asked, seemingly oblivious to the drama playing out between Ruby and me, while we sped across the Bay Bridge. "No? You should check it out. Definitely."

*   *   *

The following afternoon, with a resistant Ruby riding shotgun after school, I circled A Woman's Place three times, until at last I found a parking spot across the street. Then I stood, watching the bookstore as cars whizzed by. "Mama," Ruby said plaintively, "I mean Lizzie. What are you doing? Let's go home. I don't want to be here."

"Sweetie, this will only take a minute."

She rolled her eyes. Summoning courage, I clutched her hand and jaywalked over, dragging her, then darted in, muttering, "Wait a second," and scurried to the corner marked LESBIAN. There, slipping two books off the shelf, I pressed them under my arm and hurried to the cash register, hoping Ruby wouldn't ask. For once, caught up in her teenage annoyance and relief at leaving so soon, she didn't.

At home I tore open the bag, lay back on my bed, and began to read. Sexuality exists on a continuum, Adrienne Rich said; most of us are inherently bisexual. Kinsey's research confirmed it. I rolled over to my stomach. It made sense.

Wherever my sexuality lay on the scale, my emergence as a proud woman-identified woman could only be good for Ruby. The last thing I wanted was for her to repeat the life of a squelched mother, one who passed down the classic women's inheritance: a model of submissive, second-class living. And Abi, I was beginning to understand, could help me with this. Help us. With relief, I envisioned our friendship as a joint project to support Ruby's emergence as a strong black woman. Solomon wanted to see his daughter as often as possible, certainly, but with his disparaging position on "women's lib," I was sure that Abi could offer far more.

So I thought until the morning Abi visited me shortly after Ruby had left for school. We'd seen each other two or three times since the expedition to hear Gwen Avery, but always accompanied by a noncommittal Ruby, who I understood was Abi's primary interest. "Oh, I have the morning off," I said, pleased, although taken aback to see her small frame through our glass door. It was eight forty-five. "Come in." I opened the door wide. "This is a surprise. But Ruby isn't here."

"I know," she gulped, shifting from foot to foot. Her dark eyes gleamed more brightly than I'd noticed before.

"What?" I asked, confused. "Are you all right?"

"There's something I need to talk to you about." Her eyes darted around the empty living room. "Is anyone else home?"

"No," I said, baffled by her nervousness. "Ruby's at school. Are you all right?" I repeated. "What's wrong?" My stomach lurched. I hadn't realized how much her well-being meant to me.

"Che's not here?"

"No, he's probably at school, too." My puzzlement was growing into irritation. "You know he doesn't live here. What's up?"

"Do you have any coffee?"

"Sure, but, Abi, what's going on?"

"Let me tell you over a cup—you know I can talk better with a cup in my hand."

"Just a minute and I'll make a pot." I led her through the kitchen to the back deck, where a small wrought-iron table and two matching chairs had worn dents in the wood. It was late December: a magnolia tree next door shed petals onto the deck. Its fragrance wafted over on every gust of wind. The branches of our plum tree formed a silhouette against the morning sky, like a Japanese painting. The cornflower blue sky was clear of clouds. "A perfect California morning," I said, still amazed at the early blooming season.

Five minutes later, when I returned with a pot of coffee and a cheese Danish, I asked, "Abi, what's wrong?"

"What about Solomon, Lizzie?"

"What about him?" Such a complicated question. What about

Solomon, and his place in my life? It was gigantic; the hole his absence left could easily hold my old VW van, her MG, our aging Volvo that Solomon had taken, and fifty other cars, with room left over for a bulldozer or two. Exasperation flared up, battling for space with the pain any mention of Solomon caused. Why the fuck did she come over here before nine in the morning, knocking on my door to beg for coffee, and then question me about my ex-husband? This was absurd.

She picked up her Guatemalan bag and twisted the handle, looking flustered. "I thought maybe you two would get back—"

"I told you, it's over," I interrupted, letting myself feel the stab of regret at the same moment that I noticed, for the first time, the attractive streaks of gray hair at Abi's temples. In the early light, she looked wizened and wise. "We haven't formalized it yet with a divorce, but we live in two separate spheres. It became impossible. You know, he says women are just 'jumping on the liberation band-wagon.' That we're going to slow down the progress for black men." I stopped and leaned back, staring, trying to read her. "Is that what you came to ask me about?"

Abi's eyes darted around the yard and she gulped her coffee, which wasn't like her. Her style was to sip, sip, sip, then refill the cup, right into the late hours. "Café culture," she'd reminded me, when I asked how she could sleep after all that caffeine. "That's my people. We don't go to bed at ten p.m. like you Anglos. We know how to have a good time!" She brushed a magnolia petal from the lip of her cup and poured a refill. "Since we've spent these last days together, I'm starting to—" She narrowed her eyes. I saw her gulp and, unbelievably, heard her come out with an outlandish question. "Did you like sex with Solomon?"

"Sex? Abi, what kind of question is that?"

"I'm asking for a reason. It's not prurient interest." She tried a weak chuckle.

"Oh, really?" I mimicked her half chuckle. "Well, I did, if you must know." I shrugged. "It wasn't the sex with him I didn't like. It was the sex*ism*."

"Oh. Right." As she nodded, my annoyance gave way to gratitude. How comforting to have a friend who understood my political shorthand. Most people would have been puzzled by my statement. In this time of turbulence, her easy knowledge meant I didn't have to explain it.

"Do you think you could choose . . . ?" Her voice trailed off.

"Choose . . . ?"

She reached out one small hand to touch my leg, and began to gently stroke it. Up and down, her light touch tingled my legs until I felt a quiver shudder through my body. She cupped my cheek, slid the other hand behind my neck, and leaned over to kiss me on the lips. Hers were as soft as Solomon's had been that first evening. In sixteen years I hadn't kissed any other lips, excluding puckers for the children or a visiting relative. When we pulled back to stare in each other's eyes, I blinked, took a deep breath, and asked, "Is this what you came over for?"

"Yes." She smiled tentatively, still looking uncharacteristically nervous. Her left cheek twitched. "This was it. You. I haven't been able to get you off my mind. When we held hands for that minute on the way to the car after we heard Gwen Avery, your touch burned me." She held up her left hand and shook it, with a coy look. "I didn't even want to wash it, corny as that sounds. You don't believe people are born gay or straight, do you?"

"It doesn't seem like it," I said hesitantly. "Not the way that kiss felt. And I do believe we can choose, but this is scary, Abi. I thought you were hanging out with us because of Ruby."

"Ruby's mama," she said as she took my hand and tugged me inside, pulling me to the living room.

"I'm on the rebound, you know," I demurred. "In a very strange state. *Needy* wouldn't begin to do it justice."

"Who cares? I see who you are, Lizzie." With that she pushed me onto the couch. Then, awkwardly, we lay together on the old stuffed sofa, tentatively moving until my generous hips pushed against her smaller ones. My family legacy—an ability to leap into unfamiliar terrain—propelled me; my hunger for warmth inched me forward; and my genuine pleasure and respect for Abi kept me moving. When I let myself relax into the pleasure of her softness, I flashed again on the first time I'd melted into Solomon's lips. But now, sinking into the small pillow of Abi's body, I was stunned by how supple, how yielding she was. "This is what men have been getting all these years!" I sputtered. "This softness . . . these breasts . . . and what do women get? Hard bodies like boards!" I couldn't believe the inequity. "And that stick poking me, all the time poking, poking." I jabbed my finger into her stomach until she roared.

We remained on the couch for nearly three hours, until just after noon: talking, kissing, exploring silky skin. I was astonished at how smooth, how satiny her inner lips felt, exactly like my own wet pleasure. "Abi," I asked, nibbling on her ear, echoing words I'd murmured to Solomon sixteen years before, "how can something this good be bad?" A part of me hung suspended in shock—*me, with a woman?*—but lying with Abi felt so comfortable I could easily flick aside the scandalized witness. For the moment, anyway.

"Lizzie," she murmured, "you're the woman I've been dreaming of all my life. Political, sensitive . . . and with two fantastic children . . . three for one." She put her tongue in my mouth, averting any answer.

Two weeks later, settling in for a long evening chat with Ruby, I took a deep breath and wondered if the words would come. "Honey," I said, curling my hands together, trying unsuccessfully to soothe the ragged, painful cuticles. "Abi and I are more than friends. We're—" I sat on the side of Ruby's bed.

"What?" She glared, with that new, but already familiar stare, unnerving me further.

"We're—" But I stopped myself. It had only been thirteen days. Should I tell her? My civil liberties background could only lead me to one answer: everyone, I believed, has a right to knowledge, and children, generally denied it, have a special, incontrovertible right.

"You're what?" Her eyes opened wide, the sheen of anger disappeared, and I felt I was peering into her vulnerable soul. She looked frightened. Where had that sunny child gone whom I'd known so well, the one who used to flash the radiant smile that lit up the room, laugh, tease, "Mama-mama," grab my waist and twirl me around the room? Was it the split with Solomon that caused the change? Or was this descent into negativity simply a preview of the difficult "teen years" my friends had warned me about?

"We're lovers," I said quietly, reaching out to cushion the shock.

"Lovers!" she screamed, shaking her head, hair flying. "I knew it. When those yellow roses came." Her body heaved as she turned to the wall. "This is so unfair."

"It's okay, sweetie." I reached out, reflexively, to hug her, throwing my chest against her back, attempting to encircle her with my arms as a cushion against this latest blow. "Abi's a wonderful woman, who cares about you . . ."

"You don't love me anymore," she wailed into the wall, muffling her words. "I'm going to live with Daddy."

"Oh, honey, I do. You won't." I tried stroking her back. "Abi and I both do. You're not losing anything, you're only gaining," I said with a swirl of emotion: tenderness mixed with guilt for the pain I was inflicting, fatigue, and grief, still, about Solomon. All churned against my own bursting desire for an independent life.

When she rolled over her eyes were squeezed shut. "You can't . . ." She opened them and squeaked, "You can't. You're my mother!"

"I know I'm your mother, sweetie. But I'm more than that, too. And now I'm in a new relationship. I don't know what will happen with it, but I'm happy."

"*You're* happy! What about me?"

"Sweetie, this was all about you, if you can understand, that's why I—"

Her face abruptly took on another expression, one of horror. "Does that mean you're a . . ." She scowled. "A lesbian?"

"I don't know, Ruby. I just know I really, really like Abi, and she likes me, and you. And Che."

"Mothers can't be lesbians." Her tears flowed again; watching her, I felt a trickle down my own cheeks, my body empathizing the way it did whenever she cried.

"I'll still be your mama," I assured her. "I'll still love you, don't worry, everything's the same."

"No," she repeated, snot running out of her nose. "It's not. Nothing's the same, ever since I came back from Grandma Jean's. Daddy's gone, Che's gone, and now you're a lesbian! I wish I could run away. Far away, and never come back!"

"Yes, love," I kept saying, stroking her, but nothing proved calming until moist exhaustion claimed her and she fell asleep exactly the way she had as a young child, a damp heap in my arms.

Worn out, I called Abi. "I told Ruby. She's so upset. I can't bear to see her in pain like that." I groaned. "And here I thought you were going to be *her* friend, her mentor. What are we doing? Our friendship was supposed to be helpful to Ruby, not cause her more grief. She's been through enough already."

"She'll be all right," my new partner assured me. "We need to take it slow. Give her a chance to get used to the idea. We won't push anything."

When Che lugged his suitcase in the door the next afternoon, I waited until he'd snuggled into the couch, tossing his green tennis ball back and forth from hand to hand. He often sat like this, contentedly perfecting his skill with a ball. "Honey," I began, dropping down by him, sinking into the deep cushions. "You know how sometimes people who are the same sex—like girls and girls—well, they can like each other a lot," I stumbled.

He looked at me as if I were crazy.

"You know how Daddy and I were married," I tried again.

"Mama . . ." His puckered face showed his bafflement and discomfort.

"I've got a girlfriend." I plunged ahead. "Not like just a friend, more like Daddy and I were, kind of, but not really. A special, special friend."

Now he simply looked confused.

"Somebody that you've met. Remember Abi, who drove us to your soccer game? She's my new special friend."

Silence.

"Lover, really." I swallowed hard. "Have you heard of lesbians?"

"*Lesbos?*" The word fell out of his mouth as if he were spitting dirt.

"Che, that's not a nice way to say it. Lesbians. That's when two women love each other the way a man and a woman do."

"Mama, you can't be a lesbo." He stared at me as if I'd grown two heads. "You can't."

"I don't know what I am," I said. "Except I'm your mother. And I really like Abi. In fact, I might love her."

"Don't tell anyone," he begged, triggering every ounce of my civil libertarian we-have-a-right-to-announce-it-to-the-world rebel spirit. "Maybe you're not a lesbian," he said out loud with hope.

"I don't know." I steeled myself, jaw set. "We'll see."

"I don't want to talk about it," he said, and fled, running to his room, where I heard his door slam shut.

CHAPTER 9

Ruby

1979

I lay daydreaming on top of my red star quilt one evening around nine, not really doing anything, when I heard Mama stagger down the hall. I thought about turning off my light, pretending to be asleep. But instead I grabbed a book from the floor and propped it on my stomach. It was my social studies text, big and heavy. I yawned, trying to brush a drowsy look over my face, as if I'd fallen asleep while studying. The last thing I wanted was a heart-to-heart. With her. I had way too much to think about and my feelings about her were way too complicated. Half of me was missing her like hell and pining for Che and Daddy, aching for our old life together as a family, like a distant memory now. But the other half was mad, kind of a general fury at everything and she was right in the center. When we were together everything inside me felt all jumbled up and bouncing around, and not in a good way. Every once in a while there was a glimmer of the deep, deep comfy feeling we used to have, but only a glimmer. It would disappear before I could hold on to it for long. Most of the other times I wanted to run away. Or live with Daddy and Che. I missed them so much that sometimes my stomach felt as if it were turned inside out. But I couldn't talk to her about it or she'd start crying, like she did when I tried to tell her a couple of times.

But tonight she barged in like she did ever since they'd moved out—without any respect for my privacy, which used to be important in our family—and she dropped onto my bed, pushing Cesar off. He fell on the floor and yipped, pulling on the edge of my quilt with his teeth. I yanked it back up.

"Oh, Ruby," she started out, "it's been so long since we've spent any real time together."

Yeah, I thought. *And?*

"We're not even cooking together. . . ."

I could tell by the way she was gulping and sniffing that she was holding back tears. It was pretty obvious, as if she wanted me to know she was secretly crying so I'd rescue her. She seemed to count on me that way lately. I was tempted. Who wants to see their mother cry? I'd even gardened with her in those ridiculous plots she dug up, pulling weeds while we waited for the flowers that hardly ever bloomed. Maybe the gophers got the bulbs, I don't know, but she loved to be out there poking and sniffing the dirt and examining every little sprout to see if it was going to grow into a flower. I'd done everything to distract her, like even slamming a door just to get her attention and shake her out of her sadness. Maybe she was missing me, too, like she said. Or maybe it was just Daddy and Che she missed so much. But I was pissed. *I know, I know, you're hardly cooking at all, alone or with me.* My stomach reminded me every night I stir-fried another batch of veggie and rice or opened endless cans of tomato soup and broiled open-faced cheese sandwiches. Or whipped up yet another batch of cupcakes. *Let's talk about that,* I wanted to say. But I didn't say a word, and she didn't even notice. She kept talking even though Cesar was yipping and yelping right along. Her green eyes were cloudy, which I knew was trouble.

"You know, we hardly spend any time together anymore," she repeated. She didn't ask me how was everything for *me* in this weird new universe, with just the two of us here instead of the whole family or the friends that used to crowd around our dining table.

Instead she settled herself in, getting comfy. "You know Hannah's going through a lot too right now."

Uh, what did the troubles of her best friend have to do with me? And did I really need to know about them? I had my own troubles. Did she care about those?

"Oh, sweetie," she said before she put one hand to her forehead and rubbed it like she was trying to rub out a really giant pain. Her pain, not mine. "I need you right now."

The disgusting smell on her breath made me nauseous. I could tell by that and the way she was enunciating, real carefully, that she'd been listening to records and drinking wine, probably a whole bottle. When she was high, her words got very pre-cise, and her eyes were that murky green like a pond full of leaves. I hated the fuzziness blurring her face. It was like she wasn't really there with me. A "mama clone" had invaded her body.

"I know you need me, too. Life is so strange," she started out, and I could see that we were headed for a long meandering meditation on "the meaning of life," which she loved to talk about. "You never know what's coming. When I went down to Mississippi that summer of '63, I had no idea what was ahead. No idea."

Oh no, I thought, *where is this going?* I'd heard the story of how she and Daddy met. He was sitting outside this broken-down shack where they were both staying for the summer to register voters. How scary it was for Black people and white people to even talk together. I'd heard all about it, right down to the flock of sparrows or whatever they were, flitting around Daddy while he played his guitar. They used to hoot and bust with pride when they told about "our Mississippi introduction," like it was this huge deal.

She was still talking. ". . . no idea at all, and here I am, all these years later, in Berkeley, California, with two kids, divorcing . . ."

I hadn't said a word since she clumped into my room.

". . . one never knows what's ahead, do we? And look at you. . . ." She did then, as if she'd noticed I was there. ". . . almost grown. I can't believe it." Tears fogged up her eyes. "So beautiful and talented. Oh, Ruby, I love you." She leaned way over to give me a hug, and the sour alcohol smell was so strong I gagged. Even Cesar inched away.

"Mama!" In my panic I pushed her off, forgetting to call her Lizzie like she wanted me to. "I hate it when your eyes are like that."

"Like what?" Her face pinched.

"Like when you're drinking. Your eyes are all crazy." I didn't want to have this conversation. I wanted her gone.

"Drinking? I had a glass of wine with dinner. A couple . . . I wouldn't say I've been *drinking,* Ruby."

"That unit I studied on Problem Drinkers." I screwed up my courage and blurted it out. "Along with the one on smoking you never paid attention to. They said if you drink every day, you're a problem drinker. Lizzie . . ." I could feel myself whining in a familiar way that I hated but I couldn't stop myself. I wanted to beg, *Please stop drinking.* "I told you about it."

"Goddamn it, that's ridiculous. I am not a problem drinker." She sighed and shook her head. "You know, I have enough problems without having you—and your prudish little generation—telling me I can't even have one fucking glass of wine with my dinner."

Okay, okay. Stop swearing. Just go.

"I am still the adult around here, and I'm not going to have you telling me what I can and cannot do, Ruby Jordan. I am not drunk." She tried to pull her back up straight, but she wobbled.

"You're high."

She didn't say anything, just focused on her hands. "Yeah," she said, surprising me. "You're right, I am a little high." She gave another sigh. "Not that that's a sin." She paused. "My heart still hurts about things not working out with your dad. And after two glasses of wine, the heaviness lifts. It's amazing. I feel better. Nothing else relieves the pain. So . . ." She had the oddest expression, and I watched her eyes clear like a sky when the fog blows away. "You're right, I probably should cut back. Woman alone, drinking . . ." She smiled, staring like she was back. It was my mother again in her body there on the bed. I could see how she loved me and I felt a tug. Before, when I was young, I'd thought she was beautiful, with her wild red hair and green eyes and white skin. Like an Irish goddess. I hadn't felt that for a long time, but a wave of the old worship swept me.

"Mama," I started, not realizing I'd slipped into calling her Mama instead of Lizzie. After Daddy left, she told Che and me to call her by her name. All the time. "I'm not a role, I'm a person," she'd said. "And Lizzie is who I was before I met your father. I'm coming back to myself." But now I wanted to say, *Mama, remember when I was three, and I told you I wanted to marry you when I grew up. It was summertime, we were up in Mendocino in the country visiting Cookie when she rented that house by the ocean for her birthday, remember? We had so much fun on the beach, Che and me running into the edge of the waves, and making sand castles, digging moats. You laughed and said kids couldn't marry their mothers, but we had a special bond forever that was like a marriage, but even better. A mother-daughter bond that would never go away. Remember that?*

"Mama," I said again, craving her with that old hunger, wishing we could cuddle up and she'd tell me everything was all right. I'd be a kid again and know she could make any problem disappear. And I'd know that she loved me.

"What, honey?" she asked, not correcting me, only reaching out her hand to rub my arm, like she always did, as if that stroking erased any troubles. Her fingers were tender. She touched me so lightly it made my back tingle, even though she was only touching my arm. When I was a young child that was how she put me to sleep, caressing my arms while she told me a story.

That night it was as if she could read my mind. We were in sync the way we hadn't been for a long time, and I was lulled into a drowsy mood. I half expected a story.

"Honey," she said, her eyelids droopy like mine. "I have to tell you something."

"Hmmm?" I was nearly asleep.

"Abi and I—"

My spine told me to wake up.

"We're more than just friends."

"Oh no." I'd wondered why the yellow roses had been delivered to our front door, why Abi sent them for no reason at all. "What are you? Like—*best* friends? Instead of Hannah?"

She gave me a long look. Her eyes darkened from their usual green to a hazel brown. I couldn't see inside them.

"We're . . . more than just friends," she repeated, looking at me with an intense gaze, like I should understand without her saying the words.

"What are you then? If you're not friends." I gulped.

"We're, well, I think we're becoming lovers."

"Lovers! What about Daddy?"

"He doesn't really enter into this, Ruby. Not anymore. You know he and I are working out a relationship, a friendship—you know we're both your parents—"

"I don't want her here!" I couldn't stop the tears from flowing. "You can't do this to me."

"I will have whomever I want come in this house, Ruby Jordan," she spat. Her face was so contorted and her eyes so dark I hardly recognized her. One minute she's stroking me, the next she's yelling at me. She never understood what I felt. Everything, everything was about her. Why didn't she ever think about *me*? She couldn't do this to me.

"Lizzie." What could I say? "Lizzie," I repeated. She'd been drinking a lot lately, and I wanted to snap her out of that glazed state. Sometimes just saying her name did it.

"I want to have a life, too." She crumpled and began to cry. "You have your friends over. What about me?"

I sat up, but instead of slapping her to sober her up like I wanted to, I sat there, helpless. Mama leaned over onto me and I propped her up until my head throbbed, and then *I* began to cry. But she didn't notice.

Instead she kept moaning, "The world is so complicated," with her face buried in my neck. I sat, frozen, until finally she stood up, sniffling. "I'm sorry, Ruby. I don't know what to do anymore sometimes." She pulled a Kleenex out of the box by my bed and blew her nose. "Do you have more homework to do?" she asked, acting all of a sudden as if I were a kid and she were a normal mother and we'd never even had this crazy conversation. As if I hadn't been crying myself.

"Yeah," I lied. "A lot of social studies. We're having a quiz tomorrow." I spoke like a robot.

"Well, you'd better get to work," she said, leaning over to kiss me. She tiptoed out.

The last thing I could do was study! She'd come in here, drunk and weepy, and dropped a bomb in my lap. How would my life change, now that she and Abi were "official" lezzies? Ugh. What would my friends think if they found out? And what would Daddy say if he knew?

One thing for sure, though, was that I couldn't count on her anymore. All she thought about was herself. I cut the light and tossed in bed, pushing my quilt off and tugging it up again, all night. How could I stop wishing we could go back to how our family used to be? The way *she* used to be? I held my breath, trying not to feel sore in my stomach, trying not to feel anything, until I squeezed my body closed. After this moment, I swore, my mother would be Lizzie, exactly as she asked. I'd call her by that cold name, or maybe even Elizabeth, like Daddy called her. I knew she hated it. I'd deliberately train myself not to need her. I lay there practicing not wanting to have carrot-colored hair and not caring if she couldn't make the world safe. I'd make it safe for myself, I thought, clenching my fists under the covers. And when I couldn't I'd turn to Daddy.

I held all that inside, squashing down the ache all over my body, and the fury, the disappointment. When morning came, I would *not* need my mother anymore.

PART TWO
1980–2000

CHAPTER 10

Lizzie

1980

When Tyrone strolled into our lives, I was thrilled. A diminutive, fortyish African American hippie, he taught fifth grade at a co-op school in North Oakland and he did child care, after hours, for Stevie, a friend of ours up on Claremont Avenue. Since I'd just been hired to teach three night classes, back-to-back, at Merritt, I thought, *Aha, I'll demolish racial* and *gender stereotypes in one fell swoop.* Delighting in the prospect, I phoned the slim teacher, whom I'd met once at Stevie's.

I waited to tell Ruby until after dinner: hot and sour soup from the Victory Peace Café with spring rolls, spicy ginger, and sushi, which she liked. We were wiping down the counter together when I told her about my plan, prepared for objections.

"I don't need a sitter. *Baby*sitter. I'm not a baby. I'm almost four-teen! People my age are babysitters themselves." She tossed the yellow sponge into the sink and begged, "Lizzie, please. I know how to take care of myself. I'd be so embarrassed."

"I know you do, honey," I told her, reaching out to pat her arm. Her eyes reflected her hurt. "It's just someone to be here. I'll be gone until almost midnight. If it were just a few hours, yes, or if it were earlier in the day. But I don't want you here alone at night. Late at night." I turned on the hot water and rinsed my sponge, preparing to wash the plates. "Here, you dry." I tossed her the blue dish towel.

"I can take care of myself," she argued, grabbing it. "I'll have the dogs. What could happen?"

"This isn't the safest neighborhood. I don't want to scare you, but you know it isn't. I think it's actually getting worse. And what if there were an emergency? A dog can't handle that." I turned off the water and leaned over to pat her arm again, wanting to end the conversation.

"What about Imani? Can't I stay at her house?" She ducked away from my comforting hand.

"Not three nights a week, Ruby. That's too much to ask. And they're school nights. No."

"Pleeease!" She sounded desperate. Crinkling her nose, she shocked me by asking, "What about Abi? Couldn't she drop by or something?" Wow, she really didn't want the sitter if she was willing to ask for help from her nemesis.

"No, sweetie, we really need some regular presence here with you, late at night, and Abi has too many other commitments to come every single week, three nights every week. I can't ask her. We'd always be having to fill in. It's too much to ask. I need to keep this simple. I've got way too much going on. Lots of people know Tyrone, I've gotten nothing but great recommendations. I think you'll end up really liking him."

"Why don't you ever listen to me?" she persisted. "What I want."

"Because sometimes a mother has to make decisions, honey, for your safety. Even if it's not what you want." I blasted the water in the sink full force.

"It's embarrassing. A babysitter!"

"I know, sweetie. Try to think of it differently if you can. He'll be more of a companion. An adult companion. Lots of people have them," I tried.

Despite Ruby's angry opposition—and she didn't let go, keeping up a daily stream of complaints—the following Tuesday Tyrone showed up at four, eyes carefully lidded, hair tucked under a white stocking cap. As countless other liberal whites had no doubt done before me, I offered a dollar over the going rate, insisted that Tyrone address me as Lizzie ("We'll be on a first-name basis"), and made a point of asking about his family before I left that first day. I wanted to show Tyrone that I regarded him as a person, not a servant. He had his job, I had mine, which, I knew, glossed over the pay gap—of course, I had my own pay gap, I wanted to say, compared to the male faculty at Merritt College—but what could I do other than be kind, respectful, and pay a bit extra?

While we chatted that first day, Tyrone confided in his quiet voice that he and his son lived in a small housing project out in East Oakland. The very name of his neighborhood, East Oakland, signaled fear. All I knew about it from reading the *Chronicle* and our Panther friends were gunfights, stabbings. Police brutality. Poverty. Violence. This was where Tyrone climbed on the first of two buses each morning, hooking his bicycle on the back. Fervently hoping he would be all right with Ruby, I flashed a tight smile, one I hoped was reassuring to both of them. My farewell words, "Have fun," sounded hollow in my ears as I fled out the door, leaving a glaring Ruby watching me go.

Yet apparently Tyrone did a fine job of heating the leftovers I'd set aside and monitoring Ruby's evening until I staggered in at 11:30 or 12, too tired to say anything but "Thank you, good night," and hand over an envelope of cash. And in the morning Ruby, surprisingly, had little to say other than he'd been "okay."

The next afternoon Tyrone strolled in again, this time with the food in hand that I'd asked him to pick up, since he rode right by a Chinese restaurant on his bike. Ruby greeted him warmly, too, in spite of her grumbling to me. *This is perfect.*

All proceeded smoothly as the weeks passed. However, Tyrone told us with increasingly grim eyes and tight lips that his nineteen-year-old son was unable to find work. Knowing the statistics on black male unemployment, especially for those from the ghetto, I could offer little encouragement, and had to helplessly observe Tyrone's growing desperation as the weeks passed. Each day he looked more concerned. Nonetheless, Tyrone soon became a fixture in our house, showing up promptly three afternoons a week. I was beginning to feel assured that Ruby's objections had been fully overcome and that I had a steady sitter for the rest of the semester until the Friday morning when she wailed, "Oh, I can't find my watch." It had been a gift from my mother, a watch with multiple clip-on faces, nestled in an oblong gold box. Ruby loved to snap on red to complement her crimson pants, Prussian blue on days the sky, she said, was especially blue, and yellow for her bright golden jacket. She even wrote a poem, a haiku published in the school paper, about the magic watch that matched her mood.

Now it had disappeared.

Even though we were in a hurry to leave the house that morning, we tore apart every shelf that was high, as Solomon had taught us to systematically search for lost objects. "Look high, look low," he used to say, with a field marshal's discipline. Ruby stretched to the top of her closet, clogged with old board games, books, and clothes, while I stood on a chair, reaching deeply into the highest ledges of her bookshelves. A page of paper covered with typing fluttered down. A letter from Solomon, I imagined.

"It couldn't be there!" Ruby rushed to pick up the paper, hustling it away into her book bag.

"Look, I have to leave. You might have put it somewhere without thinking, when you were distracted by something else." I stared pointedly at her book bag.

"No, I know I didn't. It's not there, honest. It was on my bureau. Please help me look, just for one more minute. I really want to find it." She was so anxious that I relented. But the watch was not high. We hurriedly swept the lower half of the house, pushing aside piles of newspapers, dirty dishes, and clothes. We poked into low shelves and even opened the silverware drawer in the kitchen, staring into its stainless-steel clutter. "We'll look again tonight," I promised, rushing to grab my jacket and keys before we charged out the door.

That night we hunted again: high, low, and in between. "Listen," I finally said, exasperated, while we kneeled, panting, next to the couch we'd just peered under for the third time. "Are you sure you didn't leave it at school? You didn't take it off for some reason? Try to think."

"No, I had it on when I came home yesterday. I took it off when I changed my clothes, before I went out to meet Imani on the steps. I remember I put it on my bureau. Honest." Her voice was so confident, I had no reason to disbelieve her. Yet I didn't want to consider the other possibility. Only two people had been in the house with Ruby the day before.

"Did you ask Imani?"

"She didn't see it. I took it off before she came over." Ruby stared straight at me while we rose from our knees, dusting our pants. "And she never came in."

With a deep sigh, I said slowly, "I'll talk to Tyrone next Tuesday when he comes. If it doesn't turn up before then." Reluctant as I was to distrust him, when I considered every possible scenario he was the obvious suspect. I turned away to hide my confusion and marched into the kitchen, running the tap to get a drink of water, then changing my mind and pouring a glass of Chianti. The watch wasn't here; he'd been here; I could draw only one conclusion. And I was angry about it. Damnit, why did he have to blow it? Life was tough enough without stealing from friends. He can't have been that hard up. I wondered if he did drugs—*What kind, hard or soft?*—and needed money for them. Funny, I hadn't noticed any effects of a high in his behavior, but I guessed I hadn't been looking. *I should count myself lucky that all he took was the watch; something could have happened to Ruby.* Or was it his son, who'd somehow slipped in?

I'd have to make a clean break, that was all. Simple.

"Ruby, let's work in the garden," I invited her the next afternoon, a Saturday. I'd noticed how much she enjoyed hanging by my side poking in the dirt, and how nurturing the gardening was, since she often appeared calmer after we worked outside together. Whenever I stumbled out alone to weed or dig in a new plant, Ruby generally followed. Nature, I understood, was a healing space for both of us. And Cesar had taught Rosa to dig, so once Ruby and I were set the dogs howled to join us. Since the yard was unfenced I was wary, but in their old age they were staying close by, so the four of us often wallowed out in the yellowish dirt together.

"Look." That Saturday afternoon Ruby pointed out a green shoot sprouting from the earth, miraculously sporting an orange flower. Despite our sandy soil, a bouquet of orange California poppies bloomed, right next to our sparkling blue lobelia. In the early dusk Ruby and I watched the poppies fold their petals, coiling into tight buds. I knew that when the sun hit in the morning they'd open wide, uncurling into flowers, and I wondered if Ruby might be following a similar rhythm, closing up during this time of transition: her own puberty and her family's dramatic changes. I had no doubt that soon, if I held my patience long enough, she, too, would open her arms wide, returning to the sunny, open child everyone had loved. As we dug silently next to each other I thought back to her early childhood, when her radiance dazzled strangers on the street. She'd been such a bright, chatty child that she drew people to her as naturally as flowers turned their faces to the sun.

Right from birth, Ruby had been the kind of baby whose rosy face peeking out from the carriage had stopped passersby. They invariably exclaimed in admiration at my child's bright cheeks and warm brown eyes. Although, and my heart quickened to remember it, there had also been the other kind of comments. Frequently, when I walked the children in their heavy double stroller, after strangers cooed and ahhed they grilled me, looking dubious. "How did they get so tan?"

This is 1968, I'd think, startled every time. *How can race still be that complex?*

Now, as Tuesday and my meeting with Tyrone approached, my mind flew about like a crazed bird in a cage. What about Tyrone's son? Would he try to take revenge for his father? Could he have been here the evening the watch disappeared, after Ruby was asleep? Should I tell Stevie my suspicion, in order to protect him, too? After all, he left his kids with Tyrone. But I had no proof. What was ethical?

Each day I poured myself more glasses of Chianti and chewed every raggedy scrap of cuticle skin. I even made arrangements for a colleague to take my first class on Tuesday evening, giving me extra time after Tyrone arrived, which he did, right on the dot, at four o'clock.

"Hey, Lizzie," he said when I opened the front door. "No class?" He appeared puzzled, probably wondering why, if I were home, I hadn't canceled.

"Oh yes, I'm leaving shortly." My face felt as if it had been cast in plaster.

"Gotcha." He gently swung a bag of take-out Chinese food—he brought it every Tuesday—and loped toward the kitchen, walking with what now looked to me like a pimp walk.

"Tyrone," I confronted him nervously, starting indirectly. "Wait a minute. Can we talk for a minute?"

"Sure." He looked wary. A sign of guilt?

"Something's come up, uh, that I need to, uh, talk about." We stood three feet apart in the living room. The white plastic bag hung limply from his hand; I clasped mine together and twisted them nervously.

"Yeah?" His face was closing, his eyes lidding down as they had the first day we'd met.

"I'm not sure how to begin. Look, I hate to say this, but Ruby can't find her watch." I paused, let my eyes flit about, then watched him closely. "Do you know where it is?"

We both froze, as in the game of Statue, facing each other. Afternoon light slanted in from the bay window, lighting his tan face and sleeveless ivory shirt. I was struck by how slender and short he was, not more than five foot three; his eyes were a half foot lower than mine. Even Zoe, lying on the windowsill, was motionless, her tail perfectly still while she eyed us.

"No," he said, his jaw visibly tightening and his shoulders rising. "What happened?" He stepped to the side and set the bag gingerly on the coffee table, where it leaked a thin brown fluid.

"We can't find it anywhere." I took a deep breath and tumbled on, willing myself to do what needed to be done. I kept my gaze on him, while his eyes flitted over the room. "Ruby wore it to school last Thursday. She definitely remembers. She had it on and then she took it off when she got home and put it on her bureau. But in the morning it wasn't there." I recalled how my kind mother had steeled herself and charged ahead even when the way was hard. He stood immobile. At last I asked directly, "Did you take it?"

Tyrone's restless eyes locked on to mine. "Did I what?"

He forced me to say it again. "Tyrone, do you have the watch?"

"Why would I have your daughter's watch? Is that what you think?" He bit his lip. "You've known me for two and a half months. You entrusted your daughter to me. And now you think I took her fucking watch?" He shook his head, said, "Goddamn," and sauntered toward the front door, strutting in an exaggerated walk, with a deep roll to one side. Was he mocking me? Before he opened the door he pivoted, shook his head lightly, said, *"Son of a bitch,"* and was gone. Zoe's tail twitched back and forth while I stood motion-less, staring at the door.

I slogged to the refrigerator, reached for an India Pale Ale, and shouted back to Ruby's room, "Come into the kitchen!"

"Did he have it?" she asked, her eager face searching mine. "Does he?"

The cap popped off the tall brown bottle; cold liquid bubbled over and I lifted it to take a long soothing drink. "No, he said he didn't. I don't know." I sipped. "But we won't have him here any-more." I didn't understand why a hairline crack opened in my chest; I simply chugged the entire beer and reached for another, not both-ering with a glass. Liquid cement.

The next morning, exhausted after a restless night, I was pulling a box of Wheaties out of the kitchen cabinet when I heard Ruby call out, "I found it!"

"What?" My ears were muffled in the cabinet.

"I found my watch!" She sounded exultant.

I dashed back to her room.

"The watch, it was buried in my T-shirts. I've got it!" She looked at me the way she'd look in a mirror, expecting to see a relief that matched her own.

"How could you have forgotten?" In shock, I watched as if in a dream while she jammed tie-dyed shirts into the bureau drawer and tried to close it.

"I don't know, I don't know how it got there." Ruby shrugged. "I must have put it in when I pulled off my shirt to get ready for bed. But I've got it!" She smiled, clutching the precious watch.

"Ruby, do you know what you've done! How could you have not remembered!" I was stunned. My brain hadn't even begun to measure the significance of the discovery, much less grapple with the ramifications. My body bore the impact. I stepped back. "How—"

"I forgot," she said breezily.

"How could you?" I repeated numbly, with rage building inside the walls of my chest.

"I just did. But now I found it." Despite ten years of lectures on race, despite immersion in civil rights politics since infancy, she obviously didn't understand the consequences of her mistake, and mine. Didn't see how I'd leaped to conclusions on what, all too clearly, was flimsy evidence. Didn't get how classic this was, how race-based. I was beyond livid, beyond tears. Simply beyond, already dreading the call I'd have to make that evening. All I could do was turn and stride out of her room, muttering "Oh shit," before I said anything I'd regret.

First I talked to Abi, phoning her from my office for solace, even though our time together had shrunk so much we hardly saw each other once a week. "I can't believe it," she shrieked, scolding, "How could you?" which only reinforced my sense of desolation. How could I have fallen into this trap?

"Tyrone," I said softly into the telephone at nine that evening, when I could no longer postpone the call. "We found Ruby's watch this morning. I am so sorry." I swallowed, my face burning. "I don't know why I thought you took it. I'm sorry. I'm really sorry." I wished I could stab myself; suddenly, the Japanese practice of ritual suicide made sense. Ripping out one's intestines in a bid to restore honor seemed, for a moment, preferable to this shame. *I would do anything to wipe away my transgressions*, I wanted to say to him, yet I knew too much: *I won't add the burden of expecting you to forgive me, to counsel me, heaped on the damage I've already caused.*

"Humph." The injury was in his voice. Flat.

When I trudged back to Ruby's room to tell her I'd spoken to Tyrone and apologized, her open face looked so contrite, so trusting, I couldn't stay angry. But I wondered what impact my suspicion about a person of color might have on her. Would this be a lasting trauma? It was so similar to the afternoon when the corner convenience store clerk had blamed *her* for a nonexistent theft and locked her in the store while he let her white schoolmate go. Could this be triggering a memory of that fright?

I scrutinized her face but she didn't appear upset, only relieved that Tyrone wouldn't be sitting anymore. She looked so relieved, in fact, and so eager to make her own plans that a question flicked into my horrified mind. Could Ruby have deliberately hidden the watch in hopes that I'd react exactly as I did? Could she have set me up? No, I brushed the idea away, lifting my hand to sweep it off. No, I couldn't conceive of my child being cruel enough, manipulative enough, to put us all through such an ordeal. Her joy simply reflected her pleasure in her freedom to choose. After all, she was a teenager now.

"Pleeease, let me stay overnight at Imani's on the nights you go to school. Pleeease," she implored, piercing me with her desire. I glanced outside. Late misty fall was already settling, its damp chill penetrating; there wouldn't be many more classes before winter break. And she'd turned fourteen.

"Yes." I reached over and hugged her shoulders. "You can do that, if it's all right with Imani and her parents."

Ruby ran off to call, her joy rippling behind her. Bruised, I didn't feel up to delivering the usual history lesson: the one on whites accusing blacks of theft, when, *how ironic,* whites were actually the thieves, having stolen African people themselves. My annoyance at Ruby's casual treatment of this incident mixed with a familiar feeling of perplexity, as if I'd lost something but didn't know what. How was a white mother to respond? I let the teachable moment go, put on Marvin Gaye's "I Heard It Through the Grapevine," and crawled into my nest on the couch. "Ooh, I bet you're wonderin' how I knew / . . . It took me by surprise . . . / When I found out yesterday . . . / I'm just about to lose my mind."

During the winter rainy season, twice I picked out Tyrone's puny form in the distance up on College Avenue. Once he glided alone, holding an enormous green and black umbrella; the second time he held a small child's hand, crossing the street. Shame crept up my body each time, heating me until perspiration drenched my armpits. Six months later, midspring, when I heard at a party that he'd moved to L.A., I said, "Oh, really?" and turned away, so as not to show my relief. Hiding my disgrace, I vowed never again to hire an African American in my home. While I might pay well, history pulled too hard against me, exerting too strong a tide for one well-intentioned white woman no matter how hard I smiled, trying to combat it. I soon found out, from a conversation Ruby had with Imani, that she told Cookie the whole sad tale: the loss, and my accusation, as if she'd had nothing to do with it. That helped explain Cookie's increasingly dismissive attitude toward me, which had puzzled me. Each time we met, it seemed, she grew more hostile.

But despite this disruption, mostly Ruby and I lived our daily routine quite peacefully. At least once a week we nestled on the couch doing foot rubs in the late afternoons, watching the sky darken outside the bay window, while she regaled me with tales of school, imitating surly teachers until we both giggled, gasping for breath.

Her own surly moments erupted most often, I noticed, after she received one of her prized letters from Solomon. Still, daily life pressed on, impossibly full with our two schedules and care of the dogs, especially after Rosa, diagnosed with bladder cancer, needed constant attention. Ruby and I still found time, though, to garden or sing together and keep each other up-to-date. Every day she looked more grown-up, carrying her pile of schoolbooks—plus her red leather journal stuffed with letters from Solomon, which she carried like a talisman. As she chattered with friends in lingo I barely understood, I noticed her breasts growing larger; she reeked with a heavy teenage odor, a mixture of perspiration and raging hormones. When I suggested, as kindly as I could, "Honey, you need a deodorant," Ruby bristled, blushed, and ignored me.

Mostly we managed to get along in some tentative manner, until the terrible evening she finally got her period and grew frustrated by her inability to insert a tampon. After dinner, watching her fidget while trying, unsuccessfully, to get comfortable with a giant sanitary napkin stuffed between her legs, I proposed, "I'll put one in you—a junior tampon, if you want—and show you how to do it, since you can't get it in yourself," I quickly added, seeing her look of horror.

"No," she said. "Don't I have any privacy around here? Not even with my own body?"

"Well, my grandmother put my first one in," I said, blocking out the actual horrible, humiliating memory. "Once you manage it the first time, it'll be a lot more comfortable than a pad and that awful elastic belt. You'd be surprised."

"No. How could you even suggest doing that?" She grimaced with disgust.

Yet the following afternoon, after blood had flooded her under-pants, soaking right through and staining her skirt at school, she relented. "Just close your eyes while you do it," she said, kicking a chair. "Promise me."

"Okay," I said, gagging at the thought of reaching through my daughter's heavy flow of blood. But, after all, wasn't helping your daughter through puberty a mother's job? I'd changed her poop and wiped up her bottom smeared with shit; I could do this.

When the moment came that evening in our narrow bathroom, I took a deep breath. The soggy mess was worse than I could have imagined.

"Ouch!" she kept squealing. "You're hurting me."

With my eyes closed, reluctant to probe around too much with my fingers to part her lips, I poked the tampon at what I thought might be the spot, but couldn't find the opening. Which was prob-ably tight as a drum and would never yield, even if I could find the damn place.

"You might be too small," I said, jabbing the tampon. "Lift up your leg more."

"This is so embarrassing, Mama!"

"Oh, everybody has a body," I said, turning my head away while I tried to make light of it. The stench of old blood was overwhelming; I hadn't thought to tell her to wash.

"Stop it," she finally begged, tears streaming. "You're hurting me."

"Oh, please, Ruby. Cut the drama. I'm just trying to get the fucking tampon in and you're too damn tight. You'll have to wait a couple of years." Relieved to stop my explorations, I fled the bathroom and washed my hands for five minutes, rinsing and soaping and rinsing.

For days afterward, whenever Ruby and I crossed paths, she frowned resentfully, as if I'd willingly exposed her vulnerable flesh, penetrating her privacy. And I realized I'd crossed a line, though one I'd been introduced to crossing by my grandmother, my mother's mother, who tossed off the moment with the aplomb that was so characteristic of that side of the family.

"I'm sorry the tampon thing didn't work out," I attempted once feebly, trying to clear the air before we both dashed off to school. She didn't answer but merely scowled, cutting off all rehashing of the mortifying experience.

Certainly, when I let myself fully remember my grandmother's determined frame bent under my thirteen-year-old open legs, one propped up on the closed toilet, I felt nothing but horror and shame, despite her this-is-normal-as-dust attitude. She did get it in, but it had hardly been worth it. And here I'd put Ruby through the same indignity without even succeeding at my mission. As I drove along Shattuck Avenue toward Oakland the next day, I wondered, anguished: How could I do to my daughter what my grandmother had done to me? A honking driver cut me off and, swerving, I barely avoided him. Was that how these horrible mistakes got passed down, because they were what we instinctively drew on as we raised our daughters? I vowed to triply scrutinize every action I took from then on. I would be the New Mother, free at last of car-

rying on hurtful traditions, even if they'd been started with the best
of intentions.

Ruby and I never discussed the matter again, although, as the
purchaser of her sanitary supplies, I noted that she used maxi pads
for two more years. From then on, Ruby let me know that her body
was off-limits for discussion; I never again dared to suggest deodorant, or tampons, or any other hygiene products.

Yet, despite my sensitive silence, her air of grievance festered.

With my attention focused on puzzling out Ruby, and my full
teaching load now at Mills College as well as Merritt, Solomon's
announcement, at first, hardly penetrated my exhausted haze.

"I got a job teaching ethnomusicology at Columbia," he said
huskily on the phone one evening, sounding nervous. "It's an offer I
can't refuse. A new position. Finally those bastards are going to recognize African American music as part of the classical canon. Ha."

"You're moving?" I said stupidly, for a moment not realizing that
Che was involved.

"Yes, Elaine and I are negotiating for a brownstone in Harlem."
Misinterpreting my silence, he added, "You've met Elaine."

I knew they were seeing each other, but I hadn't realized how
serious their relationship was. Negotiating to buy a house together?
Reeling from this blow, I barely heard him rattling on.

"A gorgeous old mansion on 140th Street, near City College.
It was owned by a family from Barbados who're going 'home' after
forty years. It needs a lot of work, but it has the original wood
detail, with carved mantelpieces and extraordinary ornate ceilings.
Plaster angels." His words flew by. "And working fireplaces in almost every room. Elizabeth, I want to take Che."

"What?" I mumbled, dazed. "You can't take him out of state."

"He's doing so well with us. He and Elaine—you know her parents live in New York. Not that far away. He'd have a new set of

grandparents nearby. He and Elaine get along like a house on fire. He could spend summers in Berkeley with you and Ruby, and she could visit us for school holidays." His words rushed on. "It's a great opportunity. I'd reach a generation of students who think that Bach and Beethoven are the only composers who matter, and I'd be closer to my parents, too. Mother's not doing well since her chemo."

My already full brain couldn't immediately absorb it: ethnomusicology, plaster angels, Columbia, Elaine, new grandparents for my children, Che gone, Ruby traveling. And Jean's cancer. "You can't," I said numbly.

"I can. Don't make me call my lawyer. Think about it. Let's talk again in a few days."

CHAPTER 11

Ruby

1981

Once Daddy and Che moved, Daddy's letters were *it* for me. After school I'd roll down Sacramento with Imani and Jamylle. We'd stop to check out any new display in a funky storefront window or scream at passing cars and giggle. We hung in front of the B & B Barbecue or the grocery store on the corner, then I'd rush up Ashby half a block to my house. It was bright blue, a two-story Victorian, with white curlicue trim and a front lawn full of dug-up places and weeds. Usually I could get home before Lizzie arrived from work. Once a week, without fail, there'd be a letter addressed to me in Daddy's spidery writing. I'd see the long envelope: Miss Ruby Jordan, 1507 Ashby Avenue, Berkeley, CA 94703. Usually he'd have drawn a ☺ next to my name. The envelope was thick, too. Satisfying.

Daddy told me more and more about my great-grandparents, especially Great-grandma Ella, who was a baby when her mother ran away from slavery and settled in New York before they moved, years later, to Washington.

February 14, 1981
Dear Ruby,

Happy Valentine's Day! I'm sitting down to write looking at your bright red valentine propped on my desk. Your art is developing. Thank you for thinking of your old papa.

Sugar, here is some more history. I am learning bucketfuls from Daddy. His father was one of the first Black firemen in Washington at the beginning of the twentieth century. There were only a handful of them, six or seven. It was a secure, high-paying job for colored men. Quite rare. And here's an irony: he lobbied to segregate the fire department! When he joined, the few African Americans were spread out in different stations and had a rough time. You can only imagine the harassment they faced. Once the department did create segregated stations in about 1920, after there were enough Black firemen, James Jordan rose to be a sergeant. He couldn't have gotten the promotion as long as the Fire Department was integrated, because Black men could never be over Whites.

Your great-grandmother Ella, meanwhile, was out busting restrictions, too. At that time, most downtown restaurants refused to seat Negroes. The few to do so would only seat colored people if they were placed behind a screen. (Can you imagine?) Granny Ella, an elegant woman who never left the house without white gloves, would attend a downtown meeting of the National Association of Colored Women, and on her way home she'd find a restaurant willing to serve her—albeit behind a screen. Well, don't you know, after she'd eaten, Granny Ella would kick over that screen, making quite a scene! I think once she may have been arrested. Now do you see why I wanted to name you Ella? (smile) I could tell right from the beginning that you had that old Jordan fire. I'm getting all this news right from the horse's mouth, so to speak. Daddy has taken a great interest in the family history now that he's retired.

The job at Columbia continues to be . . . what can I say? Frustrating and exciting all at once. Remember when I said it was 'an offer I can't refuse'? I'm constantly on the run, developing a new course this year in African American music (which the dept. finally approved—a chip off the old block, aren't I?) and we have our biggest crop of African American students yet (although that's not saying much, given C's past history) but I find it rewarding.

Che is sprouting up, nearly seeing eye to eye with the old man (heightwise, if not in any other way) (smile). We miss you and eagerly await your spring break. Until then, I wrap my arms around you.

Give my best to your Mother. I hope the two of you are doing well. Be good! I heard you are in the school concert. Sing pretty.

Your ever-loving Daddy

These letters nourished me and kept me going all week. I had a history. There was a Black woman I took after. A heroic woman. Daddy kept me in touch with Black Pride—on every level. And with him.

On the evenings I felt lonesome, missing Daddy and Che too much, I tried to feel close to Lizzie, as I tried to call her. Even though that fist inside had clenched closed, shutting me off from her, a trickle of the old coziness seeped through when we sang together. We were so good it sent chills down my arms. When the harmony was tight the notes sat right on top of each other but retained their distinctive tones, as Daddy had taught me. Fifths. I sat on the living room floor by the heating vent next to the couch and bay window, pulled out my guitar, and strummed a few chords Daddy taught me way back when my fingers could barely reach around the neck. I'd start to pluck, hoping she'd join me. She had perfect pitch as a soprano and we relaxed into music together in a truly inspiring way. Rosa thumped her tail in time to the music and Zoe purred right along. We had a regular band going. Cesar was the only one who didn't participate. He was our audience.

One afternoon we were singing some tight harmony and I felt pretty good, even admiring my mother's copper hair glowing in the shafts of sunlight, remembering when I thought it glittered like princess hair, and I felt some shreds of that old deep intimacy with her—until she started with a folk song, a ballad. "Oh, Danny boy, the pipes, the pipes are calling." It was a song her Irish father loved, and his parents had "sung it when I was a lad," he always told me, practically slobbering with happiness. They all sang it when Lizzie was growing up, and our family continued the tradition. I felt the pull of those ancestors like a familiar tide in my soul. Elizabeth wailed out the lines, and I threw in my second soprano, just a little lower. Then she got to a plaintive verse, "And if you come when all the flowers are dying,/and I am dead, as dead I well may be . . ." We always belted that out and really jammed, in a real sad way.

That day, in the blink of an eye, instead of feeling the warmth of Grammie Margie and Grandpa Colin, feeling wrapped by their love for me, I felt suddenly excluded. These old Welsh and Irish and English folk songs weren't really my songs. They were white people's songs. The people who had oppressed African Americans. By the time we got to "If you'll not fail to tell me you love me,/I'll simply sleep in peace until you come to me," I wasn't stirred. I was pissed.

"How can you sing this?" I asked her, feeling torn in two. Those old songs formed part of my deepest heritage. But for the first time they were bumping up against a new wall—the one that separated us. Racially. "Those are white songs. They're not my music."

She shrugged me off and began to blast it, like she was trying to blast away my question.

"Lizzie." I tried to cut her off.

But she kept singing, louder. *"I'll simply sleep in peace—'"*

"Elizabeth!" I interrupted, all tangled up—wishing she understood what it was like to be me. Wishing she would let me call her Mama. Wishing I wanted to.

She stopped short. "That's part of your history, too, honey," she said, in that uncomfortable way she acted whenever she had to defend white people. Like apologetic and mad and can't-we-not-talk-about-this all at once. "Generations of your people sang these songs." She bit her lip.

"*My* people? I don't think they were *my* people. *Your* people." I hated to be on the opposite side of the wall from her and my grandparents. But that's how I felt. Those Irish ancestors had hated Black people. Kicked us as far down the ladder as they could while they were climbing up. I knew, I'd read about it in American History.

"Ruby," she said, with a strangled blend of emotions in her voice. "What's gotten into you?" She reached over, trying to touch me, as if a pat of her hand would smooth everything over. That was her solution to everything: rub my shoulder or my arm or my feet, trying to smooth all the trouble away. Cold ripples swirled in my body until they spun into my stomach.

"What are you saying?" she asked. "That this isn't your heritage, too?"

"It's more of that 'everything white is good' crap. Glorifying it. Like European roots to something make it important. What about African folk music? Why don't we ever sing that? You don't even know it!"

"Ruby." She looked at me, exasperated. With tears in her eyes.

"I don't want to sing anymore," I said before I jumped up and headed back to my room, where I threw myself on my bed, listening for her voice, until, after a couple of minutes, she stopped singing. Soon all I heard was the ticking of the red Winnie the Pooh clock on my wall.

That night I talked to Auntie Cookie on the phone, whispering from my bedroom to her. "My mom is so racist. She doesn't have a clue, singing white folk songs, like they're the best. When there's so much fantastic Black music. I'm counting the days till I graduate. You know, Daddy thinks he can get me free tuition at Columbia."

"You poor child. I can't believe your father makes you live with her," Auntie Cookie said, her voice like honey. "Come visit me for the holidays. I'll buy you a ticket and we can go to Atlanta to your grandma and grandpa and Aunt Belle. She'd be thrilled. I know she'd have a little sumthin' sumthin' for you too."

"Che's coming home, I have to be here."

"Well, sugar, you know you can visit your auntie anytime you want. For as long as you want."

Honestly, I felt so lonely, all that kept me going some days was the dream of New York City. I'd grown up in such a noisy house, with the music Daddy played night and day—guitar, trumpet, keyboard, the violin—and Che running in and out, and lots of kids, all our friends used to hang out here. The neighbors: Ayanna practically lived here with all of her kids and all. Everybody fighting and laughing. Noise. It was wild back then. Now our too-quiet house gave me the creeps. The only people around, except for Imani, were Abi sometimes and Mama's friend Hannah, who went with us a lot to Sproul Plaza. After school, when it was getting dark, they dragged me up to campus where everybody was marching around shouting, *"Hey hey, ho ho, apartheid has got to go,"* and other stuff. Lizzie and Hannah, who was hyper, really got into the yelling and cheering. It was so embarrassing. They looked funny together, my mom so tall and big-boned with her bright red hair, she always stood out in a crowd—and Hannah real short, with a round face that looked like the moon. I pretended I wasn't with them, even when I agreed with the chants. Once two kids from school were fooling around on the sidewalk nearby, not in the demo. It looked like they were watching, making fun of it. I turned my face away so they couldn't see me. Then it was a relief to get home, even if it was like a mausoleum there. Even the dogs grew quiet. Suddenly they were old, and Rosa got sick real fast. She could hardly pad down the hall from the living room, shuffling into Che's empty room. She still looked for him. So did I.

The only way I could think of to fill up the house with warmth, if I wasn't going to sing with Lizzie anymore, was to bake. I baked so often I became addicted. Muffins, cakes, banana bread with raisins, corn bread, apple pies. Popovers. Cookies—oatmeal and ginger and chocolate chip and sugar cookies. Oatmeal cookies were my specialty, but if anything could be whipped up and stuffed into an oven, I made it. I dashed home from school, checked out recipes and ingredients—'cause Elizabeth did keep up with the grocery lists I gave her—and started to mix up a batter. When the house filled up with that sweet cooking scent of butter and sugar and bubbling fruit, for a couple of hours it felt like home. I could relax.

I had to give away most of it. We could never eat it all, except when Abi and her friends were over, so I started to supply Ayanna and the old guy, Esteban, on the other side of us, who lived with his daughter and granddaughter. That felt good, seeing how happy they were when they stretched out their hands for my plates of goodies, steaming with that happy smell right from the oven. Even when I didn't feel like trudging out in the rain or opening the front door on a cold foggy evening, after they hugged me and thanked me—*"Gracias tanto, senorita"*—I'd feel a glow.

But after that high, when I came home it seemed even bleaker. The house was freezing. Lizzie kept it at 50 degrees 'cause she always moaned about the gas bill. I wore mittens and a wool scarf. We didn't even eat hot food for dinner, except once in a while when Hannah brought over lasagna, cooked with tons of cheese the way I like it. The three of us ate by candlelight, which Hannah insisted on. They'd drink bottles of red wine and laugh. And I gulped down three plates of lasagna. Otherwise Mama and I mostly nibbled on cold cottage cheese and tuna with lettuce, or leftover deli food that she brought home from her lunch.

That winter, Rosa kept getting sicker and sicker. In December, by the time Che arrived for Christmas she couldn't even stand up, her cancer was so bad. Che took one look at her skinny body—she was like a skeleton then—and he began to cook, too. But not baking. He fried hamburger or baked chicken, anything he could mash enough that she could lick it off his fingers. Every night she slept under his covers like she did even when he wasn't there, and in the mornings he carried her onto the back porch and stood on the deck, rocking her back and forth in his arms. On his last day of vacation he held her head in his lap, stroking her while the vet gave her the injection. Che was leaning over, rubbing Rosa's ears with his tears trickling, when she shuddered, and that was only the third time I ever saw him cry.

I counted on those visits of Che's. Every Christmas and then eventually every summer he flew out at the end of June, about the 28th or 30th, and moved into his old bedroom as if he'd never left. I didn't go to New York so much, 'cause Lizzie insisted we stay with her. Che was such an easygoing guy that he lifted us all up. The whole house felt different. Mama and I didn't fight as much for one thing. Che had a chuckle that rippled on and on and he laughed about everything.

One evening over summer vacation, Elizabeth started picking on my clothes. "Why are you all dressed up like a capitalist's dream consumer?" she asked me in the living room, her eyes narrowing when she eyed my brand-new red blouse and jeans that I'd spent two hours getting just right with jewelry and lipstick to match before I went out with my friends. "You look so bourgeois."

"Stop criticizing me!" I turned away, ready to split. Until Che stepped between us and said, "Lizzie, between your tie-dyed skirts and Ruby's cool outfit we could open a clothing store. Every need served. From vintage to up-to-the-minute styles." It wasn't that funny, but he said it with that chuckle like we were both okay, both right. Just different. No big deal. And we all laughed.

The next evening after work she tried to tell *me* what Black people felt like when the police pulled them over. And how to act if it happened. "Be sure to be deferential," she instructed, like I didn't know, like Daddy had never mentioned it, like I didn't have a Black parent. She just erased him. But Che picked up on the deferential part, bowing, "Yes sir," mocking it so gently, in a way that only he could get away with. She grinned and that was the end of it. Somehow he bridged that gap between her and me, and between her and Daddy, while he stayed loyal to all of us. Maybe because he got the Black family automatically with Daddy, he didn't have to fight so hard for it. Or maybe because he was a boy he never got tangled up with Lizzie like I did, wanting her and hating her guts and hurting all at the same time.

I was so jealous of how easy his life looked, until one foggy Saturday morning that summer. We were in the backyard with Cesar, throwing a Frisbee that he was mangling. "You don't know what it's like living here alone with her," I said furiously, tossing the chewed-up blue plastic to Cesar. "Easy for you to be all Mister Nice when you've got me around. But I have to take care of her all by myself when you're not here."

"What do you mean?" He looked concerned and puzzled, like he lived on a different planet. The funny thing was he never seemed to get that much taller either, in spite of what Daddy reported in his letters. That day I stalked over and glared down at him, surprised that I could almost look over the top of his head. "Don't you get it? You think everything's always fun like this when you're off in New York? It's not!"

His eyes filled. But he answered quietly, "What are you talk-ing about? You get to be here at home with Mama and Cesar." He paused and his voice caught when he continued. "And Rosa when she was here. Living with Daddy and Elaine isn't all peaches either. I miss you guys."

He left me speechless. After a minute, once I took in what he said, it all seemed so sad that I ran into the house. Later he came knocking on my door but we never did finish that conversation. Che had some sweet way about him, some purity that made ev-erybody love him. I mean everybody. Ayanna next door, she had a wicked temper—except for when I was handing her a hot apple pie or peach cobbler—but whenever Che charged into the backyard it was, "How's my man today?" Her round face was all smiles the second she saw him and she was practically running inside to cook him his own personal fried chicken and beans and rice even if she'd been hollering at Cliff, her husband, two minutes before. She never made me fried chicken. Or beans and rice. No matter how much I baked for her.

I could tell when Mama watched Che how greedy her eyes were, how she missed him. And I did, too. If he were with us all the time it wouldn't've just been me living on Ashby Avenue as the only person of color in the house trying to deal with her. Or the only kid trying to prop her up. If only she'd kept Che and me together. I know they both thought it would be better for a boy to live with Daddy, that Che needed that man model, but honestly, splitting us kids like this was even tougher. What kind of mother gives up her own child?

I was shocked when Mama's noisy fights with Abi started up, way more than I ever heard her and Daddy argue. One night I heard Mama shout in her bedroom, "Don't throw that shit at me."

"Monogamy is ownership!" Abi screamed back in a voice that

came right through the wall. "You're trying to chain me!" For a small woman, she had a voice on her. I heard Abi slam the front door and gun the motor on her Chevy. When I heard her peel away, burning rubber, it almost made me glad Zoe had run away because Abi could have hit anything moving, she was going that fast. Bad as it was a few days later when we found Zoe's stiff little body by the side of the road a block away, on Sacramento, it would have been even more horrible if it had been Abi who killed her.

Then there was the night Abi was yelling about me. I could hear every word. "There's no room for me in your bubble with Ruby! You two are like an old married couple, sitting on the couch rubbing each other's feet and talking your private talk. How am I supposed to break in? She's like a lover, you two are so close. Even when you disagree you're in your bubble. All you ever want to talk about is Ruby, Ruby, Ruby! You let that girl twirl you around her little finger. She gets away with murder. You should stand up for yourself."

I didn't hear what Mama said, but afterward I didn't see Abi much anymore. Her smelly white lesbian friends began to invade us, though—flocks of white women. Maybe my mom felt like she needed them around now that Abi hardly ever came over. I don't know why they multiplied.

Every once in a while a Black woman appeared, or a Latina, but they all wore the same big overalls and wandered through our living room and kitchen as if it were a commune. They hung around the dining table practically munching out of jars of oats like horses, honestly, with Cesar lying around getting more fleas by the day like we lived on a farm or something. I felt so strange with them. And those women brewed nasty teas that stunk up the house. Like ginger root they boiled with garlic and red pepper, simmering it for hours. Even the couch smelled of ginger and garlic. As if that wasn't bad enough the air was thick with smoke. Grass. And patchouli oil. And week-old sweat. All together it was a nauseating mix that made me gag. Even my baking couldn't cover up the smell that clung to the pillows on the couch. Or our jackets hanging on the hallstand. At school I felt like a walking ad for the hippies on Telegraph Avenue, especially after some boy, I don't know who, yelled out in the hallway, "Ooh, what's that bad smell? Who's stinking up the school?"

Even at Imani's house after school I could smell it on my clothes, but there was no way to get rid of it, so I tried to think about our art. She and I lay on the floor drawing. She had a set of sixty-four felt pens and each one had its own slot in the box. There were eleven shades of red, my favorite color, and I could name them all. Coral pink, crimson lake, faded rose, carnelian, ruby, vermilion, wine, maroon, garnet, lobster, and carmine. While we drew the sound of Moonlight Sonata drifted upstairs to Imani's room—haunting music. Her mother, Inez, played piano for a living—that's how Inez and Daddy met and our two families became friends. The sound was magical, starting as a whisper and building to get really loud. Lying on my stomach picking out shade after shade of red and listening to the piano, my world felt like it was back in place, even if the patchouli/sweat/marijuana smell clung to me. I'd known Imani so long she was a sister, basically. I was home.

At school all our classes in our experimental unit at Berkeley High, where we both were, focused on ancient Egypt. In Math we counted using their decimal system, based on ten like ours but with different symbols. For instance, 100 was represented by a coil of rope like a snake. The number 1,000 was a drawing of a lotus plant. And 100,000 was a frog. In Science we learned that the word *chemistry* comes from Alchemy, the ancient name for Egypt. My favorite project was the papier mâché casts we made in art class, like mummies shaped to our bodies.

Imani and I were drawing covers for first-person stories we wrote trying to sound like ancient Egyptians. I never could write easily. Words came slowly, but art was easy for me. And with all Imani's colors to choose from, I was having a terrific time when, out of the blue, she asked, "What's going on with your mother?" She didn't look up from her paper and her goldenrod marker kept right on moving.

My hand slipped. I'd used lemon yellow for the face in my mummy picture, with a headdress alternating Prussian blue and lemon. Now the blue bled into the yellow, and it made a sticky pea green on one cheek. "I don't know, what?"

"All the women—" She held her eyes steady looking down and kept coloring carmine, goldenrod, and ebony in the King Tut outline she'd sketched. That was Imani. She planned her drawings. Not like me, who picked up markers real fast and began to color. No turning back. But Imani drafted her work in pencil and coded the colors beforehand.

"What do you mean?" I tried to sound tough, like it didn't matter, as if the women who hung around were cats or something. Collecting them and having them run through the house was just like a habit my mother had.

"My momma—" Imani broke off coloring and placed the markers carefully back in the metal box, keeping every color aligned in gradations with the other shades of yellow, red, and blue. She inspected the ceiling, which was low, with a crack from one corner to the middle of the room. Every house in Berkeley has cracks from the earthquakes. Her mother's music floated in, coming up the stairs. At last Imani said, sounding real uncomfortable, "My momma doesn't know what's happening with your mother since Solomon and Che moved out."

"Who does?" I tried to laugh it off.

Imani leaned over to me. "Your mother calls my momma late at night. She sounds like she's trying to talk Black but she's slurring. That's what my momma says to my dad."

"Why are you telling *me*?" Tears rose to my nose. I willed them back. I never thought I'd be defending my mother, especially not to

Imani. The mix churning inside felt so complicated, I didn't even know how I felt, except awful.

"I didn't want to tell you. Honest. Even though that wannabe thing really bugs her. 'My people hate that,' she says to my dad when she tells him about it. But that's not the main thing. It's your mother hanging out . . . with all the—" She stopped breathing. "With the—"

"Lesbians." I spit it at her.

"She doesn't want me to go to your house after school anymore. That's why I had to tell you." She spun back to her stomach, picked up the ebony marker, and smeared the entire face of her mummy black.

Now I was losing my best friend, too. What was so revolting about me? I chose leaf green and pressed it on every inch of my mummy's golden face, wanting to break the marker, but instead I created a pasty green, wiping out the face over and over, until I convinced myself I didn't care. I never wanted to bring anyone home anyway, with all that crazy smell in the house and the music! They listened to "womyn's music," which consisted of the same boring four singers: Margie Adam, Cris Williamson, Holly Near, and Meg Christian. They played "Ode to a Gym Teacher," which was their national anthem, so much that the teacher Meg Christian sang about, "that showed me being female meant you still could be strong," wove herself into my dreams. Being strong, that was all these pathetic lesbians focused on, when Black women *knew* we were strong! Hell, that wasn't the issue. We'd been out there working forever, from before sunup to after sundown, I knew that from hearing my father and my grandparents talk about it. But these lazy white women sat around, psyching themselves up, with my mother leading the "I am woman, hear me roar" chant, or singing along to "Filling up and spilling over like an endless waterfall." I'd slouch by and wish they would all plunge right over the waterfall and wash away.

Fifteen years old, a Black alien in a house full of weird white women, that's how I felt. But hearing that Inez didn't want Imani at our house? I couldn't believe it. It was one thing for me to be disgusted, another for everybody else to feel the same way. Imani and I smeared our pictures until they were smudges, mine vomit green and hers a black gash. No words cut the quiet until I stumbled to my feet clutching my drawing. "I've gotta go home."

On my way out her mother called from the piano where she was doodling chords up and down the scale, that's what Daddy called it. "Ruby, do you want some eggnog before you go?"

I didn't know what to answer. How could she invite me after what she'd told Imani? But I loved eggnog, which my mother never made. Of course. And I felt tongue-tied so I nodded. She cracked two eggs into a bowl with a butter-yellow stripe, poured in milk and added vanilla and nutmeg and sugar, and plugged in her hand mixer. I slumped at her kitchen table covered with a blue-checked oilcloth that I knew every inch of like it was my own home for my whole life, and I wondered what she thought of me if she thought my mother was so bad. Inez, a tall, thin woman with oversized black glasses and a curved back, hunching over all the time, didn't smile much and she was quiet so I never knew what she was thinking. "Thank you" was all I said after she handed me a glass of eggnog, whipped up with foam on top. But my stomach lurched so much I couldn't drink it.

Imani and I never talked about Mama again. After school or on the weekend we just drifted to her house, never going to mine. Her mother was always polite even though she wasn't a warm person, at least not to me. On the nights I stayed to dinner, she and Imani's father would send formal regards to my mother as if everything were normal, as if Imani weren't prohibited from visiting me. The sore spot with our mothers in the center remained roped off from our conversations, even during our heart-to-heart talks. When Imani and I colored in our mummies that day, we drew a circle around

Lizzie and Inez, too. After that first sting, pretty soon avoiding my house and going to hers felt normal. I didn't tell anyone about it until the week before Thanksgiving when Auntie Cookie called.

"We could have a lovely time," she purred in her soft, warm voice. "Let's fly to Atlanta for the long weekend. I'll get you an airplane ticket and I'll take you to my neighborhood soul food joint, girl"—she howled—"and soak you in some Black culture. I bet you need it, sister." She'd only lived in Oakland for a few years and I could tell she was lonesome.

Her warmth melted my miserable core. "I don't want to live here," I sobbed. "It's embarrassing. It's horrible. My mother's a lesbian, the house is full of these dirty, smelly white lesbians, Imani's not even allowed to visit. I feel like a leper or something."

"What?" Her voice sounded as if she was having a heart attack, she was choking so bad. "Who? What are you talking about?"

"They smoke grass all the time and boil their stupid stinky tea and they rub their bodies in this horrible smelly patchouli oil that makes me practically throw up and it sticks to my clothes so everybody laughs at me at school, and my mother won't even let me call her Mama. She makes me call her by her stupid name and she doesn't even care about me." The agony of the last year poured out. After twenty minutes of being listened to, at last, by a sympathetic, cooing auntie, I closed my pitiful tale with the story of how Mama had forgotten to call me last week when she'd promised she'd be "home by ten, at the latest." By eleven I'd been frantic, pounding on Ayanna's door, crying, not knowing where Mama was. I pictured her in a car accident, bleeding and broken, unable to speak. Ayanna rushed back to the living room phone with me—I didn't want to be far from the phone in case she finally called. We'd started dialing hospitals when Mama waltzed in. "Sorry. I forgot." I couldn't believe how she shrugged it off. She would have been yelling bloody murder at me if I had done that.

"Oh, Ayanna, what are you doing here? Hannah and I got to talking about the fucking land grab Cal's trying . . . ," and on she went, ripping into Cal, not caring how scared I was.

When I said, "You should apologize, and swear you'll never be so irresponsible again, it's unforgivable!" she just threw her arms around me and said, "I told you I was sorry, didn't I? What are you doing up so late, anyway? It's a school night! You'd better get to bed. Go on."

Cookie's horrified response felt so good ("No, she didn't! Oh, precious baby, how could she? . . . How can you stand it!") that I spared no detail of how terrified I was that night, or any of the other times my mother abandoned me. At last somebody was paying attention.

But the next day Daddy called and practically screamed at me, "What are you telling Cookie?" He sounded furious.

"Nothing."

"No, not nothing, or she wouldn't have called me last night at two a.m. New York time, raving like a maniac, insisting that I file for immediate custody of you."

"I just told her—"

"Don't you tell that woman one more thing. Whatever you said, that's more than enough. Did you know my sister was a founder of the National Black Social Workers, whose sole mission is to furnish Black homes for Black children? Did you ever think about how Cookie would take this case to them and they'd jump on it like bees to honey? Listen, I know who your mother is and isn't. And you are going to live with her. Do you understand me, young lady?"

"Why? Why can't I live with you and Che?"

"Because this is our legal agreement. And it makes sense. You're doing fine in school there with a world-class program at Berkeley High, you have all your friends, you'll graduate in two and a half years and move to New York then. We have it all worked out. I don't want you complaining about your mother to Cookie anymore. Do you hear me? That woman is . . ." He paused before he muttered so inaudibly I could hardly hear him. "A troublemaker. She's a wonderful soul and she thinks the world of you, but she's a maniac on the subject of Black families. If you have problems, I want you talking to me, do you hear me? Only to me. Not your Auntie Cookie. She doesn't have the perspective to understand anything you have to say."

"Did you know Imani's not allowed to come to our house, Inez won't let her? Because Mama's a les—"

"Listen, Inez is a fine woman but she's as narrow-minded as a piano string and twice as strict. I wouldn't let that bother me too much. From what your mother told me, she and Abi—"

"You knew?"

"Of course. Your mother and I talk every week about you and Che, and she told me they're not seeing each other anymore. I think this is going to blow over. You're still best friends with Imani, right?"

"Right."

"Then, sugar, suck it in, call your daddy when you need to let it out, and you know you're coming here for Thanksgiving next week."

"Mama didn't call me when she stayed out later than she said she would last week," I tried. "Much later. I was so worried." As I said it, I heard the accusation lose its explosive charge, the one I'd felt so easily with Auntie Cookie.

"You know your mother, sugar, you know she's forgetful. I'm sorry that happened but she's got a charmed life. Nothing bad is going to happen to Elizabeth O'Leary." He snorted. "She loves you, of course she does, so just go on with your life and don't give your auntie anything more to fret about. That woman is working my last nerve. She doesn't have enough to do, so please don't give her a project. Talk to me instead, please, baby." His tone was conciliatory now, almost pleading.

But Auntie Cookie didn't let it drop. When she couldn't convince Daddy to sue for custody she filed herself, demanding that she be appointed my legal guardian. I thought my mother was going to kill Auntie Cookie or have a heart attack from screaming about it. Or kill me. The absolute worst moment was the afternoon a court investigator rang the front doorbell. It had taken him a month to force Mama into granting permission for a private meeting with me. When the day came, she slammed out of the house before work ranting, shouting over her shoulder one more time, "I can't believe you ratted to that bitch Cookie Jordan, who'd steal anybody's child from a home that didn't meet her fucking almighty standards of Blackness!"

Mr. Cardiff looked like a movie private investigator, a white guy, trench coat, balding. I expected him to be chewing on a cigar. He looked like the furthest thing from a social worker, which he supposedly was. He asked so many lechy questions about the lesbians in our house—which by then, actually, had pretty much stopped just like Daddy predicted—that I started to wonder if he was getting excited by my answers, and I felt like throwing up. "What did they do again when they were here?" he asked me, his blue eyes sparkling. "Do any of them sleep in your mother's bed? Do they try to recruit you?"

He was so creepy, stiff as a rail on the edge of our living room couch, scribbling on his yellow legal pad. "How do the lesbians make you feel?" he asked, and I felt sick, mostly from him. I didn't want to say anything. "What about the drugs? Do you smoke marijuana with your mother's 'friends'?"

I never answered 90 percent of his questions; mostly I just shook my head or whispered, "I don't know." The whole situation was too crazy for me to handle and I wasn't sure what to say so I tried to play it safe. The more he asked, the more I began to feel a wall of protection for Mama rise in me. How dare he come in here and ask all these personal questions about us? I never asked for this.

Even though it was tough at home and I liked Auntie Cookie, I didn't want to move to Oakland and live with her. She never even asked me if that would help, plus she had her own weirdness. For instance, she changed her name to Keisha during the legal process. Lots of people were taking African names, even me when I tried on Aquila for a few days, but why did she do it *in the middle of the case?* It meant she had to refile every single court document. For six weeks after her name change we received batches of papers every day and each one had to be signed all over again. Whenever a thick envelope showed up from the Family Court, Oakland, with its block letters engraved onto the paper like prison bars, my mother screamed, "Look what you stirred up!"

Auntie Cookie, or Keisha or whoever, was also clean like I couldn't believe—like she took four showers a day. She was so crazy about cleanliness that she washed her hands with soap and boiling water *twice* before each meal and insisted that whenever I visited I had to do the same thing. She wiped off the seat in the dining room before she lowered herself into it in case any germs might have settled since she had sat there an hour before. Everything in her kitchen was sterile. She bleached the counters constantly with Clorox. On a cleanliness scale of 1 to 10, I admit our house was a 1 or maybe a zero, but hers was off the chart on the other end. Honestly, I appreciated that she cared enough to want to be my guardian and I understood how concerned she got when I lost it on the phone, but like Daddy said, she didn't put that conversation in perspective. Yeah, it was rough living with Lizzie, and not being in a Black family didn't help, but moving in with Auntie Cookie was not the solution. Especially when the suggestion didn't come from me! Who did these adults think they were? I wondered, remembering how Che told me they never even asked him if he wanted to move in with Daddy. They just told him.

In the court papers Auntie Cookie said I was "a victim of neglect and abuse" living in a drug den of "sexual deviates" who were polluting my brain and maybe even molesting me, and since my father had obviously lost his mind, too, as demonstrated by the fact that he was not seeking custody, she alone could and would provide "a righteous African American-oriented stable home for her niece."

"Listen, my sister is driving me crazy," Daddy complained in his basement study when I visited over spring break. "She wants me to testify against your mother." He rubbed his forehead. "I don't know what to do." His haggard, pinched face looked as if he were about to cry.

I didn't say a word.

After that Auntie Cookie pushed Daddy, she wouldn't stop until he had to take a stand for or against me living with Mama or with Auntie Cookie. Finally he ended up having to fly to California to meet with the judge, and that's when the shit really hit the fan. Double time.

On Monday morning, May 21, Auntie, Lizzie, Daddy, and I waited in kind of a dark room at Superior Court in Oakland for our judicial custody conference. We were all so miserable you could feel it, like there was sweat floating in the air. The room was paneled with dark wood, walnut or chestnut, and the only light we had was from a couple of lamps on a desk and one end table that must have had tiny 20-watt bulbs in them. My mother sat stiff as a board in her large wooden chair, her eyes glazed, staring straight ahead. She and Auntie Cookie, who spills over any seat, were at the far edges of our half circle. They weren't talking, of course. They wouldn't even look at each other. Daddy sat bent in half, looking more uncomfortable than I'd ever seen him, with his chin almost scraping his chest, in a chair next to Mama. I was wedged between him and Auntie Cookie. By then, Auntie and Daddy weren't speaking either. The night before, when she'd picked him up at San Francisco Airport, she ripped into him for his "wimpy, white-influenced ways," while he told her that she'd dragged his family into an impossible situation. She should have simply contacted him in the first place if she was worried and let it go. That was his opinion. I was the only person in the room in touch with everybody else and I didn't like it but I sat quietly, too, worried about the judge's decision and hoping I wouldn't be asked, in front of everybody, to say who I wanted to live with, because I didn't want to hurt Auntie Cookie's feelings even if she and Daddy hated each other. But mostly I was worried about whether I'd have to move in with her.

When the judge slid into the room dressed in his black robe and a bailiff announced, "Rise," we all stood, but he waved us down. His pale hand caught one little shaft of the dim light. His hand glinted and a garnet ring sparkled for a second, like something on fire.

"Now this is a most unusual case," he said, opening up, looking dwarfed inside his robe and massive chair, "since both biological parents are alive and in good health, mentally and physically."

At this Auntie chortled and burst in, "Not in good *mental* health. I speak as a social worker—"

He interrupted her with a wave of his hand.

"An African American social worker," she said firmly, "who knows this so-called family all too well." She set her lips in a line.

"I see," he said dryly. I wondered by the way he said it if the case might be going against her, even though I'd heard that lesbians did lose custody of their kids most of the time. Even though Lizzie seemed to have drifted away from *"womyn loving womyn"*—helped along by this case?—my stomach, which was always my weak point, whipped around like I was on the roller-coaster ride at Great America. I had to hold my hands back from pulling up my blouse and rubbing it.

"I have reviewed the CI report," the judge began, "but I wanted to meet you in person to confirm the investigative recommendation." He paused, looking straight ahead before he continued in a monotone that would have put me to sleep if the topic had been anything else. "The adverse impact test, also known as the nexus test, requires a clear connection between a parent's actions and harm to the child before a parent's behavior assumes any relevance in a custody determination." He cleared his throat. "We are traversing uncharted legal waters here, in relation to the biological mother's alleged sexual behavior with a female partner, but recent Supreme Court decisions in Maine—last year in *Stone v. Stone*—and New Jersey, Massachusetts, Washington *(Schuster v. Schuster)* have each applied the nexus standard to a biological mother's same-sex relationship."

I could hear Auntie Cookie praying softly, "Lord, cleanse their sins," but I didn't dare look at her for fear I might trigger another outburst.

"While California has not yet applied the nexus standard to an equivalent home situation, the current law, which requires me to find in the best interests of the child"—here he looked over at me, and I held my breath—"requires me to rule that the present home in Berkeley, California, is not a detrimental environment for this fifteen-and-a-half-year-old minor, considering that this minor has deep roots in the community, strong affiliative ties to her father and brother in New York, is close to the age of majority, and is performing well in her current school milieu."

"Not detrimental!" Auntie Cookie stood up, towering over the judge. She looked as if she could pick him up and break him in two. "Your comment indicates how corrupted, how biased, this Euro-tainted system is. What a travesty. If you can leave an unhappy, distraught African American child with that, that . . ." She threw open her arms and pointed dramatically to Mama but it seemed like she was so upset she couldn't find the words to go on.

Daddy said quietly, "Her mother, Elizabeth O'Leary Jordan, Ruby's natural mother, who is, according to everything I know, a good mother to her children." But then he added a remark he regretted five minutes later, he told me. Staring right at his sister, Daddy said quietly, "Let him who is without sin cast the first stone."

With that, he stood up, took Mama's hand on one side and mine on the other, held his head up high, and the three of us marched out of that courtroom together.

CHAPTER 12

Liz

1985

"How could you?" Ruby asked me, her voice incredulous, on one of her visits home from college. We sat at opposite ends of the old couch at twilight, the way we used to, yet were anything but cozy.

It was clear she'd begun a search in earnest for stones to throw at me, and now she dug up those pitiful two and a half months of interracial employment, when I'd hired Tyrone before making that terrible accusation of theft. "I was very uncomfortable with a black man working for us, cooking for me," she said, her tone implying I'd virtually kept him in chains.

That night, coming on the heels of her first African American Studies course, she lectured me for hours on sordid details of the terrible past—when *her* people were restricted to menial work—a past in which I, her mother, had colluded by hiring Tyrone. "My great-great-grandmother worked as a washerwoman," she railed, eyes pinning me, her voice coldly instructive. She shifted position, rustling her red taffeta skirt as she stretched out each word of the indictment, searching my face, I thought, for hints of shame. "Miss Ella washed and ironed for the white folks at the New York Barracks for twenty-seven years. Twenty-seven years!" Ruby stopped to punctuate the severity of her history and my culpability. "She took care of the military officers. Daddy just found out." The zeal of the prosecutor shone in Ruby's eyes until I could see that I was found guilty. I, a white woman, was forcing Ruby's ancestors onto their tired, sore old knees, asking them, however nicely, to care for my privileged child and polish up my shiny floor one more time. Or ordering them to wash one more heavy, steamy load of my filthy undergarments before they limped wearily back to their shacks and their own squalling, neglected children. I slumped at my end of the couch, aware, in a way I rarely was, of my grungy navy blue sweat pants.

These days I never knew how Ruby would be when we met: an angry and sullen college student bent on criticizing my every word or the sunny, generous self that recalled her childhood dazzle. On some visits when I flew to New York, we meshed as we had long ago. She'd take a taxi from Chelsea down to meet me on Barrow Street, where our friend Maria had moved from Oakland: the furniture and walls were painted rich coffee shades, spiced with bright tropical colors. "My Puerto Rican past," she laughed, pointing to the pink shower curtain next to vivid orange towels. Each time I visited, Maria was eager to see Ruby, whom she'd known as a baby, but she gave us plenty of space, too. Ruby and I lounged on her couch, one at each end rubbing each other's feet, telling stories about daily life. I marveled at Ruby's eye for the telling detail, her ability to skewer anyone in a moment simply by quoting, lending only her own thick, arched eyebrow to the scene. "Oh, but I didn't *mean* to offend you," she'd say, eyes fluttering, hand on her heart, and before my eyes she'd morph into a white New York liberal, ready to cry. How I laughed.

If Ruby couldn't meet me there I strolled up to her Twenty-third Street apartment, taking my time enjoying the noisy cityscape. I wound up to Fourteenth and crossed town on that busy boulevard, its sidewalk vendors hawking fold-up umbrellas and cheap cotton clothes—especially red "I ♥ New York" tees that hung on racks in front of the narrow stores. I moseyed over to Seventh Avenue and turned uptown, marveling as Chelsea changed: one boutique after another, selling imported French negligees or white filigreed patio furniture and expensive children's toys. They lined the avenue above Fourteenth Street until I turned left at Twenty-third, headed for Ruby's place in a prewar brick building past the corner of Eighth Avenue. Excited, I pushed her bell and heard her sweet voice through the intercom, "Who's there?

"Welcome to the Ritz," she'd say after she buzzed me in and opened the apartment door. Then we were off with her childhood game, planning ornate menus with exotic items we'd never cook. "Hand-raised baby spinach, suckled by Himalayan goats and blessed by monks," we mocked. "Four thousand dollars per serving." We ordered two plates of spinach from each other ("room service"), plus "mussels that meditate, humanely executed in butter."

One morning, during one of our visits, we headed out for an early Saturday stroll in Washington Square Park, kicking fall leaves, roaming arm in arm through the sunshine. Ruby had read Deepak Chopra; this eminent doctor of color, she said, who practiced an ancient form of Ayurvedic medicine, recommended a hike before breakfast for good circulation. So there we were.

Her eyes glowing, Ruby said, with a warmth I hadn't heard in a long time, "I'm so lucky you're my mother."

"Hmmm . . . and I'm a lucky mother." I snuggled closer, glancing at wisps of dark hair curling around her forehead, at the rosy cheeks and wide ready smile. Ruby kicked a pebble, rolling it ahead. I tapped it with my toe, aiming it in her path. Ruby booted it again, laughing. "So many of my African American friends' mothers have

kept their daughters back, out of fear, saying what they can't do."
I sideswiped the stone back to Ruby, careful not to scuff my tan
Mephistos, aiming it across the small pebbles crunching underfoot.
"Like my friend Serena. Her mother warned her that she'd never get
a job as a chemist. You didn't do that with me. You have that white
sense of unlimited possibility." She beamed over her blue Columbia
sweatshirt. A matching headband pushed her hair away from her
face, which was maturing into strong features. She looks like her father, I thought, the same high forehead and full lips. "You've always
said I could do anything." It was true. Ruby had already traveled on
student programs to Italy, Norway, and Nigeria, none of which I'd
ever seen. She'd played guitar all over the country as part of a summer backup crew for Santana—a gig Solomon helped her get. She'd
been to Nairobi for the 3rd World Conference on Woman, as part
of a student delegation networking with young women all over the
world. Now she lived near Greenwich Village in a Chelsea apartment regularly frequented, she told me, by three gay men from the
Dance Theatre of Harlem. At nineteen, Ruby was living an extraordinary life. "You're perfect," she purred, and for the rest of the day
took to calling me "Perf," teasing, but meaning it, too. Feeling an
odd tingling discomfort, I warned her, after we settled back in her
apartment, "No one is perfect. Remember"—and I began to sing—
"The very same people who are good sometimes . . ."

     ". . . are the very same people who are bad sometimes," she sang,
finishing the Mister Rogers song. But somehow I knew she didn't
believe it. With her, our absolutist family legacy—the good black
people or the good/bad union folks versus the demon racists and
bosses—had reached its perfect pitch.

Two months later, stepping over blowing papers at Broadway and
116th, I entered Columbia's McMillan Theatre for Ruby's debut
gospel concert, performed by a college choir singing Negro spiritu-

als, she'd explained excitedly. As the auditorium darkened, black-robed singers entered from the back, swaying from side to side. Ruby had instructed me to sit on the left aisle; she would process down that way. Singing "There is a Balm in Gilead," a line of African American men and women flowed by in the dim light, each holding a candle. Craning my neck, at first I couldn't locate Ruby in the crowd. Dressed in her dark robe, swinging her body to the music, Ruby appeared similar to any other young black woman in the group. As the evening wore on, with one exhilarating *"Yes, God!"* after another *"Thank you, Lord,"* I understood that my daughter had entered a whole new world, one I couldn't even envisage. *"The Gospel train's a'comin', I hear it just at hand . . . get onboard little children,"* they sang. At that moment, a chasm ripped opened in front of my feet, cracking like an earthquake striking a new fissure in the earth. And Ruby, for the first time, was firmly on the other side. I might be "Perf" from time to time, but there was no way I could hop aboard her gospel train. She belonged now to a universe where I would always be on the outside, no matter how much I tried to clamber in.

But a possible entry point presented itself when the academic dean at Mills College called to ask if I might teach a special two-semester course, "The Liberal Face of Racism." "It's an honor, an opportunity," the dean told me, softening me up to take on the new course for barely more pay. "This will be a pilot. It could make a difference."

"Yes," I agreed, despite my already full load of Merritt and Mills classes.

Preparing for the course, scanning daily life for evidence of bigotry, my conviction about the insidious nature of so-called "passive racism" grew even more fervent. The same way that households of an earlier generation spied Reds under every bed, I became adept at spotting the subtle prejudice lurking in the most trivial social encounter. Traces of discrimination, I learned, could be detected in a mere stance. Or a word. Holidays were gold mines of bias. Columbus Day? A celebration of genocide. Thanksgiving? More of the same. White people dominated conversations, I realized. We whites assumed that even educated people of color lacked basic knowledge or strategic abilities, and dared to pronounce on "universal experience," based only on our own. As I became a master sleuth, anti-racist explication drenched my conversations with Ruby, who became a willing pupil, absorbing it all.

Never again, I swore, would I make the kind of mistake I'd made years before with Tyrone. I worked night and day to expunge it, even launching a small consulting firm, Fair Play, offering workshops on bias in everyday life. I was a missionary on fire with the zeal of the reformed sinner out to purify a noxious world. Setting up a file cabinet and desk, I opened my first office in my living room. "Fair Play," Ruby learned to answer the phone when she returned home for school vacations. I never considered, while we played "office" with the dynamite of racial injustice, that Ruby could one day turn the searchlight back on me.

At Thanksgiving break during Ruby's junior year, she and I planned a late twentieth birthday celebration with a Chez Panisse lunch in Berkeley. By the morning of our festive meal she'd been home for three days, but I'd hardly seen her. I'd envisioned cozy times on the couch or in the garden, sharing confidences, but instead she slept till all hours or ran off with Imani and other friends; only one afternoon had she dropped in for five minutes at my new Emeryville Fair Play office after I insisted she visit. Even on the morning of our date I didn't see her, since she was in bed when I left home, not even waking when I shoved my noisy terrier puppies, Barley and Beanie, into their crates. The pups yipped and scratched, trying to undo the latches. Still Ruby slept. But I'd hung on to the prospect of the birthday meal, imagining our lovely, intimate time, seated across a table for a good two hours. Dashing into the restaurant at the last minute, I spotted Ruby at a back table, vivid in a scarlet shirt. She waved.

Amid the din in the crowded room, I caught a glimpse of another young woman squeezed in next to Ruby. Both of them stood to greet me. Ruby looked radiant and self-assured, her joyful self on full display. She introduced me to Crystal, a striking, gap-toothed friend "from Columbia," Ruby said before removing her oversized shirt, revealing the white tee beneath. "Her father lives in San Francisco, and we might be roommates next year." Ruby flashed a smile at Crystal. I saw Ruby was wearing her silk-screened black mask T-shirt, one of a series she designed in her African Art class, she'd told me proudly the night she arrived home.

"How's life at the Ritz?" I asked, using our code, determinedly ignoring Crystal, who had the bearing, the posture of a model, with her upright shoulders and long neck arching up to a fine-boned head, her crinkly hair nearly shaved. I still hoped to create our own special mother-daughter bubble.

Ruby shrugged, dismissing my exclusionary effort. "Elizabeth, I've been thinking about something that's really bothering me."

"What?" I asked, trying to ignore the knot in my belly and her use of my formal name, the one Solomon still used, which signaled trouble. "What's wrong?"

Ruby stared, unsmiling. "It's about your office. I was very uncomfortable there. Your secretary, Wilma, is like a slave, sitting out there in that cold room. It's not even a room, really, just a landing at the top of the stairs. Without heat."

"I pay her eleven dollars an hour," I said, thinking, *Jesus, I'm hiring black people, and Wilma is by no means a perfect employee.* I flashed on the tears Wilma dribbled onto her typewriter whenever her husband hadn't come home the night before. Wilma had jumped at the job when I opened my office in a renovated warehouse. Anyway, what kind of talk was this for Ruby's birthday lunch? And with a friend there. I couldn't believe she was twenty years old. That was the conversation I'd planned on having: who she was now, on the verge of full adulthood, with the marvelous possibilities that lay open in front of her.

"*You* have that big heated room inside. It's like a plantation," she said. I wanted to clamp my hand over her mouth. *Shut up, shut up! It's your birthday!* Instead I smiled tightly and glanced over at Crystal, wondering what she was making of all this. Crystal sat impassively, shoulders back, eyes fastened on her menu. *We are not going to fight on your birthday.*

A waiter in a long black apron smiled down, his face peering above the top of his black tie and starched white shirt. "What'll it be for you ladies today?"

"My daughter will have the . . . smoked chicken pizza with pesto, right?" Anything with cheese had always been her favorite dish, and the pizza here was reliably soft and crunchy all at once, with the most delicious freshly baked fragrance.

Ruby shook her head. "No, um"—she pointed—"the pan-seared scallops, please. With anchovy pizza appetizer."

"And you, Crystal?" I asked.

"The same. Thank you." She nodded gracefully.

"And . . . uh . . . I'll have the Caesar salad," I said. "With the sautéed scallops appetizer."

"Ruby," I said after he left, my armpits sweating. "It's not a plantation." Suddenly I wasn't sure. But wanting desperately to end this conversation, I addressed Crystal, "What are you studying at Columbia?" *And why are you here?* I wanted to ask. She didn't meet my eyes, but instead looked questioningly at Ruby, who continued her assault.

"Then why does Wilma have to sit out at that little desk, with no heat?"

"She's my administrative assistant." I tried to keep my voice even.

"There's only the one room. We can't both be in there. I need to have private meetings. And we have a plug-in heater under her desk."

"She's the field nigger and you're sitting up there in the Big House. Leading workshops on racism!" Ruby shook her head. Her long lovely curls, pulled back from her face with a red tie, shook too. "It's not a good model." Her gleaming eyes let me know she believed she had me. Crystal's penciled eyebrows rose in an indication, I thought, of antipathy. And there I was, crushed once again into the wrong corner.

My tone became ever more reasonable as my temples throbbed and I felt a headache come on like an advancing line of riot police, batons raised, tapping my skull. "Ruby, when I get a bigger space, everyone will have private offices. But for now, this is what we have. I can't share a room with her. And I can't be out on the landing."

"Why not? Don't black women always end up out in the cold?" Ruby must have read the beads of sweat above my lips as victory, because she let it drop. In a moment we heard the clink of ice in a metal pitcher as a server poured fresh water; a tray crashed to the floor on the other side of the room.

"Do you two have classes together?" I asked Crystal, but again receiving no reply—only a faint nod as Crystal pursed her red lips—I ordered a peppermint tisane to settle my stomach. Our table fell silent until I spied Rita Mae Johnson, a prickly woman I'd met years before on my Venceremos Brigade to Cuba, where we picked potatoes for two grueling weeks. She was weaving across the room, moving slowly through the tightly packed tables toward the opposite corner. I waved, not sure what kind of response I'd get—Rita Mae was always unpredictable—but was relieved to have this scrapper return my motion with a grin. *See?* I wanted to say to Ruby. *Black people love me. I don't run a plantation.*

After the waiter slid our plates onto the table, I buttered a large wedge of bread, eager to occupy my hands with movement, even knowing that my stomach would never be able to digest the thick, buttery sourdough. I gazed across the table at the forehead I'd caressed so often, the widow's peak, the familiar thick eyebrows above those furious deep brown eyes.

"How're your classes?"

"This white jerk, my core studies adviser, told me he didn't think I had the qualifications for graduate school! That's not true, is it?" Ruby unexpectedly became a hungry child, searching my face for comfort.

"No, sweetie." I was all protection now. "Of course you have graduate school capabilities. That's infuriating. Has he even read your record?"

"I don't think so. This was our first meeting."

I silently assumed he'd taken one look at Ruby's brown face and written her off. I didn't know what to say. Crystal sat coolly, with a blank expression on her good-looking face. I wondered whether I should initiate my questions to her again. Why was Crystal with us, anyway? Was she silent reinforcement for Ruby's attack? I could hardly breathe. "Leave a paper trail," I advised evenly. "Just be clear what it is you find offensive."

"I know, I will." Ruby nodded.

My key chain, sparkling on the white tablecloth, caught her eye. "Where did you get that?" she asked, biting into her anchovies, spreading red tomato sauce on her upper lip. I resisted the impulse to lean over and wipe her mouth with my napkin; I knew Ruby would jerk her head away.

The silver and turquoise beaded chain lay beside my plate. "Up on Telegraph. Last week."

"How much did you pay?"

"Three dollars." I couldn't chew my salad.

"Where was it made?"

"Egypt." Of course I'd asked the vendor, who seemed glad to tell me the small object's significance. In fact, he was Middle Eastern himself. "It's a fertility symbol."

"That's cultural appropriation. Not to mention exploitation. Three dollars!"

Caught. I pressed my lips together. My chest burned.

"I'm not comfortable with you using that key chain. I can't believe you bought it. Please throw it away." Ruby stared like a prosecutor before she shot Crystal a triumphant look.

I glanced down at the chain twinkling next to my glass. I didn't often treat myself to even three-dollar baubles, and I especially liked this one. "Um, that's not a reasonable request," I started to say. "Let's think about this a little more rationally. That's one tiny object—"

Ruby's brow furrowed. "The entire history of Africa and Asia is encrypted in that key chain. The West—"

"Ruby, it's not." I could hardly breathe. I'd never challenged her this way about racism directly. For years I'd accepted accusation after accusation, apologizing for my own sins and those of all whites. "No! That's ridiculous. It's just a key chain."

"That's what white people always say." She glared. " 'It's just this one time, let it slide.' Don't you get it? The colonizers have all the purchasing power, forcing people of little means to sell their wares for pittances. *People of little means* because they've been robbed for centuries. And you're complicit when you buy their artificially low-priced goods. Then they make so little money that the World Bank forces austerity measures in return for loans, meaning that all social services are cut—"

"Ruby, this is your birthday," I cut in quietly. "It's not the time for this kind of talk."

"Oh, white people never think it's time. 'Not now.' That's the façade of normality. Your normality. Your comfortable normality, built on the superprofits of Third World exploitation. No, it's never convenient for you to talk about these things. God forbid any of the wretched of the earth should disturb your comfortable white privilege, sitting here—"

She was so quick at every turn. Crystal maintained a neutral face during this humiliating exchange. "Ruby," I said. "Stop it. This is your birthday. I spend my life now teaching about these kinds of things and my participation in a trinket trade is hardly fueling—"

Just then three waiters arrived, one bearing the triple-chocolate truffle cake I'd called ahead for. Its twenty candles glowed like beams in the murk hovering over our table. The waiters burst out with "Happy Birthday," the white peoples' version, not Stevie Wonder's. I joined in, serenading my daughter with a lump in my throat while Crystal sat, tight-lipped. Ruby, scowling, blew out the candles. Silently we ate our cake, though I could hardly choke mine down. We stood. Ruby reached her arms into her scarlet shirt, we hugged good-bye ("When will I see you?" I asked, to an enigmatic reply) and set out in opposite directions. After glancing back once to watch Ruby's bouncing curls as she receded, I plodded to my car parked around the corner on Vine, unhooked my keys, and tossed the chain into an open garbage bin. Wondering as I did so, why was Crystal with us at that horrible meal? I'd have to ask Ruby about her.

Two months later, when all I'd learned about Crystal was "she's a friend from school, but not that close, I just thought, since she lived in San Francisco, we could include her," Ruby gushed unchar-acteristically one evening during a cross-country call. Her words, so sparse on her visit home, flowed out. "I've met a remarkable woman. Norma Smith, my African American Literature professor. I had a meeting with her after class." Ruby's excited words rushed like a cresting river. "About my paper on slavery era quilts as text. She loved it and she's invited me to her house for tea. Elaine knows her, that's how I got to have the private meeting." *Oh, great. Good old Elaine, the uber-black mother.* Over the years, I'd struggled to accept this aloof math teacher's role in my children's lives. For Che especially, who'd lived with her since he was fifteen, she fit into the position of stepmother, and I'd struggled with that; Ruby, too, on her visits, and especially after her move east, had come under Elaine's protective wing. Although Solomon frequently assured me that the children had only one mother, any mention of Elaine sent my nerves spinning.

While Ruby spoke on, excitedly, Beanie nipped at my ankles, frisking in the kitchen while I hung on to the phone trying to nudge her away with my foot. But Beanie thought we'd invented a delightful new game: she attacks my foot, fearlessly wrestling the squirmy beast to the ground while I push back. Repeat. She and her brother were "full of beans," I'd thought the moment I met them, and thus Beanie gained her name, leading, somehow, to Barley's. Miniature bull terrier pups from the same litter, they were scratchy little clowns, with four white paws and black legs and backs, marked by white splashes on their faces. Their markings were so similar to Rosa's that I knew why Hannah chose them for me when her bitch gave birth to seven pups. Born the day after Cesar died, they seemed like grandkids, a younger set coming in after Rosa and Cesar had passed. Now seven months old, they were feistier than my old dogs, more energetic—I'd forgotten how lively puppies are—but even the sight of them standing at the ready, their pink ears stiffly erect over strong white necks on muscular bodies, made me laugh. They looked ridiculous with their short backs and stubby legs. Full of fire, they were always ready to play.

As the semester passed and I heard more about Norma, the ultimate mentor, I clung to the company of my dogs' cheery spirits and the brisk walks they forced on me. "She's married, with three grown sons but no daughters, and there's so much she wants to teach me about my black heritage," Ruby told me. Norma, it seemed, was warming to Ruby with alarming speed. The two spent hours together every week. Next, I heard Norma wanted to take Ruby "home" to Florida, to meet "my people, your people." The ultimate field trip, I thought, my heart receiving the news with brittle goodwill.

"Wonderful," I said to it all, gripping the phone with white knuckles while I tried to keep my eyes on the dogs, who were rapidly shredding my few intact inches of furniture legs into mulch. Beanie, especially, found her way into any mischief imaginable, from chewing phone cords to upending bags of flour she spewed over the kitchen, creating a blanket of snow. Her one black ear stood up out of the wash of flour so I had to laugh out loud before I scolded; her sweet disposition made her a lovable joker. Watching her romp with her fun-loving brother—both of their dark eyes glinting—I couldn't stay too focused on Ruby's attachment to her new mentor, although whenever I thought about them my heart contracted.

One Sunday afternoon, Ruby called to tell me that she had extraordinary news. "Norma wants to be my mother. My black mother." I concentrated on the yellow kitchen linoleum.

"Really?" I clenched the phone and felt a major hot flash coming on, an electric heat wave. It crept up my back between my shoulder blades, then gripped me until I was dizzy. I thought Elaine had provided Ruby with more than enough black mothering.

"Yes, she's so amazing. Norma is just what I need. I'm so lucky."

"That's . . . amazing." I tried to breathe, perspiration putting a mustache on my upper lip. I swiped the back of my neck with one hand, wishing I could pick up ten-pound Barley and cuddle him.

"Now I'll have two mothers. A black mother"—I could hear Ruby savoring the words—"and a white mother." The end of the sentence dropped flatly. "African Americans do this, you know, have play kin, taking on daughters and mothers. It's from slavery times and African tradition, people taking care of each other."

"I know, I've seen that with my friends," I snapped, wanting to show that I knew *something*, while a claw squeezed my chest. I could hardly breathe. I brushed damp hair off my forehead, resisting the urge to bend down and wipe my face on Barley's bristly back. I reminded myself that Ruby was finding roots I couldn't provide—

ones even Solomon or Elaine couldn't supply—and willed myself to push envy deep inside. Instead I hung up the phone, leashed the dogs, and ran outside, racing them around and around the block, all three of us ferocious with nerves, until we collapsed from exhaustion.

Two days later, Abi, whom I'd not heard from in months, called with news from her landlord, a corporation that had bought her building. "What, after all these years they're going to evict you?" I said, truly shocked. For twenty-two years she'd lived in an enchanted third-floor apartment on Lakeshore Avenue, where the floorboards had grown used to her sandals flapping across the floor, wearing a groove from front door to living room. I knew she must be paying only a fraction of market rent, but "It's outrageous!" I cried, unable to imagine Abi in any home other than the colorful nest she'd created. She'd lived there her entire adult life. "What are you going to do?"

"Start a tenants' union, of course," she laughed, "for the *gente*," twisting the word in her inimitable Hawaiian-Chicana accent. "What else are people like us here on this earth to do?"

"Yeah, you're so right," I said, thankful for my connection with this soul sister who lived for politics. After a pause I added, "Jeez, Abi, Ruby has a new mother."

"Oh, what's *bratella* up to now?" In the past, Abi's censures had irritated the protective membrane I cast around my daughter, but that night her irreverence warmed me.

"She has a black mother," I said. "Norma. I hate Norma."

"Hah," she crowed. "Me too." And I felt another flash of the old warmth, grateful for her support. Jealous as she'd been of my attachment to Ruby, she knew how to be a loyal friend.

Ruby began spending weekends, then entire weeks at her new mother's home on 144th Street, just blocks from Solomon and Elaine's brownstone. By spring break she'd moved completely out of her 23rd Street apartment to live at Norma's; occasionally Ruby and

Norma spent evenings together at Solomon's house. This "mother," a woman my age, filled her in on everything she yearned to know, Ruby told me over the spring, from Southern rituals and African history to African American ways of viewing the world, providing perspectives that even Solomon and Elaine, she intimated, didn't know about. "Like thanking God for *everything*. Even if it doesn't appear good at the time."

I couldn't envision that, but was duly impressed.

"Norma knows all about quilting, how it was done in slavery times," Ruby cooed on the phone, awe softening her voice. "And African American music, and masks. And wakes." The Florida re-union was coming up, where "she's going to introduce me to the family as her daughter."

On a hot Friday evening in late June, 1987, at the end of Ruby's junior year, I arrived at LaGuardia. Ruby had asked me to meet her the following day at Norma's, where she'd lived now for eight months, to introduce her two mothers to each other. I'd missed Norma on my last visit, when she was in Harlem Hospital for an unexplained stay. After a bagel and lox breakfast with Maria on Barrow Street, I took the A train to 145th, ran up the stairs, and stole across the broad, noisy Harlem street as inconspicuously as my height and red hair allowed. Even with my long legs I couldn't walk fast enough. Passing the corner that led to Solomon and Elaine's, where a black, yellow, and red Motherland Africa Bookstore can-opy hung, I nearly ran, hoping to avoid them. As I moved west, blowing trash gave way to cleaner vistas and larger homes. Arriving on West 144th, I found Norma's block quiet and well maintained. Stopping in front of 466, I saw an architectural gem: ornate fluted grillwork formed the railing for the front steps, which curved grace-fully; stained-glass transoms shone over each first-floor window; a stone lion's head decorated the rich detail high above the steps. The three-story brownstone boasted a tiny, neat front yard, overflowing with red geraniums and purple petunias.

In response to my knock, Ruby opened the door. I was struck, as I often was when I hadn't seen her for months, by her grace. Her face, lit with rosy cheeks, radiated joy and intelligence; her sparkling eyes were level with mine. "Elizabeth." She greeted me formally, with the name she knew I'd cast off years before, and slid an arm around my waist. I'd been experimenting with "Liz" instead of "Lizzie" as my mature, cusp of middle-age name, but her leap to the stiffness of "Elizabeth" annoyed me, as she no doubt knew. "I'm excited you're going to meet Norma," Ruby said. For her sake I wanted to be excited, too, but all I could summon was a trace of pretense.

I walked through the living room to meet my rival. She stood in an enormous, high-ceiling of kitchen at the back of the first floor, dish towel in hand. Kente cloth, blazing orange, hung across one wall. A diminutive woman, under five feet, shockingly thin, and several shades darker than Ruby, grasped my hand. "I am so pleased to meet you." We stood exchanging banal pleasantries about my trip and her lovely home. I strained to hear her over the television booming in the next room. The kitchen counter, open to the living room, held several yellow gourds and a small ebony statue. I could make out woven baskets and larger carved figures in the living room. The prevalence of polished wood, African art, and earth tones reminded me of my glimpses at Solomon and Elaine's home back in Berkeley, and I felt the same pang of exclusion.

"Supreme Court . . . resignation . . ." The television snagged our attention. The three of us moved into the living room and focused on the screen. "Justice Lewis Powell," a newscaster intoned, "citing health concerns, announced his retirement today after fifteen years on the Court."

"Oh, no," Norma and I gasped in unison. Used to viewing the Court as an ally, I felt a jab of fear at the prospect of this moderate judge's retirement. "How could he?" Norma said furiously. "Couldn't he have waited till we got Reagan out? We don't need another Scalia." With Reagan in position to appoint another replacement, the news gave me chills.

"Lord, no," I chimed in. Together we stood watching a summation of Powell's career: upheld affirmative action, though diluted, in *Bakke;* voted with the majority in *Roe v. Wade*; often a swing vote on the sharply divided court.

"Why does he have to leave now?" Norma repeated, clearly upset.

"I know," I commiserated, enjoying our unexpected bond until I heard Ruby say quietly, her voice soft with love, "Mama Norma." A chill rippled through my body. "Can we go up and see Big Mama?" Ruby placed her hand gently on Norma's arm while she spoke. My eyes swiveled, riveted to that touch. Big Mama was Norma's mother-in-law, a woman of ninety-five whom, Ruby had told me with admiration, "Norma takes care of." Big Mama hadn't left her bedroom for ten years. I couldn't imagine a worse fate than nursing someone for a decade, and guiltily understood that in this arena, too, I was lacking. Norma led me upstairs.

"Big Mama," she called into a small bedroom. "Ruby's mother is here." A small shriveled woman raised her head and gazed past me with rheumy eyes. Standing in the doorway, I smiled and nodded hello, but saw no response before we swooped down the stairs again, an awkward trio.

At last, after a tense afternoon with Norma, who'd appeared genuinely pleased to meet me, I left for a private visit with Ruby. Meandering south, we arrived at Marcus Garvey Park and wandered off the path, listening to the ground crunch underfoot. Though we chatted about familiar topics—her schoolwork, my job, the dogs, and Che— our rhythm was off. Instead of finishing each other's sentences, clumsy spaces littered the conversation. Even a reliable query—"What was your favorite class last semester?"—elicited a scornful look, as if Ruby knew it was a baby question because the obvious answer was Norma's class. Climbing the lookout in the park, we checked out the view, open in all directions. "The George Washington Bridge?" I guessed, looking north, and then pointing to the west and trying to make Ruby laugh, I asked, "Who's buried in Grant's Tomb?"

"Elizabeth!" she rebuked.

But I ignored her, continuing my game: "The Empire State Building," I said, pointing south, "and—"

"Columbia University," she answered sourly. "Where your daughter goes to school."

At least she was calling herself my daughter; I tried to savor the slender triumph. We poked around the Fire Watch Tower, an ancient iron structure with a 10,000-pound bell, we learned from a plaque at its base, but still Ruby acted as if I were a cast-iron ball shackled to her leg.

"Tea?" I suggested, hoping that sitting in a booth across a table might focus us. We trudged north again, stopping at the Amsterdam Coffee Shop on the corner of 145th Street, but the only tea the waitress could offer was Lipton's. "Hot water and lemon, then," I ordered, to her raised eyebrow and Ruby's embarrassed face.

After another uncomfortable half hour we returned to Norma's, where we stood awkwardly in front of the house. I shifted feet, waiting to be invited in again, half hoping either way; soon I left Ruby at the door with a brief kiss, reluctant to say good-bye after such an unsatisfactory visit, but when I turned to wave from half a block away, hoping for a final flash of connection, she had already vanished. In the dusky light I raced across 145th Street to the subway with my eyes on the pavement, vowing that if I reached downtown alive, never again would I ride this far north.

Before I knew it, Ruby had graduated and moved up to Cambridge to begin her doctoral program in Afro-American Studies. Struggling during her first weeks with the Harvard graduate classes, she complained, "Columbia didn't prepare me for this!" and read long unintelligible passages over the phone: "postmodern cultural criticism," she called it. But in eight weeks she'd knocked off the outline for an equally obscure paper herself: "Reproduction of Highly Condensed Signifiers and Their Ideological Work in an Array of Epistemological Systems." I was impressed.

Our conversations were alternately pleasant—with deep familiarity, when we cracked old jokes or cozily discussed classes, using our coded family language—and unpleasant. "Your entitled tone of voice," she accused, criticizing me one night. I felt low, anyway, from worry about a deafness diagnosis in Barley's left ear, with dimmed hearing in his right one. "Your house and everything in it, using Third World objects snatched out of their cultural contexts. It's all emblematic whiteness! Honestly, everywhere I look in your life I see evidence of racist symbology. It's really painful for me."

"Humph," was all I replied. Determined not to act contrite any longer, although I feared she was probably correct, I was unsure how to respond without apology. Instead, as she became harsher in her critiques that winter, I tried to get off the phone more quickly, pleading piles of student papers to grade or sudden jailbreaks by Beanie and Barley.

"Ruby's giving me a run for my money," I groaned to Hannah one evening at Suzette's Home Cooking. Our outing on Grand Avenue in the heart of Oakland was a regular treat. I'd known Hannah Goldberg for years: a short, plump, curly-haired white photographer who showed up at every movement event with two or three professional cameras slung around her neck. Solomon had met her after she hung a show on the women of the Black Panther Party, and I'd felt an immediate connection to her. Hannah, without any children of her own, had long served as an "auntie" to Ruby, one of many women who took an interest in my radiant child. After Solomon and Che moved out she used to surprise us, dropping in with an overstuffed baking dish of terrific, gooey lasagna, knowing that Ruby loved melted cheese, and plopping down at the table for dinner, she made herself ready to eat a respectable dent in the pasta.

That long-ago spring nine years before, when Ruby and I were first on our own after Solomon and Che moved out, the three of us were regular demonstrators at Sproul Plaza. We trudged up there nearly every afternoon, joining a community group demanding that Cal divest from business in South Africa, which it eventually did. And end nuclear weapons research, which it didn't. We'd wait until Ruby got home from school and dash off, rain or shine. Often my neighbor Ayanna would stride along with one or two of her sons, who were young teens then. "We've got to put our bodies on the line," Ayanna would vow in her lilting Jamaican accent, though she sometimes didn't get to the Plaza until dusk. She'd carry a black and red hand-painted banner, with doves and fists and *UHURU! FREE-DOM!* Since I was seeing Abi at the time, she used to meet us, too, sometimes on the Plaza. I'd pack a sack of peanut butter and banana sandwiches, roll up a couple *SOUTH AFRICA SOLIDARITY* signs, and off we flew. We marched for hours if I didn't have to teach, chanting in a circle to the rhythm of African drums, "Hey hey, ho ho. Apartheid has got to go!" When the regents were meeting, we shouted, "Divest now!" until we were hoarse. Things got ugly on a regular basis. The UC police used to wade in, swinging their clubs to frighten us; one particularly nasty time they aimed for kneecaps and heads. I grabbed Ruby that day and, together with Ayanna and one of her sons, we scurried off to the edge of the crowd.

I wondered sometimes if Ruby ever thought about those days, and if so, did I get any credit at all for the long chilly hours I spent protesting apartheid? We even had the photos on our wall: a series by Hannah showing police clubbing demonstrators curled up, blood dripping from their faces. AP flashed one of her shots around the country.

For years, too, Ruby and I celebrated the first night of Passover at Hannah and Jim's home. We were part of the core, among a floating group of a dozen friends. Each spring the ritual got longer because Jim kept adding new interpretations to the Haggadah. But always, no matter his latest radical spin on the traditional story of the Exodus from Egypt, we lit the candles, drank glass after glass of wine, dipped parsley in salt water, ate matzo, and tried to speak truth. Some years we read twenty pages of a "Liberation Seder" he patched onto the ritual: we included women, gays, and, depending on the year, Nicaraguans or Salvadorians or South Africans, or simply "people of color emerging from oppression." Then, still sitting around their dining table extended by boards covered with patchwork cloths to accommodate us all, we sang every civil rights song we knew, from "We Shall Overcome" to "Ain't Gonna Let Nobody Turn Me Around." One year Jim even brought in three young women who played Klezmer music. By the time Ruby was sixteen, she refused to go, but I never missed the holiday. This wasn't a matter of me returning to roots I knew anything about; but the generosity of the seder embraced me into an ancient community, and this was the warmest gathering of friends, sharing the most heartfelt of liberation rituals.

Now Aretha Franklin's voice blasted us at Suzette's restaurant. *R-E-S-P-E-C-T.* Since Ruby had left for college, Hannah and I religiously kept a dinner date the first Thursday of every month. "Every time I see her," I complained, "she has some major criticism. She's cutting me up and down and sideways. Everything I do is wrong. Remember that key chain I bought from Egypt?" I shook my head. "I had to throw it away. Now it's a tray—a 1920s *Ladies' Home Journal* cover on a tray I've had forever. It's a picture of two young blond women, and Ruby says it's 'an artifact of historic racism. The deepest Jim Crow . . .' She gets me every time. I'm sick of it."

Moving her chair closer, Hannah reached her short arm out to squeeze my shoulder. "Ah," she said quietly. "You're still letting her jerk you around."

"That's what Ayanna says," I groaned. "But Ruby's right on the facts."

"It's not about race, Liz," Hannah said slowly, her round face creasing to emphasize her point. "She's trying to separate. She has to say *'Fuck you'* and be different. You two are so much alike. You both have the same politics, you look the same: light version, dark version. Let her go. You've got to let go. Don't let her push you around."

On her spring visit home that year, Ruby and I lay stretching on the back deck. Barley and Beanie chased each other in the fenced yard below us, rolling over and over, nipping and leaping. I rarely had to worry about grooming their short coats, a relief after Rosa and Cesar's long knotted hair. Ruby, who still mourned our old dogs, her childhood companions, had taken Barley and Beanie out for a long morning walk. The three returned in high spirits.

It was an ideal April afternoon—light blue sky, a few puffy white clouds hanging along the horizon, but no hint of the rain that had pummeled us all during March. Miracle March, the weather people had dubbed it, after eight inches of water fell steadily for a month, ending our three-year drought. In perfect rhythm with Ruby, I extended my left arm to my right foot, held it, then right arm to left foot, feeling tension pull the right side of my back tight. We rose, Ruby standing in front to demonstrate a stretch she'd learned at her gym. Staring at her back, noticing the dark hair curling prettily around her ears, I thought, *She's getting heavy.* I wondered if I should talk to her about the health implications. My DNA won out over tact; with maternal passion I decided to help my daughter improve.

"You've gained a lot of weight recently, haven't you?" I started, breathless, while I held up my right leg for thirty agonizing seconds, wobbling on my left foot. Leg down and pause. "You know, that weight really puts a strain on your heart and all your organs—"

Ruby cut me off. "Black women's bodies are fuller than white women's." Ice hung from every word. She faced me, her dark eyes flashing. "Black buttocks are bigger. Most clothes are racist because they're not cut to black bodies. Akilah and I have talked about this. It's hard to find fashions for black women."

"I'm sorry," I mumbled. Akilah Rasuli, a new friend of Ruby's, seemed to have replaced Norma as the last word on black women. My shoulders hunched miserably forward and my back twitched. But over the bridge of self-reproach, resentment crept in on hot little feet. *Why can't I express a health concern to my daughter without being accused of racial insensitivity? I'm tired of this game.*

The visit faltered forward as the tension rose. I never knew when I was going to make an offensive slip and be corrected. After dinner on the third day of her planned weeklong visit, during the one evening she'd scheduled especially for us, we sat at the table drinking mint tea while Ruby told me about a new book "on cultural colonization," saying how "postmodern and brilliant" it was. Almost unintelligible, in fact, its insights were so deep.

"Oh, Frantz Fanon was the theoretical underpinning for that," I said, leaning forward, eager to help. "I loved his work. His books came out in the sixties, you should read him for the historical precedent."

"There's nothing I can read that you haven't read first!" Ruby burst out, eyes boiling. "You think you've done it all, that there's nothing new."

"You're doing amazing, creative thinking, sweetie," I said, bringing out my soothing mother voice. "Delving into cultural details with a rigor we never had in the sixties, scrutinizing the subtleties of relationships." Her vehemence shocked me. I could understand how Ruby might have felt overshadowed by Solomon; every year he pulled down some major World Music/Black Scholar prize. But who was I to intimidate her? The intensity of her rage shook me.

All that evening, as Ruby explained her theories on the devaluation of African American "craft" as opposed to Western European "art," she troubled me with her fears. "Don't write anything about my work on black women and marginality," she warned. "I plan to build my career on that, and I want to be the first to approach it in a certain way." Her admonitions hung strangely in the air while we washed supper dishes. We'd always relied on each other to think aloud together, and all I published were occasional local essays, *East Bay Express* pieces about family or neighborhood life. "People steal ideas in academia," Ruby said, bristling, soaping up a dish. "I've been warned not to talk about mine." She was so fortified and jealous, glowering, that I was sorry I'd ever encouraged her to go to Harvard. The atmosphere Ruby described, arrogant and wary, sounded repellant. But I envied her the stimulation of the highly charged environment while I drowned in the tedium of community college.

"When am *I* going to get a chance to write, to take a break?" I grumbled, taking the plate Ruby handed me, wiping it, reaching to put it away on a shelf. By comparison, Ruby had all the luxury and leisure in the world. Most semesters she didn't even teach, wanting to conserve her energies for research and writing. Each year she patched together student loans, money from Solomon, occasional small gifts from her grandparents, and, several times, substantial loans or gifts from me. Young, gifted, and black, I thought jealously. You've got it all.

As if Ruby had read my mind, she blurted, soapsuds flying, "African Americans don't have it so easy, you know. Especially black intellectuals. We're marginalized; our scholarship is overscrutinized and trivialized, if we want to write about something relevant to our community; and we have to do the work of ten, parceling ourselves out to every committee so they'll all be 'balanced.'" Ruby rubbed a pot fiercely and glared as if I'd personally hounded every black female intellectual into high blood pressure. "Nationally, the number of African American women with tenure is minuscule." Ruby slammed the yellow sponge down in the sink.

"You never let your anger out at me directly *as your mother*," I said, putting down my dish towel while I fumbled for an opening to a plain old fight, stripped to its core. "It's always about race."

"Well, race is real," Ruby snapped. "What do you mean? Are you avoiding the topic? Black women do have real issues—issues you don't understand."

"You could get really mad at me, you know," I said. "As your mother. Period. We could fight, right out, about *us,* not only about race, for once, and we'd survive it. I'd still be your mother, I'll always be your mother." Then I let myself erupt, Rosanne–style, "You know, you're so self-righteous, you never acknowledge what my generation did to help you get to Harvard, you think everything started with this postmodern shit. You know, your father's generation and mine—we made it possible for people like you to go to Harvard, to break barriers. You could show a little respect."

" 'People . . . like . . . you'?" she said slowly, her eyes widening. " 'People like you.' Who do you think I am?" Her eyes glistened but just as quickly dimmed, and she fired back. "You don't even know me, do you? I'm just one of your worthy causes, 'people like you.' " She spit it out. "But anyway, you think everything's all about you, don't you? Just like always. It's all about what your sacred generation did to help out 'people like me.' It's not about me at all. Me, your daughter. Just people 'like me.' "

"Stop it, Ruby. No, I don't think that. But just because I'm white doesn't mean that everything I do or say is wrong. I'm your mother, and you're trying to grow up. That's a lot what this is about."

"Oh yeah, typical white resistance to talking about race. This is classic. I point out something that's racist and you say, 'That's not what I meant, it's not about race, it's personality, or it's relational.' "

I tightened my lips. What a relief to voice my resentment after all these years of suppression, but how could we leave the conversation there? I knew I couldn't simply throw my arms around her the way I had when she was a child and cure everything. "Of course," I said, "you're right about what happens between whites and people of color, we both know it, I taught you a lot of that analysis"—I couldn't resist—"but I'm your mother, too, and how much of our fighting is about that? You know, we have to move forward to a new place. I'm tired of this same dance: you attack, I apologize. I'm not going to keep doing that."

She was seething, I could tell by her eyes, her furious shoulders, but she merely said, "Easy for you to say," and slammed back to her bedroom, retreating the way she had for so many years. In the morning, she was gone.

Two days later when I returned from work, my answering machine held a message. "Please don't contact me," the controlled, tight voice said, sounding both familiar and strange, almost unrecognizable. "I need space from you to sort things out. Do not contact me. It may be a while. But please respect my space. This is the most important thing I've ever done."

Stunned, I played the brief message over and over. I couldn't believe it. Ruby had cut herself off. The dogs needed a run but I speed-dialed Hannah.

"I'm not surprised," she said slowly, sadly. "That girl's got some growing up to do." Her tone grew impatient. "Maybe when she saw she couldn't twirl you around her little finger any more, she couldn't accept that."

"I don't know. Maybe not," I said, flat.

"You can't hurry growing."

"Yeah. I guess." All energy had drained from my pores, sucked into the air like moisture on a hot, dry California day. "These children." Beanie was whining at my legs, anxious for her regular evening exercise.

"Hey," Hannah said after a pause. "Did you hear about that boy in South Africa being beaten to death, and they think Winnie Mandela might have had something to do with it?"

"Oh, they're always accusing her of something."

"After all that woman's been through! You know they'll throw the book at her. The judge will be white, of course," she clucked.

I was silent, too lost in my thoughts, for once, to join the chorus. Beanie, now joined by her brother, pushed against me, rubbing, insistent, until it was hard to keep my balance. Still I ignored them.

"Oh, Liz," she said, "I'm sorry about Ruby. Give her space, though. You have to listen to what she's asking for. You've always been good at that."

"Yeah." But as soon as we hung up, instead of taking the dogs out I called Solomon, reminding him when I'd be arriving for Che's Columbia celebration. I couldn't believe he was already finished with graduate school. How had this happened so fast?

"Haven't seen the boy in weeks," Solomon said. "Elaine and I will have to hunt him down for the ceremony. Ever since he's been seeing that girl, Cynthia, we can't catch a glimpse. When we call his apartment he's never there, and you know how he is about returning calls."

I ignored his referring to Cynthia Harding as a girl rather than a woman, although it irritated me. I wondered if he did it on purpose and whether calling him had been smart: if the tiff with Ruby blew over in a few days, what was the point? But halfway into the call, I said, still stunned, "Ruby's cut me off. This is the last thing in the world I expected."

"Don't worry." He sounded unconcerned. "She'll be back." For an intense person, he certainly was mellow when it came to our children. "Don't worry" was his standard line. What insight, really, had I expected?

Unmoored, I floated until the dogs' barks forced me to give

them a perfunctory walk. My vacant self moved through the motions of early evening: preparing a salad from spinach and a bag of wild herbs, chopping red pepper and a hard-boiled egg, drizzling olive oil, squeezing a Meyer lemon from the tree hanging, laden, over the back deck. Solomon and I had heaved it out of a ten-gallon pot when we'd first arrived in California. Now, twenty-five years later, it towered over the deck and I had to continually trim it back, though I hated to cut any branch with a lemon, or even the bud that signified a lemon to come. My gardening lacked the resolution of vigorous pruning; I was too sympathetic to make the deep cuts that were needed. The garden displayed a definite overgrown untidiness now, much like my frizzy hair. Or, I would have said only a week before, my garden was wild and free just like my children, those self-expressions of creativity. Now I hardly knew how to think about that.

I forced myself to sit and eat my salad. Normal life, I counseled. Continue normal life. And only one glass of merlot. I peered out the picture window into the darkening backyard and spotted a blue jay shimmering in the early-summer evening light. Cracking open the window, I listened to a quiet song emanating from a branch of a purple passion bush. The song was as variable as a mockingbird's, but gentler. What bird was making that lovely music? All I could see was the improbable jay. It shrieked, then began its quiet song—yes, that was the source—as though it were singing to itself, ending with a flourish.

While I held Beanie in my lap, letting her lick my face, I tried to focus on the blessings of daily life the way the Buddhists said to, but it was hard, as tears trickled, to come up with any others beyond loyal Beanie and Barley. After I cleared the dishes I phoned Hannah again. Someone had to sit at the kitchen table with me while I cried. Solomon's "Don't worry. She'll be back" was no help at all. What did he understand of my complicated, intense relationship with Ruby?

When Hannah opened the front door I slipped over to fall into her arms. "I'm here for you, Liz," she said while I wept, sobbing, "Why?"

We headed instinctively toward my old couch, which I'd re-upholstered only the week before. I'd chosen a fabric as similar as I could find to the original. This one had smaller pink flowers but the same silky white background. That night as we sat in the twilight, the dogs snoring at our feet, I listened to the first of what would become many stories about other women's breaks from their mothers. "When I was in my early twenties, I didn't contact my mother—and you know how close we are—for almost three years," Hannah said, staring evenly at me, as if to gauge the impact of her words.

"Three years!" I banged my cup of chamomile tea on the coffee table. I couldn't imagine not seeing Ruby for that long. Three months would be too long. "Three years," I repeated numbly, shaking my head. Dazed, I rose with my empty teacup, shuffled to the kitchen, opened the refrigerator, and placed my dirty dish on the chilly shelf before I realized my mistake.

"Do you think Akilah is behind any of this?" Hannah called in. She followed me into the kitchen, picking up a yellow napkin and toying with it. "Or her new boyfriend, what's his name, Asa?"

"I don't know," I answered, thinking of the harsh lawyer training Asa Plummer was getting. "Maybe." I'd only met him briefly: once in New York when Ruby had invited him out to dinner with us, and once when they'd flown into San Francisco for a two-day conference, then spent a night with me. He'd been polite enough, obviously smart, well educated, and he appeared smitten with Ruby. I'd been inclined to think he was a good guy, but now I hardly knew what to believe.

"My ex-husband provoked the break with my mother. He wanted me all to himself and he prejudiced me against her. It took me years to see that. I had real issues with her that had to be worked out, but the estrangement didn't have to happen the way it did, so terribly painful for everybody. I'm not sure it even helped. We still had to do the work later."

I sat, numbly listening. Should I try to fight back against the influences on Ruby? Contact Asa and try to bond? Or give him hell? But my way, I understood, was to give my daughter total freedom, to wait and trust. I knew I didn't want to apologize, didn't need to, for what I'd said our last night together—when hadn't I simply suggested that our fighting wasn't only about race? But beyond that, I'd do anything to get her back.

Miserable days passed, each interminable. Three weeks and three days. A month. *Two, three, four months.* Time stretched heavily behind and in front, a muddy, indistinguishable bog. Even Beanie and Barley's antics failed to rouse my spirits. Our twice-daily outings became a dreaded chore instead of the pleasure they'd been.

"I'd go kick her butt," Raphael, a colleague I briefly dated, advised one morning, hands folded over his hefty belly, when I told him how Ruby had cut me off. He leaned against my office door and snapped his fingers. "In the African American community, we'd take this crap for about one minute. I'd like to go and have a good talk with her." He threw back his head, evidently imagining himself shaking a finger in her face. "Who the hell does she think she is? You changed her dirty diapers, you raised her all these years. And now she's disrespecting you." He shook his head, showing off the fashionable jagged line shaved into his close-cropped hair. "She's an adult. She has obligations."

I sighed and muttered a quiet, "Yeah." He was right. But at this late date, how could I switch my child-raising strategies?

"Do you want me to go?" he asked, shifting his burly frame from foot to foot. "I'll knock on her door. I've met her. She knows who I am."

No, I shook my head. Let her be.

Time blurred, but I always knew exactly how many days had

passed since Ruby had been gone. In early September, when she was scheduled to take a rigorous qualifying exam, I sent flowers. "Delivery refused," the humiliating message came back. In November, when the count was ten months and two days, I crept barefoot to the kitchen early one morning when it was still dark and punched in Ruby's number. Beanie, surprised by my appearance, jumped up trying to lick my face. "Sweetie," I cooed, shivering, when Ruby answered.

"Why are you calling?" A flat voice, with hints of Ruby.

"Because I'm your mother. Because I love you."

"Don't contact me."

"It's been *ten months*."

"I don't feel comfortable continuing this conversation," Ruby said, sounding like a woman I had never met.

My body felt as if gravity had lost its pull and I floated, weightless above the chilly floor. My heart was behaving oddly. Was that an irregular beat? I lay down on the cold floor.

"I told you not to call."

"I just wanted to see how you are." My whole being concentrated on the cord running from my telephone to Ruby's, focusing my concern. With my hand on my heart, I whispered, "And to say I love you."

"Do you?"

"Of course I do!" I gave a chuckle of incredulity, wondering how my daughter could ask such a question, with that disbelieving tone.

"Then please respect my request for space. I can't be in relationship with someone like you. . . ." Her voice drifted off.

I said quickly, "This is ridiculous, Ruby, you can't just cut off this way," trying to rush my words before she hung up, but by the time I ended my sentence, a dial tone sounded in my ear. I hoisted myself to stand by pushing against the stove and picked up a hot teakettle bare-handed. Holding my burned fingers under cold running water, I let myself collapse while Barley and Beanie howled in solidarity.

January arrived, pushing up yellow daffodils. Delicate early pink rhododendrons edged the front walkway. When I admired their fragile shapes and buoyant colors, joy bubbled for a moment, until a nagging unease in my chest forced my attention. Then I'd remember why I was holding my breath: *Ruby's gone.*

What is my responsibility as a mother? I wondered. Should I fly to Cambridge, try to barge into her apartment and yell, "Stop it! This is nonsense. Get over this childish behavior." Half of me wanted to stage a sit-in at Ruby's building, while the other half counseled, *Leave her alone, be patient, and she'll be back in her own time.* I harangued Solomon, "Do something, please! Can't you tell her to contact me? This is horrible, I can't stand it. I'm her mother!" But he only repeated, "She'll be back when she's ready." No matter how I pleaded, "You're in touch with her, you have influence, tell her I'm not a racist, tell her that I'm her mother and she needs to contact me," he remained cool to my suggestions.

All month I staggered through the days. Hot flashes tore at my body. I sweated through the nights, threw sheets off, then shivered and pulled the damp sheets back over my head. My clammy body felt like the perfect temple for a dripping heart.

After a long, bewildering nine months, Ruby's letter arrived.

CHAPTER 13

Ruby

1990

I snatched my pen and yellow pad from the crowded bureau, crawled back to bed, bundled myself in my red star quilt, and began. "Dear Elizabeth," I wrote, and inhaled a deep breath, smiling when the tight band around my forehead lifted. I took that as a sign, even though I'm not a person who relies on magic. But the absence of that chronic pain released a rush of energy. Today was the day. At last, freedom was just around the corner. And wasn't that what they'd brought me up to seek? Surely it was in my blood after all these generations. I was programmed to move inexorably toward my own best interests.

"You're not a mother to me," I wrote, gulped, and leaned back against the headboard. What more, really, could there be after that? Did I have the nerve to actually say it, even though I could imagine how my words would devastate her? I gazed across the room and out the window at the gray sky. The window was cracked open and a cool breeze blew through the half-inch space onto my naked body.

I couldn't tell if rain or snow was coming. Even after two and a half years in Cambridge, the changeable New England weather was hard for me to predict. Remembering the day Daddy drove me up for my first look at the apartment, I marveled again at the lack of density in that relationship. With Elizabeth, no matter her outrageous, neglectful behavior, some inexplicable yearning washed over me at her most inaccessible moments, dragging me to the bottom of the sea. With Daddy, no push–pull. If he pissed me off, I told him, "Daddy, I'm grown now." He'd listen and receive my complaint without complexity, either a flat-up yes or the old "As long as the bills come to me, sister, you ain't grown." Everything was clear as see-through glass. With her, the glass wasn't only smoky, it changed shades every five minutes.

"Long-term sublet, one bedroom, older building with natural light, single woman preferred," the listing had read.

"That's you," Daddy told me with a sly chuckle. "Better keep it that way awhile, too."

When I called, a quavery woman's voice with an accent had answered the phone. "Yes?"

"Is the apartment still available?"

"Oh yes," she answered. "I'm waiting for the right person."

Daddy, Che, and I drove slowly through the unfamiliar elm-lined streets, checking out the neighborhood, until we came to the four-story brick building, rising incongruously from single-family homes and two-story duplexes. Daddy snooped around the lobby. Its scuffed marble floor implied a faded glamour, an impression reinforced by the doorman's well-worn suit. Once we stepped out of the creaky elevator on the third floor we met Miss Hennessy, a retired British secretary who looked exactly like her voice: hesitant steps, drooping bosom under a floral rayon dress, sensible shoes, firm eyes. She planned to rent out her place on "this quiet side street," she said, for six months while she traveled to Italy with her sister. "An extended holiday," she'd giggled.

I loved the two rooms on sight: shabby and compact, just a bedroom and living/dining room, where a green marbled counter separated a two-burner kitchen in the far corner from the miniature Queen Anne dining table. Three diminutive chairs lined up around the table, all in the same shiny hardwood veneer, with graceful curved backs and white brocade seats. The fabric, like everything else about the building, was frayed but elegant. A matching curio cabinet stood on short bowed legs, bursting with china, adjacent to the tiny "front hall." A three-panel Queen Anne folding screen separated the dining area from the study corner, just a small cherry desk with swivel chair upholstered in the same white fabric. Taking five steps to the left of the living area, I was at the doorway of a crammed room, filled with a double bed wedged in by a dresser.

I peered in, smelling musty lavender. Five steps to the right side of the living room brought me to an immaculate bathroom, with a stall shower and a set of fancy white towels that belonged in Buckingham Palace. The whole place was like an ornate dollhouse, comfortable, safe, and possibly all mine. The decorating wasn't to my taste but I figured that once Miss Hennessy got her personal belongings packed up and I Africanized the walls, the place would be home. It was small and I wasn't but still I wanted it. The question was, would she let me have it? Her expression, when she'd seen Che, Daddy, and me at the door, indicated surprise, and not the pleasant kind. She'd stepped back and appeared apprehensive, asking us first, "Yes, may I help you?" although I'd set up the appointment. Once she let us in she'd been polite enough, and after we looked around, she even let loose that giggle about her holiday, but the tone of her formal questions—"This will be only your *first* year at Harvard?"—made me doubt that I fit the bill for "the right person."

"I'd need first and last month's rent," she finally said, those firm eyes sharpening as she waited politely by the front door. "And"— she paused for that telltale fraction of a second—"a security deposit of two months' rent." I wondered if our color doubled the security risk or whether she simply thought she'd put me off that way.

"Fine," I responded, not daring to look at Daddy. "That wouldn't be a problem." I scrutinized the apartment again, complimenting her dining table, "fitting so charmingly into the space. I love to read and that would be the ideal spot. There or in the study." I pointed to the corner. "Quiet, with a lamp close at hand." I flashed my most captivating smile. "Such a calm atmosphere you've created in the midst of the city." Then I waited, willing Daddy to be quiet, sending him and Che an invisible message without looking their way: Don't say a word. Please.

But my taciturn Daddy suddenly couldn't stay still. "My daughter's a remarkably responsible person for her age. I think a double security deposit's a little steep." He scowled.

I could have shot him. Why remind her about my youth? And don't act like we don't have the money!

"Of course, Ruby won't even be here that much, with school and her social life," Che chorused, enviously, I thought, given his squalid four-roommate cold-water flat back on the Lower East Side.

"I'd love this place," I burst in. "It would be a perfect home for my quiet life. Reading. Listening to classical music." I tried to look demure and studious, casting my eyes down.

"Well," Miss Hennessey demurred, sagging, glancing around at her furniture, her books, her china. "I don't know. I'll have to think about it. I'll call you, dear."

"I'm looking at a few other places today," I chanced, knowing that if we left without the apartment I'd never get it. "But I could give you the money now. All of it." Then I did look over at Daddy. He shook his head.

"After I confer with my father," I amended. We stepped into the hall.

"Daddy," I whispered urgently. "I want this place!"

"You haven't seen any others."

"Shh. Don't let her hear that." I pulled him away from the door.

"Well, you don't know what's out there. And you don't have that kind of savings, do you?" He stood, finger pointing, looking dubious.

"I've got most of it from my summer job and the Christmas money Grandma Jean sent. My fellowship check will come in two weeks, so if you can loan me—"

"Sugar, maybe you should think about it." When I saw his large hands drop, I knew he was softening.

"Yeah," Che jumped in. "Like check out a few places."

I gave him what I hoped was a withering look. "Daddy, please, lend me just half the security and I'll be cool. I'll pay you back, with interest, when I get the check."

Silence. "Let's walk around the block to consider it. You don't want to be too hasty."

I knocked on Miss Hennessy's door to tell her we needed a little time to reflect, but we'd return in five or ten minutes. "Dear," she said with that accent, "I believe I could let you sublet the flat for only a one-month security deposit. Plus, of course, first and last month's rent."

I signed on the spot. At $425 a month, I had enough money of my own.

Two weeks later, I felt like I was on top of the world. Twenty-one years old, a Harvard doctoral student with a Cambridge sublet. Life couldn't get better. I had no idea then that Miss Hennessy would end up staying in Ravenna with her sister, and that I would inherit the apartment. Once she made the decision not to return and cleared out the last of her belongings, I bought a Salvation Army metal bed frame and white glass table, and spiced up the generic student look with original art: my own black-and-white stencils on red fabric, two iridescent green Cuban paintings on loan from Daddy, and a white plaster cast of a traditional Ghanaian mask that Imani brought when she drove up to visit. Living in that wonderful old Cambridge brick home, I truly grew into myself. Sammy, the part-time doorman, became a friend, I hosted African-themed salons for classmates, and now, finally, I was gathering courage to cut the cord that wrapped me, bound like a mummy, entangled with the strange, complex woman known as Elizabeth—or Liz—O'Leary.

I shivered from the icy breeze blowing through the window crack, but my rage held steady, heating me from the inside. Elizabeth had separated me from my brother and father, my Black kin, and when they moved, she acted as if I were an exotic stuffed animal she could drag to events with no volition of my own. She paraded me as her mocha doll, her ticket to the inner circle at multiracial events. "In every sense one thinks of a mother as a nurturer, who tends to the well-being of her young," I read my indictment aloud as I wrote it, as if to convince myself of its truth. "You did not fulfill your responsibility."

I'd rehearsed my denunciation countless times, yet when I pictured my mother, with that cloud of red hair streaked with gray jiggling around her head, I had to focus on hardening my heart. *Remember how she was never there for you*, I reminded myself. *How she abandoned you time after time*. Today I was determined not to cave, as I so often did, unable to bear her suffering face when we fought. That distraught look that came into her eyes, mixed with a kind of tenderness that seemed to surface most often during our fights, hooked me every time. Maybe it was because at the moment we battled I had her complete attention, unlike every other second of every day, when she let herself be distracted by every single "cause" in the world but me.

If I could only fully separate myself, wall off my bruised heart, I'd never be disappointed by her again, never be let down by her erratic behavior. During the four years I'd gone to Columbia, half the times she planned to visit me in New York she canceled at the last minute, citing some "really important tenant strike" she was organizing that had to stage a "critical picket line." Or it was the dogs; they were sick or something. Or simply exhaustion from her work. Each time, I was crushed. That was the story of my life.

Ever since Daddy left I'd been the responsible one, the one who *did* remember to call when I stayed out later than expected, so *she* wouldn't worry. But she merrily went her own way at all hours, forgetting all about me at home alone, frantic that she must have been knifed on the street or who knows what? Even though the times she forgot to pick me up, or buy food she'd promised, or call home became habitual, I never got used to it.

No wonder she didn't want me to call her Mama after Daddy moved out. That's exactly what she was running from, with her selfish notion of liberation. So different from women of color. For her it was "*My* liberation" that mattered, not community or family. Women of color have always had to band together to make it. We've always nurtured not only our own young but each other's. She never understood that and mistook leaping out of a solid marriage into a confused lesbian affair for true emancipation. Then she dragged me along on her adventures, using my skin as radical cover.

My opening line, "You're not a mother to me," said it all, but I wanted more.

"What time is it?" Asa grumbled, edging his long body away from me. "The alarm didn't go off, did it? What are you doing?"

"I'm writing the letter to Elizabeth." Suddenly there was a lightness in my chest, the same one that had lifted me when I'd gotten into the doctoral program at Harvard. For so long I'd imagined this moment, when I would finally have the courage to tell her off once and for all. I inched closer to Asa. "I'm about to be a free woman. Stop those pathetic calls from you-know-who."

"Ruby." He turned to face me, his eyes puffy with sleep, and threw off my old quilt. His sleepy voice sounded concerned.

"Free at last." I rubbed my hand over his bare hip, rolling my voice with Dr. King's cadence. "Free—" I boomed.

"Ruby." Asa cut me off. "This is a tremendous step." He rubbed his eyes and started to scold in his gentle way. "It might be irreversible. Nothing to make light of. Think about it, take time. This is serious." He reached out and stroked my leg. "Words on paper are hard to take back. Families are forever, you know."

"Not this one." Elizabeth's face swung into view again and I could feel that wild red brillo hair poking into my nose when she held me close. It pricked the enjoyable sensation I'd just had, as if the balloon floating in my chest leaked air until I sank back to ground. "She's got to go, permanently," I said, surprised by the moisture behind my eyes. "This is the only way I can grow up." I sniffed. "I can't take that racism anymore. Not in so close. I forget, and I begin to trust her—" I couldn't go on. I didn't want to cry, not now, not on one of my most liberating days. I wanted to celebrate. I'd worked as hard toward this day as I ever had to get into Harvard. Maybe harder.

Week after week I'd sat, every Wednesday at four, in the cozy orange chair that brightened my therapist Claire's office, leaning forward, trying to unravel my life as a kid, stunned to discover that misery was not an inevitable component of childhood. I learned that not every kid thought constantly about running away to New York City. Not every fifteen-year old fed on contact with her father or her brother like a squirrel holding nourishment in her cheek to survive. I'd discovered that not every mother was a narcissist. Or a racist. "She didn't have to slight you the way she did," Claire said, over and over. "Or ignore you. How does understanding that make you feel?"

I'd reach for the Kleenex box on the bright arm of the chair, cry into it, ball it tightly, lift my arm, and heave it across the room, wishing it were glass or lead with Elizabeth's face at the point of impact. "No, she didn't have to." I shrugged. "But she did." And no one else filled that spot. "Even Norma let me down in the end," I bawled, "when I found out she drank like a fish. That was so frightening and so much like Elizabeth." I stopped to blow my nose. "Norma taught classes totally bombed. Before I lived with her, I didn't have a clue. But at her house, night after night, I saw her drink herself into a coma on some horrible, sweet-smelling brandy she hid under the sink. Before she passed out on the couch she'd stagger around the house saying the most maudlin things. 'You're the daughter I never had.' It was so much like Elizabeth it gave me the creeps. Fortunately right about then it was time to move to Cambridge."

Claire nodded. "I'm sorry," she said softly. "Two selfish mothers in a row. But your stepmother was different, wasn't she?"

"Elaine was a good listener." I paused to consider, wiggling in the chair. "When I asked, she'd be there if she could take time between teaching and Che and Daddy and the house and all. But when I was a kid I was stuck in California, and later—you know how it is at college—I was off with my friends partying or studying at the library. She's a very private person, too. So even when I stayed at their house she'd be up in her bedroom a lot of the time, meditating or reading. I can't say she was the mother I needed."

"Now you're an adult. You have power in the relationship with your mother, in exact proportion to the power you take. What do you want to say to her?"

My fingers reached for the pen again.

Asa looked at me with the patient, kind gaze that was already familiar, drying up even the suggestion of tears. He was the one I wanted to focus on, not the woman who had borne me. She was my past, he was my present. And possibly my future.

"She's got to go, but you can stay." I turned to Asa and moved closer so I was leaning above him, my breasts hanging over his chest. My hand wandered, tracing circles on his smooth skin. Soon he was erect. "If you're good," I teased, slowly, "very, very good, I'll let you come back tonight."

"Ruby," he said. "Are you sure you want to do this? It's an immense decision. Maybe you should focus—"

But I had my mouth on his, and soon we both forgot Elizabeth. On this day, I was going to celebrate my way. Asa was my party, my victory, and my prize all wrapped up in one. I couldn't believe how tender he was, how nurturing. Not a day went by when he didn't tell me he loved me, or how fine I was, how intelligent, how copasetic, and what a lucky man he believed himself to be. After the years of loneliness I'd endured, Asa was my reward.

"Hey," I called later, hearing him step out of the shower, "wanta get Chinese tonight? I could meet you at seven." I had to keep rejoicing, mark the day with celebration. How we label things is significant in how we understand them, I'd learned, studying dismissive Eurocentric names for people like traditional African healers, denigrating them as witch doctors. Today I was naming this entire day: Ruby's Freedom Day. My own personal Juneteenth.

"Will you pick it up? I have a late meeting," he called out. I could hear the hurry in his voice. "It'll be more like eight. At least."

The words *late meeting* always gave me a quiver of alarm. Even with all his endearments, was he seeing someone else? It was unlikely, but anything was possible in life, I'd learned. I brushed away the thought.

Once we made our plan for the evening, he admonished me once more before he rushed out the door, "Ruby, please, sleep on this. Write a draft, it'll do you good, but don't send it. You might regret this for years. Please."

No. I'd firmed up my heart, tight as a fist.

When I sat down to finish my letter, phrases flowed—from me, who's never been a writer—as if I'd been waiting all my life to write this good-bye. My verbal practice with Claire was working. Once I finished and reread the page, I saw it was the most accurate text I'd ever written.

"All right," I said aloud, "that's it," and escaped onto the windy street, determined to close the door on all ambivalence. Five minutes later I dropped the letter into the blue mailbox at the end of the block, surprised somehow when the box swallowed my letter as if it were any ordinary paper. Once the clank confirmed its disappearance, a familiar pain pricked my chest. *Not now,* I swore, wrestling it down. Elizabeth had told me once that white people used to have a terrible saying: "I'm free, white, and twenty-one." *Well,* I thought, snapping my fingers as I strode down the block, *I'm free, Black, and twenty-three. Catch me if you can.*

In that instant, the letter and my mother were both out of my life. By the time I'd gotten halfway around the corner of Pearl Street, I'd forced my thoughts onto the lecture I planned to deliver on the Dialectic of Race in the class where I was a TA. The material came easily to me, given my long home training, but even so, I needed a couple of hours culling citations in the library.

During the rest of that morning, whenever my mother floated into my mind I told myself firmly that my predominant feeling was relief. I was sure, as Claire had predicted, that my energy would now be freed for the exciting life ahead. As she'd often reminded me, I truly was Young, Gifted, and Black at a remarkable point in history. I was ready to claim the moment. My moment. Not Elizabeth's, with her fantasy of the perfect mixed family, where she starred as the archetypical white heroine out to save the colored of this world.

For once, this was all about me. And before long the lump in my throat would surely dissolve.

CHAPTER 14

Liz

1990

My eyes kept roving to the brass slot that had shot this bomb into my life, addressed in Ruby's neat round script. I held it at arm's length, blinking slowly, as if when I opened my eyes the letter would have vanished. She'd said, in that distant voice on my message machine, that she was "taking a temporary time-out from our complicated relationship." But now, Ruby wrote, the break was "permanent and irrevocable. You treated me like your colored accessory, the latest radical fashion. My childhood was crazy-making, everything always about *you*. I'm tired of certifying your anti–Miss Ann credentials while you play at revolution. I need be on my own to claim my fertile Black self. Do not expect to hear from me again. Don't try to track me or trace me. Leave me alone! I am no longer your daughter. I declare myself free of you, forever."

I dropped heavily onto our old couch, where Ruby and I had spent so many foggy evenings nestled in its cushions, watching the sky darken out the bay window as we talked over her day. "Promise

to keep me safe," she used to beg, burrowing deep into me. "I will,"
I'd pledged. "I promise." Now her letter threatened, "If you try to
contact me I will take every step, legal and otherwise, to prevent
you from doing so." I had to take her at her word. Asa, her boyfriend, was a hotshot Harvard lawyer. Together those two Afrocentric dynamos could tear up any life. What role did he have in this
break? Outside agitator, I tried to reassure myself, remembering the
charge hurled at us Northerners who'd flowed south in the sixties.
It was impossible that a being who had emerged from my body
could act this way of her own accord. Was this a result of her father's
influence? Or Asa's? I pressed myself into the sagging coach as my
chest heaved and Beanie, staring intently, licked my face. What had
gone so terribly wrong? Had Ruby lost her mind, and should I fly
to Boston to try to save her?

At age ten, Ruby had once thrown down her books after school
and screamed, "Mama, the KKK is in Southern California, in Riv-
erside." I vividly remembered her brown eyes stretched wide with
fear. "Until now I always thought being black was better. I never
knew people hated me."

Ruby's innocence, I thought then, had been my triumph; I'd
provided space for her to grow unfettered by fear. But after I read
her letter, all certainty withered. Had the harsh world unhinged
her? Maybe I should have been stricter and toughened her up for
trouble, the way black parents did. Maybe . . . My mind floated.
As the sun shrunk the block of light on the floor, I lay frozen with
grief. A gust fluttered a Japanese maple by the front door, splinter-
ing the leaves into dancing shadows. Nothing had ended up the way
I'd expected. Not my marriage, not my child, not even socialism.

Yet some instinct, some ancient call of peasant blood, of the Irish
ancestors who gave me my big bones and broad shoulders, pulled
me to my feet. It was January 27, late in Northern California to
plant bulbs, but I'd put off digging in the lilies I'd bought: Stargaz-

ers, Ruby's favorites, promising pink blooms and sweet fragrance; Royal Sunsets, described on the packet as "bi-color of deep apricot centers, flamed brilliant red on tips"; and Sun Crests, yellow flowers with burgundy speckles. I switched on the kitchen light, grabbed bags of bulbs from the back of the refrigerator, and stumbled outside in the winter dark to search for the shovel. There it was, a square of rust tucked under the back porch.

In the glow of a half-moon I leaned on the spade to turn over damp earth, again and again, jamming bulbs into every inch of dark wet soil, saturating the yard with mounds of sodden earth like newly dug graves. My back ached, my fingers grew stiff with cold, my nails filled with loam. Still I jabbed at the dirt. Tears clogged my throat. Unaware that words had come to my lips, I chanted, "*Togaidh mi mo Sheolta*," sniffling the half-remembered tune my grandfather used to sing while I forced my shovel, over and over, into the earth. "I will make my way." My ancestors' song held me upright while I spaded fifty-five lilies into my narrow back garden, each patted down in its own circle of earth. I tore open a pack of tulips a neighbor had left on my steps and furiously dug yet another trench, this one along the side yard, crowding the small bulbs together. I excavated one pit after another, tossing in bulbs, tamping down the soil with muddy feet. My sobs drowning out even the traffic, when at last I trudged to the back door, a thought lodged itself in me like a willful weed: *At least I'd go down surrounded by color.*

Each afternoon, the second I slipped my key into the lock of my front door and heard Beanie and Barley fling themselves against the door, barking, the tears I'd held back all day flooded out. What was happening to Ruby? Though she'd sworn all family and friends to secrecy about all details of her life, Che, anguished, broke the code and read long portions of her letters aloud. Then I crouched on my living room floor slumped against the wall, the phone wretchedly pressed to my ear. Beanie, always true, curled in my lap, black tail wagging, smooth tongue licking my cheeks, my nose, my neck, before tugging on my pants to urge me outside for a run.

"Why is she doing this?" Che asked after each allegation, which she'd carefully spelled out for her brother. Ruby cited me for how I'd introduced her to friends ("showing me off like a safari trophy") to my speech ("white, uptight, full of pretense") to the smug way I smiled and fawned, she said, over people of color. My racism was intractable and impossible: "I can no longer take Elizabeth's unaware, persistently offensive behavior, which leaves me bleeding after every encounter. And then she wants me to explain why, as if I'm her racism coach!" She indicted me—after all these years—for the few times I'd forgotten to pick her up from some sports practice! Or not called home late in the evening when I was out. It was amazing she'd held on to these paltry grievances for so long, in the sea of everything I'd done right. What was the matter with her?

"You were there, a lot of the time. What do you think?" I asked, bewildered.

"It's confusing. She sounds so positive. And where was I?" He tried his trademark rueful chuckle. "I thought everything was fine."

Weeks later, desperate to touch the solidity of my son, I flew to New York. Sitting with Che in a crowded SoHo café on Spring Street, waiting for veggie omelets and lattes, I shivered. "What is it really about, with Ruby and me?" I looked into his dark eyes, so much like Ruby's. "What do you think?"

His eyes fluttered and he glanced down. With his short build, so unlike the rest of us, in his uncertainty he looked like a teen again. "I don't know, Mama. She doesn't say that much to me about it. And when she does, it's the same old story." He reached over to squeeze my fingers. "You know Ruby." He shrugged. "Why don't you try to see her?"

"I've thought of it. But I doubt I'd be able to get into her building. She doesn't answer my letters and when I called last week, for the first time in months, she said, 'Don't you know you're not supposed to call here?' and hung up on me."

Che's eyes filled.

"Couldn't you ask her to see me? Maybe plead my case?" I asked, as lightly as I could, wanting to spare him the intermediary role but frantic for intercession. "She's always looked up to you."

"Liz, you know she won't listen to me. She threatened to cut me off, too, if I kept seeing you. I can't even tell her you're here with me! It's crazy."

We ate in silence, picking through the limp vegetables in our omelets. Che, scowling, forked his broccoli over to me; I traded my spinach.

"Well, now you have me all to yourself," I tried to joke. Yearning to reach inside that shuttered face and open it, to bond securely with at least one of my children, I snatched at conversation. "Remember when we used to go to the carousel in the park? And the Little Farm? You'd drop your celery on the ground by the cow, remember, and pull your hand back? You hated for the cow to lick you. Remember that huge tongue?" I grimaced. "It made you cry."

"Elizabeth." He tightened his mouth into an oh-no-not-again line and pushed me back with Solomon's formal name for me. I'd forgotten how he disliked these reminiscences. Whenever I dug one out of the muck of the past, he was unwilling to float back with me to his raggedy, tie-dyed childhood. Today, as if to emphasize his distance from that time, he wore his khaki pants and button-down blue shirt uniform. I still favored granny dresses or a batiked sweatshirt and any jeans at hand; my idea of dressing up was to wear a pair of beaded earrings, throw on a pretty scarf, and, for extra-special occasions, add a black velvet blouse fringed in purple silk. We were all so different. While Che typically adopted some version of prep-casual clothing, Ruby's style was New York chic: fashionable but not preppy. The last time I'd seen her, the morning she'd zoomed away in a green BayPorter Express van, she'd worn a black A-line skirt, fishnet stockings, and a tailored three-quarter-sleeved crimson shirt. Where had these soigné children come from? Hardly from Solomon, who'd impressed me right away with his scruffy, existential stance, and, from what I'd seen, he'd hardly changed in that respect.

"I'm twenty-five," Che said, not looking at his plate. "Being your only kid for the moment, it's all on me now." When Che looked that confused, that upset, I'd learned that the only course was to pull back, give him time to settle down on his own. "I don't want to be in the middle of you and Ruby!" he erupted, surprising me with his vehemence. "All my life I was man-in-the-middle. The only one who got along with everybody. This time you have to work out your stuff with Ruby yourself."

Shocked into silence, I bit my lip, determined not to cry in front of him. Damn it, he wasn't going to have to take care of me.

"She'll come around," he finally said. When we parted, I had no greater insight into what to do and no better connection with my son, either. What kind of mother was I?

Constantly I worried: Should I try to crash into Ruby's apartment and free my daughter? But from what? And was it my right? By now Ruby was twenty-four years old. Friends offered conflicting advice: "Leave her alone," some said. Others urged, "Kidnap her, if you have to, and deprogram her." As the months slipped away, Solomon, despite my frequent requests, gave only brief, occasional reports. "Let her take her time. She'll be back," he counseled. Still I felt negligent. What if she were having a breakdown and cutting me off was part of it? I'd heard of bizarre therapies—Adlerian, in particular—which required severing relations with mothers. Solomon let it slip once that Ruby was in therapy; could an unscrupulous therapist be behind this? Che, who'd reverted to his easygoing warmth with me, rarely spoke of her, and after his outburst I was reluctant to ask.

Other mothers were no help. My neighbors practically raised their hands in a hex sign when they saw me, turned their heads away, and couldn't stop themselves from blurting, "I'd die if this happened to me," before they scuttled away, acting as if my affliction were contagious, like a virulent flu. Their pitying looks gave no solace. "You've got to say good-bye to Ruby," a few friends advised. "She's doing what she has to do to grow up." But their wide-eyed horror undermined the advice.

"Kick down her door if you have to," Raphael urged. "I can't believe you'd let her go this way, not after what you've done for her. You're her *mother*!"

"Ruby has to figure out her life," Hannah frequently countered. "Leave her alone. Let her go. Whatever she's doing, she has to do it by herself." She and I had settled into my couch one evening after work, discussing my constant topic while twilight dimmed the room. Neither of us rose to turn on a light. In spite of my ache of irresolution—to go or not to go?—finally that night a surprising feeling began to penetrate my grief, spreading like a bloom of fragrance around the couch. For the first time in months I was fully in the present moment, without half my brain circling the What to Do About Ruby question. I nestled contentedly between Beanie and Barley, one pressed tight against each thigh. Their strong breath on my legs, sturdy chests expanding and releasing, steadied me. I was able to absorb the presence of a dear friend nearby, and the glass of rich red cabernet in hand. We watched the sky darken, from light blue to a deep cobalt, with puffs of pink clotting the horizon. Eventually the entire sky faded gray, lit like a stage by the streetlights outside my windows. Quietly we moved into my kitchen to throw leftover wild salmon, brown basmati rice, and asparagus onto plates, heat our dinner in the slow, aged microwave, and plunk ourselves at the kitchen table to savor the fish, an expensive delicacy.

Our talk turned to Carol Moseley Braun and her rough ride in the Senate. "The good ol' boys don't cut her any slack," I said, relieved that for once I could focus on another topic.

"I know," Hannah agreed. "They're riding her ass."

"Yeah. But she doesn't make it easy on herself. She's giving 'em a good target." I sighed. "Even if she were perfect, they'd find a way to get her out. It's definitely a club. And she's not in it."

After we polished off the cabernet, we returned to my obsession. "Shouldn't I try to see her? If she saw me, don't you think she'd snap back to her senses?" And thus, after my brief reprieve, the internal debate resumed.

"She'll be back," Solomon calmly advised, repeating the "Ruby's fine" chorus every time I asked. For a decade, I'd seen him only at graduations or other family events. Each time, I was shocked to watch this tall, thin man grow heavier, balder, grayer. Years passed between our conversations. But now, when my suffering over Ruby spread like spilled ink, he and I often talked.

I sat in thin sun on my front stoop, listening to the rustle of leaves blowing, holding the black cordless plastic to my good ear as I drank his words, letting them seep through every cell, warming my bones. "She's doing well, wonderfully well. You have a lot to be proud of." He still had a rare deep voice; once again I wrapped myself in it, clinging to what I hoped was truth, wanting to believe the surety in those melodious tones. "You've got to let her grow up in her own time. There's nothing I can say that's going to change the situation. Believe me, I've thought about it. It might only backfire if I pressure her."

When I argued, "You could tell her she's being a disrespectful little brat, and you won't have it," he quietly demurred, with a constant, "She'll be back in her own time."

I did a slow burn, demanding, "Solomon, you're her father, she'll listen to you," but nothing moved him from his mantra of "She'll be back in her own time."

One winter day I opened a letter, typed, from Solomon. "Family histories are strange things," he wrote, "and in my family I had a great-aunt Nancy. She was my grandmother's sister and looked white. She disappeared from the family and went north. It is believed that she decided to pass for white. She came back once in the middle of the night to visit her mother, my great-grandmother, who was secretly married to the white man Jeremiah, and that was the last anyone ever saw or heard of her. So maybe there's something in my family history that has called Ruby away; a reverse path of sorts, in which she has to traverse her blackness back to the core. Historical redemption."

Soaking in the comfort of these words, which provided some possible reason Ruby had left, I recalled Solomon's and my first meeting when he had crooned "Wade in the water. . . . God's gonna trouble the water." It had sounded so hopeful, as if God would stir a great pot, releasing the pain of oppression like steam rising. But the water, it had turned out, was full of heartache, welling up in surges that overtook me at odd moments. Waves pulsed so strongly my skin should have burst. I'd be jerked from any task—standing erect in front of a classroom or slicing carrots for dinner—by a flood of anguish: What if Ruby were unhinged, deranged? Wasn't it my role as her mother to rush to her side, to fix her?

"Ruby's at Princeton for a year," Solomon tersely informed me by phone late one night, months later, after I begged for news. "She's exploring race theory as cultural text with some notable professor there."

"The apple doesn't fall far from the tree," I said bitterly.

"Do you want her address?" he offered, ignoring my comment but surprising me with the kindness.

"Yes."

"It's near the university, twenty-seven Butler Road," he said, while I scrambled to scrawl it in pencil on a scrap of paper. Later, when I tried to imagine Ruby's apartment in the college town, I pictured her rooms upstairs—perhaps two rooms, a bedroom and sitting room—in a gray, clapboard house, similar to the faded one I'd grown up in. I even conjured a front porch and contemplated planting myself on its top step so Ruby would find me waiting when she returned home one afternoon. For months I toyed with the idea, imagining her rounding the corner, a spring in her step, her shock when she saw me. Was it fair to impose myself on my daughter that way? But I was her mother. Wouldn't she be happy to see me?

Wasn't it only a moment ago that a nurse had handed me my baby, all eight pounds ten ounces wrapped in pink? Ruby's face had picked up a glow from the blanket, rosebud lips opened, and her round brown eyes watched me. Enchanted, I'd let my hospital reading—Frantz Fanon's *The Wretched of the Earth* and Simone de Beauvoir's *The Second Sex*—fall to the floor while I cradled my baby in the crook of my arm, not wanting to look anywhere else but at that heart-shaped face. If hospital staff or other patients stared at our family with curiosity, I didn't see. For once, with my brown-skinned baby in my arms, I'd been oblivious to race.

Until I took her out for her first walk on Shattuck Avenue.

"What a lovely baby."

Charmed, I was sure, by Ruby's radiance, the tall white stranger stooped to admire her rosy cheeks and sharp brown eyes. But as he inspected the infant in her carriage bundled in the multicolored bunting Maria had knitted, the man's eyes darted to my red hair and pallid skin, then back to Ruby's creamy apricot face. "Where did you get this baby?"

Surely I'm not the first in the world? I'd stiffened and pulled myself erect, towering over him.

"Where did she come from?"

"From my body. Like every other baby is born."

"I thought maybe adopted. What's her father?"

"A man."

"But you look like such a nice girl . . ."

"I am." *Fuck you*, her father is a *black* man. "And you looked like such a nice man . . ." Cheeks burning, I'd whipped around and wheeled away, furious that Ruby had heard this questioning about her complexion, determined to wrap my arms ever more tightly around my baby, shielding her from surveillance. So attuned already to my body, my moods, Ruby must have resonated to the intrusion. I'd wished then I could erect a shelter around my daughter, grasp her so tightly she'd know, instinctively, that she was perfect. Every time people grilled me about her complexion—"Does she have a tan?"—I wanted to tell her, "Don't listen to them. You're fine."

But was she? Shouldn't I try to see her?

My heart briefly stopped when, after three impossibly long years since I'd heard from Ruby, Solomon told me, in his mellifluous tones, that not only had she returned to Cambridge with Asa, but he and Che had attended her "lovely marriage ceremony, held in the garden of Cambridge friends, with poets and saxophonists and African drummers. You would have loved it. I'm sorry you couldn't be there. But she will be back to you, in her own time." That night, heart pounding, I grilled Che by phone about the wedding: "Why didn't you tell me?" ("I couldn't," he said.) "Was Imani there?" ("Yes.") "Inez?" ("Yes.") "Tell me everything." ("Like what?" he said.)

My urge to fly to Boston grew into an overwhelming torrent of heartbreak: my daughter had married and I hadn't even known, hadn't been there to bless her. What if Asa was keeping my letters from Ruby, à la Mister in *The Color Purple*? Didn't I owe it to my daughter to try at least once? I ached to see her, to hear her voice, but as I contemplated actually going, I imagined every possible dilemma: What if she weren't home? What if Asa blocked the door?

The odds of talking to her seemed slim, but, after years of indecision, I decided I had to try. I thought I was ready to survive a rejection, should one come, although I suspected it was far more likely that Ruby would be relieved, once I appeared in the flesh. "At last you've come," she might say, "I've missed you so much, I just had to know you loved me" before she fell into my waiting arms. Someday we'd look back and be amazed, maybe even chuckle about this terrible misunderstanding.

After suffering last-minute doubts and twice canceling plane reservations, I finally made definite plans to scale the fortress, as I'd come to think of Ruby's walls. On the morning of September 19, five years after I received The Letter, after so much speculation and discussion, I was going to Cambridge to see Ruby.

As I packed on the eve of the flight, Hannah sat on the edge of my bed, determined to ensure that this time I took off on schedule. For the hundredth time, she wondered aloud, "What if you can't get in?"

Abi, whom I'd asked to come over for this momentous send-off even though we hardly saw each other anymore, echoed the worry, cautioning in her lawyerly fashion, "You have to get in. But it would be illegal, remember, if you try to penetrate her defenses by jimmying the lock. You don't want to end up in jail." Her small face was scrunched with concern, the gray hair pulled into a severe bun accentuating the lines on her face. "I wonder if there's any way you could get the police to let you in. No . . ." and I could see her mind ticking off possible modes of entry.

I could imagine nothing more frustrating than flying all the way across country and arriving at a locked building. Would Ruby buzz me in if there were an intercom? I harbored a hope that there was one: if she actually heard my voice, surely some memory of kindness, of reality, would kick in. Again I imagined her embrace. "Maybe I could sneak in behind someone who lives there," I ventured, not for the first time. But with only five apartments other than Ruby's, the likelihood that anyone would enter at a specific time was slight; the chance that they would allow me to barge in, even more remote.

"What if Asa answers the door and cusses you out, and won't let you talk to Ruby?" Hannah worried while I held up two long-sleeved shirts, one sparkling lime, the other a softer green, my favorite color, as I tried to imagine the Boston weather. I'd heard it would be rainy and cool. And I wanted to look beautiful for Ruby. I folded the soft green.

"I'll go when he's at work."

"How do you know his schedule? And what if Ruby's teaching, too?"

"I called the law school to find out what courses he teaches," I admitted. "It was so weird to pretend I was a former student trying to catch up with him, wanting him for a panel. I found a chatty secretary who told me everything. But the Afro-American Studies Program wasn't so helpful. I couldn't find out anything about Ruby's schedule."

"What if she's there but she doesn't answer the bell?" Abi asked, twisting a straggly hair through her fingers.

I shrugged.

"Just keep pushing the buzzer," Hannah laughed wildly. "Drive her crazy, the little bitch."

I threw my long white gauzy nightgown into the suitcase, followed by my faded pink-flowered plastic toiletries kit, the one I'd carried on trips since the summer I flew to Mississippi the year I met Solomon. And it had been secondhand then. My mother had found it, looking shiny new, at the Ladies Aid thrift store downtown.

"You should make a scene, scream outside the building if you can't get in. Let her know this is serious business." Hannah snapped her pudgy fingers. "Damn it. Underneath, she wants you to come. You know that. Anyway, you deserve to be there."

I hoped it was true.

"Demand that she see you," Abi insisted, "without doing anything illegal. But don't take no for an answer. Just *decide*."

After they'd flung every bit of advice they could and at last departed in a flurry of hugs, tears, and good wishes, I called everyone I knew. "Send good vibes, please, I'm actually going to see Ruby." At midnight, awash in camaraderie, I fell into a dreamless sleep and awoke surprisingly refreshed, ready to tackle my adventure. After a hurried breakfast, off I went, scrambling up the high step of the green BayPorter van. Soon the airplane swallowed me and I let my mind float free, but by the time we landed at Logan in a howling wind, my heart began to miss beats. Guiding a taxi driver through the storm to the friend's home where I'd be spending the night, I found it hard to believe: the moment had come. As we emerged from Sumner Tunnel, rain lashed the windows. The taxi driver slowed, apparently unsure where to go. When he lowered his head to consult his map, the car skidded onto a shallow curb; the driver swore, but managed to bump us back down onto the street. "Where now?" he asked grumpily, as if it were my fault that our destination was still miles away. "Stay on Storrow Drive," I instructed, as my friend had told me, "until the Kenmore Square/ Fenway sign." At the last minute he veered to the exit, then steered us into one wrong turn after another, complaining the whole time—"It's a terrible night to be out"—until we arrived at the home of Julia Bartlett, a former Mills College colleague now teaching art history at Simmons. It was 10:30 p.m. In less than twelve hours, I hoped, I'd see Ruby.

"Elizabeth," Julia greeted me formally, wrinkling her nose with distaste at my dripping slicker. "There." She pointed down a stark hall. "Hang it in the bathroom. Would you like a drink?" She rubbed her eyes.

Huddled on a thin futon in a small bedroom up a crooked flight of stairs, I lay awake most of the night, listening to wind rattle the windowpanes and whispering my own quiet plea. "If it is right, let me get into the building, let me talk to her. I don't know how to make it happen," I prayed to some benevolent spirit of the universe. "But here I am, doing my part. I'm showing up. If it's right for us to meet, please let it happen." At last entering a calm state, I drifted peacefully, though by morning my heart thumped hard with expectation, skipping beats again in a worrisome way.

I woke to a clock radio announcer's excited voice exhaling news of a massive category 3 hurricane "pounding the entire Eastern Seaboard with roaring winds and torrential rain. At six thirty this morning, Mayor Menino ordered Boston virtually shut down." His voice rose. "Only emergency personnel should leave their homes." Everything was closed: government agencies, schools, and businesses. Since the driving rain meant walking to the Fenway Square T would be impossible, Julia, groggy before her morning coffee, hunched by her wall telephone in the deeply brown kitchen (chocolate walls, tan floor, bronze pottery dishes, oatmeal napkins) and ordered a taxi. I had planned to time my arrival so that Asa would have left for school. Now, with everyone staying home, wouldn't he, too? Were all my careful preparations ruined? I called his department at Harvard. Eight thirty and he'd just arrived. I thanked the universe and hung up before the call went through to his office. Hopefully my luck would hold and Ruby would be home when I arrived.

Riding in a grubby taxi reeking of stale cigarette smoke, I could hardly believe she was here in this city, nearby. Gusts blew the taxi sideways, rain pelted the windshield, smearing the grime. The driver had trouble finding the small street they lived on, Williams Street, but after stopping twice to consult his map and once to call headquarters, he pulled up in front of a large brick building. When I managed to push the back car door open, wind almost tore it off; I staggered out into the storm, both hands clutching a borrowed umbrella as a shield against the heavy rain and wind, and skidded up onto the front patio. "There used to be a doorman," Solomon had volunteered, grudgingly. "But now it's an intercom system." Seeing six bells, none with names, I rang them all. My heart pounded ferociously against my chest.

The buzzes brought no answer. I stood dripping outside the front door. Was anyone home?

Above the howling weather, I heard a faint voice from above. Ruby's voice. I peered up, but my view was blocked by an overhang. The wind roared; I ran out to the street but was unable to see, with water pouring into my face and my poncho hood blocking upward vision, nor was I sure which side Ruby's window was on, or even what floor. Solomon and Che had both refused that detail. I hadn't wanted to pump them too hard when they resisted; they both suffered, I knew, torn between Ruby and me, and I couldn't risk alienating anyone. Especially Che. I returned to the front door. There, my heart pounded so violently I wondered if this was the first sign of a heart attack. *Don't let me die on this patio before I see Ruby.*

No one came to let me in. I pressed all the bells. Again. And again.

A middle-aged woman in a shimmering blue housecoat appeared, stepping carefully down the stairs directly in front of a glass panel in the door. She opened an inner door, and approached the outer, locked one. Like the Red Sea parting, the door opened and the hand of God picked me up. I stepped over the doorsill and was in the building. Mail lay on a curved side table in the marble entryway.

"I've come to see Ruby," I said. A slight pause. "She doesn't seem to be answering her bell. Maybe it's broken," I added, smiling in what I hoped was a friendly way.

"I'll take you," the woman said pleasantly. Her hair, that telltale rust color of henna, caught the overhead light for a moment before she turned to lead the way up the stairs. "It's a miracle I'm home at all. I've been a teacher in the Boston schools for twenty-three years, and we hardly ever close for weather. We pride ourselves on it." She swiveled her head and smiled.

We arrived at the second floor. The hallway was painted a faint pastel yellow; two small oil paintings hung on the wall; a folded *New York Times* lay in front of one door.

"This is Ruby's place. But of course you know."

I nodded.

"I live on the third floor." The teacher pointed up and left me in front of Ruby's door. A grassy doormat lay under the newspaper. A black door held a peephole with a brass plate and a brass knocker. Was anyone home?

I took a deep breath and tapped with the knocker.

No answer.

I rapped lightly with my hand.

Still no answer.

I knocked again.

"Who's there?" It was Ruby's voice, clear and melodic, sounding exactly as it always had.

I gasped. "It's your mother."

"Go away. Why are you here?" Her voice was low.

"Because I love you. I want to talk to you." I had anticipated this conversation through a closed door so often, the words flowed out. "I came all the way from California to see you."

"Get out of here. How did you get in?"

"A neighbor let me in. Ruby. I want to talk and hear what you have to say. I'm ready to listen. Please open the door."

"No. I don't want to talk. You have no right to be here." Still her tone was even, and rebuffing though her words might be, she wasn't calling the police or screaming. And while she kept saying she didn't want to talk, she was talking.

I heard a bolt slide, then the click of a lock, and, unbelievably, as in slow motion, the door opened a crack. Through the two-inch opening, I saw Ruby's blazing brown eyes.

"I love you," I said. "There's a lot happening," I added, trying to entice her. "You're missing out. Sweetie."

"Go away," Ruby said, although I thought her eyes were searching my face.

I tried to keep up the conversation, anything to keep open the crack in the wall Ruby had erected. "I miss you. I . . ."

"Get out of here!" For the first time, Ruby's voice level rose. "I'm going to move away from the door now." Still she left it open.

"You'll always have a place, whenever you're ready to come home," I pleaded, drinking in the thin slice of Ruby's face and body that I could see. Tiny streaks of gray highlighted her hair, which hung below her shoulders. I remembered my own first gray hairs at thirty.

"I don't want to talk to you," Ruby said, while the door remained ajar. "I'm going back into the apartment," she warned. And then her tone turned steely. "If you don't leave in one minute, I'm going to call the police."

The door slammed shut. I heard rustling, an inner door close, and the sound of retreating footsteps.

I stood on the doormat, stunned. After all these years, I'd talked to Ruby. I'd even seen her, for several delicious minutes. Reaching into my brown leather tote, I took out the yellow pad I'd brought in case I never got into the building. "Dear Ruby," I wrote. "It was wonderful to hear your voice and get a glimpse of your face. I'm sorry you won't see me further, but I want you to know how much I love and think about you. I support you in whatever path you walk, and there must be something good in this one. When you are ready, let me know. Much love, Liz." I crossed that out. "Mama." I slipped the note under the doormat, stole a last glance at the hallway, walked down the stairs, opened the front door, and stepped once more over the threshold. The universal gate that had swung open closed behind me. I had had my moment.

Stumbling out into the rain and heavy wind, I was surprised

by how light my heart felt, how filled my soul. I had heard my daughter's lovely voice, the one that had lilted through my life for twenty-three years, until she'd withdrawn it. Ruby was alive. She sounded sane, she appeared as radiant as ever, she lived in an attractive, well-kept building. And now, I thought, I've done all I can do. For the first time in years, I felt complete, as if I'd taken care of some necessary business that was forever waiting just out of sight. I had personally delivered my message of love. There was no possibility that she had not received it, however she might interpret or distort it. And though the next-to-worst had happened—she hadn't let me in—I felt surprisingly successful.

But now that I'd given my all and no pebble remained to worry in my fingers, rolling it back and forth—*Should I go, shouldn't I?*—I flew back to San Francisco, wondering numbly if I'd ever see Ruby again. Once home, my body began to empty itself of hope. Slowly drops of anticipation oozed from my pores until I was drained. No more heroic actions loomed in the distance, holding out the possibility of retrieving Ruby.

As the days after the visit ground on with no redemptive vision on the horizon, I relived the despair I'd felt after her letter, when she'd first cut me off. I knew I was in trouble when Beanie and Barley, those reliable twins in mischief and loyalty, couldn't hold my attention, when their pink tongues licking my face or tugging on my sleeve, and their adorable twirling gymnastics as they leaped in the air, only irritated me. Instead of rubbing their velvety muzzles, I pushed them away. No matter how they romped and chased their tails or thumped the rubber balls I'd wrapped in socks, their antics failed to lift my spirits. Even when Barley did his special trick—gripping the sock with his teeth he flung it from side to side, then dropped it and barked at his sister to do the same, until they were slinging these heavy socks in unison—even then, I didn't laugh.

*   *   *

When I emailed Solomon news of my attempted visit, I received an immediate reply.

She told me you'd come and I was surprised she didn't let you into the apartment. Ruby has made her choice and she is the one who must live with the consequences, and I fear that they will be greater than she can imagine. You might as well know, I've told her over and over again that she will regret this rupture for the rest of her life. Having lived with the death of my mother for ten years this coming winter, there are still times when there'll be something I want to ask her or share with her and it is not possible. Don't worry, Ruby may think she has excised you from her life, but a mother is never cut from the psyche of a child. I hope for her sake as well as yours that she will get in touch with you one of these days, but it was always hard for her to admit that she had made a mistake. (smile) This is the karma she is creating for herself. You were a good mother and someday Ruby will recognize it. She's on some other trip now. I hardly understand it myself even though she and I share long conversations about everything under the sun. You know she's a night owl like her father. (smile) But she's a hard one to fathom. Don't blame yourself. Take care. Solomon.

His words gave me a solace I hadn't expected. Yes, God had indeed troubled the waters, though not with the impact I'd once imagined. Instead another miracle had taken place: Solomon and I were communicating with an intimacy I hadn't imagined we'd ever share again. At last the tide had washed away our youthful mistakes, leaving only a residue of sweetness, like that first time we kissed. Well-meaning friends had tried to console me over the years with stories about "gifts that come wrapped in strange packages," but I'd sniffed, thinking, *They don't know shit about pain.*

Renewed friendship with the soul mate of my youth was a gift I never expected.

As the broken months completed their cycles, winter rains came and went, sprouting bright green grass on the hillsides. One late February afternoon as I pulled weeds in my back yard, I was shocked to notice a sprinkling of grass creeping over my inner landscape, too, covering the wound. Where there'd been merely scarred earth, a protective groundcover had begun to appear. How had it grown while I'd grumped my way through winter? Like my new intimacy with Solomon, it seemed a gift I'd done nothing to deserve, nothing to create, but a blessing sent from that same benevolent spirit I'd prayed to the night before I visited Ruby, asking to be let into her building. I tiptoed gingerly around the healing, afraid that my poking might disturb it, and merely observed with awe. Is this what grace meant, an inexplicable moving out from under the weight of suffering? Yes, I still ached—unbearably when the pain caught my breath and threatened to squeeze the life from me. But now I also had instants when a lifting heart caught me unaware, surprising me with its intensity, too, until I hardly knew how to react. What kind of mother could experience joy after her only daughter had abandoned her? I'd dutifully lash myself then back into misery, suspecting that any happiness, however brief, was a sure sign of guilt, just as an accused seventeenth-century "witch" who failed to drown when thrown into water tied up was proven guilty. Surely the innocent could not survive unscathed. Witches were supposed to float; was my floating now a sign of my evil, selfish nature, exactly as Ruby charged? Would I ever escape the torment of second-guessing every minute of my mothering, searching for clues to Ruby's behavior?

All that early spring of 1996 I watched my garden obsessively, damning every gopher or mole that might even contemplate eating the bulbs I'd dug in that awful evening of The Letter. Each spring since then, fewer bulbs had survived the winter rodent munching, but those remaining were hardy and had produced offspring to replenish the slaughter. The spring after my visit to Ruby, the more I waited for the sprouts, the more sacred the bulbs became, my own talisman of guilt and innocence; if they grew, I would survive. In early March, when the first tulip shoot poked through the soil, I treated it like a baby, hovering, tending to its every likely need. Slowly more tender shoots appeared, then lovely green folds, until by April I was rewarded with the colorful affirmation I craved. During subsequent months, an abundance of lilies flowered. Though not every plant produced a blossom, a profusion of tints—lavender, violet and cherry, mango and tangerine, gold and plum and ginger streaked with pink—welcomed me in the cool evenings after I arrived home. When I sat on my carved wooden bench whistling, the dogs prancing nearby, I had to dodge hummingbirds swarming the garden; they dove, buzzing me, before darting into the bright blooms.

One foggy morning while I dug in my yard, planting a tight row of green bean seedlings, I imagined the indictment Ruby might hurl. "Miss Ann playing farmworker," she'd probably snarl if she were here. "Privileging whiteness." But instead of the hot rush of shame that used to flame through my body, I simply felt—what? I had to think about it, pull the strands apart. Sorrow at the truth of it: white people playing, yes, all too often, while African Americans chopped and dug and broke their backs. Sorrow that this was her only lens, and grief that we weren't together. Relief that Ruby wasn't here saying it, and awe, too, that the imaginary charge triggered only a trace of the old defense: "I'm not like those other Miss Anns," I still wanted to murmur. "The oblivious ones." But it was a shred left in a well-worn groove. How had I emerged so far from its grip? I recalled my nights at the No Name bar on Telegraph Avenue, a place I'd frequented after Solomon first moved out. At nine or ten o'clock I'd head up and console myself for an hour or so in the warm company of friends from Merritt College. We'd press around a battered black table, drinking and laughing. Imani's mother Inez was part of the group, and even though we'd worked together, hanging out at *No Name* was where I learned to appreciate her wit. Raphael, another teacher who was briefly my lover after Abi and I broke up, used to join us, too, often with a young man I found out later was his *other* lover.

As I dug in the bean seedlings I remembered how, whenever I arrived in the noisy, smoky bar, I tried any trick not to sit by Molly, the other white regular. Desperate to blend in, as had been my habit for so many years, I needed to be buffered by at least one African American on either side. This was challenging because Molly had the opposite impulse. When she strode in she chose an empty chair by me or pulled one over to wedge in beside me. Suddenly I'd feel visible, as if we were two gleaming headlights in the smoky fog around us. "It's too thick right here, even for me," I'd cough, making a show of waving the haze away with my hand. "I understand, dearie, it is a wee bit smoky," she'd say with her brogue and pat my hand, wanting to soothe and befriend me, but instead driving in my guilt at leaving her until I had to pull my hand away. Or I'd get up, saunter to the restroom, and upon my return I'd casually grab a chair from another table to push in somewhere else, anywhere else, so long as I was surrounded by black. My people, I thought, only half ironically. Since I couldn't see myself except in a mirror, it was easy to imagine I faded into the dark. But now, tamping down earth around my green beans, I had to acknowledge that I was irrefutably white. Breathing hard, I stamped, one heavy foot after another, on each side of the row. *That's* my people. White folks, with all our ugly contradictions. From slavery to John Brown. That's us. That's me. What a relief to admit it, even for a second. I felt my body relax. Beanie, digging happily by my side, seemed to agree. She jumped up with her muddy paws, streaking my jeans with dirt, yipping. "Okay, we're white," I laughed. "You and me, baby." Had I truly forgiven myself the accident of my skin?

Even though waves of grief still overtook me when least expected, I admitted I was enjoying my independence, too. I flirted, guilt-free, with strangers, men and women of every hue, at the Berkeley Bowl while I picked through broccoli or cabbage. I began to savor pleasures like the union songs I'd long ago given up as racially suspect—even though I instinctively glanced over my shoulder every time I whistled "Union Maid" or "The Banks Are Made of Marble." But, reassuring myself, "I'm an ally," I discovered deep comfort in those tunes from childhood. Despite the mostly exclusive history, that message of solidarity, of hope and perseverance against the overwhelming power of the bosses, still resonated. Wasn't there a way to blend the best of union tradition with our new awareness, layering the civil rights spirit of inclusive community over that old rough courage?

When I heard from a Merritt colleague that the teamsters' union was recruiting volunteers to turn out the vote for President Clinton's reelection, I urged Hannah and Abi and Ayanna: "Come on." The next Saturday the four of us showed up at eight, a heavily laden quartet: Hannah lugging two cameras slung over her shoulders; Ayanna hoisting her baby girl, Florenza, in a carrier on her back; Abi with armfuls of posters, just in case; and me carting Beanie, who was ailing, in an improbable canvas bag. At fifteen pounds she wasn't easy to transport, but her cries, when she heard me preparing to leave the house, had haunted me so much I'd stuffed her into a sturdy white tote and hauled her along. Inez and a few other faculty members plus two students from Merritt College joined us that morning. Soon we were set for door-to-door campaigning, with our voter lists and leaflets and door-hanger flyers. But after our orientation, at the last minute before we set out from the Sacramento Street storefront, a block captain burst in the door to ask whether any of us in the crowd standing by the entryway could sing in a sound truck. "Okay," I called out, raising my hand, "if I can run home and get my guitar. I only live three blocks away."

Once aboard with the guitar Solomon had bought me thirty years ago, and Beanie left whimpering at home with her brother, I slipped into the comfort of the familiar union atmosphere. Standing as we inched through the crowded streets of working-class West Oakland, I harmonized with a young white man, updating Woody Guthrie tunes with topical lyrics. I prefaced "This Land Is Your Land" with Woody's words. "'I hate a song that makes you think that you are not any good,'" I quoted from memory, plucking my simple chords. "'I hate a song that makes you think that you are just born to lose. Bound to lose. No good to nobody. No good for nothing. Because you are too old or too young or too fat or too slim. . . .'" My voice rose, I intensified the strumming and called out Woody's famous lines: "'Songs that run you down or poke fun at you on account of your bad luck or hard traveling. I am out to fight those songs to my very last breath of air and my last drop of blood. . . .'" When chills ran down my arms, I knew I was where I belonged.

Every Saturday I rode again with the truck. Once we ventured all the way to the Central Valley; each time I felt a surprising sense of wholeness. We were all pulling together—whites and blacks and occasional Latino migrant pickers who joined us—to elect a white man who, however flawed, was acting in our interests. Being white didn't automatically seem like such a sin. I laughed among white men and women with an abandon I hadn't felt in thirty-five years, not since I discovered what "they" had done to black people.

Again I felt the surprise of a lifting heart, one I hadn't expected. As if I'd been in a coma for six years, not expected to regain consciousness, my renewed sense of life—*even without Ruby*, I kept marveling—seemed like a bestowal of grace. I hummed during the week, sweeping the front stoop and weeding my garden. I hummed while I prepared my classes for fall. At first I was afraid to allow this peace to escape my lips in any form save a hum or whistle. If I left it unspoken I could secretly taste it, like a piece of Halloween candy savored for months, with a token lick each day sweetening the tongue. Verbalized, it might evaporate, or be the sure sign of a faithless mother. My unspoken calm was punctuated by swells of grief that swamped me each time a mother and adult daughter passed on the street, their features so similar to each other, arms casually circling one another's waists. Their intimacy caught in my throat, my chest.

But one evening when Hannah and I ate our Thursday dinner at Café de la Paz, sweltering in the second-story restaurant, I confided quietly, "I'm so at peace, more content than I've ever been."

"You look it," she reflected after studying my face. "Even your shoulders are relaxed, not pinched up to your ears. You almost look like a woman in love, you look that happy."

"Not because Ruby isn't in my life," I said quickly, "but in spite of it." Like Ruby, I was learning to make my way alone. I thought of the old Celtic words, *Togaidh mi mo sheolta*. I will make my way. Somehow a river of joy was rushing through me, flowing over the loss as if it were a boulder on the streambed, changing my life's course but not its vigor. "Ruby and I share a bond that can never be broken, even if I never see her face again," I swore to Hannah. Yet as soon as I affirmed it I yearned, with that ache I thought I'd banished, to walk down a street with her, any street, casually draping an arm over her shoulder, chatting and exchanging ideas about everything that mattered. If she called I'd fly in a second to any airport in the world just to glimpse her face for five minutes or share a conversation. Just to find out what the hell was going on.

When Che and Cynthia announced their plan to marry that August—the same month my beans would ripen—I anticipated another chance for a healing, "or at least a sighting," I tried joking to friends. But Ruby, I heard from Che, insisted that if I were attending, she would stay away. "That girl is dug in," Solomon apologized in advance. "I can't explain it. In every other way she seems to be doing fine, but she has this thing about you up her butt. Nobody can move it."

Still, the wedding in Cynthia's mother's lavish Los Angeles garden was a celebration for our whole extended clan. My aging parents and Irish cousins and Jewish uncles and aunts, all dressed to the nines in an array of crumpled clothing, faces daubed with off-color lipstick, arrived en masse. Since Cynthia's divorced parents had, like Solomon, each remarried, the family cast, Che announced at the rehearsal dinner with his typical chuckle, "requires a flowchart." On the big day Solomon and I, one on each side of our son, walked confidently down the aisle created between rows of folding chairs under a white tent. I had wondered how it would feel to perform this ritual together; the healing between us was palpable when we stood behind Che as his parents. After so many years apart, at last the situation felt normal. Yes, we were his parents, still and always. It was Ruby's absence that caused the sharp pain, one that no amount of excellent wine and music could dull that day.

But by spring Che had fathered a baby girl, Mia, energizing me with her sparkly new life. My burping technique resurfaced intact, Solomon and I exchanged baby photos by email, and that winter I sent holiday cards with photos of a granddaughter cradled on my lap, looking up at me with intense blue eyes. As she grew, though, I felt a familiar worry. Unmistakably, the child looked white, like her mother, with blond hair and a pale pink face. Just as visibly, Che was brown. Watching the two of them in public, my anxiety sizzled until, during one of my visits, it bubbled over. Mia was just days shy of turning two. I'd come for her birthday.

"Catch me, Daddy," she squealed, after Che drove us to a New Jersey mall. The gaudy shops dazzled her, I could tell by the wild look in her eyes, and the expansive hallways were perfect for a girl who loved to run. She took off squealing across the polished tile floor. Che, dressed in sweats, waited a moment before he followed, running slowly before he closed in to scoop her up. To my race-trained eye, this was an alarming scene. While I waited for a white passerby to scream, one who'd be "saving" the white baby from the long-legged black man about to snatch her, I flashed on the grim moment years before when a teenage Che and I had been actors in our own running scene. Once more I was flooded by gratitude that the white men who yelled "Stop!" didn't have guns, since it was clear from their cries that they assumed Che was snatching my purse. In fact, he was racing me to our car and, being so much swifter, had handicapped himself by carrying my heavy leather bag. I wondered whether times had changed so much that he never had to worry. Maybe people walking by *did* see a loving father delighting in his child. "I'm coming to get you," he laughed as he gave chase, running with exaggerated steps. Passersby didn't show the bewildered faces I'd witnessed long ago—faces that had scanned my own young children, then me, and come up empty of explanation. Now, at the Pleasant Valley Mall, Che didn't appear concerned, nor did anyone else. And not wanting to burden him with my ancient fears, I remained silent.

Perhaps the new world that Solomon and I had tried so hard to birth did exist in this modern family. Like Solomon's and mine, this one contained a black father, white mother, and biracial child. But thirty-five years later, in the midst of Che and Cynthia's hectic professional lives, race seemed a footnote. I wondered, would Mia someday call her pale body and upper-class life lived mostly among whites African American? Mixed race? Or not describe herself in racial terms at all? And what did Ruby make of it? Though sixteen months younger than Che, by temperament she bridged the old and new generations, whereas he, the elder child, seemed inextricably woven into the new, more relaxed biracial cohort. I imagined she'd be torn by this merging into "colorless" identity. Not that Che avoided race. But it wasn't the screen he used to filter his everyday world, as Ruby, Solomon, and I habitually did. Were we three legacies of the old world, necessary bridges who helped show a path to the new but were already anachronistic? And what was Ruby thinking about it all now?

Back home I sat in my tangled garden sipping a cup of peppermint tea, marking the ten-year anniversary of our rift with a special meditation, as I did each year. For an instant I wondered if there ever was a Ruby, she seemed so far away. Would I ever be fully resolved about her?

I opened the book on my lap and read Rilke's words.

I beg you . . . to have patience with everything unresolved in your heart and to try to love the questions themselves as if they were locked rooms or books written in a very foreign language. Don't search for the answers, which could not be given to you now, because you would not be able to live them. And the point is, to live everything. Live the questions now. Perhaps then, someday far in the future, you will gradually, without even noticing it, live your way into the answer.

Scenes from my young adulthood and years of mothering hovered like images from a story I'd once read. Did I make up my memories of this child? The last time I'd seen Ruby, other than the glimpse at her door, George Bush was president. Ruby and I had missed the Clinton presidency. What did she make of the impeachment? When I thought of her, Ruby appeared like a distant friend, an intimate from long ago. Was there ever an exuberant girl who strummed lovely peace songs, or laughed with me on the old stuffed couch covered in white flowered silk? This warm, sunny child seemed like a memory from another life. It was hard to imagine her existence. But whenever the phone rang and I heard a silent open line, the familiar presence rushed in, as close as if I'd seen her this morning. As I repeated "Hello" to the echo, I imagined that my daughter simply wanted to hear my voice.

Perhaps this time she would say, "Liz?" Or, more likely, because she'd rebelled against calling me the name I asked her to use, she'd say, "Elizabeth?"

I held the phone against my left ear, tilting my head slightly.

"Hello," the familiar voice would say, sounding like honey.

"Ruby! Is that you?"

"Yes. I want to talk." I could hear the bubble, the warmth that used to suffuse her voice.

And then I was fully into the fantasy. My body relaxed as if sedated. Shoulders loosened. Energy spun in curls down my arms. Every cell rejoiced. "Oh, sweetie, I'm here. I'd love to talk to you." My eyes were wet. I smiled. "That's what I've been wanting to do all these years." Thank you, universe, for letting me live this long. I inhaled deeply.

"It's not easy. I've been suffering so," Ruby would say. I couldn't imagine it otherwise.

"I know, honey. Me too."

"But this is not all about *you*."

I chuckled softly. "Just tell me about you, sweetie. I've been so upset. I'm so sorry for any pain I ever caused you." My heart hit my chest wall. There was that familiar edge in Ruby's voice, even in my fantasy. And I wasn't going to put up with any bullshit. That I had vowed. But the unbelievable had happened. Ruby had called.

Wanting to keep her on the phone and without a way to call her back, I was trying to remember advice for people talking to suicide threats when the miracle occurred.

"I'm sorry, too, Elizabeth."

Could this really be happening? After so many dreams, where my daughter saw me from across a room. Sometimes she took my hand, in others she glided silently away. In my dreams Ruby had been an infant, a toddler, a teen, a woman. But now this would be her real adult voice on the phone, sounding as she always did.

"I love you, Ruby. I never stopped." I paused. "Do you want to get together?"

"Yes. But there's a lot to talk about. A lot to work through."

"I know there is. We can do it. We're still a mother and daughter. Ruby, I love you so much." My hand, wet with sweat, slipped on the phone. Yes, there would be a lot to talk about. Ten years of separate insights and all the previous years of our bond to understand.

"Will you come to Cambridge?"

"Yes. Just tell me when."

"I will. I'll call you back. I've gotta go."

Click.

That evening I'd tell Hannah: "Ruby called." I'd feel a tight, crooked smile pull one corner of my mouth to the side. Hannah would know what I meant—there was an open line—and if we were together she'd smile fondly back, shake her head, and wish, with me, that it were true.

Someday, I believed, it would be. A letter, a call, or a knock on the door. Ruby would be ready to talk or eager to yell. She knew where to find me. "Even if it's only a story I'm making up," I joked to Hannah, "it keeps me going, day to day. So why not tell that one instead of the one where she never comes back? And I've imagined this one so often, I really have come to believe it."

By then, the words that had so chilled me in Ruby's parting letter seemed merely histrionic. Dramatic. Everything in me was gentle toward her. *You were doing the best you knew how to do,* I thought, about her, and myself. *Brava, Ruby! I taught you to be strong, and you are, although not with a result I could have anticipated. I'm proud of you, my daughter. Just as I have been for all these years. I hope you are doing well.*

Every day I sent blessings and wondered, astonished anew by our separation, what Ruby's life held now.

PART THREE
2005

CHAPTER 15

Ruby

"Ruby, can you take Ella? She's chewing on the phone cord again!" That bitter January day I heard Asa before I saw him bounce into the living room, shaking his head in mock horror. Ella, bundled in a black and red striped sweater, clung to his hip. "I can't get any work done; I have to get this damn speech finished tonight or I won't sleep at all. She won't give me one second of uninterrupted work," he complained. But as he squinted down at his daughter, obviously unable to take his eyes off the charming wiggler in his arms, I noticed, once again, how like Che's his infectious personality was. Such a contrast to my own serious ways, although Ella put a song in my heart.

"Wait a sec, I'll take her," I told him, marveling, for the millionth time, at the contrast between my medium brown husband and our sandy-haired baby. "Give me five minutes." *Those recessive genes sure are something,* I thought. White people make their way into the room no matter what. No wonder they rule the world. *"United we stand,"* those genes must proclaim when they bump up against each other, *"united* we can break through any amount of brown." Maybe I could do my lecture on that one day. The power of white to penetrate Black. Look at what's happened to Africa. Now here in my own home . . . maybe because Asa's grandmother was white, too. That, in fact, was an initial bond. The white-lady ancestors, we named them. So the genes had a head start.

It was more than a passing thought since every time I gazed into Ella's green eyes I saw Elizabeth staring out. And now my baby was sprouting red hair. No matter how much I tried to "wash away the white," I told myself ruefully, here it was in my arms. I adored my daughter, but sometimes it was hard, damn hard, to see past my mother. I hadn't talked to Elizabeth in years. Which was just the way I wanted it. I didn't know if she was dead or alive—well, actually I did, because I knew Daddy would tell me if she passed. He dropped bits of news from time to time, but, to be honest, I wasn't sure I cared.

Yeah, I had those moments when the old lump would rise in my throat if I saw an African American mother and adult daughter stroll arm in arm on the street, engaged in an intimate tête-à-tête. I wished then I shared that kind of bond with my mother; there was nothing like it, having a heart-to-heart with someone who cared as much as the pair I watched visibly did. But since my mother was a self-centered bitch, what was the point of wishing for that intimacy? She was incapable of that kind of love. Claire had confirmed it when she'd diagnosed Elizabeth as narcissistic. I'd turn my head away from the sight of Black mother-daughter love and force myself to focus on the beauty of a leafy tree, to really take it in and enjoy nature's splendor. Or gaze into a shop window and choose my favorite item. Discipline—that's one knack I've had ever since I played sports as a kid, when I saw what willpower could accomplish. Or when I put my mind to baking cakes and muffins and pies and handed them out to the neighbors, creating joy instead of feeling sorry for myself. I had lots of practice diverting my attention from unwanted events when I lived with Elizabeth those last years.

Now, whenever that lump rose from my chest until sometimes it nearly choked me, I reminded myself of my closeness with Asa and how it nurtured me. I didn't need somebody who didn't need me.

"Ruby!" Asa stood in the middle of our Persian rug, watching me with the puzzled face I knew so well. He should have been used to my spacing out by now, but he still wondered where I went.

"Maaa . . ." Ella squirmed and reached out her arms.

"Five minutes, you said," he reminded me.

"Okay, okay, let me finish these notes for tomorrow. Honestly, one more minute and I'll take her to the park." I blew a kiss, watching while Ella reached her chubby arms to catch it, and turned back to my desk, a lovely white counter built into a sun porch that opened out from our living room.

In a minute I filed my notes, the final touches on the following day's lecture, "The Semiotics of the Dozens." Peering out at the gray day, though, I saw drops of sleet spatter the window and chose a bath for Ella instead of a walk. She loved to splash in one side of the double kitchen sink, swatting Ivory soap bubbles and chomping on her rubber duckie. I selected an Ella Fitzgerald CD, placed it in the Bose, nuzzled Ella's sweaty hair with my nose and toted her to her room off the kitchen. While she gurgled at the clown mobile and kicked her plump legs, I held her down with one hand. "'A-tisket a-tasket,'" I sang along, pressing my face into Ella's tummy, "'A green and yellow basket.' That's Miss Ella Fitzgerald." I blew hard on her stomach, creating a rubbery sound, until she let loose the cascade of giggles that triggered my own. Lifting my head, I saw my brown arm thrown across her tummy—white-white we used to call that pasty shade—and flashed on a startling question. Is this the way it was for Elizabeth when she undressed me? Was she shocked by her own alabaster arm against my robust copper body? For the first time, I wondered what she felt. Was it as strange for her as for me? For a brief, painful second I longed to ask her, before I resolutely turned my attention to the wiggly baby under my arms.

Ella, round and pudgy, twisted hard under my hands, shrieking and lifting her hands, signaling *up, up.* Holding her tight, I ran warm water in the sink, slid her in, and waited for the spray. She splashed the counter, me, and the floor while I willed myself to shake off my lapse. Imagine wanting to ask the witch anything! I wasn't going to put myself in that vulnerable spot, only to get the Lecture of the Week on who-knows-what about brown arms and white tummies. It's a clichéd image, she might say, one designed to comfort white liberals. If I were to press her—*How did you* feel?—she'd turn it into something abstract: *We were making the new world, blah blah blah.* Nonetheless, I felt that familiar lump and tears form behind my eyes, moistening my nostrils. *I want my mother.* The words flowed unbidden into my mind.

But it was impossible to ruminate for more than a moment with Ella. Every ounce of attention went to this slippery, giggling creature. I couldn't keep my eyes off her, and that new-baby joy flooded every part of me, washing away all thoughts of Elizabeth. "Sudsy," I giggled. "Sudsy, sudsy Ella."

Later, after Ella had been snuggled dry and I'd read a picture book, pointing to the mama bear and papa bear and grunting appropriately, I was seated at my slab of a desk, finding my way back into my work in the precious minutes while Ella napped. When we'd first moved into this place I was surprised at how familiar it felt. It took me a month to appreciate that I was back in Daddy's airy third-floor apartment, his first one back in Berkeley after he and Che moved out from our house. When I understood that I'd moved back into one of my most beloved homes, I doubly appreciated our new place. Now I was just settled into work when the ringing phone penetrated my happy concentration.

"Want me to get it in here?" I called to Asa.

"See who it is."

I glanced over. The number was Che's. We hadn't talked in weeks, maybe a month, but I had no time that afternoon. Still I decided to pick up just to say hello and set a phone date.

"Hey, bro."

"Ruby," he said, and I knew instantly from the tightness in his voice that this was not a let's-catch-up sibling call.

"Ruby," he repeated. "I just got a call from Dad's doctor. Sneed." He paused to let this sink in. "He's had a heart attack. It might not be serious but he's on his way to Harlem Hospital. In an ambulance."

Harlem Hospital. I felt the tears rise. It's the call every adult dreads, even though I believed my dad was indestructible. Other people's parents were felled by heart attacks, but not my sturdy father. "Oh no."

"Yeah, 'fraid so." His voice sounded as if every bit of vitality had been crushed out. "But he'll probably be okay. He was conscious and all. . . ."

"Shall I come down?" I swallowed while an odd pressure built in the bridge of my nose.

"He's only sixty-five. That's not old, these days. . . ."

"Do you want me to come? I've got a class tomorrow." *Tell me no,* I was thinking. *Say it's going to be all right. I'm really jammed right now, beginning a semester.* But while I was thinking schedule, the tears started down my cheeks.

"Why don't you wait and see. He could be out in a day or two. I'm going over now. I'll probably get there right after he does." Che attempted a feeble laugh, which only accentuated his flat tone. "Fortunately I don't have any gigs for the next coupla days. Lots of prep work, but I can manage. . . ." His voice, usually so bright and vigorous, kept trailing off. "I'm not going anywhere till next Tuesday. I've got a seminar in Chicago. I'll call you from the hospital. Gonna be home? Or on the cell."

Then his voice was gone. I sat stunned before I ran back to Asa, who was munching a bowl of cereal at our narrow kitchen counter.

"It's Daddy," I screamed, and hurled myself into his arms. Ella woke and we could hear her in her room, howling in sympathy.

Ten days later, on a Saturday morning, I was stepping off the Acela at Penn Station, pushing through the crowd. Nothing had gone as it should have. Another heart attack, a mild stroke, and then a respiratory infection they took too long to diagnose. He was still in the Acute Heart Care Unit, or whatever it was called. I'd talked to him three times a day. I couldn't believe how easy it was to reach him after I told the nurse I was his daughter. He was usually in his room except when he was off having interminable tests. Or new "procedures." Each day I could hear his voice grow weaker. Still I was not prepared for the sight of Solomon Jordan, the stern titan of my childhood, lying shriveled in a hospital gown, his wrists tied to the sides of the bed which were pulled up like a crib. Plastic tubes hung snaking their way under the covers. Tubes attached to needles stuck out of his arms.

"Daddy." I lunged for him, reaching over the metal bed frame. "Daddy, what's going on?" I was fighting tears, resolving, *I will not, will not cry in front of him.* "How are you feeling?"

"Pretty good. Come 'ere, baby." He reached out with his head, his neck stretching like a wild turkey's. "Untie these damn things." He wriggled his wrists, growling.

A smell of ammonia overwhelmed me. "I don't know, Daddy . . ." I leaned over and stroked his head, gently pushing it back on the pillow. "They must have them there for a reason." But my mind was blank. What could I possibly say that would be true when what I saw—before my very eyes—could not be happening?

"Let me loose!" He rattled the bed with his arms, struggling to shake off the restraints.

"We better ask someone. . . ." My voice kept dropping off.

Before I could speak again we were interrupted by a nurse, who walked in carrying a white plastic tray in one hand, reaching up to slide the curtain around his bed closed with the other. "Only going to take me a minute," she said, nodding me out toward the hall.

"I'll stay," I told her with my characteristic firmness, the will persisting through my shock like a decapitated chicken flapping on. The nurse ignored me. She was fussing with Daddy's blankets, yanking out a yellowish square of rubber sheet from under his buttocks. A strong smell hit my nostrils. I turned my head from the sight of his emaciated loins, embarrassed to catch even a glimpse of my father's naked body. When I looked back the nurse was reaching over to unhook a tube that was probably a catheter. "I'd like to speak to the doctor privately," I said when she finished. I had to get answers, tell them to take off the restraints, demand that they make him better. *This is not some old Black man who wandered in off the street!* I wanted to cry. *This is Solomon Jordan, who* . . . My thoughts kept wandering. But I had to do something. "Or . . ." I started to say, *"Or someone in charge"* until Daddy cut me off.

"Nothing you can say alone that you can't say in front of me." His low voice sounded stronger. "This is Judy. She knows all my secrets." He laughed like an old roué.

"You can try to catch the doctor in the morning," she replied calmly, her back to me, her eyes fixed on the monitor high up over the bed. She whipped out a pad and jotted a note, which I couldn't decipher, over her shoulder. "He does rounds about eight or eight thirty." Judy adjusted one of the tubes hanging from a large upside-down bottle and kept her eyes averted from mine. Che had filled me in, but why should my father, a healthy man, be lying in the hospital with a respiratory infection—one he didn't have ten days ago when he arrived here? It was making me crazy. I wanted to blow up the whole place if that would get them to notice: my dad is here and he doesn't look good.

"Remove the restraints please," I asked her. "They're agitating him."

"He was already agitated," she replied sharply. "That's why he has them. So he won't pull out the drip again."

"I'll speak to the doctor about it," I said after a long silence.

At last, after Judy left, I lowered myself onto a blue plastic chair I'd dragged over next to the bed so I could hold Daddy's hand. His breath was shallow, his eyes fluttered, and within minutes he seemed to be sleeping. We sat for an hour like that, me in a daze, he perhaps in a trance. When he looked firmly asleep I left his room, waiting until I was in the hall to cover my face with my hands and let the sobs engulf me. Feeling a hand on my back I peered out. An aide wrapped in green said quietly, "I know, I know." But he didn't.

That night, back at Che's apartment, when I relaxed with him, Cynthia, and their seven-year-old, Mia, over dinner, I found the child's presence reassuring. Her bubbly chatter, reciting the Spanish numbers she'd learned in school (*uno, dos . . .*), and her questions about the peanut sauce pasta, while she wrinkled her nose and pushed away her salad, distracted me. Next to Mia we held an empty chair open for her invisible friend, Diana, "seventeen years old," who visited every day, according to Mia. Cynthia's and Che's fears about Mia's fantasy had recently been allayed by Adam Gopnik's *New Yorker* essay about his daughter Olivia's imaginary playmate, Charlie Ravioli, which several friends had passed on to them. Now they actually set a plate for Diana, with bits of food spooned onto it by Mia before she recycled them into her own mouth.

After dinner Che took Mia into her bedroom, starting his hour-long bath and bedtime story ritual, while Cynthia and I cleaned up. Later, the three of us sat up for hours in the kitchen, reviewing the ten days Daddy had been in the hospital. "They can't figure it out," Cynthia told me unnecessarily over her fifth cup of coffee. Her blue eyes, usually vivid, were lidded, underscored with dark half-moons. Her teeth chattered, clicking and clacking. "But the doctors say it's typical for old men to get respiratory infections in the hospital. The viruses are rampant. So when people are older and weakened by illness they catch it." She shuddered and reached for the coffeepot. I'd heard of pneumonia as the "old man's friend," but never before had the odd designation sounded so cruel.

Che said less, sitting slumped in his chair, staring vacantly with hollow eyes. He sipped cognac, silent like a zombie. At midnight we agreed that the following day I'd be at the hospital before eight to catch the doctors on their rounds. I'd try to get all the information I could and impress upon them that Solomon Jordan had a family who cared and was exercising oversight. We hoped this would encourage their diligence and that at the very least they'd remove the humiliating, painful restraints.

The next two days were a blur of invasive tests. "Just give your permission, Mr. Jordan, for us to put this catheter into your heart. . . ." or "One more X-ray" and "A scan that should give us some answers . . ." The doctors kept trying to identify the virus that was running through Daddy's body, tearing it up like a war zone ravaged by bombs. Or maybe, they hinted darkly, he had some new strain of TB? All so mysterious and confounding; they shook their heads and clucked.

Forty-eight hours later Daddy started to hallucinate. "Where's the car?" he asked when I shuffled into his familiar room and bent to give him a kiss. His hands, untied by then, twitched, plucking at the white blanket covering his thin frame.

"I came by taxi," I told him, trying to stay calm.

"No, the car. To take me home."

"Daddy, you're too sick to go home today. . . ." Tears must have filled my voice. They weren't leaking from my eyes but my body felt jam-packed, as if the water level were up to my nose and I was gasping, starting to drown.

"The car, so you and Che can lift the bed in . . ." The jerking motions increased. "It has to be big enough . . ." His eyes roamed the ceiling while his hands were in endless motion, tugging at the blanket, trying, perhaps, to lift him out of this hell.

"Don't worry," Dr. Sneed told me when I tracked him down later that afternoon. "Your father is experiencing what we call ICU psychosis. It's a temporary condition from being confined in the hospital too long. It often occurs after a week or ten days in one room."

I remained silent, furious, letting my rigid body show my rage.

"And the plucking motions at the covers are simply random motions, a side effect of the morphine. Paradoxically, anxiety. Once he's home again, that will pass."

"Home?" I couldn't imagine Daddy pulling out of this. He was weaker every day, dozing in fits and starts. He never slept at night.

"They come in every hour . . ." Daddy explained, patiently, "opening the door, checking the monitors, rubbing my back. It's a regular spa." He attempted a chuckle, but all that emerged was a feeble snort.

By Wednesday Daddy had shrunk another five pounds. He was a long, frail weed. "Everything tastes sweet," he complained, turning his head away from the spoonfuls of Jell-O and cottage cheese I held in front of his mouth. A nurse dashed in and told me, sotto voce, shaking her head as if she were describing a naughty child, "He's not eating anything." I could see why. The oxygen mask he wore constantly made every mouthful, every sip, an ordeal. There was no doubt he was significantly weaker, with fluttering eyelids.

That night I ran to a health food store I'd seen on Broadway around the corner from Che's apartment and demanded their highest-protein drink mix. The clerk handed me a large green cardboard container guaranteeing "immediate health. The body responds to nature, to the sea where we come from. Only one spoonful—" The text gracefully looped over a picture of splashing blue-green sea drenched in sunshine. The next morning I whipped up five tablespoons in the blender, determined I'd get Daddy to drink a cup of green nourishment. This would give him vigor, I was sure, to fight off the infection. Hours later I carried the precious drink to the hospital in a Starbucks thermos and as soon as I reached the room I begged Daddy to take a few sips. "Here, Daddy." I pressed the bent straw to his lips. "You need your strength," I pleaded, remembering how he'd cajoled me into spoonfuls of oatmeal when I'd turned my head and buttoned my lips at age five or six, gagging at the sight of the gelatinous mess. "It's natural spirulina and kelp, no sugar." But he tightened his lips and twisted his head from side to side, waving me away. "Everything's sweet," he mumbled through the mask, his face contorting with distaste. "Horribly sweet."

Each morning Che, who'd joined my nutrition-will-cure-Daddy crusade, and I attempted another "treat." We came up with a dyna-mite chicken broth that Che made from scratch, boiling a chicken until the kitchen reeked with the stench, then pouring the broth into the trusty thermos. "Jewish penicillin," we reassured each other. "It's what he needs." Hey, if the doctors couldn't figure it out, we would. Chicken broth, we learned from an online site, "contains the essential nutrients and trace elements needed to heal any infec-tion." This was going to do the trick. Within days Daddy would rally, gain strength, and be out of the hospital in a week. But try as we might to get more than one spoonful of magic broth into him, we failed.

Obsessively we conducted frantic nightly searches to find the latest research on herbal and nutritional cures for infections. If only we found the right one, we were convinced, and could locate it in time, Daddy would get better. One day we tried a spoonful of brown rice (all those essential B vitamins) with a drop of gravy on it; another day, a strawberry health powder stirred in "smart water"; the combination was supposed to generate miracle powers. Then crushed garlic, "a natural antibiotic," we assured each other. Each day, Daddy would take one bite or sip before we'd hear the piteous refrain, "Too sweet."

All right, I thought, *here's something that's not sweet: cod liver oil,* which "checks the development of emaciation," I learned online. I ran out of the hospital to buy virgin-pressed, organic cod liver oil and rushed back, my elixir in hand. But upon hearing what it was, Daddy refused to even try it. The next day he refused again, our final offer: oatmeal porridge, also alleged to have medicinal properties. When he wrenched his face away, lips clamped shut, we gave up our attempts at a dietary solution.

At our wits' ends, Che and I initiated a twenty-four-hour watch. We thought it might reassure Daddy, who acted increasingly agitated, to have one of us there. And we still attempted to get a spoonful of food into him at odd hours. The first night, Che sat up in a huge brown vinyl chair he dragged in from the waiting room. Deep into the dark, he read aloud essay after essay from that masterpiece of poetry and scholarship, DuBois's *The Souls of Black Folk.* Toward morning, he said, Daddy couldn't stop moaning. At one point, just as dawn came crawling in on slow feet, when Che couldn't take any more of that deep whimpering sound, he was afraid Daddy was about to slip away. But the night nurse, Carol, the one we liked so much, whispered to him that Daddy was the strongest person his age she'd ever seen. She definitely expected to see him again the following day after her night off. That sounded promising, even though he resembled a sack of bones strung loosely with rope. "She must know what she's talking about," we said, bolstering each other. "She's a nurse." We tried to ignore his raggedy, gaunt demeanor, the eyes drilled back in their sockets.

Saturday night at the apartment, Che told me Elizabeth had called from California that afternoon. When she heard of our all-night vigils, she offered to fly out and take a shift, staying over one or two nights. "You wouldn't have to see her," Che offered, his face gray with fatigue. "But I'd like her to come. Obviously she wouldn't stay here."

"No," I said instinctively. "I'm sorry, bro, but I can't do that now.

I'm stretched thin as a rubber band. It's way too complicated." That was one person I refused to run into. Not now. My reserves were on zero.

"She wants to say good-bye." His dark eyes implored. "Just in case. That was her husband you know. And they've become good friends—"

"Che, I can't. She abandoned him all those years ago, how does she think she can jump in now when everything is falling apart? *Now* she wants to say good-bye. It's a little late. He's our Daddy, he's not her anything. If she comes I leave." I began to cry. "She can't . . ."

He stared at me as if I weren't making sense, but clearly he was too exhausted to fight. All he said, quietly, was, "She's my mother and I'd like her to be here. I think Daddy would, too."

"All right, all right," I relented. "One night, one morning. I'll sleep in. Let me know when she's coming and when she's gone."

"Thanks, sis." He patted my shoulder and staggered off to bed.

Three days later, after I'd been in New York for the longest week of my life—talk about not sleeping—I sat in the blue plastic chair next to Daddy's bed holding his icy hand, lifting the bones to my lips. It was a Sunday. Elizabeth had come and gone and I'd successfully avoided her, refused to allow myself even the thought of her nearby. But when I'd caught a whiff of a ripe purple plum at the health food store on the morning she was supposedly in town, childhood memories of my mother slurping the juicy fruit, her favorite, tumbled in, one after another. I saw her face suffused with pleasure, juice spilling from her lips while she feasted. I remembered the taste of this sweet fruit on our backyard tree, which I too had loved, but not allowed myself for decades. When I excised my mother, I'd excised plums, too. Now I stifled the sob gathering in my chest before it rose to my throat. This was no time to allow my mother anywhere near my bursting heart. Elizabeth O'Leary or whatever she called herself these days was not going to waltz in and ruin these moments with my father, not going to hog up the limelight. I stormed out of the store, nearly running from the tantalizing smell of purple plums.

Now the fluorescent light over Daddy's bed wouldn't shut off and the oxygen mask slipped onto his chin. When I reached over, for the tenth time, to pull the band tighter, he told me, "Your mother . . . if anything happens to me . . ."

"What mother?" I muttered, gagging on the smells in the room: disinfectant, unwashed body, and an uneaten tray of food—a puddle of beef, mashed potatoes, wilting salad, and the omnipresent Jell-O, which a young woman in blue delivered three times a day and left moldering until the next meal arrived.

Daddy squeezed my hand and murmured faintly, "Come closer. This is important." I hopped up on the edge of the bed and perched there, leaning down so my face was six inches from his lips. "I want you to hear me. Contact her. You'll need each other. Ruby, don't be a fool and spend the rest of your life estranged from your own flesh and blood."

He stopped, exhausted. I didn't think he'd have the strength to say more until I heard a mumble through the slippery mask. "Our people have too much history . . . of that . . ."

Oh no, I thought, *I can't believe it, he's fucking dying in here, and he's talking to me about "our people."* But I listened.

"Slavery ripped mothers from daughters. And later, people hopping the train north fast as they could never had the money to go home." Miraculously, the reedy, frail voice emerged, slowly, each word an effort. "Or they were passing, so they couldn't go home. Ruby, baby, that's one tradition of the Black family I don't want you to inherit. Cookie—Keisha"—he attempted a feeble joke at her expense—"tried to tear you once—"

"You say, 'the Black family.' She's not even Black. Just a wannabe!" I burst out, trying to mock Elizabeth in the easy way I often did, but my voice sounded shrill, sharp, even to me. It didn't come out with the casual scorn I'd intended. "She's an egomaniacal, neglectful—" I stammered.

"Ruby, she's part of our family and we are a Black family. You, me, Che." He stopped. "Elaine . . ." I was surprised that he put her in the family list, since they'd split a couple of years before, after she'd moved around the corner to take care of her mother. He paused again, sounding as if he couldn't possibly go on. But he did. Each word took an eternity. "And Elizabeth. The white part of our Black family." He stared at me over the mask, unblinking, as if he intended to impale the words in my breast. "You've got some white in you, too, girl. Deal with it." He paused to let it sink in. "She's your mother, Ruby. You can't escape that, no matter how far you run and how deep you hide. Elizabeth O'Leary Jordan . . ." He was out of breath. ". . . is your mother, the only one you've got." He paused again and rasped, "Make the best of it. Someday you must reconcile. Show some mercy. It might as well be now." His eyelids fluttered and closed. The effort had clearly exhausted him. But he continued murmuring, even more softly. I leaned in so I was lip-reading as much as hearing. "She didn't do a bad job, either. You. Che." He stopped, out of breath. "It's time to reach out, my God, after all these years. Open your heart, let her into your life. " The words were as faint as soap bubbles coming from his mouth, nearly vanishing into thin air before I could get to them. "Ella," he mumbled. "Ella . . . a grandmother."

"She has Elaine," is all I said, wishing again that Asa's mom hadn't passed away only three months before Ella's birth. It was so horribly unfair that she never got to see her first grandchild. She came so close. Dying at sixty-six, like Black people do. I closed my heart like a clam. How's that for legacy? But I listened.

"Promise me," he said then, raising the stakes impossibly. "Promise me . . ." He waved his long hands and grimaced. ". . . you'll contact your mother."

I took the biggest breath in the world. "I don't want to talk about this now, Daddy."

"Promise me." His eyes were closed, his voice so feeble that I couldn't imagine how he was going to live another minute. Each word arrived on a feather of air. "Promise." This sounded like the last breath he could marshal.

"But she . . ."

"Promise," I barely heard.

"She's not my—"

He tightened his grip on my hand with surprising strength.

"I promise." *Don't die.*

"Remember. Or I'll haunt you." He uttered a hoarse laughing sound.

A chill rippled through me. *Please don't die.* But how much more of this hospital could he take? The doctors still hadn't figured out what strain of pneumonia was wasting his body, his muscles melting like butter on a hot afternoon. The cardiologist and the pulmonologist had thrown every drug they had into his poor body. He was refusing our natural remedies, and nothing was working. The next day, if he still wasn't eating, they were planning to insert a feeding tube, an intervention we'd all resisted.

Now he said, with astonishingly renewed vigor so I could actually hear the words, every syllable formed perfectly, even through the dreaded mask, "Remember *agape.*"

"What?" He'd gone completely around the bend.

"Dr. King's *Agape.* Unconditional love. Willingness to forgive, not seven times, but seventy times seven." He was clearly forcing the words out, but they were flowing, softly.

I couldn't believe he was talking this bullshit now, when all my life I'd heard how he and Elizabeth had blown off that crap. Elaine, too. *Dr.* King? They'd nicknamed him "Da Lawd." They had clucked when he swept into one town after another with his entourage, vowing, in that deep velvet voice, "We shall not be moved." Then, after he got the sheriffs good and mad, he'd fly out of town the next day to hold yet another press conference while the hometown folks had to deal with the backlash. I never knew Daddy had changed his mind about King. He was a stone Malcolm man. Maybe he's having a deathbed conversion, I thought. But that ain't me. No sir, you can leave agape where you found it, as far as I'm concerned, back in Greece or wherever the hell it came from.

Agape . . . I remembered my parents doubled up with laughter when Daddy quoted King. "Since the white man's personality is so distorted by segregation, and his soul is greatly scarred, then he *needs* the Negro's love." Daddy could make his voice sound just like King's, with that deep, slow roll, and all that southern timbre. "The Negro must therefore looove the white man, to remove his tensions, insecurities, and fears." Daddy would make a face, and they would howl. "Damn! Who's gonna looove the Negro?" they'd ask each other. Then Daddy would mock in his scriptural tone: ". . . a way through the sea and a path through the mighty waters." All from agape, they'd sniffed. And now Daddy was quoting the good Dr. King. I was surprised he didn't say "the *Reverend Dr.* Martin Luther King Jr."

"You've made up a story," Daddy panted. "About your mother. We all do." With one last effort he pushed out, "That's how we live. She used to say that all the time. She's probably made one up about you, too." He closed his eyes, and within moments he was asleep at last.

That night in Che's overheated study, which doubled as a guest room, I wrote Daddy a letter retracting my commitment. We'd corresponded for so many years by mail that it was a familiar means of communication. Even though writing didn't come easily to me he was an easy audience. It used to feel as though I were with him. I could hear him listening as I wrote, hear his mm-hmms. Exhausted,

I simply penned a note: "Dearest Daddy, I love you so, but I cannot do this thing you are asking. I cannot contact Elizabeth. Too much water has gone under the bridge for us to get back together. My life is going along smoothly. I have you and Che and Asa and Ella, plus all my friends and my work. I don't want to complicate my life by engaging with Elizabeth's weirdness. Please understand. Much love, Ruby." Then I tucked the note in my pants pocket and hurried back to the kitchen where Auntie Cookie and Auntie Belle, having just arrived from Atlanta, were solemnly holding vigil. Despite the ten years when Auntie Cookie hadn't spoken to Daddy after that court case in my childhood, she was fully on the scene now. No one would ever know how bitter that estrangement had been, how much suffering it caused them both.

"You're so thin," Auntie Cookie greeted me, her bent body showing her anguish. Auntie Belle simply embraced me, saying, "Sugar," and as soon as her heavy arms circled my back, she hung on and wept.

At dawn the next morning when I staggered into Daddy's room with the day's new nutritional drink, a fifty-dollar shake I'd had overnighted from an online pharmacy, my hand reached in my pocket, feeling for the note I was prepared to deliver. Daddy gave me a hoarse, "Hey, baby." His eyes were closed and it sounded as if he were talking in his sleep until he sighed and I heard a quiet bark, more like a squeak. ". . . a time to be born and a time to die, and I think my time has come." His fingers were grasping air. He was twitching, moving without stopping. I heard him cry out, "Mama Jean!" and moan, "Mama, Mama."

Terrified, I ran out to the hall to call Che on my cell. "Get over here now, with the aunties. Daddy's losing it." Then I ducked into the bathroom for a quick cry. The tears only stayed inside for brief periods by this point. Afterward, I leaned over the sink to splash my face with cold water; my face tingled and I felt better, surprised to catch sight of myself in the glare of the mirror. The bright bathroom lights showed a haggard, gray, scrawny woman with puffy eyes. *Hell,* I remember thinking, *I'm so drawn I hardly look Black. Maybe that white is busting out.*

When I pushed open the heavy door to the Critical Care Unit and peered into the heavy fluorescent lights of that surreal world, the pulmonologist, on his way out, mumbled, "Oh, they just paged you. Jordan family." He gave me a quizzical squint, which I didn't know how to read. When I dashed into Daddy's room—I must have been gone no more than five or six minutes—a new nurse, a white girl who looked fifteen, was holding his wrist and staring up at the monitor. The number 0 showed in neon blue light.

The young nurse held me around the waist while I screamed. I leaned into her, furious, bawling, until she faced me, eyes level with mine, and declared, "He made the choice to go. It was his choice."

"No!" I kept shouting, while she was steady telling me, "He made the choice. He was ready."

"No! How do you know? You didn't even know him. No!"

"He made the choice to go alone. When no one was in the room. That's how they do it. Either they pass when everyone is standing around the bed or they wait until they're alone. Lots of old people go that way."

"He isn't old. He's only sixty-five," I sobbed, shrieking for maybe ten minutes, surprised by this young girl's strength. Even when I flung myself on Daddy, she never wavered from her point: he had chosen to go.

After I stopped screaming she asked, "Would you like to be alone with your father?" My tears fell on the sheets while I kissed his still-warm face, the top of his balding head, the long hands I'd held so many times. I stroked him, wild, groping to touch him while I could. "I love you, Daddy," I repeated. When Che and Auntie Cookie and Auntie Belle burst in we started kissing Daddy all together, crying.

"You did a good job, Dad." Che spoke softly. "Fly away home. Blessings on your soul, peace, my father, move along, do what you need to do."

Auntie Belle and Auntie Cookie looked as if a stun gun had blasted them into a horrified silence. Their mouths hung slack, their eyes stared uncomprehendingly. They hadn't arrived at the hospital in time to see their younger brother alive: this gaunt skeleton would be their final image of Solomon Jordan, the baby brother of their youth. My heart went out to these two loyal sisters: Daddy and Cookie had finally effected a reconciliation after years of uncomfortable family gatherings where she passed messages to him—"Don't hog up all that corn bread!"—through others, and now, when she could have enjoyed her old age with her brother, he was gone. Out of her original family of five, only she and Auntie Belle remained.

"We love you," I added, hugging Daddy. I wanted to squeeze and pinch him, slap him back to life. I was still sitting on the side of the bed kissing him when Che started to rifle through Daddy's wallet. He found a card with the name of a Harlem funeral home ("Thank you, Daddy") and called on his cell, even though it wasn't allowed in Critical Care. I heard Che's monotone "Yes, the name is Solomon Jordan," and knew that he, too, was struck, every nerve cell deadened so he could function. We all four must have sat with Daddy for a couple of hours. It didn't seem long, but an older nurse came in eventually, carrying a white shroud in a transparent plastic bag, and said that she had to put Daddy in it before her shift was over at three and she had lots of paperwork to do. We asked her to wait until we could gather up his belongings, but first: "Could you take off his gold ring?" Auntie Belle asked quietly. It was Grandpa Jonah's; Daddy had worn it ever since his father's homecoming. The nurse tried, twisting the ring back and forth, but it stuck fast, giving me horrible visions of the undertaker sawing off the finger. At last, patiently wielding a bar of soap, she slid the ring off and handed it to Auntie Belle, who sprang to life, burbling through the tears that streaked her face. We hurriedly crammed a suitcase and a plastic bag with the clothing and remnants of healthful drink mixes that Daddy had accumulated during his two-week stay. The young nurse ripped the Get Well cards off the wall where Elaine had taped them, and several other nurses and aides wandered into the room to hug us good-bye. Che and I hauled everything down to the ground floor on a cart, using the large service elevator covered with a gray quilted carpet. We met the aunties in the lobby. For the last time we walked out the front door of Harlem Hospital, numb and in shock.

Flying home from the homecoming five days later—the memorial celebration, Daddy's pastor called it—I was still shaken. It could not be true. My father could not be gone. At one point in the service, jammed with musicians and civil rights activists, an old friend sang "You've Gotta Sing What the Spirit Says Sing." When he inserted, "You've gotta Solomon when the spirit says Solomon," Che and I clung to each other. It was small consolation that Daddy had died on February 1. Speakers at the memorial repeatedly pointed out that this man who lived and breathed the Movement had died on the forty-fifth anniversary of the Greensboro sit-in, the historic day when, one speaker said, "On February 1, 1960, four brave students marched down to Woolworth's and struck the match that fired up a whole generation of Solomon Jordans."

It wasn't fair. Daddy was a healthy man. The hospital had killed him with their incompetence. I knew it and Che knew it, but he didn't want to bring a suit, even when I promised to find a pro bono lawyer. "That would corrode years of our lives," Che argued with me. "And it won't bring Daddy back. Let's spend our time remembering him, honoring him. That's what he'd want." He was probably right. But on the way home all I could think was: *It'll take years to absorb this blow.* I was trying to remember the words of the Twenty-third Psalm, which Auntie Cookie had sung, beautifully, in a strong singing-in-the-choir-all-these-years alto. No wonder she still sang the lead at her church. "He maketh me to lie down in green pastures." I wished I could.

"It was so weird to see Elizabeth," I murmured to Asa, snuggling against his shoulder. We'd upgraded to the first-class bulkhead, which each time felt like its own private universe, with its roomy gray leather seats and no one in front of us. "So strange. Her hair's half gray. She's old. Did you see how her neck is sagging?"

He hardly knew Elizabeth, really, but ever since that day when I'd written her the cut-off letter and he'd cautioned me to reconsider, he continued to question my refusal to see her, no matter what I said. And Elizabeth was always so *nice* to him the few times they'd met—"to colored people in general," I'd explained, "she smiles and carries on. 'Please' and 'thank you,' she makes sure to say, again and again. The lower their social class, the nicer she is, tumbling over herself to convey that she *understands*—good white savior that she was—that you all are *people*." All that awkward niceness she exuded made me sick, but Asa, who underneath that nonchalant demeanor of his didn't have any more patience than I with white liberals, still reminded me, each time I brought her up, that someday I might regret this decision.

Today he said, "That's your mother, Ruby. Mine wasn't perfect either. Moms aren't." Here he looked at me significantly. "But I'd give anything to see my mother for one day. For one hour."

"I could see her inspecting me." I nuzzled on the rough wool of Asa's jacket, oddly comforted by the abrasion against my face. The scratchy sensation reminded me that I had a body, with feeling.

"Staring. That hungry look. God, the last time was . . ." I crinkled my nose trying to remember, while the flight attendant brought me a china cup of steaming water with lemon.

"At Che's house, after Mia had that accident," Asa said, finishing my thought, as he was often able to do. "You didn't talk to her then either, did you?"

"No."

I hadn't told Asa about the promise—the classic pledge extracted by a dying man—or how I didn't have a chance to hand Daddy my retraction. I wondered again why he did it. God! Had Elizabeth asked him to intervene, when he was so sick, so vulnerable. Is that why she wanted to say good-bye? That was just like her disgusting egocentric self. My mind twisted back and forth, trying to escape the knot. Who could I turn to for help? Normally when I was stuck, Daddy was the one I'd ask. Or Asa. I opened *The New Yorker* to bury myself in its nonsense. The red-lettered headings for The Talk of the Town reassured me: some things stay the same. At Shouts & Murmurs I nodded off, dreaming that Daddy was calling. I heard his voice on the telephone and rose up to shout, "He's alive!" When I started awake, I panicked. I'd sneered at the platitude that a person's spirit lives on. But the mood stayed with me. Daddy *was* alive. *Baby*, he was saying inside me still, in a voice as strong as ever. *Respect yourself, all of you. Respect your family.*

I opened my eyes and stretched my neck, side to side, before I burrowed deeper into Asa's shoulder. So this is what my quiet husband had meant after his mother passed, the things that I'd thought were bullshit. Her spirit lingered around him, he swore. Daddy was here, but everything had changed, even time. Now it was moving slower and faster, all at once. Me and Che, me and Asa and Ella. And . . . the problem of my mother. May she fade away. I drifted back to sleep, craving my father's voice, hungering after those familiar tones warming my ears.

*   *   *

"Maa," Ella cried, moving quickly, her right leg sticking out in the odd way she crawled, scooting down the hall when she heard the front door latch. "Maa!" Moving ahead of LaDean, our part-time nanny, Ella grabbed my ankle until I scooped her up. She locked her legs around my waist and leaned over to Asa, squeezing herself between us. "Daa!"

I glanced over at LaDean. "Did you pour Miracle-Gro on her?" Could Ella have grown in two weeks? She looked inches taller, longer in the torso, and her whole body felt more solid. The smooth baby skin rubbing against my face amazed me anew. Her Raffi CD wafted into the hallway, I started to clap along, and it all felt like home, normal life, until I flashed on an image of myself jumping on Elizabeth after she'd been away. I was a small child then, clinging to my mother. A new fear shocked my frayed nervous system like a lightning strike: What if someday Ella were to cut me off? I couldn't imagine what would cause her to run from me, but the alarm was a novel sensation. *Is this grief?* I wondered, while my lips smiled into Ella's sunny face and my ears listened to LaDean telling me that Ella had just eaten "a big-girl supper." Would sorrow worm its way into my every vein now, popping up when I least expected it, lending even ordinary moments an undercurrent of doubt? What if Ella decided to pass when she grew up, I suddenly worried. And wanted to disown me, the telltale African American mother. She'd certainly be light enough. Or, I fretted, cradling my precious girl in my arms, was I already a dinosaur, clinging to outmoded racial categories? What will this pale-skinned child call herself when she grows up? A chill ran through me until I willed my whole self back into the moment, back to Ella's strong arms pushing against my embrace as she tried to wiggle free.

Days later I found myself furious at an old man shuffling by our house. He limped slowly, hunched over, listing to one side while he dragged a fluffy white dog on a pink leash. Why should *he* live when my father had died? He was ancient, decrepit, years older than Daddy, who had stood up straight and tall until his final days. It was unfair that this feeble white man should have the luxury of living on when my healthy father was cut down.

I fiddled with the dozen death certificates we'd ordered—what an awful invention—and was appalled to realize that while I was sitting at my desk watching the grizzled guy on the street with his stupid battered tan hat tugging on his dog, I was wishing he would fall down dead. Or the disobedient dog would dash into the street and be smashed by a car. As if that would bring Daddy back. But I wanted the grief to spread, seep over the world. I had too much to hold inside. Everyone should suffer.

Asa walked up behind me and leaned over. "How're you doing, honey?"

I whipped around in my seat and glared. "Not very well." If he loved me enough, he'd reach through the veil and pull Daddy back.

"Whoa," he said. "We're in a mood, aren't we?"

I hated that patronizing tone. "My daddy died!"

"I know," he snapped. "Everyone's daddy dies, eventually. Join the human race."

"Thanks for the support." I turned away.

"Look, I've been damn supportive." His voice was cold. "I've taken care of Ella, way more than my share, so we didn't have to pay extra to LaDean. I went to New York for the service, I . . ."

"I don't need the list," I interrupted. "When your mother died, you weren't exactly heaven to live with. It took months."

Silence. "I know. Let's take it from the top. How 'bout a hug?" He stretched his arms out.

"I'm really busy getting all this stuff out." My voice was tight, ripe for a fight. I pointed accusingly at the unruly pile of *death certificates* stashed on top of photos of Daddy and articles about him to paste up. As if Asa had created it all. Or that old-timer on the street. If only I could find out who had created this nightmare, making Daddy suffer in the hospital and die, I could shake them, rattle their bones. If only I had someone to blame, I'd get them to do right, confess, make it up. And Solomon Jordan would reappear.

"I know," Asa said, his voice cracking. "I'm sorry."

I stood up and let him squeeze my shoulders, allowing a few tears to trickle out of the sea inside. "I miss him."

He gripped me harder. "I know you do."

"No you don't!" I exploded, pushing him away. Nobody had a Daddy as good as mine.

"Your dad was a wise man, and you're lucky you had him for thirty-eight years," Asa said, trying to put his arms back around me. "His vibration was high. When he returns, he'll be at an even higher-level vibration, strengthening the next generation."

This talk, coming from my lawyer husband, always bewildered me. How could a lawyer, for God's sake, be that airy? But even though I was skeptical—my atheist gene, a legacy from Elizabeth, kicked in—his words soothed me. Shaking Asa off, I crossed the floor to the altar he'd erected on our antique credenza near the front door and saw my favorite photo of Daddy, taken years before: he was smiling directly at the camera, fist in the air, a radiant warrior. In front of the picture a prayer candle flickered in a glass. To the side, sweet grass and sage rested on kente cloth. At the back of the credenza a sepia-toned baby picture in a cardboard frame sat propped against the wall. Grandma Jean held him in her arms, gazing down with pure adoration, and here, too, he stared at the camera, looking like a sparkle on the Fourth of July.

I smiled back at Daddy through a film of tears and decided to add the letters he'd written me when I was a lonesome teenager, bereft after he moved to New York. If I reread them with a prayer, maybe our ancestor Miss Ella, the one he wrote about, would inspire me. Hearing about her perseverance had given me direction years ago, when I didn't know which way to turn, and simply put my feet, one in front of the other, every day, just like she and her mother, Rose, did. In my case, it had meant staying in school and living with my mother. Every day had been a struggle.

Retrieving the packet of letters from my study, where they rested in a place of honor next to a first edition of *The Souls of Black Folk*, I placed them on the altar. But I slid one out of the batch and scanned it. Calmed and once more enchanted by my father's words, I flipped pages, remembering how comforted I'd been by Ella's mother, Rose, who had lost her own mother to the Louisiana cotton fields as a teenager, at a time when I was losing my mother: a mama who, after her divorce, seemed to drift away, into a world of adulthood, a world of loneliness, of drunkenness, of whiteness, of activism—a world I didn't know how to follow her into any more than Rose knew how to find her mother buried in the cotton plantations of the deep South. My eyes locked on Daddy's familiar words while my heart skipped a beat.

Tears trickled onto a page already puckered. This time the salty beads were for Daddy, dying too young, but the ache blended into grief for Ella and all the nameless others who'd lost parents in a sudden, brutal moment. Now that I was a mother my heart clutched, too, for the countless mothers torn from their young. And I was crying for myself, still feeling the sting of being suddenly fatherless as well as motherless. Trembling, I read aloud, the spoken words blending with the memory of my young teenage voice, so that I heard layers of sound:

The horse began to pull the creaky buggy along the rutted dirt road, is the way the old family tale goes. Rose's last sight of her mother was of her face, partially covered by her bonnet. Her mother, whose name we sadly do not know today, never was seen or heard from again.

A nonsense rhyme flitted into mind. We'd recited it when I was young, slapping hands and jumping rope: "Blood red, ruby red, this way, that way, old Joe fled." Coded knowledge, I imagined, passed down through the enslaved generations. Perhaps one of the ancestors was speaking to me after all. Even though the clue was faint, it gave me solace. But what was the way?

A week later Ella was dozing in her jogger, her sweet head with its copper curls lolling off to one side, and I was nodding, too, sitting on a bench in Hastings Park, down near the river. In summer it's my favorite shady spot. But that early March day, when I thought of the Charles River, Miss Rose came to mind, following her river and then the underground railroad to New York so long ago. *Thank you, ancestor,* I wanted to say, *thank you for making it.* The willow branches in the park swayed in the breeze. I gently rocked the jogger, tilting my face up to catch some late winter afternoon sun, which felt pleasantly warm on my cheeks. I was reaching over to touch Ella's forehead, checking whether she was too hot, when a well-dressed white woman with four-inch heels and a black Tumi briefcase accosted me.

"Do you have other days available?" she asked brusquely, glancing down at Ella.

"Beg your pardon?" My head jerked up, startled out of my sun- and fatigue-induced trance.

"I was wondering if you had other days available," she repeated, tapping her foot. "And references, of course."

I had no idea what she was talking about. For a second I thought she might be from the department, or the administration, and she was asking whether I could teach another class. But that wouldn't be happening here, not like this.

"We've been trying to find a nanny for weeks," she began, her impatient foot beating time with her quick words.

Still my mind wasn't grabbing on.

"We have . . ." I started to say, "We have a good one, but I don't think she has any more time," when, like dawn breaking at one specific moment, after half an hour of creeping light, I understood and, in a flash, I saw what she saw: a brown woman in jeans and head wrap, rocking what she thought was a white child's stroller. I decided to complete the sentence as I'd mentally begun it, maintaining my dignity by refusing to acknowledge the picture she perceived. "We have . . . a good one, but she's fully booked." I smiled coolly, dismissing her, while instinctively I bent over to give Ella a protective touch.

And now it was the white woman's turn to be thrown off balance. I could actually see her puzzled, quick brain working: it was like observing a cutaway science graphic, watching the synapses—painted red for the illustration—firing, one after another, with tiny explosions, until the necessary connections had been made and she, too, understood our exchange. Eyes averted, she mumbled a brief apology for the "misunderstanding" before clicking away, briefcase lightly swinging with each stiletto step.

The nanny. This was the second time it had happened, but evidently the first incident had left such a light groove in my brain that I wasn't prepared. Thank goodness Ella was asleep. She would not have understood the words, but might have picked up the discomfort. Again, involuntarily, I thought of Elizabeth. What had happened with her, back in the sixties? She never spoke about it. People would not have assumed she was the nanny, but what did they think? I do remember how tightly she held me when we went out in public, a habit I'd construed as part of her neurosis, her need to be publicly identified with African Americans. It had never occurred to me that she might have been trying to protect me by indicating, without speaking, that we were family. A wave of visceral memory flooded me; I heard her high soprano voice warbling out, "I'm stickin' to the union," when she tucked me into bed, smoothing back the hair from my forehead, and my breath relaxed into the deep comfort of her hand, her song. Shaken, I rose, swiveled the kelly green jogger in the direction of home, and began to run. As I turned the corner a black dog lumbered across our path. The way its shaggy body moved, limping slightly, reminded me of Rosa in her final years, and a longing rose in me like a tide.

CHAPTER 16

Ruby

"Imani," I said breathlessly, catching the phone on the last possible ring before voice mail kicked in. Ella and I had just come home from giving out bread on the street. It's a thing I still do: bake loaves and loaves of oat bread and a tray or two of muffins. I love kneading the dough and the baking aroma that wafts through the house, filling it with a sweet smell of home, security. Safety. This day, after I'd kept one loaf for us and a couple of muffins, I stuffed the rest in the jogger—jamming a few loaves down by Ella's feet—and rolled out the door to give them away to homeless people. Not *the* homeless. I can't stand it when people say "*the* homeless." Like "*the* poor," as if that's all they are, instead of people, first.

I've loved cooking ever since Elizabeth stopped doing it when I was a kid. It was a way I took care of myself, whipping up treats in huge batches for me and Che and anybody else who was around, neighbors and even, sometimes, passersby. Massive cooking is still a habit. It's how I take care of people, one of my ways of giving back. Teaching is cool, too, but this is so immediately satisfying. And since I cook in huge quantities, especially baked goods, years ago

Asa suggested I take "the extra" to the street. Now I like to do it with Ella, giving her a taste of community and generosity.

"Imani, damn, girl, I'm glad to hear your voice."

She'd been calling for weeks, ever since she missed Daddy's service because of her job at the new National Underground Railroad Freedom Center in Ohio. This was the first time she'd caught me. "Oh, Ruby, I was so sorry to hear about your dad. Wow . . . these dads." Imani's voice sounded full and rich like it had forever, and immediately I was pulled into the warmth of her orbit. It had been too long.

Ella was yanking books off the shelf, causing a crash that put a worried look on her face. Her lips fell down at the corners and I could see she was about to cry. I held out my arms, but when she didn't crawl over and I saw that she'd recovered, I pointed to the center of the room where she had a basket of toys. "Go there," I mouthed.

Imani's dad had passed a few years before. It hadn't seemed significant to me then, especially because they'd never been close, but now I understood that their emotional distance might not have made a difference. Or possibly even made the loss worse. "Yeah," I said. "These big spirits. It's tough."

Ella plopped down, *whoosh,* in the middle of the living room. Sitting, she turned over a wicker basket of toys, pulled out a pile of red stacking cubes and a pop-beads necklace in black and yellow and green and red, the one Imani had sent her, that Ella took on and off, on and off, working it over her head with difficulty, but obviously pleased, each time. After Imani and I chatted—Ella content with her toys and necklace—and we fell into our old groove, I felt an urge to tell her about the promise. My body had been aching constantly, with knots in my shoulders and back, no matter how much Saint-John's wort I took. I was having trouble breathing, too. I'd wake in the middle of the night, sweating and gasping for breath, with my heart pounding. It felt as though someone was sitting on my chest. I hadn't told anyone, not even Asa, about what Daddy made me pledge. Instead I'd kept the panic deep inside, like a canker sore that my tongue could worry over in private. But bathed in the consolation of Imani's familiar voice, the entire hospital stay spilled out. When I got to the last days and what he'd whispered about Elizabeth, Imani shrieked.

"No, he didn't," she said.

Relief wasn't flooding me the way I'd hoped. For a second I regretted my impulse. But once having started I plowed on. "Yeah. I don't know what to do. You know, a deathbed commitment. But if I get in touch with her, what would I say after all these years? What is there to say? I mean . . ." As I started to rant, I felt familiar righteous ground under my feet, and every wisp of nostalgia I'd felt for the woman, especially the waves since Ella's birth, floated away. "What, really, is there to say? And as for that agape stuff . . ." My blood flowing, I felt warmer, more relaxed. "Fuck agape. Elizabeth's a bitch. End of story."

"I don't know," Imani started out, cool. "After all is said and done, she is your mom."

Oh no, we'd had this conversation before, which somehow, in the warmth of the connection, I'd forgotten. Maybe because her mother and Elizabeth had inexplicably become close friends later on, she didn't get it, even with everything I'd told her. But how *could* she, with a Black mom who was born Black, always been Black, wore a dashiki every day for damn near twenty years. She didn't know what it felt like to not have an African American mother to guide her, only a wannabe who mortified the hell out of me. Yet Imani had been right there all those years to watch how Elizabeth neglected me, time after time. And put me through that whole horrible embarrassing affair with Abi. What about the lesbians who'd invaded our house, so she wasn't even allowed to come over? She of all people should understand.

"Hmm, this is deep," Imani continued. "She is your mother, though, Ruby. Maybe you could ask that ancestor—remember, the one your dad wrote you about. . . ." She stopped and laughed. "Of course. *Ella*. That's who you named her for. So much like *Elizabeth*, hmm . . . who named you after Ruby Dee," she muttered, an aside I chose to ignore. "Call on the ancestors, Ruby. Ask them. Are you doing any ancestor work?"

I was surprised. Imani had really changed from the party girl she'd been years back, from what I'd heard, at Spelman. She'd gone home to her roots, that was for sure. "I have an altar," I said defensively, noticing that suddenly I felt the need to establish my Black credibility. Me, with Imani! Me, a professor of African and African American Studies! While I tried to get my bearings, I wondered, was this grief? Asa interpreted every feeling I had as one more manifestation. But I heard Imani's voice. "Put something about Miss Ella on the altar—she'll send you a sign."

"I'm listening," I said, as offhandedly as I could. "I already put Daddy's letters about her there."

"You could write her a letter yourself, ask her what to do. She's your great-great-grandmother, right? Ask your dad's spirit, too. Maybe he's with her."

I felt an overwhelming urge to scoop Ella into my arms and feel her smooth baby body against me. The touch of reality. "I've gotta go," I said. "Thanks, Imani, I'll catch you later. Call you soon. Love ya."

But I did write a letter on one of my yellow legal pads. I imagined it was only going to be a sentence or two, but as soon as I started the words spilled out, the same as when I'd written Elizabeth, telling her to go to hell. Did that mean Spirit was working through me?

Dear Miss Ella,

If you can hear me, please tell me what to do. I am so carefree without my mother in my life. She makes me crazy with her need and wanting to show me off, and I'm still so angry at her. And hurt. Honestly, I don't know if she really loves me or not, if she ever did, or if I'm merely a good-looking brown accoutrement to her lefty lifestyle. Her racism drives me wild, and so do her erratic ways. I don't trust her. I don't even know if I like her, strange as it may sound. I know she's my biological mother, the woman whose body I came out of, and she raised me. Daddy's been reminding me of that for years. I can hear him saying, "She's your mother, you have a responsibility to her, you can't ever change that."

I think maybe I have, though. My parents taught me to be tough and to go for what I want. They said that a million times. "Ruby, you can do anything you want to in the world. There are no barriers for you. None at all." Elizabeth was always telling me, "You're brilliant, be exactly who you want to be. You get to create the life you want, the one that suits you, that's tailor-made for you. It's one of the first times in human history when women can do that," she said, "when women can do anything." She pushed me and pushed me, just to be me.

And now I am happy. I've never been this satisfied, with my teaching and Asa and now little Ella. Even without Daddy I can say this, though I miss him to the point of insanity sometimes. We have a comfortable home, everything's going fantastically well. I don't need any changes to upset our lives. But your great-grandson, your son James's grandson, Solomon Jordan, my father, made me promise to contact my mother, whom I haven't talked to basically in fifteen years. Now he's passed, so I can't retract my word.

I'm not sure why he did this. In his last few days my father talked a lot about healing and I guess his wanting me and my mother to make up was part of it, even though this isn't about him. It's about me and his first ex-wife, my biological mother, who's white. So give me a sign please. I know I haven't talked to you or had a dream about you for many years, but I haven't forgotten you. I even named my own daughter Ella Jordan-Plummer *after you. As soon as I knew she was a girl your name floated into my mind. It was the only one, and never left. You have a great-great-great-granddaughter namesake. Could you have imagined this, after all you went through? She is a wonderful, healthy girl, a worthy namesake in every way, and we will do our best to raise her with integrity and respect for her ancestors.*

I'm not sure what else to do, but I will put a plate of food for you on the altar every day for the next month, and ask for your blessing. Thank you for your grace and for giving me some guidance.

Your great-great-granddaughter,
Ruby

I folded the letter into a square, bent my head and kissed it, walked to the altar, and placed it there carefully, tucking it under the prayer candle, which burned twenty-four/seven. Asa did that, lit one of these tall white candles in a glass jar, every time someone died. Obeisance to the spirits, he called it. Elizabeth's cynicism popped up in me, of course—"opiate of the masses"—but somehow I was moved now to honor my ancestors. Must have been Daddy's spirit moving in me. Didn't this show how much more his daughter I was than hers?

I touched the corner of the paper again, releasing my plea to the spirit world. *If one exists, may it help me, please. I can't dishonor Daddy, but I just can't see calling Elizabeth, either. That would be asking for a whole lotta trouble, getting me back into that old push–pull of emotion that Claire helped me leave behind. Please show me the way.*

*   *   *

Day after day, whenever I passed the credenza on my way in or out of the house, I sent a silent appeal—I wouldn't call it a prayer, more like a mental request—in case someone was listening. *Please, help me know the right thing to do. I want to act with integrity, and I don't want to call trouble into my life. Daddy talked a lot about forgiveness, but I don't know how to do that. I don't even know if I want to. Can't I go on the way I have been? I don't want to put myself back in the maelstrom of all that vulnerability that formed such a painful strand of my child- hood tapestry. I've pulled all the threads out, I've unraveled it, and I'm so much better off exactly the way I am now. I've worked hard to get here. Don't I deserve this peaceful family life, without that woman's drama?*

Each time I glanced over and made my silent plea, I saw the photos of Daddy and my eyes filled with tears. It was automatic, like a sprinkler system. I saw photo: *boom,* switch turned on, water- works. First I felt a warmth in my eyes, they tingled and smarted, then water. What surprised me most was the idea that the tears must always be in there, just under the surface, if merely the sight of his face released them so quickly.

But even though I made my appeals as sincerely as I could, at home and while I was jogging, nothing came back. *Nada.* No mes- sages from Ella, nothing from Daddy. Spirit either did not exist or, just like my mother, didn't care about me. Was this to be my fate? Instead all I heard was my own whirling mind obsessing on the promise I'd made to Daddy, keeping me awake in the early-morning hours. I fell asleep easily enough, about eleven, but at three I woke, my brain alert. As I turned from side to side, my mind raced. *You were delirious,* I reasoned with Daddy, *high on every antibiotic they could pump into you, and morphine, too. You were out of your mind those last few days. If you weren't, you never would have inflicted this weight on me, a pledge like that, when you know how much I don't want to be connected to that woman you were married to. Yes, the one who gave birth to me.*

As I argued and sweated, the sheets grew clammy. Over the silent hours I refined my arguments—I'm good at that—until I pretty much had myself convinced that I could forget the deathbed ramblings of one dying old man, even if that man was my father, and go to sleep. I tried deep breathing then, in and out, belly breathing. Come on, alpha state, let me go. Let me sleep. A grown person has a right to make a decision like the one I made. That's my right!

But something had me snagged. No matter how much I persuaded myself that I was foolish to spend another minute on this so-called "promise," one that maybe Elizabeth herself had engineered, my body wouldn't let it go. I'd throw the covers off, then pull them on, tossing and turning until finally, each night, I imagined contacting Elizabeth. Okay, I'd tell myself, I'll honor the oath, but he didn't say I had to go any further than that. One contact. I'd write a letter—and tell her Daddy made me do it. I visualized the letter, written in blue ink on my classic pad of yellow lined paper.

Dear Elizabeth,

Daddy asked me before he died to contact you. I'm not sure why. But here I am. I have a daughter, as you no doubt are aware, and have created a wonderful life. I'm an academic, tenure track, which I know you never got to be, at the finest university in the country. . . . Why would I say all this? She knew it, I felt sure. So I'd start again.

Dear Elizabeth,

I know you tried *to be a mother to me. And you were, after a fashion. I just think we're both better off not having an adult relationship. I don't believe you ever really cared for me,* qua *me . . .*

Why rehash this old ground? Finally, exhausted, I'd fall into a light sleep shortly before dawn. When I bolted up, bleary, to the rat-a-tat-tat of the alarm, Asa sometimes pulled me back down. His hand stroked my legs, my buttocks; when he reached around and began to squeeze my thighs, I knew what he had in mind. Usually the whole area tingled from his touch—fondling the tender skin of my inner thighs was a guaranteed turn-on. But lost in mental arguments, one morning I batted his hand away. "Not now, honey."

"Another sleepless night?" he asked, weariness lining his face. He was sure it was all heartache about Daddy. "Grief." He'd become the expert. "And insomnia. They're closely linked," he said authoritatively, annoyingly, until I'd see the affection shining out of his brown eyes, warm pools I wanted to dive into and float in, then swim far away. One of these mornings, I thought groggily, when we've got more than five minutes before we have to grab Ella and dash out of the house to drop her at LaDean's, on a morning when he hasn't left for the gym at 5:30, I'm going to tell him what's going on. My exhaustion was causing me to lose all perspective. Every muscle ached. I wasn't too caught up on sleep before Daddy passed anyway, with Ella waking us up, and since that time at the hospital and every minute afterward crammed with classes, I was seriously sleep deprived. I thought I might be losing my mind. Nothing appeared solid anymore.

It happened, the first time, after my Intro to African Studies class, during that last gray hour before dark. I was rushing across Harvard Yard, pulling my coat tight. A bitter wind cut into my neck. The light was dimming fast, with huge black clouds billowing on the horizon. Snow was predicted. Two students who'd walked out of class with me, one on each side, begging for extensions on their papers, with, actually, some novel excuses, had just scurried off toward Mass Ave and I was headed toward Quincy Street, when I heard her speak right behind me. "Ruby!" I knew that flat Midwestern voice so well, even after all these years. This was absolute delight I was hearing. "How wonderful to run into you like this, sweetie."

I whipped around, trying to snare that familiar voice in its lair, prepared to yell, "Why are you following me?" Stalking, even, sneaking up behind me like that. So close, in fact, I felt a warm breeze on the back of my head when she spoke. It must have been her breath on that cold evening.

At first I didn't see anyone. Maybe she'd jumped behind one of the towering elm trunks. She really had lost it if she was preying on me, hiding behind trees. Shadows danced about, gnarled branches blown by the wind, silhouetted against the darkening sky. Gusts swirled around me. She could have been anywhere. Or was this Daddy's ghost? He'd vowed to haunt me if I didn't contact her.

"Elizabeth!" I shouted into the wind. "Stop it."

No one emerged.

"Where are you?"

A tall shadowy figure, hard to make out in the dusk, appeared on the walkway, coming toward me. Where had she hidden? I saw only flat lawn, broken up by the huge, twisted trees.

"Stop following me!"

The cloaked form, burdened with a large package, came closer, lifted its hood, and I saw a young woman's curious, worried face. Blond bangs, cut sharply, hung over blue eyes. "I'm not," was all she said before she dashed past me and disappeared into the dark.

Feeling ridiculous, I put my head down against the blasts of frigid air and half ran toward the Barker Center. But I hadn't taken ten steps before I heard it again: "Ruby, I've missed you, you know. Terribly. You were my angel. . . ."

I covered my ears with my hands. What was she doing, tracking me down at school? I doubled back, lunging behind the closest elms, trying to catch her. But the vast Yard appeared empty.

Am I losing my sanity? I thought. *Or has she lost hers?*

*   *   *

Late that night, after two glasses of pinot noir failed to fill my body
with the sleepy fluidity that one glass usually gave, I turned to Asa
in bed. "Honey." I poked him. I couldn't hold this in. "Asa."

Snores. "Huh?" he grumbled. I knew how much he needed sleep.
He was the one who'd been getting up with Ella—she still woke at
least twice a night—and he'd been attending weekly emergency meetings at the law school, so I put my arm over his shoulder, curled into
his back, and tried to put the whole bizarre episode out of my mind.

But at dawn the next morning, when I heard water running in
the bathroom and knew he was brushing his teeth, I knocked on
the door. Asa was hurrying, I could tell the minute I saw the deep
line between his eyebrows and the way he was throwing water on his
face, splashing over the edges of the sink, which I'd reminded him
not to do. It was ruining the grout, which was crumbling and yellow. But in spite of his harried frown, I rushed to say, "The strangest
thing happened last night. I thought Elizabeth was talking to me, in
the Yard, right near Mass Ave."

He glanced up, as if to say, *Why are you telling me this now?* while
metaphorically turning his eyes down to his watch. I recognized the
gesture. But I needed a listener, so I walked over, bumped my hip
against his in the sexy way we'd perfected, and continued, "Listen,
she was talking right in my ear, but I don't know if she was really
there or not. I heard her so clearly, but I couldn't see her."

"What are you telling me, sweetie?" I had his attention now. We
moved back into the bedroom. "Was Elizabeth there or not?" His
tone was weary, patient. "Did you see your mother?"

"I don't know if I'm hearing voices, honestly, or if she's stalking
me. Or what." I exhaled noisily and leaned into him, falling, pushing him down on the bed. His shoes slipped off, crashing noisily to
the floor. "Shh . . ." I put my finger to my lips. We needed those few
minutes while Ella was sleeping.

"I doubt she's following you around Harvard Yard, honey." He rolled over to search my face. "You know I've gotta go in a second. Get to the gym. You're dropping Ella this morning, right? Listen, Elizabeth hasn't tried to force herself on you in years. Maybe you heard someone else calling out . . . or the wind was playing tricks, whistling, and you imagined it." He started to get up.

"No, it was her voice." I rose, too. "I don't know, though . . ." I trailed off. "It's over . . . I'll just leave it alone."

"Yeah, you're exhausted." He gave me a quick kiss on the cheek and hurried out of the bedroom. "But someday you might want to consider giving her a call . . ."

I scowled.

". . . when you're not so tired," he hastened to add.

"Don't ever tell me that again." I was serious. "Please."

The second time, she came in a dream, I guess, although at that point I couldn't swear that she hadn't climbed into our second-floor bedroom, where, even in winter, Asa insisted we sleep with the windows open, minimum two inches. It was late March, the day before her birthday, in the quietest time of the night, when I heard that familiar twang so clearly she *must* have been in the room. By then I was so used to being constantly groggy I didn't know whether I was sleeping, dreaming, or awake. Lying on my side, I heard her voice again right at the back of my head, and felt a breath flutter on my neck. "Ruby, I'm glad we're going to talk. . . ." It was the same as before: she was there, behind me.

This time it spooked me even more. "What the hell's going on?" I muttered, not knowing whether I was drowsing or not. "I never said we were going to talk, didn't even contemplate it. The most I was going to do, if anything, was write you a brief letter. One short letter. That would've fulfilled my pledge to Daddy." End of story. Promise fulfilled. Duty discharged.

But now she was talking to me as if we were all set to begin a marvelous conversation. I didn't get it.

"Ruby, I have a lot to explain," she said. I heard her clearly, even though I saw nothing but familiar dim shapes in the darkened bedroom, with only the night-light shining from the bathroom. "How hard it was, being a single mother all those years—"

"Oh, shit," I cut her off. "I've heard your self-pity for years. Don't you have anything new to say? You weren't the only single mother in the world, for God's sake."

"I'm so sorry," the disembodied voice whispered, "I do love you, though. I've always adored you, and I did my absolute best. And look at you now." Even her voice sounded proud. Then she was gone. Although I'd seen nothing, I *felt* her abrupt departure.

In the morning, after I told Asa he suggested I call Claire, whom I hadn't seen for ages. Anyway, I'd heard she retired. "No time," I told him. "I can handle this. It must have been a dream." But privately I wondered how abnormal it was, experiencing phantasmic visits. Each time I'd been convinced Elizabeth was with me, in the flesh. I didn't understand what was happening, but I didn't want to delve too deeply into it, either. *"If it ain't broke, don't fix it,"* Daddy used to say. And I wasn't broken.

Asa's suggestion started me thinking about Claire, though. Years before, in graduate school, all my friends had been seeing her, the only African American therapist on staff. She was a real guru on campus during our most militant negritude phase.

After my first six months of therapy, Claire had concluded that not only was Elizabeth narcissistic, she was "iceopathic," a term she coined to describe the quintessential selfish mother. Not to mention the racism; we used to laugh about Elizabeth as "the white glacier." Elizabeth was definitely a mother to let go of, she'd assured me. "Make the break," she'd advised, "it's grow-up time, my dear," while her pen scratched on a small yellow pad of paper. A Nubian princess, she called herself, reveling in her own dark, almost black-purple skin. I felt loved in that magical weekly space, comforted by the strips of bright African cloth—especially one deep red and gold print—draped around the room. "Cut the cord to the white glacier," she'd said. "Come home where you belong."

At last I had the unequivocal love, the care I'd only dreamed of during those lonely teenage years: succor from a formidable African American woman. "I'm remothering you," Claire promised while I gratefully wiped my eyes. "Giving you what you should have always had as a cherished daughter of the tribe. Believe me, she didn't do you any favors. Now you can experience what it's like to have a generative Afrocentric figure on your side, one who is truly listening and loving you. You don't have to feel alone in your growth journey. You were undermothered, Ruby, by a woman too self-obsessed to be capable of mothering. I am absolutely dedicated to co-creating a deeply trusting bond, nourishing you to create the fantastic, creative life you were meant to live."

Each week I drank in the nourishment, working toward the day when I'd be strong enough to release that other mother. The false one.

CHAPTER 17

Ruby

As spring semester unfolded with the Larry Summers scandal eating up our precious bits of time—though I had to admit to some satisfaction, watching an arrogant white guy catch his—I occasionally caught Daddy's eyes in my rearview mirror: the deep brown color, heavy eyebrows, shape, everything, right down to the crease in the same place between our eyes.

I had plenty of distractions. The law school seemed to have nonstop parties that March. One week we had two must-attends. Since our next-door neighbors, a male couple, had a girl Ella's age and assured us it was easy to care for one more child, we'd take Ella over and go through our bedtime story/song ritual, tuck her into a Pack 'n Play portable crib in the study, and gratefully creep out. She'd whimper, but not for long, and was quiet by the time we left the house. One party at the dean's home was especially interesting. When we arrived the spacious rooms hummed with conversation as well-dressed academics gathered in the living and dining area, people in the jam-packed crowd reaching across each other for canapés and wine from trays passed by white-jacketed waiters. Asa and I mingled easily. He knew many of the guests, who were attached, one way or another, to the law school. We joined several small groups, sequentially, as knots dissolved and re-formed. Soon I found myself at the edge of a conversation near the kitchen, where an energetic dark-skinned woman introduced herself to us as Susan Barker, literary agent. My ears perked up.

"Do you handle academic writing?" I asked when I had an opportunity.

"Rarely," she said, laughing. "But sporadically I do, when a project compels me. An agent has to be ready to go to the mat for her client's work, and most academic writing, frankly, doesn't have a broad enough audience for me to fight for. Use up my chips on. Or get interest from a publisher."

"Oh," I said, deflated.

"What did you have in mind?" she asked, raising her voice. The crowd around us, which had grown, exuded an even louder, excited buzz. I'd heard that the young Illinois Senator, Barack Obama, was scheduled to appear. But so far no sign of an entourage.

"My field is semiotics," I told her. "It's the study of signification, the process where signs communicate meaning to an observer. I'm focusing on the construction of race in art—examining the symbols that connote white supremacy, like aristocrats, past and present, who chose to be shown with their Black servants in paintings while they covered their own faces in white paint and powder. Which happened, by the way, to be highly toxic," I added with an ironic inflection.

Surprisingly, Susan winked. "How accessible is your writing?" she asked. "It's the impenetrable style that usually sinks interesting research."

"I'm working on writing for a general audience. This is not meant to be a textbook."

Susan removed her card from a gold case, extended it, and said, "Call me. Let's talk," before Asa drifted by, took my elbow, and nudged me to an opening in the crowd. I glanced down at the card in my hand. Susan's address was on 138th Street in New York, not far from Daddy's old place. Ours now. Che was getting the house ready for sale, with painters and drywall installers. Daddy had let it go after he and Elaine split. His heart just wasn't in the house anymore, he said. He rarely even ate at home those last few years.

Just then I could tell by the quieting murmur that a program was about to begin. The dean, flanked by the provost, stood in one corner of the bookshelf-lined library, where red Oriental rugs covered the floor. But I tugged at Asa. "We've got to get home," I said. "I have to work. And we need to pick up Ella while she's still in that early-stage sleep. Otherwise, she'll be awake half the night."

"You're right," he agreed, moving quietly toward the door with me. On the way home, I told him about my conversation with Susan Barker. Even if the contact came to nothing, her interest in my topic was encouraging, and I vowed to devote at least an hour a day to the manuscript.

Now that Daddy had passed, though, my other so-called parent moved in. Her third visitation occurred one chilly morning while I was running at dawn, pushing the jogger. I'd started mile six when I heard her familiar voice call, "Ruby, I'm thinking about you, I hope your life is good," right at the corner of Williams Street. The sound was sharp and close, startling me. I jumped; the sudden stop jolted Ella awake. She squealed and Elizabeth disappeared.

Later that morning, when I was frying pancakes and turkey sausage and trying to keep Ella away from the popping, sizzling grease exploding over the edge of the pan, I thought about what Daddy had said: that we all make up stories and live as if they were true. But this one, I'd swear on any Bible in the land, was not a fairy tale, and it was not my imagination. Maybe I should call Claire, on the off chance she was still seeing a few patients, or would consent to come out of retirement for a couple of sessions. Perhaps this was grief after all. There might be a remedy she could suggest.

But caught up with midterms, Ella, and life, I didn't call. Several weeks passed with no "visits" and in the crush of events I forgot. When I did occasionally remember what had happened, I was relieved. *That's over. It must have been a symptom of strain.*

At the one-month mark, however, Elizabeth resumed her visitations. Every few days at the oddest times I'd hear her—in my office, outside, or at home late at night—that familiar voice sounding full of pleasure that we were "about to talk." The clarity of sound was unambiguous. If I were a different person, less grounded, less efficient, I'd have believed I was losing my mind. But there were no other signs, no hallucinations. My life, in fact, was hitting a new high: my students were completing their work, a few brilliantly; I wrote consistently well, late every evening, filling in the outline for my book; Ella was progressing in her few hours a week at campus day care, where her teachers assured me she was a star; and Asa and I were fine— more than fine, considering the year we'd had. Except for missing Daddy so intensely, with a searing physical pain in my chest—where it felt as though someone had kicked me—life was ideal. There was no way to account for this voice other than the idea that somehow that terrible woman had managed to project her utterances into our home, my office, and every place I regularly frequented.

Soon I began telling Asa, jokingly, as if it were a matter-of-fact, everyday occurrence, "Elizabeth visited today." I had no way to explain the hauntings, as I came to think of them, although they didn't frighten me. He was the only one I confided in until one morning when I impulsively shared the voices—diminishing their number— with Mercedes, a colleague from the Art Department with whom I'd collaborated. Mercedes had a Down syndrome toddler two months older than Ella, and she was pumping breast milk, too. We tried to meet weekly at Starbucks for even forty-five minutes, to commiserate about pumping and share baby stories or talk shop. When I told Mercedes, over a quick latte, what had been going on, she wasn't as concerned as I was afraid she would be. "The sounds could be auditory fantasies," she speculated, rolling her eyes up while she thought. "Like an apparition of the ear." She imagined they might be simple illusions induced by stress—from Daddy's death, the strain of nursing, teaching three classes, and the Summers drama that was shaking everything up. "Whatever is causing it," she urged, "I think you should call your doctor. Have some tests. Maybe you have an inner ear infection. That could produce unusual effects."

Although her assumption that I was not crazy encouraged me, I was intrigued but not convinced by her infection hypothesis. I knew what a person's voice sounded like, I knew my so-called mother's voice, and I'd been hearing it. I couldn't account for it—the woman lived in California, for God's sake, what was she doing in Cambridge?—but I was open to plausible explanations. Asa, in a fit of wonderment late one evening, even suggested I might have stumbled into a bleeding over of universes. String theory, he told me, posited eleven dimensions, with zillions of parallel universes operating simultaneously, so maybe I "really" was hearing her talk to me, whatever "really" meant in this context.

One thing I found the strangest—amid all the weirdness of it— was why she invariably sounded pleased, confident that soon we were going to talk. *Ain't gonna happen.* I'd pretty much concluded that Daddy was out of his mind when he'd extracted my commitment, and anyway, the sentimentality of it, deathbed pledge and all, rendered it moot, I'd decided. No court in the land would morally sustain it. In his right mind, Daddy would have disdained the entire conversation as "cheap theatrics, baby." I could see him dismissing the entire maudlin hospital scene with a flourish of his hands.

Stranger still, by the time the semester wound down in late April, I was getting used to Elizabeth's visits, no longer alarmed when I heard that twang. The first few times I'd yelled, *"Shut up, we're not going to talk. Not now, not ever!"* But I'd strangely gotten used to her voice in my ears, or my head, or wherever it was in my body I heard her. The sound even started to remind me of the comfort I'd once felt being around her, before those awful teenage years when everything about her grated. All she'd had to do by then was utter a word, and I was all over her. There *was* a lot to criticize. She'd slur her words over dinner, and afterward pass out on my bed if she came to sing some drunken ditty and "tuck me in."

Oh my God, when I remembered that time. She'd fawn over every Black person we knew, it was embarrassing whenever anybody came to the house, even Imani or Inez. Elizabeth threw in Ebonics in all the wrong places, or with the wrong pronunciation, trying to be "hip" when she only sounded ridiculous. "Sister," she'd mumble to Inez, throwing her arm around her shoulder, especially when she'd been drinking. "I'm a soul sister, let's get down, girlfriend." The only thing I felt then was the strong desire to get away from her and the sound of that preposterous, humiliating, irredeemably white voice.

Once I confided in Asa, early one morning, that Elizabeth's visitations had become a part of my routine—and were almost reassuring in their regularity. He tried again to convince me to call Claire. "You're hearing voices, Ruby," he said emphatically, shaking his head in disbelief. So much for parallel dimensions, which he'd evidently abandoned. We sat on the edge of our high bed together, his arm around my shoulders, while with the other he brushed hair out of my eyes. "Don't you think that warrants an appointment with a psychologist? Or a physician?"

Each time he brought it up, usually late at night or just after dawn, when we had a few moments alone, I saw the concern in his eyes, along with the fatigue that showed in new creases crinkling his forehead. "At the very least, try meditating," he begged. "That should calm you down. Take a class at the stress clinic."

"I haven't got time," I replied, though it was hard to say no to him.

Imagining how weird it would sound—*"I'm hearing my estranged mother talk to me every week, though I never see her, and it's not happening on the telephone"*—I hadn't mentioned the visits to anyone other than Asa and Mercedes. They were so brief, just a whisper sometimes, that, honestly, they'd almost started to seem normal. "That's scary," Asa said worriedly, giving me his famous visual inspection. "Silent interrogation," I began to call his heightened scrutiny, telling him he should sign up for the CIA.

In the crush of daily life, with Ella adding hours of tasks each day to our already impossibly stretched minutes, it was easy to ignore the vague whisperings. To celebrate our May 25 anniversary, Asa and I planned a dinner at Legal Sea Foods, our first "date" since Ella's birth. On the appointed evening, we put her to bed—hurrying through the bath and story/song ritual—and at seven thirty opened the door to LaDean. Asa and I were more than ready to have an evening's private conversation, with no cooking or clean up. Legal Sea Foods wasn't the most romantic setting, but I'd loved the restaurant ever since discovering it at its original Park Plaza location on our first date. I'd savored the legendary thick and creamy clam chowder, with its chunks of clam and potato, and been equally stunned by the sight of miniskirted prostitutes in doorways only a block away. Now the nearby Legal Sea Foods was our place, noisy and crowded though it was. "The food *is* fabulous," I argued with Asa whenever we had an occasion for celebration. "And remember how romantic our first meal was, when we sat down in the well and you told me about New Orleans, how romantic that environment was, and your mom and dad?" He nodded. Any mention of his late parents was sacred.

The warm spring evening was lovely, still light, so we set out on foot to Pearl Street, passed our neighborhood market, turned again on Cottage Street, and strolled, admiring the blooming blue and purple iris. "I love it here," I told him, tucking my right arm into his left one.

"Hmm . . ." Asa seemed distracted.

We walked silently all the way to the Charles. Then I couldn't contain my pleasure. "We're so fortunate to live here," I said, snuggling into his arm, pulling my shoulders in against the chill of the river.

"Hmm, we are." He nodded.

"'Hmm . . .' is my line," I teased. "Usually I'm the vacant one. You're taking my spot!"

"I know." He shook his head. "Just department crap. Sometimes I think about going off on my own, hanging out a shingle. . . . The students inspire me, but . . . same old, same old."

"Maybe someday you will. But tonight, let's talk anniversary talk. Married for ten years. Can you believe it? Asa, this is so good."

"It is, honey." By the time we turned onto Eliot Street, almost at Legal Sea Foods, I had his full attention. The restaurant was crowded for a Tuesday night, with waiters shouting as they hoisted their trays high through the swarm, but we got the seats I'd requested out on the quiet patio. Over a decent chardonnay, oysters on the half shell, and creamy bluefish pâté, we reminisced all the way back to the morning we'd met. I'd been new on campus and he, the seasoned student, had offered to show me around. "What if you hadn't volunteered to be a mentor for incoming African Americans?" I said teasingly. "I know what you were looking for."

"And I found her, didn't I?" The joke we'd repeated for years never lost its luster. We basked, each time, in retelling our story, the origin tale of our own personal culture.

"No us, no Ella. Imagine, she wouldn't even exist."

He reached across the wooden table and took my hand. "This life with you is what I always dreamed of." He looked around at the nautical décor and added, "Life on a boat, in the courtyard of the Charles Hotel." He squeezed my hand, then freed it to tackle his steamed lobster. "No, honestly, honey, it's better than I dreamed. I couldn't have dreamed you, how we can share everything. You are a true partner, in every sense of the word. Thank you." He raised his glass. "To us, and to fifty more years. May we live to see Ella grow up and bounce our grandchildren on our knees." His voice trembled and I wondered if he were thinking about his mother, who hadn't lived to see Ella.

"Hear, hear," I said. "And to all our ancestors, whose struggles helped us be here tonight."

After we'd eaten our fill, lingering over a too-sweet amaretto custard, Asa said,

"I don't want you to work as hard this summer as you did last one. You need some time off."

"I know." I shook my head. "But I have to finish the draft of my book."

"You're exhausted. Look in a mirror, Ruby. The circles under your eyes. Which, by the way, are closing. Let's take a taxi home."

He was right. I fell asleep in the cab and had to be half carried like an overgrown child into our bed, where I enjoyed my best sleep in months.

By mid-June, when we took down the altar for Daddy, I'd had no signs from the ancestors. Daddy was simply a huge, painful absence. Elizabeth seemed to be the only ghost who was speaking to me and she always said essentially the same thing: "Anticipating our talk." Which was not about to happen. Asa and I had had an unlisted number for years and I guarded it like the devil watching over hell.

Asa kept bugging me about calling a psychologist, a psychiatrist, "or somebody. These so-called voices have gone on way too long to ignore." He hunched over his plate one night after a Moroccan dinner he'd whipped up, courtesy of a friend's recipe. Ella played contentedly at our feet, occasionally trying to pull herself up using the table legs, each time falling back down and rediscovering her brightly colored blocks. Dishes were strewn over the table. One of the candles had guttered out; the other still flamed in its brass candlestick. When I rose, wearily, to clear the plates, I shrugged him off with a noncommittal "Hmm . . ." but he persisted. "I'm not going to let this drop, Ruby.

You can't go around hearing voices and not deal with it. Maybe this is the sign you've been waiting for from the spirit world, telling you to contact your mother. You can't not deal with this much longer."

Just watch me, I thought, trudging with an armful of dishes to the kitchen. There are worse things in life than spectral visits from one's estranged mother, though what they might be I was too tired to conjecture.

At last, though, by midsummer, with the voice following me even to our corner coffee shop, one morning as Asa passed me in the hall after his shower, he finally wore me down. "Ruby, this is serious. Promise me you'll do something about it. I'm worried. This can't go on."

"Promises! You men in my life, all you want is promises!"

"Ruby, stop it. This isn't funny. What about Ella? If you're hallucinating, it's not safe . . ."

He didn't have to finish his sentence. "I promise, I'll call a professional."

Sharply at nine the following Monday morning I called Mental Health Services. As I thought, Claire had retired. For an instant I envisioned tracking her down, trying to convince her to take me on for a few private sessions, but while I was fantasizing the intake person talked me into scheduling with a new guy. "He's African American, too," she assured me, like Black people were interchangeable. Yeah, the race of a therapist was important to me, but when a person who sounded white brought it up, why did I feel thrust into a ghetto? Anyway, Dr. Timble's first opening wasn't for more than a month, which was fine, because we were going to the Vineyard for a couple of weeks. I took the appointment.

It wasn't until one lazy August afternoon in Oak Bluffs, after I'd finished the first draft of my manuscript and was wallowing in the perfection of its final paragraph, sitting back in my chair listening to the ocean breeze ruffle the trees, that I realized I hadn't heard from Elizabeth in weeks. Maybe a month. Just as inexplicably as her voice had started haunting me, it had stopped. Good. Now I could keep my focus on the manuscript. Susan Barker was eager to see it and I'd promised to send a draft in good shape by Labor Day, only three weeks away. Writing, so long one of the more difficult aspects of my academic existence, was getting slightly easier. I actually almost relished the search for the exact right word, and found my own logic in the book irresistible: for all of recorded history, people had used signs, however injurious such signifiers might be, to associate themselves with the most successful groups within their societies. In cultures where pale skin was valued, members modified their behavior to avoid acquiring a tan (indicating field work), or used face paints and whitening creams, even when they were lethal. This applied from the Middle Ages, when aristocrats used cosmetics to create the lustrous white complexions seen in portraits, right up to the present. Chronic users like Queen Elizabeth I, who covered their skin with ceruse, a lead-based makeup, eventually acquired gruesomely diseased features. Michael Jackson was our present-day version. I found this research infinitely more fascinating than thinking about Elizabeth, who, in her topsy-turvy world, had tried all during my childhood for a signifier of exalted status by virtually appearing in blackface. I vowed to forget her again, especially now that her visits had passed.

Still, on the appointed afternoon, a sweltering, sticky one at the end of August, I set off for my meeting with Dr. Timble because I'd given my word to Asa, despite the current lack of Elizabeth's visits. Perspiring, almost suffocating in the intense heat, I made my way, first through honking rush-hour traffic, then on the T, until I arrived at the familiar old brick building. Ushered into his office, the first thing I noticed was its spaciousness. Already I missed Claire:

the African prints, the masks, the cloth, the sense of relief every time I entered that cozy room. Even the Kleenex on the arm of the chair, which had welcomed my tears. Here, no tissues were in sight.

Dr. Timble was a short, rather formal man in a black suit and red bow tie, with a pink shirt that set off his ruddy cheeks; the starched collar had been pressed for days. He strutted, chest out above his paunch, to the center of the room to pump my hand, then quickly motioned me toward a chair miles from his huge polished desk.

"How would you like me to address you?" was his first question.

"'Ruby' will do," I said, preferring not to be Dr. Jordan here.

"All right, Ruby, what brings you to see me?" His voice was crisp, cool, all business.

This could be aversion therapy. I chuckled inwardly. *I already don't like him.* But forcing the feeling down, I rationalized, *I'm here, I might as well go for the gold.* Briefly, I described my estrangement from Elizabeth, Daddy's death, the promise, and at last, hearing her voice, although I downplayed that, making it sound ambiguous, perhaps mere whisperings, or even vivid thoughts.

"How does hearing the 'voice' make you feel?" he inquired, peering over his glasses from his perch across the room.

Shit, freaked out. "Uneasy," I said. "Strange." My mouth was dry.

"What feels strange to you?" His tone was even, impersonal.

Oh Lord, wouldn't it be strange if you were hearing voices? What the fuck can I say? So I was silent. And consequently, so was he. Stand-off at the OK Corral. After what's got to have been five minutes—of my valuable time and money, I was fuming—I decided to say something, anything. "I'd like some help here." I intended my tone to sound as aggrieved as I felt.

"What kind of help do you want?" he asked, remotely.

Why did I think this session was not getting anywhere? "Help with these voices? Is this normal? Have other people had them? What's going on? Could it be an inner ear infection?" I blurted out. "My husband thinks it's a symptom of grief."

"Lots of good questions," he said. "What do *you* think?"

"I came to get help, not play twenty questions," I snapped.
"How do *you* feel about that?"

"Hmm . . . We might want to explore your reluctance to answer
inquiries further," he said evenly. "It sounds as though there could
be several major issues at play here."

Oh God, I know. That's why I came.

"Perhaps you need to absolve *yourself* in order to be open to
your mother." He leaned back and pressed his fingers together in a
steeple.

"Absolve *myself*? You've got to be kidding. She's the one who
neglected me——" My rush of words grew heated. "She's the one who
treated me like a Black doll to pull out for her friends, she's the one
who didn't care, who was selfish——"

"Ah, that might be a fertile avenue to explore," he said smugly.
"Methinks the lady does protest too much. What do you have to
forgive yourself for?"

"How can you ask that?" I shot back. "She's the one you should
be asking!"

"Ah, but you're here, aren't you? And she isn't."

Finally, after more verbal fencing, while I was sweating like a
pig, and he was Mr.——oops, make that Dr.——Cool, he asked, "Can
you imagine a reconciliation with your mother? Perhaps that is
what these 'voices' you describe——which, of course, are your own
internal projections——are seeking. A part of you wants to reunite.
But your mind has resisted her for so long, you can't accept that
desire."

Oh, bullshit. I heard what I heard, and I know what I heard.
They're no fucking projection. And I couldn't imagine initiating
contact with Elizabeth——the real person——after what she'd put me
through: her selfishness, her desire to show me off like a Persian
rug, except in the coin of her realm only a Black-and-white girl
would do. I knew her. She pretended she was doing things for other

people's good—like her children, for chrissakes—yet it was only for
her. Letting Che go, even though in the end that might have been
the best thing for him, getting away from *her*. But splitting us up;
that was incredible! He was my best friend. My protector. My big
brother. I could never forgive her for that. Only narcissism could
explain it. Two children were simply too much bother when one
colored child would do all she needed quite nicely. What about that
would I have to forgive myself for? She was the adult.

I didn't know why Che had remained in contact with Elizabeth—he really had stuff to be mad about, getting sent away—but
he'd always been a go-along-to-get-along guy. That wasn't me.

"I don't believe that," is all I said, adding, "My mother is not
a person anyone would want to reunite with. She's rough, really
rough. A lush, a racist . . ." I was having trouble swallowing. "A
narcissist."

"Then why do you think you're creating her presence, immediately after your father died?" He paused, indicating with his eyebrows that his utterance carried such significance that we should
both ponder it. "Your inner child is, unconsciously perhaps, seeking
out your other parent for comfort in this time of grief. That's not
a bad coping strategy, believe me." For the first time, he smiled.
"Ruby," he continued, patiently, as if speaking to a slow ten-year-
old, "everything you're thinking and feeling and even imagining
you're hearing is coming from inside you. Your mother is not pro-
jecting her voice long-distance. You are creating her being with
you—auditorially. Only you can know the reason why."

"No, I heard her," I responded immediately. "And it's freaking
me out," I admitted, losing control right on the spot. "Completely.
I'm ready to burst. I wake up in the middle of the night, wide
awake, crazy, and I hear her talking to me."

"Anxiety reaction formation is not uncommon after a death,"
he said pleasantly. "There are a number of medications that would
probably give you some relief."

Oh, man. A few seconds of silence went by and he continued, his eyes focused above my head. I wondered what he was fixated on. "It's a form of introjection. On the unconscious level, one assumes the attributes, or, in this case, the auditory hallucinatory persona, of another, acting as if these were one's own." He was droning. "And then, as a defense mechanism, you've projected this distressing desire, to be with your mother, onto *her*. She's now the one who's seeking you." He paused and closed his lips tightly, satisfied. "It's a reaction formation, because you're defending against an unacceptable feeling—desiring your mother—by exhibiting the opposite of your true impulse. You feel that you're *fleeing* her, when in fact you're pursuing her."

This was worse than Asa's gobbledygook. Give me spirits any day. Eleven dimensions, wormholes I can crawl into and fly away. But there was more.

"Defense mechanisms protect the human psyche from raised levels of anxiety, which you experienced after the loss of your father. So in some sense your husband is right. This *is* a form of grief."

"And what am I supposed to do about this?"

He glanced up at the clock on the wall, strategically placed so it was visible to both of us. "Our time is almost up. What would you like to do? We could make another appointment to explore this further, and/or I could suggest several medications that might help calm you down."

Whew, I wasn't sure what I expected, but whatever it was, this wasn't it. What a bust. I couldn't picture "exploring" my life with Dr. Thimble—ha! my joke gave me a second's pleasure—and I wasn't about to take drugs. I'd seen and read about what the so-called "side effects" of drugs had done to too many people. I stayed away from medicine, except every six or seven years when an unrelenting bronchitis had hold of my lungs and I settled for a short course of antibiotics. But a psychotropic drug? No, I wasn't going to mess with that. "Let me think about it," I said slowly, standing up.

He rose, we crossed the Sahara Desert to shake hands, I escaped into the long corridor and fled the building.

Walking back across campus to the T, shaking, I simmered, furious at the waste of time, livid at Elizabeth for creating this havoc. So much for "missing" her voice. Ha. I realized how close to the surface my rage still was, my childhood hurt, ever ready to bubble up. At least I had learned that. Again. Would it ever let go? My mind spun. I certainly had nothing to forgive *myself* for. What an idiot. As for absolving her? Wouldn't that betray my wounded child self? No, I'd stay strong.

I crammed myself into the throng at Harvard Square. Pressed into the crush of sweaty bodies on the T, jerked from side to side, I enjoyed a few minutes to myself. Since Elizabeth's voice wasn't coming anymore anyway, I decided to put this whole time behind me and plunge back into my life. I certainly had plenty to occupy my mind. Ella had begun walking—brilliantly, she could toddle from one end of the living room to the other before crashing on her bottom—so a whole new world of childhood was opening up. The train jolted. Crushed between a perspiring giant pulling a cart of bowling balls and a well-dressed Indian guy trying to read a book jammed up under his nose, I mused on Ella's rapid changes. How could she have grown so much in thirteen months? It was hard to remember the eight-pound, squealing infant she'd been now that her toddling presence filled the house. The clatter of the train, its steady rhythm, became almost a pleasant background drone, calming me while I pondered Ella's growth.

With thoughts occupied by my daughter, my gaze drifted over the crowded car until it rested, alarmed, on the familiar figure holding on to a pole not twenty paces away. Instantly I recognized the back of her flaming auburn head, now laced with gray, as it would be, I thought, startled. Her head tilted, as ever, slightly to the left. Her hair was shorter, trimmer than it used to be, not so wild and frizzy, but with the same curl. And she was shorter than I remembered, wearing a pale green sweater that I didn't recognize—but then I wouldn't, would I?—with a frayed brown leather pocketbook strap looped across her back, just the way she always did. Except for her shrunken stature she was exactly as I remembered her, down to the magazine tucked under her armpit. Yup, that was Elizabeth—an aging version, but still keeping up on the news. Maybe it's *Essence* or *Ebony*, I thought. Yeah, she'd be carrying one of those for show, anyway. Saying to the world, "I may be a white lady, but I'm your sistah, for real. Yo, bro, it be's that way sometimes." Putting up her hand for the slap.

How dare she come to Cambridge, following me? Had she gotten a job here? What was she doing on the East Coast, anyway? Did she move here simply to torment me? This had gone on way too long. *Go back to California where you belong!* Fired up, with furious tears smarting my eyes, I lurched between passengers, pushing past one bruised white man who stank of piss and perspiration and I don't know what else; I had to shove through a group of suburban teen-agers swaying to headphones, popping fingers—snap, snap—and holding up baggy pants with their free hands.

She was still facing away from me. Very clever. Then she flipped open her magazine—ah, I should have guessed, the sophisticated *New Yorker*—and I heard the rustling pages. Coming up behind her—*Ha, let's see how you like it, when you least expect it*—I whispered, as harshly as I could, "Get out of my life, for once and for all. Go back to California."

I expected her to twist around mischievously and continue her regular patter: *"How wonderful to see you, and here we are, talking, isn't this lovely?"* But instead she ignored me, didn't turn at all. In fact, she lifted her head from her magazine, her back still to me, and studiously read advertisements on the wall.

"Elizabeth O'Leary, go home! Stop following me!" I whispered with more urgency.

Still she didn't turn, didn't even twist her neck one inch in my direction.

Infuriated, I said, in almost a normal tone, "I hate you! Listen to me!"

And finally she did. She inclined her head toward me, ever so slightly, glancing out the corner of her eyes while she slipped away, hurrying through the crowd. As soon as I saw her cheek, heavily rouged, and the eyelids larded with blue shadow, the painted mouth and the wrinkled, protruding forehead, I understood my mistake.

Mortified, trembling, I slunk off at Central Square, stumbled up to the chilly air, and dragged myself along Pearl Street. After several blocks I felt life return to my limbs; home would be a haven. Turning right onto Williams Street, my eyes sought our house, and the cloud of nurturance that floated over it.

When I arrived, drained, at the front door, and pushed it open, I heard Asa and Ella rush to greet me. "Good thing you're home, honey," Asa said loudly. "The smoke detector in the kitchen went off, it's so damn sensitive, and it set Ella off. For the last twenty minutes." His smooth, worried face glanced in my direction as he handed Ella over. "How was your day?"

He'd forgotten my appointment, but I halfway forgave him when he reached out and put one firm arm around me. I'd have time to tell him later, and I knew how the combination of the smoke alarm and Ella's high-pitched, terrified scream could drive out any thought except how to stop the noise. Catching a glimpse in the oval hall mirror, I turned to watch us: two tall light brown people with rosy cheeks, wide mouths, each with an arm around the other, and copper-haired green-eyed Ella clinging between us. Asa and I could almost have been twins; we were both freckled, and the top of his handsome, well-shaped head was nearly even with mine, only an inch or so higher.

Ella's eager face tilted up to me, while she "spoke" in urgent syllables I couldn't understand—"Daging," it sounded like; perhaps it was a Jamaican word she'd picked up from LaDean. There was no way for me to be in this family and not be grounded by their love. Indebted, I strode to the back of the house and stepped down into the kitchen, planning to whip up a huge, celebratory meal. Just what we were celebrating, I wasn't sure; I only sensed that some internal shift had occurred. I felt lighter. Perhaps Dr. Thumbelina had imparted some wisdom after all.

Once school started the following week and I was back in my familiar fall routine, teaching a mere two courses so I could finish my book, I wondered if the projective "auditory hallucinations" would begin again. I was still convinced, even after all the conjectures, that what I'd heard *was* Elizabeth's voice. I didn't understand it; I couldn't comprehend it; but I surrendered to the phenomenon. Asa's hypothesis of parallel universes, with the one where Elizabeth existed leaching into mine, made as much sense as anything else.

All of September and into the beginning of October, I noticed, in my one minute of free time a day, that Elizabeth, who had not reappeared, was occupying a small psychic space inside me that felt new. Mostly I ignored it. But one afternoon on my way to class, as I rushed by the window of a tiny Tibetan shop on Pearl Street, a silk scarf caught my eye. Actually it stopped me in my tracks. The stunning green-and-gold intricate pattern was exactly my mother's pastel color palette. Without thinking, I darted into the narrow shop, inhaled its fragrant incense, and quickly inquired, pointing to the scarf, "How much?"

"Only twelve dollars," the diminutive woman said. "Isn't it lovely?" She reached over and fingered the silk. "Are you looking for yourself?"

Without answering her question, I simply nodded noncommittally and said, "Please wrap it for me."

Was I acting out of some long-ago habit, when I used to buy scarves for my mother's birthdays? Even though I occasionally wore silk scarves now, too, especially one long brilliant crimson one,

Elizabeth had a passion for them: she wrapped her neck for warmth in the foggy Bay Area weather and believed that simply draping a beautiful scarf over any old shirt was enough to dress up her jeans for a party or a show.

But I looked horrible in that shade of soft green that had so caught my eye in the shop window, and muted gold had never been my favorite color either. What had possessed me? At home I quickly shoved the scarf, still in its elegant silver box, inside a brown paper bag and into the back of my closet. Maybe someday I'd give it away as a gift. Meanwhile, I put it out of my mind.

During my weekly tête-à-tête with Mercedes over coffee, I never again mentioned the voices. The absence was hardly missed. Between interpreting the signifiers in European and American art, which fascinated us both, and an infinite reservoir of baby chat, we never ran out of topics. In fact, we'd stand up still talking as the last second approached for us to leave and race to class. One morning that fall, though, we actually sat back down again.

"Can you believe it?" Mercedes was saying, horror rippling across her face, draining the blood until she turned two shades lighter right before my eyes. "He said, 'You're going to have to think about putting her in an institution.' Henry and I are still in shock."

"What a bastard. Has he seen Lulu lately?"

"Yes, it was after her two-year exam. That battery of tests." She started to cry. " 'Lulu's not going to go much farther,' he told us. 'You might want to consider alternatives now, before you get more attached.' Ruby, *more attached to her!*"

"What a monster," I said, fighting a well-honed urge to rise from my seat again. If I left at this exact second, I might still make class without being late. "It's bizarre. I wonder if he has kids of his own. How could he think you wouldn't be attached to a two-year-old? I don't get it."

"Me either."

We sat for another five minutes, me trying desperately to absorb some of her shock, the rage and fear. I stroked her hand, whispering over and over while she cried, "Lulu is going to be fine, you're a great mother." Then I sprinted all the way to class, arriving as the students were still settling themselves down.

"Imani," I murmured quietly into the kitchen telephone late that evening, twirling the tight curls of the cord. My habit drove Asa crazy, since the cord got hopelessly twisted every time I used the phone. "It's the oddest thing." A cat's meow from the street drifted through the window, which was open a crack, and I heard a raccoon scratching at the garbage cans. "I almost, but not quite, almost . . ."

"What?" she screamed.

". . . I'm not committing, but I might want to talk . . ." I started to say "to Elizabeth" but instead over Imani's "What? What?" I continued, "Want is too strong a word, but there's some shade of that meaning, think a microcosm of it . . . that, well, wishes I could, maybe, just once, have contact with Elizabeth. Very brief, and only because Daddy died. There are some things I'd like to ask her." I let the words fall into Imani's shocked silence and didn't even try to retrieve them, although I was afraid they might be disloyal. To who? Claire? The younger me? To . . . Asa? My great-great-grandmother? To the threads of blackness I'd so carefully woven, creating the texture of my satisfying life? To my students, for God's sake, who relied on me to be Ms. Dr. Black America? But Daddy wouldn't have led me on to this point if it weren't okay, I had to believe. I'm faithful, I tried to reassure myself, trying to tamp down the anxiety rising in my chest. Breathe in, breathe out. Isn't this what he wanted?

"Ruby." Imani was choked up. When she did speak, her voice was hoarse. "This must be the ancient Ella speaking through you. Moving inside you. Or else it's your father."

Not really. Since we'd taken down the altar months before, I hadn't asked any of the spirits for guidance. Even though I kept the baby photo of Daddy and Grandma Jean on my desk, and glanced at it every couple of days, I wouldn't call that summoning the ancestral spirits. "I don't think that's it," is all I said. "I can't explain." But even as I tried to recover the sentiment, it vanished. "And maybe it doesn't mean anything." Since I couldn't summon up the feeling I'd been describing, I tried to make it into a game, the way we'd done when we were children: "Oh, forget it, Imani. I didn't really mean it. I got you good, though, didn't I?" And I laughed, letting her know that I'd tricked her.

By the time we hung up, I'd convinced myself.

October 18 was my thirty-ninth birthday, and I ended up with an unusual hour to myself at home. Late in the silence of the afternoon, when Ella was out in the park with LaDean and Asa was at school, I turned up Wynton Marsalis's "Down Home with Homey." Show me someone who has his horn more together; in a trance I crossed over to the white cordless telephone on my desk and, in what felt like a spontaneous gesture, extended my left hand, gripped the receiver and lifted it up to my ear, ready to punch in Elizabeth's number, which I knew by heart, since it was my old number, too. But what, really, after fifteen years, could I say? That I was sorry? That I felt like an orphan, even though I was entering my fortieth year, and what could she do about it now? That I missed my daddy so much my chest felt as if it had been pounded with spiked steel bars? That maybe hearing her real voice in my ears might console me? I doubted it. I wasn't a kid anymore, and I knew her too well. Way too well.

The impulse to call her on my birthday puzzled me. I, who am so used to providing reasonable explanations, could come up with none for this unplanned urge, any more than I had one for that impulsive purchase of the silk scarf in her colors. Or, for that matter, for anything relating to Elizabeth O'Leary anymore. I stood in my study surveying the yard through the windows, my mind a blank. A robin scrabbled in the dirt, pecking. It felt like the weight of the receiver was going to break my wrist. A fly buzzed, until I squashed it with a used sheet of paper, leaving a smear on my white laminated counter. The antique desk clock ticked, maddeningly loud.

I can't call her; not today. Maybe tomorrow. I placed the receiver back into its cradle and had turned to walk into the living room when an image stopped me: Daddy's gaunt hospital room face, eyes full of pain beseeching me. I heard his tired voice rasping, "Seven times seventy." But how could I forgive Elizabeth even once, never mind . . . I did a quick calculation . . . four hundred and ninety times?

Haunted by the memory of Daddy's pleading expression, I turned back to my desk, lit a stick of rose incense that Asa had handed me that morning for my birthday, placed it in my Ghanaian incense holder, and sniffed the warm aroma. Dark, sweet-smelling smoke curled into the air. Rose, I recalled, is a heart opener.

Taking an enormous breath—in, out, in, release—the words echoed in my ears: "Seven times seventy." That's what King asked us to do, Daddy said, as part of our healing journey. Not for the white man, but for ourselves.

Breathe in, breathe out. Now the tears had passed, my mind felt clearer. Turning toward the window, I noticed a faint wash of rose paint the sky. In a moment the splash deepened to crimson, edged with green. Staring out the window, I watched the robin flit about in the yard, and caught a whiff of rose incense. Other robins fluttered down, settling on branches of an overhanging maple, their red chests puffed up. A flock of sparrows flew into our carved stone birdbath and began to splash, two at a time, puffing up, spattering water over the sides of the basin. They circled it, nudging each other out, flapping their wings in the water, splashing and trilling. Soon I saw a flurry of brown and black and white, beating their wings against the water. The last rays of daylight, gold and purple, glinted in the overflowing water until I began to laugh. Okay, Solomon Jordan, you old wizard, I give up. I should have known you'd be as good as your word, Mister Old School.

That man got me to howling, shaking my head in disbelief. Even though I had no idea what I'd say if she answered, I sat down at my desk, picked up the receiver again, punched in Elizabeth's number, and waited to hear it ring. For the first time in years I actively tried to picture her rather than brushing her image away: she'd be lying on that ratty old broken-down couch she loved so well, buried in what was left of the saggy feather pillows. And something stirred, brushing against the walls of my chest.

"Elizabeth," I planned to start if she answered, with no idea where I'd go from there but trusting the words would come. I gulped and held my breath, listening to the ring. Once, twice, three times. When her voice mail kicked on I listened for a few seconds, dropped the phone, pulled out my laptop, and leaned back against the headboard of our bed, ready, I realized, to write my mother. As soon as my fingers tapped the keys a barrier burst, jolting me, and all the warmth, the longing that had gushed through my childhood and been dammed up so long, rushed out like a mighty river running home to the sea. The words flowed the same as last time, but even faster, surprising me, the nonwriter, all over again. Once I typed "Dear Mama . . ." the fist in my heart unclenched, the words "I miss you so much" flew onto the page, and the rest of that letter wrote itself.

Acknowledgments

Many people have generously supported me over the decade I labored, intermittently, on the numerous iterations of *Mama's Child*.

My first appreciation goes to the readers who thoughtfully gave feedback, some on a chapter, some on draft after draft: Muriel Albert, Betsy Blakeslee, Lan Samantha Chang, Faith Childs, Jewelle Gomez, Nellie Hill, Sydelle Kramer, Zee Lewis, Janis Cooke Newman, Wendy Lichtman's writing circle, Jonathan Poullard, Achebe Powell, Lesley Quinn, Rebecca Saletan, Mardi Steinau, Dorothy Wall, and Maxine Wolfe. To all, I offer a heartfelt *Thank you*.

A special shout-out to my writing partner, Marissa Moss, who edited every version as the novel sprawled and contracted. And to my beloved partner/spouse, Carole Johnson, who enthusiastically listened to me read every revision aloud, through all the years the novel sought its form.

Gratitude to Donna Korones, who suggested I enter the 2010 Bellwether Prize for Fiction competition, where this manuscript ended up as a Finalist, encouraging me to persevere in yet more revisions.

Other friends and allies have sustained me with their faith that this novel would find its right home at the right time: Mandy Aftel, Nina Brown, the Reverend Robert Collins, Sandee Dennis, Ruth King, Julius Lester, Viola Pickens, Elaine Seiler, Alice Walker, Leonie Walker, Brooke Warner, and Ellery Washington. Thank you for holding me in the light!

Appreciations, too, to my fabulous agent team, Judy Hansen and Cynthia Manson, who loved the manuscript on sight, recommended key tweaks, and found *Mama's Child* the perfect publisher with senior editor Malaika Adero at Atria. I have long admired Malaika; her gentle suggestions for revision ("Take another look at . . .") significantly improved the narrative. Todd Hunter kept production running smoothly, while copyeditor Judy Steer deftly scrutinized the final draft. Thank you all.

My extended family has been uniformly supportive of my writing career; it is wonderful knowing that my home team has my back. Thanks to all for your steady encouragement.